House of Correction

House of Correction

A Novel

Nicci French

HARPER LARGE PRINT

An Imprint of HarperCollinsPublishers

FIRST HARPER LARGE PRINT EDITION

ISBN: 978-0-06-302948-4

Library of Congress Cataloging-in-Publication Data is available upon request.

20 21 22 23 24 LSC 10 9 8 7 6 5 4 3 2 1

To Lucca

House of Correction

PART ONE
Inside

One

The screaming started at three in the morning. Tabitha had never heard a human being howl in that way before. It was like the screeching of an animal caught in a trap and it was answered by shouts, distant, echoing. Tabitha couldn't tell whether they were cries of comfort or anger or mockery. The screams subsided into sobs but even these were amplified by the metal, the doors, the stairs and floors. Tabitha felt they were echoing inside her head.

She sensed a movement from the bunk above her. The other woman must be awake.

"Someone's in trouble."

There was silence. Tabitha wondered if the woman was ignoring her or really was asleep, but then a voice came out of the darkness. She was speaking slowly, as if she were talking to herself. Her voice was low and gravelly, a smoker's morning voice.

"Everyone's in trouble," she said. "That's why they're here. That's why they're crying, when they think about their children or what they did. Or what they did to their children. When there's real trouble, you don't hear any screams. You just hear the screws running along the corridors. When it's really bad you hear a helicopter landing out on the field. That's happened three times, four times, since I've been here."

"What's that for?" asked Tabitha.

"What do you think?"

Tabitha tried not to think about what a helicopter landing in the middle of the night meant. She tried not to think at all. But she failed. As she lay staring up at the bottom of the bunk above her, as she heard the sobs and the shouts and then another burst of crying from someone else, she had a sudden feeling of absolute clarity piercing the murk: this was real.

Up to now, it had all been so strange, so completely outside her experience, that it had felt like a lopsided fairy tale about someone else going to prison, someone she was reading about or watching in a film, even when she herself was experiencing it. When she was sitting in the tiny, windowless compartment in the van that brought her from the court; when she took her clothes off and squatted and was stared at and examined and heard a woman laugh about her small breasts and hairy armpits; when she stood in the shower afterward. She had been issued sheets and an itchy blue blanket and a thin towel and escorted through door after door. The doors really were made of heavy metal. They really did clang shut. The wardens really did carry huge bunches of keys attached on chains to their belts. The prison was so prison-like.

Yesterday afternoon, as she was escorted through the central hall, lined with cells on both sides and on the floor above, she felt stared at by women standing in groups. She wanted to say: "This isn't real. I'm not one of you. I don't belong here."

She lay there on her bunk trying not to think of that, trying not to replay it in her mind, over and over again. But even that was better than thinking of where she was, right now, this minute, in this space.

Tabitha had never liked lifts. What if they fell? What if they got stuck? She always took the stairs. When she went to London, she hated the Underground. Once she had been on a train during rush hour, standing up, crammed among the hot bodies, and the train had stopped between tunnels. There had been a muffled announcement, which she couldn't understand. It had stopped for five minutes, ten minutes. It was in the summer and the heat was stifling. Gradually Tabitha had thought of the solid clay and brick between her and the surface. And then she had thought of how she was in the middle of a train that was stuffed with people in carriage after carriage in front of her and carriage after carriage behind her. She had felt an impulse, which she could barely stifle, to scream and scream and fight her way out.

Now she was in a cell, four paces long, three paces wide. There was a tiny, barred window. It looked out on a yard, beyond that a wall topped with barbed wire, and beyond that, you could just make out the hills, hazy in the distance. Yesterday she had looked out of that window and she had thought that she saw a little shape moving on that hill. Someone walking. Someone outside. Someone free. But now it was dark and there was nothing but the spotlights illuminating the yard. The door of the cell would stay locked until the middle of the morning. When she thought about it, she felt like she was buried alive and wanted to yell for someone to come and rescue her. Perhaps that was what that woman had been howling about.

If Tabitha couldn't scream, then perhaps she could cry. But she knew that if she cried, she wouldn't be able to stop. And probably it wasn't good to be seen crying.

It was very cold, and the single blanket was inadequate. She drew her knees up almost to her chest and lay hugging herself in the darkness. She smelled different. Of prison soap and hair that needed washing, something slightly moldy. She closed her eyes and thought of the sea, waves swelling and cresting onto the rocky shore. Thoughts came in long dark curls and she tried to push them away. There was another scream, then someone banged on a door far away.

Although it felt impossible, she must have slept a little because she was woken by the woman sliding down from the top bunk. It seemed to take a long time. Her feet came first, long, with purple-painted toenails, a tattoo of a spider on the right ankle. Then her legs in gray jogging pants, on and on. Then a black tee shirt riding up to show a ring in the belly button. Finally, a smooth oval face, long thick dark hair with a fringe, circular hoops in her earlobes. She was very tall, maybe six feet, and looked strong; in her late twenties perhaps, although it was hard to judge. Tabitha hadn't seen her last night, not really. She'd just climbed into her bed and pulled the blanket over her head and lain there.

"Hi," she said now.

The woman didn't reply. She went across the cell and opened the little curtain.

That was another thing. The cell had been built for one person. Now it had bunk beds, two chairs, two narrow tables, two tiny chests, a sink and a toilet with a little curtain rigged up in front of it. The woman tugged her trousers down and sat on the bowl. Her face was quite expressionless; it was as if she were alone. Tabitha turned to the wall, wrapping herself in the blanket so that she couldn't hear.

The toilet flushed and taps were running. Tabitha waited till the woman was done, then climbed out of her bed and washed herself under her arms, splashed water on her face. Then she pulled on canvas trousers, a tee shirt and a sweatshirt. She slid out her sneakers from under the bed.

"I'm Tabitha," she said.

The woman was methodically brushing her hair. She looked down at her. *She must be almost a foot taller than me*, thought Tabitha.

"You told me that last night."

There was a pause.

"What's your name?" asked Tabitha.

"Michaela. I told you that as well."

There was a rattling sound at the door and it was unlocked and the door pushed inward. A stringy, colorless woman was standing next to a trolley with two stainless steel urns on it.

"Tea," said Michaela.

"Tea," repeated Tabitha.

The woman filled two mugs and handed them across.

Tabitha's breakfast pack was on the table. She opened it and laid it out: a plastic bowl, a plastic spoon, a miniature pack of Rice Krispies, a small carton of UHT milk, two slices of brown bread wrapped in polythene, foil-wrapped butter, a little tub of raspberry jam. There was no knife so she spread the butter and the jam on the bread with the handle of her spoon.

She couldn't remember when she had last had a meal and she ate the sandwiches in quick bites. The bread was dry but she helped it down with gulps of her tea. She tipped the cereal into the bowl and poured the milk over it. The milk was warm and had a sour under-taste. It almost made her gag, but she ate it all and when she was finished she tipped the bowl to drink the last of the milk. She still felt hungry.

She sat on the toilet behind the thin curtain. She felt like an animal. As she sat there, her trousers around her ankles, she felt as if lights were flashing and there was a ringing in her ears. She suddenly thought of smashing her face into the wall, over and over again, something that might bring relief, that might make all of this stop.

Instead, she wiped herself, pulled up her trousers, washed her hands and sat back on her bed against the wall. She didn't have anything to read and she didn't have anything to do. The day felt shapeless and vast. Anyway, if she had sat there reading, that would feel like this was now her life instead of a nightmarish mistake, a mistake that would be corrected when everyone realized that she didn't belong here and let her go.

Michaela was leaning over the sink, brushing her teeth. She was taking a long time over it. She spat into the sink, bent down and drank straight from the tap. She stood up, leaned her head back and gargled noisily. Tabitha felt like everything was turned up too high: the noises, the smells, the physical proximity of the other woman. Michaela pulled her hair back in a ponytail, then walked out of the cell. A few seconds later she walked back in. She leaned back on the table and looked down at Tabitha.

"Don't just sit there."

Tabitha didn't reply. It felt too much of an effort.

"It's worse if you do that. I know, I've been here for fourteen months."

"What did you do?"

Michaela stared at her, her face quite expressionless. "Did they give you the bit of paper with all the shit about exercise and showers and when the library's open?"

"I've got it somewhere," said Tabitha. "But I don't care about all that. It's just a mistake."

"Yeah? Well, don't think you can just hide in here and get through without anyone noticing. It's like a school playground. The little girl who stands in the corner wanting to be left alone, she's the one who gets picked on. You need to get up. You need to get up and get a shower."

"I don't feel like it. Not today."

Michaela reached under the little table that was reserved for Tabitha.

"Here." She tossed Tabitha the towel she'd been issued on her arrival. "You take the towel and the soap and you have a shower."

She went out of the cell, leaving the door open. Tabitha got to her feet. She was cold to her bones. She looked out of the little barred window again: the sky was white. *It might snow*, she thought. That would be something: feathery flakes falling thickly just a few inches from where she stood, covering everything in a blanket of unfamiliarity.

She took the towel and the soap from the side of the sink and walked into the central hall that was echoey with sounds: footfalls and doors and voices raised, laughter, coughs, the slap of a mop. A very thin woman with long white hair and her face a muddle of wrinkles hobbled toward her. She wore a thick brown dress to her shins and her hands were swollen with arthritis. She was holding a bundle of papers clutched to her chest.

"You're here too," she said, smiling.

"Yes, I'm here too," said Tabitha. She walked the length of the hall and into the little wing reserved for showers. The showers were in a row of stalls. Along the far wall was a wooden bench and hooks. Women were pulling clothes on and off. The tiled floor was wet and there was the smell of soap and sweat and bodies. She had a memory of school changing rooms that was so pungent that it hurt. She slowly took her clothes off, looking at the wall so she didn't catch anyone's eye. Before she took off her knickers, she wrapped herself in the thin worn towel, like a shy teenager on a beach, and then eased them down.

Inside a free stall she pulled the curtain across and hung the towel from a hook. She turned the tap and a tiny trickle of water emerged from the showerhead. She tried to twist the tap further but it wouldn't go.

"You need to bang it," said a voice. "Bang the pipe."

She tapped the pipe. Nothing happened.

"Harder," said the voice. "Really hard."

She made a fist and hit the pipe. There was a little spluttering, coughing sound and the trickle became a faint stream, just enough to wet herself all over. But there was nothing good about it, nothing to lose herself in, nothing to comfort her.

Two

"This way." The warden was solid with a bored expression. When she walked, her feet slapped down, flat and hard.

"What?"

"Your brief's waiting."

"My brief?"

"Your lawyer. You were told about this yesterday."

Tabitha couldn't remember that. But then she couldn't remember much of yesterday, nor of the days preceding it. Everything was a jumble of faces, eyes staring, questions she couldn't answer, words she couldn't make sense of, people saying her name over and over again—her name and her address and her date of birth and then pieces of paper pushed toward her, machines clicked on to record what she was saying, long corridors and strip lighting, doors and keys and bars.

"In the visitors' room," the woman was saying. Keys jangled at her waist. "It's not a day for visiting."

The visitors' room was large and square and too brightly lit. There were small tables in rows with a chair on either side, two vending machines by the wall. The room was empty except for a middle-aged woman who was sitting at one of the tables with her laptop in front of her. She took off her glasses and rubbed her round face and then replaced them, frowning as she read. As Tabitha approached, she looked up and briefly smiled, then stood and held out her hand, which was strong and warm. She had peppery-gray hair and a steady gaze and Tabitha felt a surge of hope. This woman would sort everything out.

"I'm Mora Piozzi," she said. "I've been asked to represent you."

"What happened to the other one?" He'd been young and cheerful in a blustery, unreassuring way.

"He was the duty solicitor. He referred your case to me."

They both sat and faced each other, their chairs scratching across the linoleum.

"How are you?" asked Mora Piozzi.

"How am I?" Tabitha resisted the urge to shout at her. What kind of question was that? "I'm locked up in prison and I don't know what's happening."

"It's my job to bring clarity to this and to help you."

"Right."

"First things first. You need to tell me if you agree to me representing you."

"Yes."

"Good. I've got your prison number, in case you haven't been issued it yet."

"A prison number? But I'll be out of here soon. Why do I need a number?"

"Here."

She pushed a card across to Tabitha, who read it out loud: "AO3573." She looked up. "So I'm a number now."

"It's just bureaucracy. You'll need it for people who are going to visit."

"Visit?"

"As a remand prisoner you're entitled to have up to three visitors a week. Has nobody explained all this?"

"Everything's a bit of a blur."

Mora Piozzi nodded. "It's hard at first."

"I just want to leave here as quickly as possible."

"Of course. Which is why I am here. But, Tabitha, you do understand what the charge is?"

"I know what they say I did."

"Good. So this is what we're going to do today: I am going to lay out the summary of the case against you. And then you are going to tell me, in your own words, what happened on the twenty-first of December."

"Can I ask something first?"

"Of course."

"What day is it today?"

"Wednesday, the ninth of January."

"I see."

Christmas had gone by, and New Year's Eve, and now she was in another year and another world.

"So," said Mora Piozzi, looking down at her laptop. "In brief: you are charged with the murder of Stuart Robert Rees, on Friday the twenty-first of December, between the hours of ten-forty in the morning and three-thirty in the afternoon."

"Why?"

"I'm sorry?"

"Why those times?"

Piozzi flicked through her notes.

"There's a CCTV camera. It's attached to the village shop. His car drove past it." She looked down at her laptop. "At ten thirty-four. And as you know, his body was discovered at half past four that day."

"Yes," said Tabitha faintly. She paused. "But there's a spare hour then, between half past three and half past four."

"I understand the forensic pathologist is satisfied that Rees had been dead at least an hour when his body was discovered."

Piozzi continued speaking in a low, calm voice, as if it was all routine. "His body was found by Andrew Kane in a shed outside your back door, wrapped in plastic sheeting. You were in the house at the time of discovery. Stuart Rees's car was parked round the back of your house, out of sight of the road. He had been stabbed multiple times by a knife, but the cause of death was the slashing of his carotid artery." She looked up. "That's in his neck. His blood was all over you and all over the sofa where you were sitting."

"But that was from after he was dead," said Tabitha.

Piozzi tapped on the keyboard of her laptop. "The police have interviewed everyone who was in the village and—"

"Wait."

"Yes?"

"There must have been lots of people coming and going. They can't have interviewed everyone."

"Not on that day."

"What do you mean?"

"Don't you remember? The village was blocked off. There was a big storm and a giant chestnut tree that had blight was torn up by its roots and fell across the road. There was no way out and no way in. Apparently it took most of the day to clear it."

"I didn't know."

"But you were there, Tabitha, all day. You must have known."

"I didn't know," Tabitha repeated. She felt like the last fragments of memory were flowing away like water through her fingers. "I don't know if I knew."

"The police have a list of everyone who was in Okeham on the twenty-first of December. They also have your statement saying that you were in your house most of the day. They have statements from other witnesses, but I haven't seen them yet. All we have at the moment is a police summary. I'll get the rest later, well before the first court appearance."

"The trial, you mean?"

"No. On the seventh of February you will be officially charged. That's where you plead. You know, guilty or not guilty."

"Isn't there a chance they'll realize that this is all wrong and let me go?"

Mora Piozzi gave a smile that didn't look like a smile. "Let's not leap ahead. I want you to tell me what you remember about the twenty-first of December. Take your time."

Tabitha nodded. She closed her eyes and then opened them again. What did she remember? It was like looking into a night full of snow, a dizzying half darkness, when even up and down seemed reversed and the ground tilted beneath her feet.

"I woke up early," she began. "But I don't think I got up at once. It was cold outside, a horrible day. I remember it was half snowing and then it was sleety, with a hard wind blowing. I started to make myself breakfast, then I realized I'd run out of milk so I just put a jacket on over my pajamas and went to the village shop. I bought a paper, I think."

"What time was this?"

"I don't know. I wasn't looking at the time. Then I went home."

"Did you go out again?"

"I had a swim. I always have a swim."

"How?"

"What?"

"Where's the nearest swimming pool and how did you get there? Remember, the road was blocked after ten, so you would have to have gone and returned before then." She spoke with a warning tone.

"In the sea."

Piozzi's eyebrows shot up. "You went swimming in the sea, in the middle of winter, on a day you describe as horrible."

"I do it every day," said Tabitha. "It's a rule. My own rule. I have to."

"Rather you than me. You have a wetsuit, though."

"I like to feel the cold water on my skin. It almost hurts." She saw Mora Piozzi purse her lips slightly, as if Tabitha had said something she didn't like. "People in Okeham probably think I'm mad. Anyway, I swam that day." She thought she could remember the bitter splash of waves on her body and the sharp, icy stones under her feet, but perhaps she was making that up. She swam every day. How was she meant to tell one from another?

"What time?"

"I don't know. I can't remember. In the morning? I think it would have been the morning. That's when I normally go."

"Did you meet anyone?"

"I don't know. Maybe. I can't think. I go every day, so things blur together."

"And after your swim?"

"I went back home."

"Did you leave again?"

"I think I did, but I don't know for sure anymore. People have asked me so many questions that I can't tell things apart."

"What did you do in your house?"

"Not much. I can't really remember."

"Did you speak to anyone on the phone?"

"No."

"Or send any texts, or use your computer—you have a computer?"

Tabitha nodded. "I didn't do any of that."

"Did you send emails?"

"I don't think so. I might have done some work." She knew she hadn't worked. It had been one of those terrible days when she simply had to survive.

"So you have no clear memory of what you did during that day?"

"No."

"But you remember Andrew Kane coming round?"

"Andy, yes."

"Tell me about that. Be careful, take your time."

Tabitha wondered why she kept saying that: "Take your time." Anyway, it didn't matter. She had so much time.

"He knocked on the door. I was in the main room and I opened the door. Or maybe he opened it himself. It was already dark and very cold. I remember the icy wind rushing in. He was all wet. He was dripping onto the floor."

"Were you expecting him?"

"No. But he often just comes round." She saw the questioning look on Mora Piozzi's face. "He's helping me with the house. It was a wreck when I moved in, back in November, and we're doing it up together. I pay him by the hour and he fits me in between other jobs. We were going to lay some floorboards the next day and he just wanted to check on everything."

She stopped and took a deep breath. This was where her memory became clear, like a shaft of light in the gloom.

"He went outside to the shed where the planks were stacked and I heard him call out. I don't know what he said, maybe it wasn't even words. I went out to him, and he was sprawled on the ground inside the shed, on top of something." She swallowed hard. Her throat was tight. "I bent to help him and I felt something wet and sticky, it was everywhere, and I pulled him to his feet and he kept saying, 'Oh God, oh God,' over and over. I think he was crying."

Tabitha stopped but Piozzi didn't speak, just waited, her eyes narrowed.

"It was dark. We couldn't see anything really. Andy got his mobile out of his pocket but dropped it on the ground and had to scrabble around to find it. Then he shone it downward and there was a body. Andy had blood all over him, even on his face. I looked down at my hands and saw I did too." As she spoke, she could see it all: the little beam of the mobile's torch picking out the stare of open eyes, the gaping wound in the neck, an unnatural twist of limbs.

"Did you see who it was?"

"I don't know what I thought. Andy said it was Stuart, I realized he was right."

"Just to be clear, you knew Stuart Rees?"

"Yes, he's my neighbor now." She stopped. "I suppose I should say he *was* my neighbor. And years ago, he was one of my teachers."

"So you knew him well?"

"What can I say? He was a teacher."

"Were you on good terms?"

"We weren't on bad terms. I didn't really see him much, though, just to say hello."

"What happened next?"

"We went back inside. Andy called nine-nine-nine.

We waited. The ambulance arrived and the police and it all started. You know the rest."

Mora Piozzi closed her laptop.

"So you see, it makes no sense," Tabitha continued urgently. "Why would I have sent Andy outside to look at the planks if I'd just killed someone out there and left the body for him to trip over? Why would I kill Stuart anyway? It's just crazy. You see that, don't you?"

The solicitor glanced at her watch. "We've made a good start. I'll be back quite soon, by which time I hope to have a more detailed knowledge of the prosecution's case against you."

Tabitha nodded.

"In the next few days you'll have a medical assessment."

"Why? I'm not ill. I might be small but I'm strong. It's that swimming." Her voice jarred. She tried to smile. She was cold and shaky and she didn't want to go back to the central hall, where everyone watched her and shouts echoed, or to her cell, where she was trapped with herself. The day ahead seemed endless, but the day led to the night and that was even worse.

"It's just part of the process. And I want you to write down everything you can remember that you think might be useful."

"What kind of things?"

"Timings. People you saw or talked to. Give me a list of the people in the village you're friendly with."

"I only moved there a few weeks ago."

"You should tell me anything you think might be helpful to your case, or relevant. I would much rather hear things from you than from the prosecution."

Tabitha nodded.

"Make sure you arrange visitors. Family. Friends. Have you any of your things here?"

"No."

"Get someone to bring them. Keep yourself occupied. Keep healthy."

"And you'll get me out of here? Won't you?"

"That's my job," said Mora Piozzi. "I'll do it as best I can."

Tabitha watched her leave, the door opening and then shutting. She imagined her going through a series of doors, each one locked behind her, until at last she reached the exit and stepped out in the world, breathing in the fresh air, free.

Three

Tabitha couldn't remember the last time she'd queued to use a public phone. Okeham had an old red telephone box but it didn't have a phone in it. It was used to store secondhand books for people to borrow. Now she was standing third in the queue waiting for the burly woman at the front to finish an argument with what sounded like a feckless husband or boyfriend on the other end of the line.

Tabitha kept looking around nervously. It was nearly lunchtime. She'd heard that a warden might come and send them away at any time. She'd been told by the warden with the grim face, whose name, she'd discovered, was Mary Guy, that she needed to fill out a form and that each telephone number had to be recorded in advance and approved. She didn't know anybody's number, apart from her own. Her numbers were in her phone. How could she be expected to know them by heart? She asked Mary Guy if there was any way she could get access to her phone, just to get the numbers. That got a laugh.

She had no parents to phone. No other close relatives. She tried to think of friends, contacts, but she had been abroad for several years and lost touch with people. They had moved, drifted away. She had one number. The solicitor, Mora Piozzi. That was a start. But was there anyone else? She went through the people she knew in the village. Stuart's wife, Laura. That wouldn't be appropriate. It probably wouldn't be legal. There was Andy. She could get his number from Mora. Who in the village did she actually talk to? There was Terry, the woman who ran the village shop. They used to chat a bit when she bought a carton of milk. But they weren't exactly friends.

Then she had a thought: Shona Fry. Shona had been at school with Tabitha and had stayed on in the village after everyone else had left. Tabitha didn't know Shona's mobile number but she did know her landline number because it was a mirror version of her own: 525607.

When she got to the front of the queue, there was just five minutes before lunch.

"Tabitha! They told me you were going to call," said Shona, who sounded breathless with excitement.

"I know."

"They asked if it was all right. They wanted my permission, which is a bit odd, isn't it? Obviously I said yes. You must know that because—"

"I'm sorry," said Tabitha, interrupting. "I've got almost no money for the call and almost no time. I need to ask you a couple of favors."

"Yes, of course. Anything at all."

"First, can you come to visit me?"

"Me?"

"Yes."

"Absolutely," said Shona. "Yes, fine. I mean, of course I will, sure . . ." She didn't seem to know how to end the sentence, so Tabitha cut her off.

"That's brilliant. Could you bring some things for me?"

"Yes, yes. I suppose there are rules."

"I need clothes."

"I thought people in prison had a prison uniform."

"No."

"Right. Oh, this is so weird. What clothes?"

"Just comfy things. Another pair of trousers, a few long-sleeved tops and jerseys. It's freezing in here."

"So you don't mind which ones I bring?"

"Not really. I'll be out soon, so it's just for the next few weeks. Underwear."

"Like knickers and things?" Shona sounded almost embarrassed.

"Yes. And socks. Thick socks."

"Where do I find them?"

Tabitha pictured her bedroom. It was at the top of the house, under a sloping roof. She'd chosen it because one window gave onto the sea, and the other onto the cliffs. She still slept on a mattress on the floor, and there was only one chest of drawers in there. The rest of her things were in suitcases and boxes.

"In my room upstairs," she said. "You'll just have to rummage around."

"Anything else?"

"Some pens. And pads of paper. And soap and shampoo. More toothpaste."

"I need to write this down."

"The pens and the paper are the most important. There are several pads of paper in the kitchen, on the table, I think, and pencils and pens in a big jar on the windowsill."

"Got it."

"And could you buy me writing paper and envelopes? Also, the village shop sells notebooks; they have black or brown covers and unlined paper. Could you get one for me?"

"All right." But now she sounded grudging.

"I'll pay you."

"Sorry, it sounds awful but I'm completely skint. Is that it?"

Tabitha thought for a moment. "Books. There are a few next to my bed. Can you bring them?"

"Sure. But how do I get in?"

"There's a key under a stone next to the front door. Oh, and stamps," Tabitha said.

"How many?"

"Ten. No. Twenty."

"First class or second class?"

"First class, I guess. I haven't got time to wait around."

"Are you doing all right?" said Shona. "I mean, this is so awful. I can't believe it's happening."

"Me neither. I don't know how I'm doing. I'm trying. How are things in the village?"

"Yeah, well, obviously there's only one subject people are talking about."

Tabitha had a sudden thought. "Could you bring phone numbers of people in the village?"

"Which people?"

"Anyone. People who might be helpful. Landlines if people have them. Calls are really expensive here and I haven't got much money."

"I don't know who you're talking about. Could you suggest some names?"

Tabitha started to speak and then a hand appeared from the side, disconnecting the call. She looked round. It was a male warden she hadn't seen before. He was pale, slightly puffy and overweight, as if he had been overinflated.

"Hey! What the fuck? It was important," said Tabitha.

"Lunch," he said and turned away.

Four

She lay tightly curled up in her bed, dimly aware of Michaela moving around the small cell. She heard her use the toilet. She heard taps running, soft footsteps. She kept her eyes shut and her blanket pulled over her so she was in her own sour cave; she didn't want to move and she didn't want to see the light of day. Her thoughts were thick and sluggish.

"Get up." Michaela's voice was matter-of-fact.

Tabitha didn't reply.

"Get up, Tabitha." The blanket was pulled from her face.

"Can't."

"You can. You have to."

Tabitha opened her eyes. Her mouth felt furry.

"Up," said Michaela.

"How are you?"

Tabitha looked at the laminated plastic name tag
that the psychiatrist was wearing round his neck. Dr.
David Hartson, with a photograph that showed him
when he had more hair and different spectacles. The
stringy warden with long, limp hair, who she had seen
that first morning, had come to her cell and led her
downstairs past the rows of other cells, unlocking and
locking a series of doors, along a corridor and then into
a room that didn't feel like it was in the prison at all.
It looked like a rather shabby doctor's consulting room
that you might find anywhere.

"Can I ask a question first?"

"Of course."

"Who is this for?"

Dr. Hartson gave a slightly uneasy smile. "I don't
know what you mean."

"You're a doctor. Are you here to help me or are you
here to assess me?"

He nodded. "That's a good question. I'm really acting for the court. But obviously if I see anything of
concern, I'll do what I can. So, how are you?"

"I'm in prison. I've been accused of murder. I guess
that means I'm not doing so well."

"Do you have any feelings about self-harm?"

Tabitha shook her head. "I've been here two nights. I still feel like I'm in the middle of a car crash and the crash is going on and on and on. But soon they'll realize that all of this is crazy and let me go."

Dr. Hartson reached for a form and straightened it in front of him; took a pen from his pocket and clicked it. He took details of her schooling, of her parents, of her father's death from a heart attack when she was thirteen and her mother's death just two years ago. He asked if those deaths had been difficult and she said, yes, they had been difficult. He asked if she had been close to her parents and she had thought for a moment and answered that there had been ups and downs. He didn't seem to show much engagement with anything she said; just frowned with concentration and wrote on the form. Tabitha couldn't make out what he was writing.

"Do you work?" he asked.

"I'm a freelance copyeditor of science textbooks."

"Any episodes of mental illness?" he said.

"What kind of mental illness?"

"Anything that needed medical treatment?"

"I've been a bit down sometimes."

"Are you currently on medication?"

"Not anymore."

"Were you treated with medication in the past?"

Tabitha mentioned one or two names although she wasn't sure if she had got them right. Dr. Hartson wrote them down.

"How did they make you feel?"

"They were different."

"Did you have lapses of memory? Blackouts?"

"I don't remember." She gave a nervous laugh. "Sorry, that wasn't a joke. I didn't like them."

"Were you ever hospitalized?"

"I had a bit of an episode when I was at college." She tried to speak casually. "I dropped out."

"And you were hospitalized?"

"Briefly. But not in a hospital. It was a kind of clinic." She heard the scratching of his pen once more. "It was years ago," she added.

"Of course. Did you go back to college?"

"No."

"What were you studying?"

"Architecture."

"And now you're a copyeditor?"

"Yes."

"Do you like it?"

"I'm my own boss."

"You like being your own boss?"

"I don't like *not* being my own boss," she said, and

he looked at her searchingly. She wanted to poke him in the eye.

"How have you been recently?" he asked after a pause.

Tabitha shrugged. "I'm like everyone. I have good days and bad days. The village can be a bit grim in winter. You know, when it gets dark at four."

Hartson smiled but it didn't reach his eyes. "I know exactly what you mean. Why did you move back to the village?"

"I got an inheritance when my mum died. I bought this wreck of a house. It was a kind of dream I had."

"Interesting. How was the dream turning out in reality?"

"I like the house. I like making it whole again. I like using my hands, making things."

"How was your mood in the weeks before the murder?"

"It wasn't really any different from usual."

"Up and down?"

"Yes. Probably more up than down." That was a lie.

"And on the day of the murder?"

"What?"

"How was your mood that day?"

Tabitha looked at his pen poised above the paper;

she looked at his small, wet mouth. She didn't want to tell this man anything at all.

"So-so," she said.

"Do you have a clear memory of it?"

"Nope."

"You don't remember the events of the day?"

"It's a bit of a blur."

"I see," he said. "I see."

"I doubt it."

"Sorry?"

"I doubt that you see," said Tabitha. She knew she should curb herself. "It was just one of those days. One of those days to get through. Most people have days like that. Don't you?"

"This isn't about me, it's about you and your mental state."

"Yeah, well, I'm just saying I don't remember much and that doesn't mean anything. Right?"

Dr. Hartson waited before replying. "Right," he said neutrally. He turned back to the form. "Do you have friends in the village? People you talk to about your troubles?"

"I don't really talk about my troubles."

"Did you feel that returning was a mistake?"

For a moment Tabitha found it difficult to speak.

"Just at this moment it feels pretty much like a fucking mistake."

He raised his eyes and looked at her. "I meant in the days before the murder."

"It was early days. I was doing up the house. I was thinking about things."

"What were you thinking about?"

"What to do with my life. I think that problem has been settled for me for the time being."

Tabitha meant that as a sour sort of joke but Dr. Hartson didn't react. He stopped writing and looked reflective.

"I think that's everything." He moved the form. There was another one underneath. "Would it be all right to access your medical records?"

"Can't you just go ahead?"

"I need a signature." He rotated the form and pushed it toward her.

Tabitha took the pen he was offering and signed.

"Does everything seem all right?" she said.

"It all seems straightforward enough."

"What are you going to say?"

"What would you like me to say?"

"That I couldn't possibly have done something like this."

He didn't reply. He just gave the sort of smile that people give at the end of a social occasion before they say: "I think I'd better be heading off." But in this case it was Tabitha who ought to be heading off. She looked around. She didn't want to leave this room and go back into the real prison.

"It doesn't seem real," she said.

"That's natural." They both stood up. "Goodbye, Miss Hardy."

"Nobody calls me Miss Hardy. It's Ms. Not that it matters. By the way, if I'd said that I was suicidal, what would you have done?"

Dr. Hartson looked surprised by the question. "I would have recommended that you talk to the prison doctor."

Tabitha was tempted to make an angry response, to say, wasn't he a doctor? Wasn't he supposed to help people in distress? But she knew that she needed this man on her side. She walked out from her brief encounter and met Mary Guy and saw the heavy bunch of keys dangling from her belt.

Five

Tabitha was in the library. It was still cold, but better than in her cell. It didn't feel quite so much like being in prison, although through the window she could see a peeling white wall topped with barbed wire. The librarian, tall with bony hands, pale brown hair, welcomed her with a smile.

"I haven't seen you before."

Tabitha nodded, suddenly unable to speak.

"I'm Galia. I'm glad you found your way here."

"Tabitha." Her voice came out gruff.

"And you like reading?"

"Yes. I've none of my own books yet. A friend's bringing them soon."

Galia nodded. "Well, you've come to the right place. I wish more people would use the library."

Tabitha looked round. Apart from a woman sitting at the table reading, the room was empty.

"Can I take whatever I want?"

"If you're reading in here, of course. If you take books back to your cell you have to sign them out. And if there are particular titles you want, I can order them for you."

"Like in a real library?"

"This is a real library."

Tabitha looked along the shelves. It was mainly fiction but there was also a true crime section and another devoted to erotica of different kinds and tastes. Tabitha turned to the librarian.

"Is there anything that's *not* allowed?"

"Not really. Except for true crime books about crimes committed by people who are actually in the prison at the moment."

"I get that," said Tabitha.

"And books with maps of the local area. But I don't suppose you want books of that kind."

Tabitha looked back at the barred window, at the walls topped with spikes and barbed wire. "No," she said. "I won't try to escape. Anyway, I won't be here long."

Galia nodded. "I'll leave you to have a browse."

Alongside the novels and the pornography, there were a few classics, a large foreign language section.

There was a small area devoted to gardening and to DIY, another to well-being. There were books of crosswords and sudoku, many of which had been filled in. Tabitha found a book about Iceland, a country where she had always wanted to go. She took it over to the central table and sat opposite another woman. She was middle-aged, with dark hair, streaked with gray and neatly cut, and she wore a skirt and a flecked turtleneck sweater. Tabitha wondered if she was another librarian. She looked at the book she was reading and the woman, noticing, held it up. It was a recipe book.

"My guilty pleasure," she said. "Ridiculous, isn't it, to be poring over recipes when I'm stuck in here?"

"Doesn't it make things worse?"

"I fantasize about the meals I'm going to cook when I get out. What are you reading?"

Tabitha held up her book. "It's about Iceland."

"The same thing."

"I guess it is."

To imagine whales and glaciers and wild spaces in a poky cell; Tabitha looked down at the book, sick with longing for an open sky and the salty wind in her face.

"Why are you here?"

The woman put her head on one side. She had a curious smile on her face. "You mean, what did I do?"

"Yes."

The woman looked suddenly reflective. "It was stupid, really. I worked for a company that got caught up in a financial mess, and I didn't see what was happening until it was too late. They needed a scapegoat and I was in the right place, or the wrong place. That's my story anyway. Everyone here has a bad-luck story and everyone says they didn't do it."

"I see," said Tabitha.

"You're new here, aren't you?"

"It's all a mistake," Tabitha said. "I think my solicitor will sort things out soon."

"What's your name? I'm Ingrid, by the way."

"Tabitha."

"All right, Tabitha, I'm going to give you some advice. I wish someone had given it to me when I first arrived. Rule number one: never ask anyone what they're in for."

"Oh. Sorry! I didn't mean . . . I mean I didn't know . . ." And she'd asked Michaela as well, she thought, remembering the way her cellmate's face had closed on her.

"I don't mind, but lots of people do. Rule number two: if you have a problem, if you think something's unfair, if someone's got it in for you, don't go to the warden."

"Who do I go to then?"

"You don't. Rule number three: the prison governor is a dreadful woman. Don't rely on her for anything and don't get on her bad side."

"These rules aren't making me feel better about things."

"Rule number four: if you're in trouble for some reason, think of what it was like in the playground." Tabitha grimaced. Michaela had said the same thing, and she'd had a brutal time of it in the playground. "You don't get people to like you by being weak."

She seemed to have finished.

"Is that it?"

"It's advice more than a rule. Keep active. Oh, and the food here is terrible. Go veggie."

"I am anyway. Is the vegetarian good?"

"It's not good but it's a bit less bad." She leaned across the table. "You just have to keep going, Tabitha. You'll be all right."

Six

Half an hour in the exercise yard, a dingy rectangle of concrete and wired fences, and the wind was hard and cold. Tabitha didn't have gloves and her coat was inadequate. But she was outside at least, and there was a sky above her.

Women stood in huddles, most of them with cigarettes. She didn't try and join any of them. She tilted her face up to watch the clouds shift and took in gulps of air, like someone who had been drowning.

In the central hall, she came across the thin old woman with arthritic hands she had seen on her first day, on her way to the showers. She was saying in a loud voice, to everyone and no one, "I think I've found it. This will show them! Look." She fumbled through her thick bundle of papers. "Look here."

Half the pages slipped from her grasp and fell to the floor. She knelt to retrieve them and then had difficulty in getting up again. People were laughing, both prisoners and wardens. Tabitha went forward to help her, but one of the wardens—the puffy one who had ended her call with Shona—got there first, putting his hands under her armpits and lifting her to her feet like an oversized rag doll. He grinned across at Tabitha and screwed a fat forefinger at his temple.

She thought of giving his shin a good, hard kick but instead she smiled at the old woman and turned away.

"Michaela," she said in the darkness.

There was a grunt from the bed above her, then: "What?"

"I'm sorry I asked you what you'd done. I didn't know I shouldn't."

No reply.

"It's quieter tonight."

"That's because everyone's fucking asleep except you. And now me."

"Sorry."

She stared into the thick darkness while Michaela moved restlessly above her and then fell silent again. She heard her breathing. She heard herself breathing. This was her fourth night; in twenty-six days, she would go to court and her case would be thrown out. Four nights out of thirty, two-fifteenths; in percentage terms, that was 13.333 recurring. Tomorrow, Shona would come with clothes and books and pen and paper. She could do this, she could get through it. It would become like a bad dream, the kind that made her lurch awake at night with sweat on her forehead. But just a dream. It wouldn't be true anymore.

Yet still, it was so cold and so dark, and in the darkness thoughts and memories came like an ill wind blowing through her, so that her heart hammered and her breath felt shallow and hard to find. She could suffocate in herself.

She thought about how the doctor had asked her about her moods, the drugs she took, the time she had spent in hospital. She hadn't wanted to talk to him about it, or to the solicitor, because talking made it seem so decisive and clear-cut, whereas to Tabitha being depressed was like being in a swamp. A colorless, featureless swamp with no horizon, no sunlight, no way out.

That day, the one that had led to this cell that tonight felt like a coffin, she had been in the swamp. She barely remembered it, just the immense effort of hauling herself out of bed, her body as heavy and useless as a sack of wet earth; of trudging to the shop; of making herself go for a swim because that was her pledge. And now she was here and she couldn't swim in the sea or chop wood or walk in the cold rain. She knew she mustn't let herself be pulled back into the dreary horror of herself, but she was hanging on by her fingertips.

Seven

"They took everything away."

Shona was slightly out of breath. She sat down opposite Tabitha but her eyes were darting this way and that, taking everything in with an expression that was both nervous and excited. She had put on a blue satin shirt and large earrings; her bobbed chestnut hair shone under the sour lighting. Tabitha could smell her perfume. She looked fresh and pretty and out of place. Faced with her, Tabitha felt small, shabby, plain and grimy. She couldn't remember when she had last washed her hair, and it hadn't been cut for months. However thoroughly she brushed her teeth, the inside of her mouth felt furry. There was a cold sore on the edge of her lips: she needed fresh air, crisp apples, green salad, nourishing vegetable soup.

"They'll need to go through them all. Did you manage to get everything?"

Shona nodded. Her earrings swung. "I think so."

"It's so kind of you."

Shona took a little piece of paper from her pocket and unfolded it in front of her.

"I wrote down how much it cost. Is that OK? Things are really difficult for me right now."

You weren't allowed cash in prison. Tabitha thought hard.

"Talk to Andy," she said. "Andy Kane. I gave him some money for building supplies. He should be able to pay you."

"I'm sorry." Shona bit her full underlip and Tabitha had a memory, as clear as yesterday, of standing in a queue with her outside the swimming pool in town. They must have been about twelve. She couldn't remember why they had been there together; they hadn't really been friends at school. But she could remember the heat of the day and she could even remember that Shona had been wearing a cropped, short-sleeved top whose tightness emphasized her developing breasts.

"There are two types of skin," Shona had said with high seriousness. "Oily or dry. What's yours?"

Twelve-year-old Tabitha put her fingers to her cheek. "I don't know."

"I'm oily," said Shona. "That means I'll have more spots but won't get all wrinkly when I'm old." She leaned in and examined Tabitha's face. "Dry," she said.

Tabitha looked at Shona's skin now, eighteen years later. It was smooth and lustrous.

"Tabitha?"

"Sorry. What were you saying?"

"I feel really bad about asking for the money back."

"That's fine."

"I was worried I'd be late. It took me longer to get here than I thought. It's only about forty miles away but the roads are narrow and there was this huge lorry in front of me almost all the way."

"It's kind of you," said Tabitha. She could feel her familiar impatience building up inside her.

"I've got a few phone numbers," said Shona, and she took another piece of paper from her pocket. "Andy's and Terry's. I didn't know who you wanted. And I got the vicar's number as well."

"The vicar's?"

"I thought you might want it."

"Right."

They stared at each other.

"How are you?" asked Shona eventually. "I mean, how *are* you? You must be . . . I mean, just, well, I couldn't believe it." She stopped. Her brown eyes suddenly filled up with tears. Tabitha had the horrible feeling she was about to lean across and give her a long, perfumy hug.

"Nor me," she said and sat back, out of reach.

"Is it awful in here?"

"It's not great." She didn't want to talk about that. She took a deep breath. "People know I didn't do it, right? That this is just a dreadful mistake."

"Well, *I* know."

"What about other people?"

"You know what villages are like."

"What are they like? I've only been back in this one for a few weeks."

"People like to gossip. Even little things can seem exciting. And this—well, nothing like this has ever happened in Okeham. My God, on the day, well, you can't imagine!"

"You were there?"

Shona frowned. "Don't you remember? I was supposed to be at work but I got stuck because of the tree coming down. It was terrible timing—two of my mums were expecting." Shona was a community midwife. "Anyway, it's still all anyone is talking about."

"So what are they saying?"

"I don't know, just that it's awful. Things like that."

"What are they saying about me?"

A flush suffused Shona's smooth skin. She leaned across the table slightly, made as if to put a hand on Tabitha's arm, changed her mind.

"Don't think about that."

"Is it that bad?"

"No! But you've always been your own worst enemy, haven't you, the way you charge in. You put people's backs up a bit."

"Do I?"

"It's just you don't let sleeping dogs lie. I'm on your side though," Shona said. "Tell me what to do and I'll do it."

"Tell people it's a mistake. That I'll be back soon."

Shona nodded.

"Because it's mad," Tabitha went on. "I mean, why would I kill Stuart? There's absolutely no reason. The prosecution will see that."

"Of course they will. Of course."

"I've got a solicitor who seems clever."

"That's good," said Shona.

"Yes."

Silence filled the space between them. The woman at the table next to Tabitha was leaning toward the man opposite her and sobbing. She was pleading with him, but Tabitha couldn't make out the words. The man merely looked bored.

"Andy's very upset," Shona said. "He's practically the only one in Okeham who doesn't like talking about it, even though he was the one who . . . you know."

"Yes, I know."

"You two are close," said Shona.

Tabitha knew what she was saying. "He's just working on my house."

"Really?"

"Really."

"I don't even know if you . . . you know."

"No."

"Like men."

"Ah."

Shona waited a beat but Tabitha didn't say anything else.

"Does he ever talk about me?"

"I don't think so," said Tabitha cautiously. "But he doesn't talk much anyway."

Shona nodded. "Still waters run deep. Maybe if he visits you could mention that I've broken up with Paul at last."

Tabitha couldn't stop herself from giving a snort of disbelieving laughter: she was in prison charged with murder and Shona wanted her to act as a matchmaker.

"I should go." Shona stood up. "I'm on call this afternoon and some of my mothers are about to pop. But I'll come again, if you'd like me to. It must be lonely."

Tabitha tried to smile. "I'll be home before long."

Eight

Tabitha sat at the little table in her cell. It was so narrow that her back was almost touching the bed. She opened the unlined notebook. She tried to remember the last time she had written a letter on a piece of paper and put it in an envelope and posted it. Probably it had been to a grandparent to say thank you for a present she hadn't really liked. Her mother had told her that it was important to write proper letters to grandparents. Emails didn't count.

Now her mother was dead and her father was dead and all four grandparents were dead and she finally needed to write a letter.

For the past two years, she had been working as a copyeditor for a London publisher. It was perfect for her. She could do it from home. She could do it whenever she wanted, just so long as she met her deadlines. But she wouldn't be able to do it in prison.

14 January
AO3573

Dear Cathy,

Maybe you've heard by now but I'm writing this to you from prison. It's all a mad mistake. I won't go into the details. I'm sure it's going to be sorted out soon but for the moment I'm not going to be able to do any work for you.

Also, I don't think you've paid me for the Greenwood job or the psychology collection I did before that. I know there's always a delay in paying and I don't want to make a fuss, but I really need the money at the moment as you can imagine. It would be good if you could do it by bank transfer. I'm not sure if I'll be able to deposit checks from here.

You can write to me here and I'll let you know if things change.

All the best,

Tabitha

Tabitha looked over the letter. It felt like a mixture of too much information and not enough. And a bit whiny as well. It felt strange to be complaining about late pay-ment when she was in prison charged with murder.

The second letter required more thought.

14 January
AO3573

Dear Michael,

After writing this, Tabitha stared at the wall for fully ten minutes. There was a poster on the wall, a photo-graph of a pine forest with a soft green floor, dropping gently into the distance. For a tiny moment, she had the illusion that she was looking through a window and the forest was just in front of her, tantalizingly out of reach.

Michael. What could she say to him? They'd had no contact at all for nearly a year. Things with him hadn't ended disastrously, but they hadn't ended all that well either. *Just write*, she told herself. *Don't think about it too much.*

You're probably surprised to hear from me. And
you're probably even more surprised to get a
letter from me. I don't know if you've heard what
happened. The postmark will tell you something.

There's no point in me going through it all here. Just google me and you'll be able to find out as much as you want to find out.

Short version. I'm in Crow Grange Prison. What happened is that a neighbor of mine was found murdered and insanely I was suspected of it. In fact, you'll see after about two seconds of going online that I've been charged with murdering him and so I'm here on remand.

So why am I writing to you? All I can say is that I'm like someone who's just fallen in the water and you were one of the names that came into my head to shout to for help. I was wondering if you might come to visit. I know it's a lot to ask because it means coming all the way to Devon. But it would mean a lot to me.

If you can come, please write back with a phone number. I'll need to ring you because visiting is a bit complicated. You have to fill out a form and bring ID and probably other stuff. I'll check.

Let me know.

Love (if it's OK to say that),

Tabitha

Nine

And, three days later, he came.

Tabitha made the route to the visiting hall. She saw him before he saw her. He looked so familiar. The unbrushed hair that was starting to recede, the gray jacket he always wore with too many pockets, his hands awkwardly in two of them. He always had the air of seeming just a little uncomfortable wherever he was. At least he had some excuse this time. There were the usual sounds of sobbing. Somebody shouted and a warden ran across.

Tabitha sat down opposite him.

"I wasn't sure you'd come," she said.

He shifted in his seat as if he was already preparing to leave.

"I didn't know what to bring," he said. "I brought some magazines and a couple of other things. They took them away. But the woman said you'd get them. I suppose they need to check them."

"Thank you," said Tabitha. "And thank you for coming."

"Thank you for asking me," he replied solemnly, absurdly. But then he added, "I was a bit surprised that you did, actually."

She remembered the last time they'd met. She remembered shouting at him and him backing away. He had often seemed faintly puzzled and embarrassed by her. They'd met in the café where she'd briefly worked when she'd arrived in London after dropping out of university. Michael had come into the café almost every day for lunch. He had the soup of the day followed by Earl Grey tea and a flapjack. They'd both been lonely, knowing almost nobody in this huge, churning city. They'd both taken the other for someone they were not. Tabitha had thought Michael was shy and thoughtful, but actually he turned out to be quite smug and doggedly set in his ways. He had thought Tabitha charmingly kooky at first; her rages and her wretchedness had soon made him acutely uncomfortable.

"So what the hell happened?" said Michael now.

"Did you google me?"

"Yes."

"Then you know."

"No, I don't. For a start, what were you even doing in Okeham? I thought you hated the place."

"Not exactly hated."

"You said you were miserable there."

"Maybe it was me, not the place. You know I hated living in London. It was always meant to be a stopgap while I decided what to do in my life but I kind of got stuck there." He nodded. "Anyway, there was a fantasy I'd always had about this old house there and it came on the market and I bought it and I've been doing it up."

Michael leaned forward on the table and rested his head on his hands. He looked like he was in pain.

"I saw that he was found in your house."

"In a shed at the back."

"That's weird."

"Yes."

He gave a nervous little laugh. "I mean, why would you report finding a body in your own house if you'd killed him?"

"Shed. And I didn't exactly find it. It was found by this guy, Andy."

"Is he your new . . . ?"

Tabitha remembered that Michael had an irritating habit of leaving his sentences unfinished as if he were waiting for you to guess the word.

"No. He's a builder. He's helping me with the house. I guess I should say he *was* helping me."

"I suppose you've got lots of old friends in the village."

"I know people in the village to say hello to. There are a few left from when I lived there. And now one of them is dead."

"You knew him?"

"He was a teacher at my school."

"So you've got a motive," he said with a half smile.

"Don't. I'm in prison. Don't make one of your stupid unfunny jokes."

Michael made an indeterminate gesture. "I took a train across England to get here. I had to change twice and then take a bus and then a taxi."

"OK," said Tabitha tightly. "Sorry."

"Can I ask a question? A body is found in your house. Or next to your house. That's bad. But why are they actually charging you with murder?"

"I'm not completely sure. I think they have to tell the solicitor and she'll tell me."

"And what about your defense?"

"I don't know. I don't know anything about the law.

I'm just desperately hoping that the lawyers are going to sort this out and show the police that they've made a mistake."

Michael gave a shrug and shook his head.

"What?" said Tabitha.

"I don't know. It's just that it doesn't sound like you. It sounds more like the way you saw me."

"How did I see you?"

"Being passive. Not doing much. I wouldn't expect you to just be sitting here waiting for someone else to sort things out."

Tabitha took a few deep breaths. "Have you looked around?" she said. "I'm in fucking prison. How am I supposed to sort things out?"

"I don't want to get sucked into one of your arguments."

"One of *my* arguments?"

"I used to sometimes feel like we were slipping down a slope into an argument and whatever I did to stop it, I couldn't."

"Whatever *you* did?" said Tabitha. "You mean, sit there and look at me as if I was an object of poor taste?"

"Tabitha, please—"

"That's exactly the tone. *Tabitha, please.* Like you were the sensible grown-up and I was a naughty little girl who was—"

She stopped suddenly and put a hand over her eyes so she didn't have to see his face. "This isn't what I wanted," she said.

"I understand you're under a great strain," he said stiffly.

"I'm grateful you're here." Her face ached with the effort it took to look calm and rational. "I'm going to need all the help I can get."

There was a pause.

"Ye-e-s," said Michael slowly and then Tabitha knew, with a sickening lurch, what was coming.

"I'm so sorry about all of this. It's terrible. It shouldn't happen to anyone. But I'm not the right person for this."

"Oh," said Tabitha.

"I felt I needed to make the gesture. To come here and see you and bring you things."

"Magazines."

"And some other things. But we weren't together for that long—"

"Fourteen months."

"And it was a while ago."

"It's all right," she said. She looked at his mouth opening and closing and she just wanted him gone. Why had she ever asked him to come?

"I'm not a lawyer. I don't have money. I'm trying to deal with things myself."

"I said it was all right."

He looked at his watch. "I'd probably better be, you know . . ."

"Yes."

"There's a bus and a train."

"Of course."

He got up and held out a hand and then looked at it as if it didn't belong to him. "I don't know. Are we allowed . . . ?"

"Yes, we can shake hands."

They shook hands briefly and then he turned and walked away. Tabitha thought to herself: *Well, he was an ex-boyfriend, after all. What was I expecting?*

Ten

*Y*ou *just have to keep going*, that was what Ingrid had said. And Michaela. But today was one of Tabitha's bad days, when the effort of hauling herself out of bed, of pulling on clothes that were always grubby, brushing her hair that always felt a bit greasy, eating food that made her gag, seemed a monumental task. Her body felt impossibly heavy. She wanted to curl in a ball and hide. She wanted to howl.

But at least her solicitor was coming to see her.

"So have you any good news?" she asked. Her voice came out too bright, almost jocose.

"I have your medical assessment," said Mora Piozzi, tapping on her iPad. She looked older than Tabitha remembered, and more unyielding.

"You don't look particularly happy about it. I hope I'm not dying." She winced as she spoke at the sound of her false cheerfulness.

Mora Piozzi didn't smile. She was studying the screen in front of her, swiping through pages. Then she looked up.

"I'm not particularly happy," she said.

Tabitha felt a lurch in her stomach.

"Do you remember I said you should tell me of anything relevant—anything I'd rather hear from you than from the prosecution?"

"Did you say that?"

"You didn't tell me about your history of depression."

"It's not really a history."

"You were hospitalized in 2010 and then again in 2013."

"It was more of a clinic."

"You were sectioned."

"Only the once. The second time was voluntary. And it wasn't for long. I was going through a bad patch."

"Tabitha, I'm not judging you, but don't you see that this is relevant information?"

"I'm sorry, I didn't even think of it."

Mora Piozzi looked down at the screen again. "Over the years, you've been prescribed a variety of medications: Citalopram. Paroxetine. Most recently—in fact until ten days before the murder—Zoloft and amitriptyline."

"I didn't get on with them, though."

"Which is also relevant. And you've had therapy."

"That was a waste of time."

"Did you think all this wouldn't come up, Tabitha?"

"Why should it?" Tabitha bunched her fists up and leaned forward. "Why the fuck should it? When I was younger, I had a hard time and I dropped out of uni. That's not a crime, just a wasted opportunity. I've had drugs and therapy to help me cope. That's not a crime. I don't like people knowing about it because then they put a label on me and I hate that. I know what I have to do to deal with it. I make myself get up. I walk. I swim in the sea. I eat healthy food. I do practical things, like fixing my house. I put one foot in front of the other. I have my bad days, sure, but I'm doing all right. I was doing all right."

Mora Piozzi briefly put a hand on Tabitha's bunched fist.

"I am sure you were and in normal circumstances, of course, you can keep it all private. But these are not normal circumstances. You've been charged with murder. Your whole life will be scrutinized. The fact that you have been seriously depressed is relevant. The fact that you have been on a regime of strong antidepressants, some of which are associated with memory loss, is relevant."

Tabitha's mouth felt dry and her head hurt slightly. The lights in the room were too bright; it was like being in a laboratory.

"Dr. Hartson says you were resistant to his questions."

"I answered everything he asked," said Tabitha. "What did he want me to do? Break down and weep? Tell him all my troubles so he could be the good doctor? Where would that get me?"

Mora Piozzi was looking at her as if she was a problem to be solved. "Was that day one of your bad days?"

"It wasn't great." Not great at all, she thought: a day that had been heavy and colorless and grim.

"And you say you can't remember much of it."

"It's a bit of a fog. But I'd remember killing someone." Tabitha laughed harshly. "That's not something I'd ever forget."

Piozzi didn't smile back. She started to write and then stopped.

"You believe that I'm here to do everything I possibly can for you?" she said. "Don't you?"

"I have to. It's not like I've got many other people on my side."

"You've got to trust me," Piozzi continued. "But I also have to trust you. I need to know the problems, the weaknesses. I need to hear them from you, not from the police, not from the prosecution. You have to be straight with me."

"Just ask me anything," said Tabitha, "and I'll answer it."

"That's not enough. You need to tell me the things I wouldn't even think of asking about."

"I've told you everything, everything I can think of."

Piozzi put her pen down.

"Good," she said, very softly.

Eleven

"There's a visitor for you," said the warden.

Tabitha looked up from where she was lying on her bunk.

"Who?"

"How should I know?"

Tabitha got up and quickly walked past the warden and along the corridor. She would have liked time to prepare mentally for a visitor, collect her thoughts, think of questions. She would have liked time to prepare physically. She hadn't looked in the mirror but she suspected that her hair was disheveled and greasy. She probably didn't smell too good either. She hadn't showered today, just a quick wash under the arms. But it was too late. The important thing was to get there on time.

She was so used to the noises of the prison—the clanging of doors and footsteps, the shouting—that it took her a moment to notice a scuffle taking place across to one side. The old woman with the papers was being jostled by two young women. Some of the papers had fallen to the floor.

Tabitha continued walking. She remembered the advice she had been given. To get through this just keep your head down, don't get involved, don't make trouble. Besides, she was in a hurry, someone was waiting for her. Anything she would do would only make things worse.

She stopped. She muttered to herself angrily. She felt a familiar sensation, as if something were tearing apart in her head. A wave of anger was curling and cresting inside her. *Don't*, she told herself. *Just don't*. She knew she would.

She turned back. The old woman was on her knees, trying to collect her papers, but more kept falling.

"Excuse me," said Tabitha. "You never told me your name."

The old woman looked up. "Vera," she said.

The two younger women looked round. One of them had tattooed tears down one cheek. The other had hair that was shaved, leaving a ribbed pattern across her head.

"Fuck off out of it," said the tattooed woman.

"Leave her alone," said Tabitha.

The shaved woman pushed Tabitha's shoulder.

"What's the point of that?" said Tabitha. She was crackling with rage and it felt good. "Stop bullying her and fuck off," she added.

The woman pushed her harder. Tabitha pushed back, hard, and then she was immediately lost in a whirlwind of blows and punches. She pulled herself free and swung her right fist, her left fist. She didn't know if she was making contact. There were shouts and screams and she felt herself held from behind and a blow against her face that felt like an explosion of white and orange and red. She kept trying to wriggle free and was forced down onto the linoleum and even then, when she couldn't use her arms she managed to flap her legs. Gradually it all subsided. Her face was forced down and she was held down and saw the boots of a warden beside her face. Her mouth felt full and she spat on the floor and saw that it was blood.

Standing in the prison governor's room, Tabitha felt like she wasn't in a prison anymore. It was more like the headmistress's office. There were paintings on the wall of a deer and one of a moonlit lake. There was an embroidered rug, a leather chair. On the desk was a nameplate: Deborah Cole MBE. Sitting at the desk was Deborah Cole herself, a woman in her late forties, her hair neatly styled with blond streaks. Tabitha could only see her top half: gray jacket, white shirt with a brooch at the throat. Her face was made up with a surgical precision, as if she were about to appear on television.

Tabitha had been led into the office by two female wardens, who stood on either side of her. Cole looked up from a file she was reading. Tabitha assumed it was hers.

"What happened?"

"I don't know," said Tabitha. "It was a bit of a blur."

Cole barely reacted. She just tightened her lips. "Orla Donnelly," she said. "Jasmine Cash. Were they the girls you were fighting with?"

Girls. Tabitha almost found the word funny, as if this had been a little bundle on the hockey field.

"I'm new here. I don't know people's names."

"Could you identify them?"

Tabitha knew that she should just say no but she couldn't stop herself.

"Are you saying that I should inform on other prisoners and then what? You'll protect me? Keep me safe?"

"We keep everyone safe."

"Yeah, right, OK. But as I say, it was a bit of a blur." She took a tissue from her pocket and wiped her mouth. It was red. "And now I've got to go. There's a visitor here to see me."

Cole shook her head. "You've been in a fight. No visitor."

"I'm not a prisoner. I'm on remand. I've got the right to be visited."

Cole's expression became almost contemptuous. "Visits are a privilege, not a right. You can have visits when you deserve them."

"How the fuck can I prepare for the trial if I can't have visits?"

"You should have thought about that before." She looked down at the file. "Less than a fortnight and already causing trouble. We'll need to keep an eye on you."

"You'll regret this," said Tabitha.

Very slowly Cole closed the file. "Maybe things haven't been explained to you properly, Miss Hardy. I run a zero-tolerance environment here. Zero tolerance for drugs. Zero tolerance for violence. And zero tolerance for disruptive behavior. This is a house of correction." She looked at one of the wardens. "Take her away. Full search."

"What do you mean, full search? Search for what?"

Cole was already looking down at her desk and Mary Guy and the stringy woman seized an arm each and pulled her out of the office. In the anteroom she saw the tattooed woman and the shaved woman, each with a warden, seated.

They dragged her along the corridor and into a room, completely empty with gray walls, no pictures, a window high up. All Tabitha could see through it was the blankness of a gray sky. They let her go and she stood between them in the middle of the room.

"You know this is crap, right?" she said, panting with anger rather than the effort.

"Wait," said Mary Guy.

"For what?"

Neither of them answered. After a few awkward minutes, the door opened and two more female wardens came in. They were dressed in the same uniform but were clearly younger, much younger. They were like schoolgirls. The two of them stood to one side, right by the wall. Mary Guy turned to them.

"Watch," she said. "This is what we do." Then she turned to Tabitha. "Take everything off and put it in a pile."

"This is crap," said Tabitha. "I was just on my way from my cell. You've got no right to do this."

"We can make you do it. And I promise you won't like that."

"I'm not a convicted prisoner. I'm just on remand. You can't do this."

"It's going to be done, one way or another. If necessary, I'll send for more people and they won't all be women."

Tabitha tried to make her mind go blank. She pulled her sweater and her tee shirt together over her head. She wasn't wearing a bra. She kicked off her shoes. She pulled off her trousers.

"Everything," said the stringy warden.

She pulled down her knickers and added them to the pile.

"I said, everything."

Tabitha looked down. "You mean my socks? Oh for fuck's sake."

She teetered on her left foot and pulled off her right sock, then teetered on her right foot and pulled off her left sock. She tossed them on the floor.

"You should shave more," said Mary Guy. There was a snickering sound from behind Tabitha.

"Fuck you," said Tabitha.

"I'll remember you said that."

She walked forward until she was almost touching Tabitha. Then she walked behind her.

"Squat," she said.

"I know what you're doing," said Tabitha. "You're not looking for anything. You're just doing this as some kind of punishment."

"Squat."

"No."

"Would you like a week in solitary?"

Tabitha thought of her visitor. Of her visitors. The visitors she desperately needed.

She squatted.

"Lower."

She forced herself down. Her back was hurting.

"Stay like that."

She sensed the woman behind her. "You're not allowed to touch me."

"I'm not going to touch you."

Tabitha heard a click. She looked down and saw that the other warden had placed a small pocket mirror between her feet.

"This is how we check whether they're hiding anything inside. I want you to come one by one and look."

One by one the other wardens came over. One of them squatted in front of Tabitha, looked down at the mirror and then smiled at her. It was almost a grin. Tabitha imagined her going home in the evening, being with her family. Imagined her at Christmas dinner. It was a way of not screaming.

An hour later, or it may have been two or three hours later, Tabitha was lying on the bed in her cell, facing away from the door. She heard a sound and turned round. The tattooed woman and the shaved woman had come into the cell. The shaved woman had pulled the door almost closed and was standing with her back to it. The tattooed woman took a step closer.

So this was it, Tabitha thought. This is where it all ended. She stood up. If they were going to do it, they would really have to do it. She wasn't going down passively.

The shaved woman extended her hand—it was empty.

"You did good," she said. "You didn't rat us out. I'm Jasmine. This is Orla."

Warily, Tabitha shook Jasmine's hand and then Orla's.

"Leave Vera alone," she said.

Twelve

As Tabitha approached the table, she wasn't even sure if she knew who her visitor was. The woman stood up to greet her and then Tabitha recognized her. She was the vicar of St. Peter's church in the village. For an alarming moment, she couldn't remember her name. She felt like she was searching for something in a dark room and then suddenly the light came on.

"Melanie," she said and held her hand out. "Do I call you vicar?"

Melanie Coglan took her hand and shook it with a firm grip.

"Call me Mel," she said.

"I'm sorry about your visit a couple of days ago."

"That's fine. Is your lip all right?"

Tabitha put her hand to her lip and flinched slightly. She knew it was still swollen.

"It's nothing," she said. "I'm sorry to take you away from your church."

Tabitha had never seen Mel in the church. She had never been in the church, except to look around the old Norman interior on a weekday when nobody else was there. She had only seen the vicar striding around the village and she had the look of someone who walked a lot in the open air. She was square-jawed, freckled even in the winter. She had gray-blond hair, tied back in a ponytail, and wore a gray sweater, dark slacks and solid leather shoes. And she wore a dog collar. A bulky jacket was draped over the back of her chair, the one Tabitha had seen her in so often, walking with large and energetic strides around the village to call on parishioners. She glanced around the room with obvious fascination, then contemplated Tabitha with a look of concern that also had a touch of fascination. Tabitha felt like a strange exotic animal, crouched at the back of a cage being stared at through bars.

"You're looking at my dog collar," Mel said.

"I wasn't really."

"I know, it looks funny. I'm not really that sort of a vicar. I don't want to ram the God thing down people's throats. But when I come somewhere like this, I think it shows a certain, I don't know . . ."

"That you're not trying to smuggle drugs and a mobile phone in?"

Mel suddenly looked alarmed. "They wouldn't think that, would they?"

"That's what people do."

"I did bring you some magazines," she said.

"Thank you."

She never read magazines. She had passed the ones Michael had left for her straight to Michaela.

There was a pause. Mel looked awkward but Tabitha felt no inclination to speak. She waited.

"You're probably surprised to see me here. I know you're not a churchgoer."

"I'm sorry. Well, I'm not sorry. I just don't believe in God."

Mel smiled. "It's not compulsory," she said. "Actually a lot of people come to church without really specifically believing in a God who's up there in the sky. It's more about comfort and meeting others."

"Just now I've got another problem with going to church."

"I know, I know, and if my job is about anything, it's about coming to see people in the parish when they're in distress. It's not about judging you. It's about trying to give you solace."

"It is about judging me," said Tabitha. "And realizing I didn't do it."

"You don't need to say that to me. You don't need to say anything."

"Have you been to offer comfort to Laura Rees as well?"

There was a momentary pause before Mel replied. "Yes. Yes, I have."

"How is she?"

"She's in mourning."

"Sorry. I guess it's inappropriate for you to talk to me about her. Does she mind that you're coming to see the woman who's been charged with murdering her husband?"

"She knows that I look after all my parishioners."

"You mean the goats as well as the sheep?"

"I don't really see it like that."

"And Stuart was a parishioner of yours as well."

"Yes."

"He was a churchgoer, wasn't he?"

"He was a *regular* churchgoer."

Tabitha started to say something else and then stopped, struck by what she had just heard.

"That sounds not completely enthusiastic."

"I didn't mean anything like that," said Mel. "One of the challenges of my job, maybe I should say one of the joys of my job, is that people have their own personal views of religion. And how it should be practiced."

"He thought you weren't religious enough?"

"He had certain views." Mel smiled cheerily. "Which I quite understand. I shouldn't be saying any of this. I'm here to listen to you. Is there any way I can help?"

"You can get me out."

Mel gave a nervous bark of laughter.

"All right," said Tabitha. "Failing that, you can tell me how things are in the village."

Mel thought for a moment. "I don't know what to say. Nothing like this has ever happened there before. Once the police and the television cameras had gone away, there was a sense of confusion and grief."

Tabitha felt dissatisfied with this. Confusion and grief sounded more like a sermon Mel was giving to her usual, near-empty church. Tabitha needed specifics.

"Did the police interview people?" she asked.

"They talked to people."

"Did they talk to you?"

Mel beamed at her. "I'm not sure if I'm allowed to say."

"I don't know if you're allowed to say either. Anyway, what could you possibly tell them about me?"

Tabitha looked at Mel but Mel didn't reply.

"I know this is tricky for you," Tabitha said, "but what do people think of me?"

"They don't know what to think," said Mel. "They know that Stuart Rees was murdered and they know that you have been, you know . . ."

"Charged with his murder," said Tabitha.

"Well, yes."

"I don't completely fit with Okeham society."

"I wouldn't say that exactly."

"And Stuart was friends with everyone."

Mel's amiable smile wavered. "I wouldn't exactly say that either."

Tabitha stopped to consider. "Then what *would* you say?"

"Oh, you know. Villages."

"I don't know what you mean exactly," said Tabitha. "My main impression was that I didn't really know anyone in the village and he knew everyone. Villages like Okeham probably depend on people like Stuart."

"I suppose he did know everyone." She gave another little laugh. "But then I know everyone as well. And people probably have mixed feelings about me. You know, here comes Mel again, asking how I am. That's probably what people say."

"I'm sure they don't. But what do they say about me? You're the person who talks to everyone."

Mel took a deep breath, as if she was making a resolution. "Tabitha, rather than worrying about what other people think of you, don't you think it would be helpful to reflect on what you think of yourself?"

"That doesn't sound like a good idea at all."

"I'm just here to guide you and give you comfort in any way that I can."

She leaned forward with an expression of earnest sympathy that made Tabitha want to tell her to fuck off and never come back. But she didn't. It occurred to her that she might need Mel one day.

"Thank you," she said. "That means a lot to me."

Thirteen

It was spitting snow outside the little window. It didn't look like the kind that would settle. Tabitha tried to count the days. Today was Thursday, January 31, so she had been here three weeks and one day. Tomorrow it would be February. That meant that in a week's time she would be going to the court to enter her plea. One week.

Michaela was brushing her long hair in front of the mirror that Tabitha still avoided looking into, though every so often she caught a glimpse of her face: pale, with new lines round the eyes, cracked lips and hair badly in need of a cut. She put on a clean shirt, though nothing really felt properly clean, and a cardigan that had a hole in the elbow but was better than her old sweatshirt.

"My solicitor is coming," said Tabitha to Michaela. "I hope she has news."

"Can I remind you what you said to me on my last visit?" said Mora Piozzi.

"This sounds like I'm already in court," said Tabitha.

She forced her bruised lips into a smile, which hurt. Mora Piozzi did not smile back.

"You said that you couldn't think of anything that you hadn't told me that might be relevant to your case."

"That's right," said Tabitha warily.

"Really? Nothing, Tabitha?"

"I don't think so."

"Yesterday, the prosecution received a letter that stated you had been in an inappropriate relationship with Stuart Rees when you were a schoolgirl."

Tabitha felt like someone had punched her hard in the stomach. She heard herself give a snort of laughter and put a hand across her mouth for a moment in case more laughter should escape.

"Well?"

"What do you mean, a letter?"

"I mean a letter."

"Who wrote it?" Tabitha asked indignantly. She could feel her face flaming; her whole body felt intolerably hot.

"That's hardly the point. Is it true?"

"Of course not."

"And yet Laura Rees has confirmed it."

"What?"

"I said—"

"I heard what you said. Why did you ask me if it was true if you already knew it was? You were just trying to trick me."

Mora Piozzi was white around the nostrils and her mouth was a thin, straight line.

"I think you'll have to come down from your moral high ground," she said, her voice clipped and sharp. "You explicitly assured me there was nothing you were keeping back. And now I learn from the prosecution that when you were fifteen, you were sexually involved with the man you stand accused of murdering. Are you going to tell me that's not relevant?" There was a long pause. "Well?"

"Hardly sexually involved," said Tabitha, dragging her gaze up to meet the solicitor's hard stare. She was aiming for a scoffing tone but it came out a weak squawk.

"You were underage. He was your teacher. He had sex with you. You return to the village and buy the house that is nearest to his."

"Five minutes away," Tabitha interjected feebly.

"A few weeks later, he is found stabbed to death in the backyard of your house. You don't tell anyone about the relationship; indeed, just now you denied it."

"None of that sounds quite right."

"It might not sound right—but are you going to tell me it's not true?"

"It's not *not* true. But you're putting sentences next to each other that don't belong next to each other, and it makes it seem that each thing leads to the next, but it doesn't. Not necessarily."

"Why in God's name didn't you tell me? You must have known it would come out."

"It's no one's business," Tabitha said. "It didn't matter."

Mora Piozzi bought her fist down on the table and Tabitha jerked backward. "Wake up! Do you have any idea of how bad this looks?"

"It was years ago. It has nothing to do with now."

"Don't be ridiculous."

"Don't be insulting," replied Tabitha. "You're supposed to be representing me."

"Exactly. I'm supposed to be representing you. You don't tell me about your history of depression and I have to learn about it from Dr. Hartson and from reading your medical history. You don't tell me that the murder victim sexually abused you—"

"That's not true."

Mora Piozzi gazed at her. She didn't frown so much as draw her whole face into an expression of forbidding incredulity. "You were fifteen, Tabitha. He was your teacher."

"It wasn't like that."

"So what was it like?"

Tabitha folded her arms round herself and looked away. Her mind was working very slowly. She couldn't explain to herself why it was that she hadn't mentioned to the solicitor her . . . what was the word? Not "relationship," not "involvement," surely not "abuse"?— her *thing* with Stuart. She realized now that at some level it must have occurred to her to do so. Without consciously making the decision, she had withheld the information, pushed it deep down inside her. She felt bewildered and suddenly, shockingly, scared.

"I don't know," she said.

"You don't know what it was like?"

"I don't know. I can't say. I don't want to talk about it. Please."

"I'm afraid you don't get to choose."

"Don't I? I thought I could just remain silent."

The woman sighed and passed a hand in front of her face. When she looked at Tabitha again, she no longer looked angry, but distressed.

"I'm representing you," she said. "You need to trust me. I want to help you but I can only do that if you let me. Do you understand?"

Tabitha nodded.

"You can see how this looks, can't you?"

"How does it look?"

"Frankly, it looks bad. And the fact that you concealed relevant information makes it worse."

"I see."

"Let me try again. Can you tell me what happened between you and Stuart Rees when you were fifteen?"

Tabitha stared down at her hands with the bracelet of eczema round the wrists and the bitten fingernails. She felt small and soiled and didn't want to be looked at.

"There's not much to say. You need to understand it was a whole different life. Something that had gone and I never thought of it. That's true," she added, seeing the disbelief in her solicitor's face. "When I came back and met him again, I barely recognized him, you know. It was like meeting a stranger. When I was at school, he looked normal but now he'd got properly overweight, and his hair had receded and he'd grown a beard, like he needed to compensate."

That was the first thing she'd said to him when they had met again, two days after she had moved into her house: "You've grown a beard." He had stroked his chin, as if pleasantly surprised to feel the hair growing there, and said it was easier than shaving but Laura didn't like it. He'd said she was looking well, though his gaze had never settled on her but shifted rapidly this way and that. Then he had added how nice it was that they were neighbors, and that she must come round for tea sometime, for old times' sake. She never had, though once Laura had left a lemon drizzle cake on her doorstep.

"What are you saying, Tabitha?"

"I'm saying that he was a different person and so was I and that's why it wasn't relevant. It was like it had never happened."

"Like it had never happened?"

"Yes."

"I'm not sure a jury would find that very convincing."

"I don't care. It's true."

"You need to care. How many times did he have sex with you?"

"Not many."

"Once, twice, ten times, more?"

"I don't know," said Tabitha. She could feel herself shutting down, the lights going off one by one. "More than twice," she made herself say.

"You never told anyone."

"No."

"Why?"

"It didn't feel right. It was private."

"Were you infatuated?"

Tabitha heard a snickering sound coming from her. She put her fist into her mouth and bit down on it.

"No," she said eventually.

"Was he violent?"

"No."

"Did he—?"

"No."

"Tabitha, listen to me."

"I'm listening."

"Your hearing is in a week's time."

"I know."

"In the light of this new information, we need to think about how to proceed."

"You're telling me they're not going to throw the case out."

Mora Piozzi looked aghast. "They certainly are not," she said eventually. Then she continued, carefully, as if worried that Tabitha might not understand her. "It is my opinion that on the seventh of February, we have three options: you can plead not guilty, you can plead guilty to manslaughter and you can—"

"Wait," said Tabitha.

"Yes?"

"I need to ask you something."

"All right."

Tabitha took a deep breath. "Do you think I did it?"

"I'm your solicitor. I'm here to represent you as best as I can."

"That's not an answer."

"My job isn't to find the truth."

"So you won't answer?"

"No."

"Which means you think I might have done it?"

"It means I'm acting as your solicitor."

"But I need my solicitor to believe in me." To her dismay, Tabitha felt her eyes fill with thick tears. She turned her head away and blinked furiously, feeling Mora Piozzi's steady gaze on her.

"No, Tabitha, you need your solicitor to do the best that he or she possibly can to represent you. Which is what I want to do, but I need your help."

"I'm in trouble, aren't I?"

"We're only at the beginning of a long process."

Tabitha couldn't speak. The room was bleary through her tears. She had been counting the days until February 7, but now she understood that that was only the start of it. She thought of her cell, where the sky was just a tiny square in the concrete wall and where at night she felt she would suffocate. She thought of footsteps echoing down corridors, doors shutting, keys being turned; of howls in the darkness, eyes watching her.

"Tabitha? Did you hear what I was saying?"

"No. Sorry."

"I was saying that you have to take things one step at a time."

Tabitha nodded.

"The next step is the court appearance. You have to consider your options."

"Yes, you said that. You said you thought I had three options. Not guilty. Guilty of manslaughter. And you didn't say the third."

"Guilty with diminished responsibility."

"I don't understand."

"Stuart Rees abused you when you were a vulnerable minor. Since then you have been clinically depressed and have struggled to cope."

"What are you saying?"

"I am saying you need to think about your best course, Tabitha."

"You think I murdered him."

Mora Piozzi stood up. "One week," she said. "Think about it."

Fourteen

At secondary school, Tabitha had been good at math, chemistry and art (though she liked drawing more than painting). Small, strong and wiry, she had been good at cross-country running. But she hadn't been good at making friends or joining in or keeping her head down. She hadn't been good at being sweet, or flirting with the boys, or giggling with the girls, or buying the right trainers, or knowing the latest dance moves, or going out on Friday night, or boasting about sexual experiences she'd never had, or getting the right amount of drunk or the right amount of stoned, or sharing secrets. She hadn't been good at being a teenager, especially after her father had died. At its best, school was a lonely business for her; sometimes it was much worse than that. She coped by pretending she didn't care, and bit by bit she actually didn't care. Or not really. Not so that it hurt and shamed her as it used to when she was younger.

Tabitha lay in her bunk and remembered herself at fifteen, half her lifetime ago: an awkward and fiercely cross only child, short and flat-chested and looking much younger than her age, disguising her shyness by being grumpy and taciturn. Gradually, people stopped picking on her until at last nobody really took much notice of her at all—until Mr. Rees the math teacher singled her out. For several years, he was just another teacher at the school, not one of the charismatic ones who the girls giggled about, nor one of those who were bullied, like Mr. Wheedon with hair combed over his bald spot. Mr. Rees didn't have trouble keeping order. He sometimes got angry but not in an uncontrolled way like some of the others who would shout and flail their arms. His anger was deliberate, contemptuous and effective.

He had never taken any notice of her either, until she was fifteen. Then she suddenly found herself the focus of his attention. At first, it was just about her work—she was his star pupil, and he used her as an example to others who were struggling (which hadn't helped her popularity). Then he started keeping her back after the end of class. He gave her more advanced work, told her she should study math at university. It seemed to Tabitha that he had recognized her like no one else had done.

He wasn't young and handsome. She didn't have a crush on him. She didn't think of him like that at all. He was just kind to her at a time when she was badly in need of kindness. A friendly face.

When he had put an arm around her shoulder, she had let him. When he placed a hand on her knee, she didn't push it away. When he told her she was the reason he looked forward to coming to work, she had believed him. When one wet day in winter he offered her a lift home and drove instead into the woods and lifted up her skirt and pulled down her knickers and in the muggy darkness of the car slid on a condom and deflowered her, her blood spotting the seat, she hadn't protested, just turned her head away and watched the rain. Numb, just waiting till it was over. She had never thought of telling anybody what had happened. Nor the next time, or the ones after that. Eleven Wednesdays, Tabitha thought, as she lay in her bed beneath Michaela who mumbled in her sleep, and remembered those days. Or was it twelve?

Then there was the Wednesday when she had waited behind in the class and he had walked past her without looking at her, and it was like she didn't exist anymore.

She had gone to the window and watched him drive away in his car. That was how it ended, as if it had never happened, like he had simply erased her. She sat week after week in his lessons while his glance slid over her and felt she had disappeared. In her place was just an absence, a hole where Tabitha Hardy used to be.

She had felt neither relieved nor upset. She had felt nothing at all.

It was like a dream—a dream in the darkness and she couldn't piece the fragments together into a story that made real sense.

Why had she—small, cross, fatherless Tabitha Hardy who stood her ground against the bullies and read passionate books about women's rights—let it happen? Why hadn't she thought about it for all of these years, not even mentioning it in her therapy sessions? Why hadn't she been upset, angry, ashamed? She was a fighter, but she had never once thought of fighting for herself.

She stared out into the night. Perhaps she had been wretched, she thought; perhaps she had been damaged; perhaps she had minded so much that she had pushed it down as deep as she could. Maybe Mora Piozzi was right and it was abuse and she was traumatized. Of course she was right: she had been fifteen and he, what, something like forty-five?

And now the person who had abused her was dead. Mr. Rees the math teacher. Stuart Rees her neighbor. The pillar of his little community. His body in her shed, his car parked outside, his blood all over her.

She bit her lip so hard that she tasted iron in her mouth. She put her hands over her eyes to make the darkness darker. She couldn't remember that day, or only a few snatches. It had been a day of wild weather and of a crouching fear. The kind of day she had to crawl blindly through, just to get to the end.

What had happened? Why had he come to her house and why had he died and what had she been doing?

Her solicitor believed she had murdered him. What did she, Tabitha Hardy, believe? She didn't know. She didn't know, and not knowing tipped dread through her like poison.

She didn't know what to do. She had no idea. She had no one to turn to and the night went on and on and on and when morning came she still didn't know.

Fifteen

"A re you all right?"

Tabitha looked around. Ingrid was looking at her with concern. Tabitha had been standing in a corner of the exercise yard. The prisoners were legally entitled to one hour of exercise in the open air every day. It was on the schedule; many things were technically on the schedule and available, but schedules could change at the last minute and availability was always liable to suspension without notice. Even during Tabitha's time at Crow Grange, the exercise had been suspended several times for reasons of security, because of staff shortages, and once for no reason at all.

Today, after her awful night, Tabitha had just felt grateful to get outside. The yard was surrounded on three sides by buildings and on the fourth side by a high fence, on the other side of which was another vacant yard. But you could look up at the sky and that was a relief, even on a day like this that was cold and gray.

Some of the women used the hour for exercise. One woman was preparing to run a marathon. She was serving a thirty-year sentence for her part in the murder of three gang members so she wasn't going to be running through the streets of London. Her marathon was going to be on the day of the marathon but limited to circuits of the nearby football pitch: two hundred of them. The yard reminded Tabitha of the school playground, the girls dividing into groups of the cool ones, the hangers-on, the excluded, the defiant, the bullied, the lonely. Tabitha did what she had done at school, which was to retreat to the farthest corner and hope that nobody would pay her too much attention.

When Ingrid spoke to her, she had been leaning back against the wire fence, with her eyes closed and her head tipped back.

"You don't have to be polite," said Tabitha.

"I'm not being polite," said Ingrid. "You looked worried."

"Are you going to tell me another of your prison rules?"

Ingrid looked around. "You don't want to be too standoffish," she said. "I'm not saying you should try and join one of the gangs. But if you're too much on your own, people get suspicious."

"I'm not going to be here for long," said Tabitha, though dully and without conviction. "I don't care how suspicious they are."

"Look, I'm in the same position you are. I've got my parole hearing coming up. There's always something to hope for. You start fantasizing about life outside." Ingrid smiled. "You know, food, company. But mainly I imagine just going for a walk."

"Don't," said Tabitha, trying to smile back as if they were just two women having a normal conversation.

Ingrid's expression became more serious. "Honestly, how are you?"

"I was always taught growing up as a young English woman that when someone asks you how you are, the only answer allowed is 'fine.'"

Ingrid put her hand on Tabitha's shoulder. "You can't get by here alone," she said. "You need to talk to someone. It doesn't have to be me. But you have to find someone. The people who don't, they end up cutting themselves or getting high or even worse."

"All right," said Tabitha. "The answer, just at the moment, is I'm not doing so well."

And then she took a deep breath and told Ingrid about her meeting with Mora. When she was finished, she looked at Ingrid curiously.

"More advice?"

"Yes. You can lie to everyone. You can lie to your friends, you can lie to your cellmate, you can lie to me. But you have to tell your lawyer the truth. Your lawyer is like . . ." She hesitated. "If you believe in priests, your lawyer is your priest. You tell them everything. Good and bad. Unless you're guilty, of course, and then you do lie to them."

"I don't think she believes me anyway."

"She doesn't need to believe you. She needs to get you out of here." Ingrid narrowed her eyes and looked at Tabitha with a concentration that made Tabitha laugh nervously.

"What?" she said.

"There's something else, isn't there?" said Ingrid. "What is it?"

Tabitha pushed her hands into the pockets of her windbreaker. Suddenly she felt as if the weather had turned even colder.

"You know when you're going over things at three in the morning?"

"That's another rule. Don't go over things at three in the morning."

"I was thinking about how bad it looked to Mora. I've been charged with murdering Stuart Rees and I had said that I had no reason to kill him; there was no motive. But I knew that there was a motive. He had sex with me when I was underage. People would call that child abuse. I'm not sure if I would."

"I think I would."

"Well, whatever, it looks bad that I didn't mention it."

"I hope that she was sympathetic."

"I wouldn't say she was sympathetic. Mainly she was angry. But that's not what I wanted to say." Tabitha paused. It felt difficult to utter the words out loud. But she needed to get it clear. "I've been through difficult times. I've been confused and depressed and I was given medication to deal with it and sometimes it made me feel better and sometimes it made me feel worse." She had been talking almost to herself and now she looked directly at Ingrid. "Do you really want to hear this?"

Ingrid nodded.

"It may have saved me but it also messed with my head. There are bits of my life that are blanks, things I just don't remember. Like I've been wiped. So I had this moment last night when I suddenly asked myself: what if I did it?"

"And what was the answer to that?"

"That's not really the point. I went through it in my mind. It went something like this: I suffer from depression, I drop out of college, I go traveling in an aimless sort of way. All the time, without really knowing it, I'm thinking about what happened between me and Stuart. At the time it felt a bit sophisticated maybe, or at least one of those things almost all young people go through, messy sexual experiences that are part of growing up. But gradually I start to realize that I was horribly exploited by him and I start to blame him for what's gone wrong with my life."

"I'm sorry," said Ingrid. "Are you saying this is what you felt?"

"Wait," said Tabitha. "So I start unconsciously fixating on this and it kind of takes me over and in the end I move back to Okeham. I have a vague, hidden sort of feeling that I'm going to confront him about what happened, make him face up to what he did to me. I meet him and we have words. I threaten to expose him, go to the police. I arrange to meet him at my house. I tell him there are things we need to talk about. Instead, when he gets there, I have a knife. Which I use. I have a plan to get rid of the body, but before I can do it, my friend Andy walks out to the shed at the back of the house and finds it."

There was silence, except for the shouts across the yard, the thumping of a basketball.

"You're not saying anything," said Tabitha.

"I don't really know what to say. Why are you telling me this?"

"I'm pretty certain that that's what Mora thinks happened. So I was trying to look at myself the way Mora looks at me. I know I'm a bit crazy sometimes. I brood. I get angry. Could I have done it and somehow suppressed all memory of it?"

"Surely you couldn't have?" said Ingrid. There was a deep crease between her brows.

"That's what I think. I couldn't, could I? Even if the pills mess with my memory, I'd remember. Now that I'm here, going over everything, I know that Stuart did terrible things, and it damaged me in some deep way. It was abuse, of course it was. But I didn't think that before. At least, if I did, I pushed it down deep. Anyway, none of that matters, all of that stuff about a motive. I wouldn't kill someone whether I had a motive or not." She looked at Ingrid's expression again. "I'm not asking you to believe me. I know everyone says they're innocent."

"Some of them are," said Ingrid.

"The problem is, what I know, or what I say I know, isn't going to be much help in court. This may sound stupid but I don't want someone just to do some clever defense. I don't want them to think about strategy. I want to know the truth, even if it's a terrible truth, and it's driving me crazy. You see, I can't remember that day. I've tried and tried, but it's a horrible blank with nasty fragments in it, and I don't know what I did. I honestly don't know. I don't know what I did during that day. The story I told you sounds quite convincing, doesn't it?"

Ingrid looked at her with a troubled expression.

"What was *your* lawyer like?" asked Tabitha.

Ingrid's expression hardened and then she gave a shrug. "He promised more than he delivered," she said.

Sixteen

When she woke in the early hours, she couldn't remember for a moment where she was. She lay in the dark silence, just the sound of Michaela's steady breathing, which had become somehow reassuring, and everything returned to her.

Tomorrow was her court appearance. She needed to prepare herself. She tried to imagine it and found she couldn't. Her world had shrunk to this tiny room and to the thoughts in her head that she couldn't escape. In here, time was both meaningless and relentless: measured out by doors being locked and unlocked, by meager breakfasts, unappetizing lunches and nasty suppers, walks round and round the yard. But in twenty-six hours, she would, briefly, be back in time again. She used the toilet, washed her hands and face, brushed her teeth, dressed in the same old shapeless trousers and thick top that she wore every day.

It suddenly occurred to her that she didn't have the right clothes for the court and it was too late to ask Shona to bring anything. She rummaged through her things, old tee shirts and trousers and jerseys, everything a bit wrinkled and stained. She couldn't ask Michaela—she was about twice her size; one of her tee shirts would look like a dress on Tabitha. She imagined herself standing in front of the judge in a grubby tracksuit, with her uncut hair and her bitten fingernails and her cut lip, then put her head in her hands for a moment, feeling grim and helpless.

"Can I ask you a favor?"

"Of course." Ingrid patted the chair next to her. The library was cold this morning; the heating wasn't working. Heavy, sleety rain fell past its window so Tabitha couldn't even see the fields and the trees.

"I haven't got anything to wear to court. I wondered if you could lend me something. You're always so smart."

And it was true. Today, Ingrid was dressed in dark woolen trousers and a bottle-green round-necked sweater. She had studs in her ears and her graying hair was neatly brushed. She looked like she was about to go into a meeting or stand at a podium to talk about fiscal responsibility.

"I know not to let myself go," she said. "Of course you can borrow whatever you want. Though you might drown in my things. Let's go and have a look."

Tabitha felt like a child trying on her mother's clothes. The skirt she put on slid to her hips and came down almost to the floor. The sleeves of Ingrid's jacket covered her hands.

"You're very little," said Ingrid, inspecting her.

"I'm still waiting for my growth spurt."

"What about this dress? You could hitch it up a bit."

Tabitha took off the skirt and jacket. Her skin was white and pricked with goose bumps. Her legs were hairy. She took off her socks. Her toenails needed cutting. She pulled on the dark blue dress. Ingrid rolled up the sleeves, then folded it up at the waist to make it shorter. She tutted and twitched the material, gathering it here and smoothing it there. Tabitha stood very still. She couldn't remember the last time someone had properly touched her, put an arm around her.

"There," said Ingrid at last. "What do you think?"

"I can't see myself. Will I do?"

"I think so. Have you got shoes?"

"Trainers."

"What size are you?"

"Four."

"Mine are far too big. Trainers will have to do."

"Thank you."

"My pleasure." She scrutinized her once more. "You should wash your hair and comb it back from your face. It looks a bit wild."

"I know."

"Do you want to borrow any makeup?"

"I don't think so. It's just a brief appearance." She swallowed hard. Her throat hurt. "I'm nervous."

"That's only natural."

"I mean I'm scared. Really scared."

Seventeen

Tabitha woke before it was light. She was very cold and her heart was knocking against her ribs. She used the toilet and then brushed her teeth so hard her gums bled. Michaela lay on the top bunk and watched her, not speaking. She put on Ingrid's dress and tried to adjust it so it didn't look ridiculous. She sat on her bed. Breakfast was impossible, but she had a mug of tea when it arrived. All around her she could hear the sounds of a day beginning. Doors scraping open, a cough, a dirty laugh, someone shouting boisterously along the hall. Her hands were shaking and her legs felt spindly, as if they might not hold her weight.

"You look good."

Tabitha spun round. "Oh! Really?"

"Yeah." There was a silence, then: "Good luck today."

It was so little, a few basic words that anyone would say, but tears filled Tabitha's eyes. She put a hand against the wall to steady herself.

At nine o'clock two wardens came and collected her. Tabitha thought the woman was one of those who had searched her, but she couldn't be sure. She put her old jacket round her shoulders, glanced at herself in the little mirror as she left the cell. Pale smudge of a face, blinking eyes: she looked about thirteen.

As she walked through the central hall, people looked at her. Ingrid wished her luck; Orla shouted out an encouragement. Several women banged on their doors. Tabitha tried to smile at them.

Doors opened and doors banged shut, keys turned. Past steel lockers. A vending machine. Then she was out into cold damp air. The wall ahead was high and gray, with a coil of barbed wire snaking its way along its top. There was a white van, its back opened, ready for her.

"In you go," said one of the wardens, giving her a little prod.

Tabitha climbed inside. The doors were shut. An engine revved and then she was moving, stopping, moving once more, gathering speed. She was in the world again, but the van was just another cell jostling her forward. She tried to concentrate. She had a pain in her lower back and thought she might be about to get her period, though it had been months. Out of the tiny window she could see trees, telephone wires, the sides of buildings.

The van came to a halt and the doors were opened. Tabitha climbed out. They were at the back of the court and it was only a few steps into the building. Along a corridor, down some stone steps and then another flight. A door was held open for her and she went into a small room and sat on a chair and squeezed her eyes shut.

"Tabitha."

She looked up at Mora Piozzi. She had a leather satchel over her shoulder and was holding a cardboard cup of coffee in either hand.

"I don't know if you take milk or sugar."

"Black is fine."

Tabitha took a sip, then another. Real coffee. It felt like a message from the outside world.

"How are you feeling?"

"OK."

"We have half an hour."

Tabitha nodded.

"Are you clear about the procedure of a plea and trial hearing preparation?"

Tabitha shook her head.

"It's very simple and quick. You go into the dock. That might feel scary, but don't worry. I'll be sitting at the bench a few feet away. The judge will enter. Then the court associate will read out the charge and ask you for your plea."

"Yes." Tabitha took another mouthful of coffee.

"Then the judge will fix the timetable, which includes the date of the trial, but also a series of stages. The first-stage date is the one on which the prosecution must serve their evidence."

Mora Piozzi took some papers and her laptop from her satchel, but she didn't look at them.

"I have received the advance disclosure pack," she said. "Basically, it's the evidence the police have collected so far and the streamlined forensic report. There's nothing in it we didn't already know."

She looked searchingly at Tabitha. "Have you thought about your plea?"

Tabitha nodded her head.

"Good. Have you reached a decision?"

Tabitha didn't reply.

"Would you like me to go over their case against you one last time?"

"All right."

Now the solicitor picked up a single piece of paper. "The victim was last known to be alive at around ten-forty because CCTV shows he drove his car through the village shortly before that, in the direction of his house and yours. His car was parked at your house. His body was found in the yard behind your house. His blood was on you. You have no alibi. You have a history of mental illness. You lost your father when you were thirteen and you were abused by the victim when you were fifteen. Before the murder took place, you were heard making angry remarks about Stuart Rees. You were seen after the murder in a state of confusion and distress."

She put the piece of paper down, set her coffee on top of it.

"You know what I'm going to say, don't you?"

"No."

"I strongly advise you to plead not guilty to murder, but guilty to manslaughter."

"Is that it?"

"If you plead not guilty on all counts, Tabitha, you are very likely to spend many years in prison. There is a mandatory life sentence for murder. If you plead guilty to manslaughter with diminished responsibility, we can build up a strong case in your defense. He abused you. You were traumatized and mentally dis-turbed. It is very likely you would get a lesser sentence, perhaps no more than two years, which means you'd be out in one."

"I see."

Tabitha drank the last of her coffee, which was turn-ing cold now. Her head was beginning to throb.

"There's a problem," she said. "What if it isn't true?"

"Tabitha—"

"If I do what you say, I'll never know."

"What won't you know?"

"We need to find out who did it. Whoever it is."

"That has nothing to do with any of this and it's not my job. My job is to represent your interests. This is what I advise you to do; it's your best chance. No so-licitor would tell you anything different."

"OK," said Tabitha. At last she knew what she was going to do. It made her feel vertiginous.

"What does that mean?"

"It means no."

"You want to plead not guilty?"

"You think I did it, don't you?"

"We've been through this. It really isn't the point."

"It is. You think I'm guilty so I should plead dimin-ished responsibility and try to get out as quickly as I can. But what if I'm not?"

Her solicitor gave a deep sigh; her shoulders looked heavy.

"All right," she said at last. "All right, if that's what you want, we will go in there and we—"

"No."

"Sorry?"

"I don't want you to represent me."

"What are you saying?"

Tabitha smiled. "Don't you get it? I'm firing you."

Eighteen

The stairs leading up to the court were narrow and steep and Ingrid's dress tangled in Tabitha's legs. A lace was coming undone on her trainers so she had to stop and retie it with the two police officers standing too close behind her.

The courtroom took her by surprise; she blinked in its light. There was a man in a black gown with a clipboard, and rows of empty wooden benches, and three people sitting near the front, talking to each other, as if this was just another day. Two women sat at machines.

She stumbled as she went up into the dock. There was glass on either side of it, and she didn't feel tall enough. She stared out, confused. The exultation she had felt a few minutes ago had ebbed away and in its place was a sense of helplessness.

The judge came in and he wasn't as old as she'd expected. He had a gray wig and a blue-and-black gown with a red slash across it. He called her Ms. Hardy and she wanted to thank him for using the correct title. He had a thin, clever face and a courteous tone. Perhaps he would be the judge at the real trial. He was saying something else but she couldn't hear properly.

"I was asking, Ms. Hardy," he said, "if your legal representative is present."

"No," said Tabitha. "Your Honor," she added. Was that what you called a judge?

He frowned. "Is he on his way?"

"I haven't got legal representation."

"Why not?" His benevolent expression changed to one of alarm.

"I fired her."

"What?"

"A few minutes ago," added Tabitha.

He leaned forward. "I hope this isn't some attempt to delay proceedings."

"No."

"You are charged with murder."

"I know."

"This is serious." His voice slowed. He spoke to her like she was a small child. "You don't have to pay, you know. This is a charge of murder. But you must have legal representation."

"I don't think that's correct."

"I'm sorry?"

"I don't think that's correct."

The judge pushed his wig back slightly to scratch his head and scowled at her. He looked appalled.

"For goodness' sake. This is a serious, complex matter. You need legal representation."

"They'll tell me to plead guilty."

"They will act according to your instructions."

"But they won't believe it."

"They will present your case to the best of their professional ability."

"I'll do it myself," said Tabitha. Her voice was scratchy.

"That's ridiculous." He leaned further forward. "It's worse than ridiculous, it would be a gross act of self-harm."

"It's my right."

The judge stared hard at her until she felt herself flush. Her legs trembled and she wished someone would offer her a chair. Finally he sat back. His face wasn't so benevolent now. He took several deep breaths.

"If you think you'll get some benefit by doing this, you're very much mistaken," he said.

"She just wanted me to plead guilty," said Tabitha.

"Stop," said the judge. "Don't say anything about any conversation you had with any lawyer. Do you understand?"

"I don't see why it matters."

"In court, you follow the instructions of the judge. Do you understand?"

"All right, fine," Tabitha said angrily and then tried to calm herself. "I mean, yes."

He looked across at the prosecuting team.

"This young woman says she is going to conduct her own defense," he said. "She has been advised against it, but there it is. It's your duty to get all the documents in your case to her. Everything. Do you hear?"

They nodded. The younger man with the clipboard grinned at Tabitha as though she'd just told them all a good joke. She knitted her brows at him and he looked away.

"I don't want things going astray. At the end of this hearing, I want you to give her contact numbers. She needs to have a CPS liaison officer immediately, is that clear?"

They nodded.

"How will they contact me?" asked Tabitha.

"Usually we get in touch by email," said the young man.

"I'm in prison."

"I know." He was still smiling.

"You'll need to use the phone," said the judge irritably. "See to it. I am setting the trial for Monday the third of June. In up to fifty days from now, Ms. Hardy, you will be served with all the evidence. You then need to serve your defense to the prosecution and the court no later than forty days later."

Tabitha gazed at him. She didn't have a clue what he was talking about.

"Your defense statement, a list of witnesses you want to call, written responses from any professionals. Do you understand?"

"Not really."

"Of course you don't: you're not a lawyer. This is a farce—and a reprehensible waste of time and public money, I might add."

He went on speaking. He was saying things about written applications, previous convictions, applications for hearsay, primary and secondary disclosures. Tabitha wasn't listening or, at least, she wasn't properly hearing. The words sounded like gibberish to her, and now the crown prosecution solicitors were replying with the same orotund vocabulary. She felt suddenly hollowed out by tiredness.

"Let's get this over with," the judge was saying.

"What?"

"You haven't entered your plea, Ms. Hardy."

A woman who had been sitting impassively below the judge stood up. She asked Tabitha to confirm her name, her nationality and her date of birth.

And then here it came:

"Tabitha Hardy. On count one you are charged with murder. The particulars of the offense are that on Friday the twenty-first of December 2018, you did murder Stuart Rees. Do you plead guilty or not guilty?"

Tabitha gripped the side of the dock.

"Not guilty," she said.

Nineteen

On the way back, enclosed in the van, she wanted to bang her head against the metal walls. She wanted to kick against them. She wanted to punch them. When they arrived back at Crow Grange she was led out of the van. She said to herself that if they strip-searched her again, she would go for one of the wardens, leave them something to remember her by, but she was given nothing more than a cursory pat down.

She was led into the main body of the prison and then she walked along the corridor and into the main hall. She kept her head down all the time, staring at the floor in front of her. She had a feeling that if someone looked at her wrong or if she saw someone picked on, she would get involved. She felt a terrible impulse not just to do damage to someone but to be damaged herself, to be beaten up, to be really hurt, just to stop the burning fizzing feeling inside. She arrived back at her cell, which was empty, and paused only to grab her towel.

What she normally would have done at a time like this was to walk out of her house, down to the beach, and plunge into the sea, the colder and stormier the better. A shower would have to do instead. She pulled her clothes off and stood under the shower and switched it on. Only a few drops fell onto her upturned face. She remembered the advice on her first morning to bang the pipe. She hit it a couple of times and nothing much changed. She hit it harder and harder and then she felt as if something inside her gave way. She grabbed the showerhead above her with both hands and swung from it with her whole weight until it came away. Then she seized the pipe that ran up the wall and pulled. It wouldn't move, so she put her right foot up on the wall to give her some real purchase and leaned backward. At first there was nothing, then a creaking sound and then a shattering and she fell back on the floor, pulling the pipe with her. There was a jet of water from where the pipe had snapped. The pipe had bent so the water gushed outward onto her as she lay on the floor. She heard shouts from either side; the women gathered round her, aghast, though a little impressed. Just for a moment, Tabitha laughed and felt a sense of release that was like nothing she had experienced for weeks and months.

She wrapped herself in her scratchy towel, gathered her clothes and ran, half naked, back to her cell, her wet feet slapping on the floor. She could hear people shouting, but she didn't know who they were or what they were saying.

She pushed open the door and half fell inside. She dropped her clothes—Ingrid's clothes—to the floor and pulled on some old trousers and a thick shirt. She needed to have a swim, go for a run, walk for miles and miles with a gale in her face. What should she do to get rid of this terrible energy? She jumped up and down, feeling her heart begin to race.

And then the wardens came: Mary Guy, of course, and the thin one with a face like vinegar, and someone she'd never seen before who wore an incongruous red bow in her hair.

"Stand back," said Mary Guy.

"Get out of here. This is my room," said Tabitha. "Fuck off and leave me in peace."

Mary Guy swept the flat of her hand across Tabitha's table, scattering all her meager possessions to the floor.

"You've no right!" yelled Tabitha.

"Really?" She nodded to the other wardens. "Carry on with the search," she said. "You're coming with me."

Tabitha stepped backward into the room. "I'm not."

Now the wardens were pulling her clothes out of drawers and tossing them on the ground, throwing her books carelessly. Mary Guy gripped the top of her arm so hard that Tabitha gave a grunt of pain.

"Walk," she said.

The governor looked impassively at Tabitha. She didn't ask a question. She didn't say anything at all. Tabitha just stared back at her. She wasn't going to apologize. The governor looked at Mary Guy standing beside her.

"She wrecked a shower fitting. Totally destroyed it. Pulled it away from the wall. There's water everywhere."

Deborah Cole took a deep breath. "I heard about your court appearance," she said.

There was a pause. Tabitha didn't reply.

"Aren't you going to say anything?" Cole continued.

"I don't know what to say," said Tabitha. "It didn't go the way I expected."

"You're planning to defend yourself?"

"I don't know what else to do."

"If you want to destroy yourself, that's none of my business. What is my business is what goes on in this prison." Cole pushed her chair back and looked up at the ceiling. She took another deep breath, as if she was forcing herself to stay calm. "I don't think you understand your position."

Tabitha was also trying to stay calm. "In what way?"

"You think because you're on remand that you're somehow not a normal prisoner, that the rules don't apply to you. Well, they do. You've committed an act of vandalism."

"It was not an act of vandalism," said Tabitha. "That shower has never worked. You have to bang it to get it to work. I banged it and it still didn't work. I hit it and pulled at it and then it came off the wall."

Cole looked past Tabitha at the warden. Tabitha couldn't see how the warden responded.

"I'm tempted to give you a week or two in solitary confinement," said Cole. "It might give you a chance to reflect on things."

"You can't put me in solitary confinement."

Cole's lips tightened. "Really?" she said. "And why not?"

"If I'm doing my own defense, I'm going to need help. I'm going to need a place to work."

There was a silence only broken when Cole started drumming her fingers lightly on her desk. When she spoke, it was slowly and distinctly.

"Don't you ever try to tell me what I can and what I can't do."

Tabitha felt her heart beating fast, so fast that it almost hurt. She could feel the blood racing through her veins, bulging. She was breathing faster, her eyes flickering from side to side. She saw a very slight shift in the governor's expression, a wince of concern. She understood that she was just very slightly wary of what Tabitha might do next. Was she going to fly at her? Was she going to say something reckless? It felt like a battle of wills and then Tabitha realized, almost with an ache, that it was a battle she could only lose.

"I'm sorry," she said, untruthfully. "Things have been difficult. It's been a strange day. I didn't mean to damage the shower." Again, untruthful. "But I'm sorry that it happened." She swallowed hard. She hated saying this. "I want to be cooperative."

Cole's expression was unchanged. "It's not about cooperating. It's about obeying the rules." She paused again. "Consider this a warning. I'm making allowances. I won't do it again."

"Thank you," said Tabitha.

"Thank you, *ma'am*," said a voice behind her.

Tabitha looked round.

"You address the governor as 'ma'am,'" said Mary Guy.

"Ma'am?" she said. She turned to Deborah Cole and she had a terrible impulse to laugh at the ridiculous theater of it all and then it made her so angry that she could hardly think. This woman was sitting in her nice office wanting to be called "ma'am" while a few corridors away there were women finding places to cut themselves where it wouldn't show and someone, somewhere, was looking for a way to end it all.

"Thank you, ma'am," she said.

She pushed open the door expecting to walk into a scene of wreckage but instead it was as if the past hour had been a violent dream. All her things were back on the table, in the same positions as they had been before. She pulled open the drawers of her chest. Her clothes had been folded and replaced and as far as Tabitha could remember they were exactly as they had been. Ingrid's clothes were folded and laid on top of her bed, which had been made.

She sat down with a little grunt and rubbed her eyes. The door opened and Michaela came in.

"Did you do all this?" asked Tabitha.

Michaela shrugged. "Things need to be kept neat in such a small space," she said.

"You've made it identical to how it was."

"I thought that was best."

She'd noticed everything, thought Tabitha: how she rolled her tee shirts; where she put her deodorant, her toothbrush; what order her books were stacked; how she attached her pens to her notebook by the clip on their lids.

"I don't know what to say."

"You don't need to say anything."

Twenty

Tabitha sat at the table in the library and opened the brown notebook that Shona had bought for her. She smoothed the page flat with the palm of her hand. She took the cap off the top of the blue ballpoint pen and stared at the blank paper. She had absolutely no idea where to begin.

Yesterday, the judge had instructed the prosecution to hand over all the evidence, and she vaguely remembered something about timetables and stages. After she had stepped down from the dock, legs weak as water, she had given a young man her prison details so that they could keep in touch with her. But until that happened, was she supposed to sit and wait?

She wrote "Friday, December 21" at the top of her page and underlined it. She drew a snowflake beside it.

Perhaps she should begin with everything she could remember about her movements that day. "Cold, sleety,
wet, never properly light," she wrote. She tried to recall
what she had told Mora about the day—that she had
woken early, but not got out of bed at once; that she
had started to make herself porridge, but had run out
of milk; that she had gone to the village shop; that she
had made herself swim in the inhospitable sea, but she
didn't know at what time; that she thought she might
have met people but couldn't be sure; that Andy had
come round when it was already dark, and that was
when Stuart's body had been found.

She wrote each item down beside a bullet point. The
trouble was, it was simply a memory of what she had
told Mora, which presumably was itself a memory of
what she had told the police, and that had been a memory of what she couldn't adequately remember.

Squeezing her eyes shut and pressing her fingers
against her temples, she tried to put herself into her
house. She imagined walking along the gravel track
and through the rickety iron gate that hung askew (she
could ask Andy to fix that), up the little path that was
muddy in winter, to the gray-stone building with its di-
lapidated outhouses and the old beech tree to the left
that as a child she had imagined climbing. Through the
front door, the tiled hall filled with building material,

and into the low-ceilinged kitchen with its thick walls, wide windowsills and its view of the sea. The floorboards near the door had been pulled up, ready for her and Andy to lay new ones. The walls were plastered and unpainted; one day they would be white. There was an open fireplace that she hadn't lit that day because she hadn't found the energy, and beside it a large battered sofa, bought on eBay, where she had been lying, covered in a blanket, when Andy had knocked at the door. The back door led out to the main garden, though more a muddy building site than garden at the moment, and to more falling-down sheds. Tabitha forced herself to think of that door swinging open onto the wet December darkness: the pile of boards, Andy crouched on the ground, reaching out for him and feeling the plastic cover under her hands, then the bulk of the body; the blood.

In her mind she stepped back inside, into the kitchen, then the living room that was uninhabitable at the moment. Up the narrow, winding stairs, past the small bathroom, the guest bedroom stacked high with boxes, up a few more steps and into her room under the eaves. She had chosen it for the view of the sea from its small windows; when the waves were large, you could hear the sea as well.

In her mind, she stood in front of that window now,

and she was looking at the gray water and listening to its distant sigh.

"Tabitha Hardy?"

The voice made her start. It was a warden, the thin woman with a pinched face who had helped strip-search her.

"Your lawyer is waiting for you in the visitors' room."

"She's not. I don't have a lawyer."

The warden shrugged her sharp shoulders. "Whatever. She's there anyway."

"Why are you here?" asked Tabitha.

"Hello to you as well," said Mora Piozzi. "How are you, Tabitha?"

"Confused."

"I wasn't happy with how we left things."

"It's not your fault," said Tabitha. "I know you were trying to help."

"And I'd like to continue trying."

"What do you mean?"

"You can't do this alone, Tabitha."

"Except I am."

"You mustn't. It's madness."

"Perhaps I am mad—that's what you think, isn't it?"

"If you defend yourself in court you will lose everything."

"At least I'll try."

"Try what?"

"Try to find out what happened."

Mora Piozzi wrinkled her nose. "Is that what you're intending? To conduct your own investigation from inside your prison cell. Is that your line of defense?"

"You make it sound absurd."

"Because it is absurd. Worse, it's self-destructive."

Tabitha nodded.

"Tabitha, I'm not here to get you to reinstate me. I'll recommend another lawyer to you. Just as long as you don't do this."

Tabitha looked down at her hands on the table. She had bitten all her fingernails back and the skin was dry and cracked.

"You believe my only course is to admit I did it. I can't do that." It took a great effort to say the words. Her impulse was to give up, give in, accept the solicitor's help. "So thanks, but no thanks."

"That's your last word?"

"Yes. Yes, it is. But the thing is, the thing that I don't know," said Tabitha, "is what to do now. I have literally no idea what to do."

Mora Piozzi was bending down to the stout leather briefcase on the floor. She opened it up and lifted out a thick bundle of papers.

"I thought you might say that. I've printed out all the evidence the prosecution has sent. This is where you should start, by reviewing their evidence, seeing what their case is—though I think you know their case already."

"You're being kind," said Tabitha. Her voice croaked.

"The prosecution have up to fifty days to get everything to you, including who they intend to call as witnesses, but there's a lot here already. Everything the police got leading up to your charge. All the witness statements, the copies of documents, most of the forensics, the nine-nine-nine recording. You."

"Me?"

"The transcript of your interviews. Your medical assessment, things like that." She glanced up. "Some of the photos you might find upsetting."

"Of him?"

"Yes. Anyway." She pushed the bundle across the table. "This is yours. They've been through it so now you can just take it."

"Thank you."

"After they've served you their evidence, you'll have twenty-eight days to give your defense statement."

Tabitha looked away. She thought if she met the solicitor's gaze she might start wretchedly giggling.

"Right. My defense statement."

"At which point they are legally obliged to serve you with any material that might help you or undermine their case. You should bear in mind that sometimes they don't give you everything they should."

"Why?"

"Why indeed? You can request evidence that's not included."

"How will I know what that is?"

"That's a good question. The answer is, you should have legal representation."

"Are you very angry with me?"

The solicitor tipped her head to one side. "I'm aghast. I feel like I'm watching an accident that's about to happen and I can't stop it."

"That doesn't sound good."

"My card is in that bundle. If you want to be in touch."

"Thanks."

Tabitha watched her leave. Then she stood up and lifted the bundle of paper. The top page simply had her name on it and her prison number. She carried it back to the library and put it on the table next to her brown notebook. She took the cap off her pen, thought for a moment, then replaced it. She couldn't even think where to begin. There was so much.

So she began to leaf through the pile to try to get a sense of it all. There was a sheaf of images from the CCTV looking outward from the shop. There was nothing obviously dramatic about any of them. They showed a car or a person walking past. She turned one of them round. There was no explanatory caption, just a reference number. But on the images themselves there was a time code. As she flicked through them she was stopped by a familiar image: herself, blurry but unmistakable, hands pushed into the pockets of her jacket. The accused. She even looked like the accused, hunched over, like she was trying to hide even from herself.

She lifted up the photo and peered at it more closely, then caught sight of what lay underneath it. An A4 image, beautifully in focus, of the body. Stuart's body, overweight, balding and dead. She recoiled, squeezing her eyes shut, and sat for a few seconds trying to catch her breath. Then, cautiously, she opened her eyes and allowed the photo to slide back into focus. His limbs at unnatural angles, his eyes open, his bearded jaw slack. She lifted up the photo to see the one beneath: Stuart from above. Then from one side, then the other. Then of wounds, multiple wounds. This was easier to look at for they were just marks on a surface that didn't need to be skin or belong to a body, to a man she had once known. Had once, she made herself acknowledge, been involved with or abused by, or whatever the word was for a relationship between a teacher and his fifteen-year-old student. Touched. Fondled. Fucked. She stared, her eyes burning. She felt sick with self-loathing.

Tabitha made herself look at each picture, turning them facedown afterward. Then she looked briefly at the transcript of her own interview. She couldn't bear to read the whole thing, word by word. Mostly it looked like gibberish; she had said things like "no, no" and "please" and "I don't know" and "blood" and "I want this to be over." But certain moments stood out. She was asked if she had any bad feelings toward Stuart Rees and she said no. But what was she meant to say? "Actually we slept together when I was fifteen but that has nothing to do with anything." Were you meant to spontaneously put forward information that would damage your own case? Tabitha didn't know but she did know that it could be made to look bad.

She flicked through the other statements under hers, again without reading them. What could these people have to say about her? They barely knew her. Nobody apart from her and Stuart even knew about the sexual involvement. Tabitha stopped herself. That wasn't true. At least one person knew. They not only knew but they had written to the police to tell them about it.

Who? The obvious person was Laura Rees, the griev-
ing widow. But why would she write an anonymous
letter? Why not just tell the police directly?

The other statements were from Andy, who had
found the body with her. There was Dr. Mallon, the
local GP. What did he have to say? He wasn't even
her doctor. There was the vicar, Melanie Coglan. At
the top of one of the forms, she saw the name Pauline
Leavitt and she had to pause for a moment as she made
herself remember who that was. Yes, she said to herself
finally, she was an old woman who walked around the
village with her fat Jack Russell and a stick she would
wave at cars if she thought they were driving too fast.
They used to nod at each other vaguely. But did she
even know who Tabitha was?

She was so curious that she actually read that statement. The language was strange. It sounded like it
had been filtered through the police officer she had
talked to:

Sometime in the days before December 21 I saw
Tabitha Hardy talking to Stuart Rees while I was
out walking with my dog. They both seemed agitated. She was saying something like: "I'll get you.
I promise that I'll get you."

Tabitha put the paper down and thought for a moment. Her first impulse was almost to laugh at the absurdity of this. She couldn't possibly have said anything of the kind. If she was going to kill Stuart, just for the sake of argument, would she threaten him in the middle of the village with an old woman and her dog walking by? It was ridiculous.

But it didn't matter what Tabitha thought was ridiculous. The police hadn't thought it was ridiculous. They had taken it down as a statement and offered it as part of their prosecution. What would a jury think? Tabitha tried to concentrate hard. Had Pauline Leavitt really seen and heard anything like that? In a way it didn't matter what Pauline Leavitt had "really" seen. She had given a statement that she had seen Tabitha and Stuart and that Tabitha had said those incriminating words. Presumably she was willing to go into the witness box and repeat the accusation under oath. Was there any way that Tabitha could prove that it hadn't happened? What would proof of that even look like?

Tabitha read over the words again. Perhaps she could claim that the words referred to something else, that they had been taken out of context. It didn't look good, though.

She wrote her first note: "Pauline Leavitt: threat?"

Right at the bottom of the pile was a single sheet of paper. At the top, underlined, it read: "**Tabitha Hardy. Prosecution Case: Initial Details**."

And there, below it, in a few paragraphs, stark and surprisingly short and matter-of-fact, was the case against her:

Charge:

That on December 21, 2018, between 10:40 A.M. and approximately 3:30 P.M., Tabitha Hardy unlawfully killed Stuart Robert Rees.

The body was found in the outer shed of Miss Hardy's house, Aston Cottage, Okeham, Devon, by Andrew Kane, a local builder.

The body was found shortly after 4:30 P.M. Death was placed at sometime between 10:30 A.M. and 3:30 P.M.

A number of witnesses have placed Miss Hardy at or close to the murder scene during the relevant period.

Motive:

Under questioning from detectives, Miss Hardy had denied any past problems with the murder victim. It later emerged that she had had a clandestine sexual relationship with the victim while she was at school. This has been confirmed by the victim's widow, Mrs. Laura Rees. There is credible evidence that Miss Hardy had threatened to publicly accuse the victim. There are further credible testimonies from friends and neighbors as to the state of mind of the accused. Medical evidence showed that she had recently been under treatment for mental health issues. Miss Hardy made no mention of this when questioned by police about her state of health.

Forensic evidence:

Forensic examination suggested that the murder occurred where the body was found. Forensic examination also found numerous traces of blood on the accused's clothing, hands, under fingernails.

The contention of the police is that as a result of her sense of victimhood, Miss Hardy returned to Okeham with the intention of revenging herself on Stuart Rees. As witnesses will show, she approached him on numerous occasions, threatened him, lured him to her house and murdered him. Her plan to dispose of the body was only thwarted when Mr. Andrew Kane discovered the body.

Miss Hardy's guilt is suggested by forensic evidence, her own statements in the presence of witnesses and clear motive, which she has lied about and obscured.

Tabitha read this statement over and over again. She wrote in her notebook "between 10:40 A.M. and about 3:30 P.M." but her hand was trembling so much that the figures were barely legible.

She read the page once again. It all looked bad, so bad that she couldn't even think of what to write a note about. There was so much. She decided to start with a list of all the bad things.

Motive

She had a motive to kill Rees, she had apparently lied to cover it up and nobody else seemed to have any motive at all.

Location

The body had been found on her property. Who else would or could have killed the man in *her* house? It might have looked a bit better if she had found the body and reported it to the police. But Andy had found it. So it looked as if she had been interrupted before she could get rid of the body.

Witnesses

Tabitha had felt that one of the good parts of her life in Okeham was that she was basically invisible. It was as if there was a silent agreement that if she didn't bother anyone else, then they wouldn't bother her. It was a simple life. Working, swimming, walking. Once a day she would go to the shop and get a newspaper. It was another of the weird things she did. Who spends money on a newspaper? But she liked it. She liked the feel of it. She liked to do the crossword, or fail to do it. She nodded at people, sometimes even exchanged a muttered word. But there were witnesses who were giving evidence that she had actually threatened Stuart.

Forensics

That felt like the most obviously bad. She had his blood on her. She had his blood under her fingernails and God knows where else.

It was the most obviously bad but it was the easiest to explain away, wasn't it? She had followed Andy and the two of them had struggled with the body. Andy had got Stuart's blood on him as well. That was where the blood on her clothes came from. Or plausibly could have come from.

But the problem wasn't any individual detail. It was the whole story. Everything fitted together and the only plausible explanation was that Tabitha had killed Stuart Rees. There were two ways of looking at it and both were terrible: everything pointed to her and nothing pointed to anyone else.

She sucked on the end of the pen and realized she was sucking on the wrong end. She rubbed her mouth with the back of her hand and looked at it. It was blue. Her mouth must be blue as well.

What she needed to do now was to go through everything. All the photographs; all the statements. She needed to construct a timeline. She needed to know who the witnesses were, what they'd said about her.

But it would take time. She needed time and quiet. Just then, as she turned to the first sheet of the pile and started reading, she heard the librarian say that it was time to go and then she heard a voice shouting and realized that the voice was hers.

The expression on Deborah Cole's face when she saw Tabitha was not so much anger—although there was anger as well—but weariness.

"I need a room," said Tabitha.

"What?"

"If I'm going to be working on my case, I'm going to need a quiet, secure space, some kind of office where I can read and not be interrupted and chucked out and where I can have access to documents."

"Stop," said Cole. "Stop right now. You don't seem to understand the situation. This is not some kind of negotiation. You were brought here for causing a disturbance. Again. Access to the library is a privilege. If you can't behave appropriately, then you will lose that privilege. I don't know what this talk of an office is." She held up her right hand with her thumb and forefinger almost touching. "I am this close to giving you a week in solitary confinement. With no books and no papers. That might give you time to reflect on your behavior."

"That's not going to happen," said Tabitha.

There was a pause. Cole looked at the wardens standing on either side of Tabitha. She had an expression of disbelief.

"What did you say?"

"I'm looking at my case. In a few months I'm going to be on trial for murder. If I can't look through the evidence properly, then the case will be halted. I don't know what happens when a big trial can't go ahead, but I guess that people will get angry."

There was another pause.

"Is that some kind of a plan?" said Cole.

"What kind of plan?"

"You think you can get away with this by delaying things?"

"You've got this the wrong way round," said Tabitha. "I don't want to delay things. I want somewhere to read my files, to work on my case."

"I've seen people like you before," said Cole.

"No, you haven't."

"They think they're better than other people. They think the rules don't apply to them. They're the ones after five years, ten years, fifteen years, you see in the corner, talking to themselves."

Tabitha stared straight at the governor. She felt like a firework that was about to go off.

"I just need a space," she said.

"I decide what space you get," said Cole, slowly and evenly.

Twenty-one

When Tabitha got back to her cell, Michaela was methodically putting her things into a black bin bag.

"What's up?" said Tabitha.

Michaela looked round but she didn't stop filling the bag. There wasn't much: clothes, toiletries, books, magazines, pens. She didn't speak until she was finished.

"I'm leaving," she said.

"Are you being transferred?"

"My release came through."

"Your release? From prison?"

"They just told me. Five minutes ago."

"You didn't tell me." As soon as she had spoken the words, she felt foolish. "I know. Why should you tell me? But I thought there was lots of preparation."

"Some papers went missing and then they found them and then they came and told me."

Tabitha and Michaela looked at each other. Tabitha didn't quite know what to say, or even what to feel. She had only known Michaela for a few weeks and it wasn't like they'd become particular friends. But somehow they had become used to each other. Michaela was silent, and then she seemed to come to a decision. She rummaged through her bag and produced a piece of paper. She put it down on the table and wrote on it, then handed it to Tabitha.

"That's my phone number. If you need something."

Tabitha looked down at the paper. "I don't know what to say," she said.

Michaela hoisted up the bag. "Maybe I'll come and visit. It might be a bit weird though, coming back to a prison I've just left."

"Why would you do that?" said Tabitha.

"You have to stand by your mates."

"Right."

"And we're mates now."

"Yes," said Tabitha. It didn't sound enthusiastic enough. "Yes, we are," she added. She was touched and confused. She and Michaela had shared a cell; they'd lain in bed night after night listening to the sound the other was making; they'd used the same toilet and eaten meals side by side. Yet they'd never had a proper conversation or shared secrets. *Maybe there are lots of ways of being friends*, she thought, *and they don't have to involve words.* The thought cheered her.

"You know," said Michaela. "Nobody has come to see me the whole time I've been here."

"If you came, it would be a great help to me."

"Don't hold your breath, no promises. You might never see me again."

"It's a nice thought, anyway. Thank you."

Now what? Tabitha stepped forward but Michaela held up a hand to stop her.

"No hugs," she said. "I don't like being touched."

"I'm not so good at it either."

"You don't say." Michaela grinned and then hesitated, searching for the right words. "Don't do anything stupid. I can imagine you doing something stupid, picking a fight with the wrong person, something like that."

She walked to the doorway and then halted.

"Don't even think of coming along with me," she said. "I hate it when people come and see you off."

Still she didn't leave. She seemed to be making up her mind about something. Finally she spoke.

"So you're defending yourself."

"It looks like it."

"Did you do it?"

Tabitha took a deep breath, then let it out. She met Michaela's gaze. "No."

"Good." Michaela nodded. "You asked me what I did."

"You don't need to—"

"I hit my boyfriend with a flatiron. Several times. He nearly died. I wish he had."

She turned and walked away without looking back, her feet clicking over the hard floor.

When she was gone, Tabitha lay on her bed. She tried to stop herself but she couldn't: she thought of Michaela going through door after door. They'd give her back her phone and they'd also give her a bit of money and then she'd go through one last door and she'd be out in the street. She would catch a bus or just walk, in any direction she wanted. Would she really come back? Tabitha put her hand against the wall. It felt cold and hard and heavy.

Twenty-two

Tabitha followed the warden across the room. It had cement floors and steel girders and long fluorescent lights and was lined with worktables, about forty in all. On each table stood an identical large black machine. Along one side of the room were broad shelves on which were stacked piles of blue drawstring trousers. In a locked cupboard with glass doors, Tabitha saw a variety of implements, including needles in different sizes, pins and safety pins and several long-bladed scissors. It was icily cold in the room. A tracery of frost decorated the windows and her breath hung in the air.

The warden stopped in front of a door, fumbled with his keys and pulled it open. Tabitha peered inside.

"Here?"

"That's right." The warden, who was enormously tall and bulky and was wheezing alarmingly, smiled at her. Not in a nice way.

"But it's a cupboard."

"Don't blame me. This is what she said."

"It's dark."

He reached his hand round the doorway and turned on a light. A single bulb glowed inadequately.

"It's still dark. And freezing. And it's full of things. What are they?" She took a step into the windowless space. "They're mannequins."

He shrugged.

"There's no room for me with those things in there."

She took hold of the first pink figure and dragged it out, then started on the next, whose plastic arm was raised in a warning gesture.

"Hey, what are you doing?"

"How am I meant to work in there if I can't even get inside?" She stood the second figure beside the first and their featureless faces stared at her serenely. "Anyway, there's no desk and nowhere to sit. Is this a joke?"

"I'm not laughing."

"Help me."

"Sorry?"

"If we take out these two as well, we can just about fit that little table in here and a chair."

"Somebody needs that."

"There's no one here."

"There will be tomorrow. This place is popular. The girls like learning to sew."

"Girls?"

"Yeah."

"You mean the prisoners?"

"Yeah."

Tabitha pushed the table, which was surprisingly heavy and screeched horribly along the floor, into the cupboard. Her spirits were lifting; she felt almost spritely with anger. She picked up a chair and put that inside as well. A single mannequin remained in the corner, its back turned to her. There was just enough room to squeeze herself in as well, though she would have to lift the chair up to get the door closed. She put her bundle of papers on the table and turned back to the warden, who was staring into the distance, whistling softly.

"I need more light."

He shrugged his large shoulders and pushed his hands deep into his pockets.

Tabitha went to the long table at the front and seized the Anglepoise lamp, then bent down and pulled the plug from the socket on the floor. At first she thought there was no socket in the cupboard, then she spied one near the door. Its cracked plastic casing suggested it hadn't been used for years. She plugged in the lamp, pressed the switch, and light pooled into the little space.

"There's a dead mouse," she said.

"It's a rat."

"It's too small."

"He's dried up. But he still has his thick tail." He prodded it with the toe of his shoe. "See."

"Can you get rid of it?"

He stared at her.

"OK, OK. I'll do it." She stared around her then spied bin bags in the corner, along with a bristle-headed broom. She ripped a bag off the roll, put her hand into it, bent down and picked up the rat in her protected hand, trying not to look at it as she turned the bag inside out with the creature safely inside. She rubbed her hand down the side of her trousers. "Can you put it in the disposal unit for me?" she asked.

He sighed, then took it. She was starting not to mind him. "What's your name?" she said.

"What?"

"Never mind. How long do I have?"

He shrugged. "Until curfew, I guess. You'll miss lunch, though."

"I don't want lunch."

He pointed to his left. "There's a cubicle." Then, seeing her bewildered expression, "For when you need to go."

"Oh."

"I'll have to lock you in."

"To the cupboard?"

"To the workroom."

"Won't anyone be coming here?"

"It only operates twice a week. Cuts."

"How will you know when I'm ready to leave?"

Once more, he shrugged his massive shoulders. "Someone will come," he said.

Alone, Tabitha felt almost giddy with the sense of solitude and space. The fluorescent lights hummed above her and the sewing machines sat there, sinister objects that she felt might suddenly stir into life. Going into the curtained cubicle, she washed her hands, shook them dry, then drank some water from the tap. On the side there was a plastic bag with several teabags in it, but no kettle; also a box of sugar lumps that were turning yellow with age. She put one lump into her mouth and sucked it. Her teeth ached. Then she walked up and down between the tables, running her hand over their surfaces, fingering spools of cotton, lifting pieces of fabric and letting them fall again. She unfolded a pair of trousers and held them out. They were thick and looked comfortable; she wondered if she could take a pair with her when she left. She knew she was putting off the moment of squeezing into the cupboard and facing all those pieces of evidence.

At last she sat down at the table and opened her notebook. For a moment she was a student in the university library, doing research for an essay. But then she looked at the remaining plastic mannequin turned to the wall, and at the photo of Stuart's body that lay on the top of the pile, and a little shudder rippled through her.

She had to be methodical. She unstopped her pen and pushed the photos away, out of sight. Underneath them was a photocopy of the anonymous letter that had been sent to the police; she had missed it yesterday. It was all in large capitals, written on a slant, everything leaning backward as if the words were about to fall into a heap. The sight made Tabitha feel slightly sick.

FYI. IT IS MY DUTY TO INFORM YOU THAT STUART REES WAS CARRYING ON WITH TABITHA HARDY WHEN SHE WAS UNDERAGE AND HE WAS HER TEACHER. THIS IS TRUE.

Tabitha crumpled the paper into a tight ball and held it in her closed fist. She wanted to throw it on the floor where the dead rat had lain, and stamp on it until it disintegrated. But at last she uncrumpled it, smoothed it out and stared down at the message, frowning.

"Fuck you," she said. "Whoever you are, fuck you."

She put the letter to one side and began with the transcript of her own interview. Though it went on for pages, it turned out that she hadn't actually spoken a great deal. She had said "I don't know" many times, often repeating the words over and over in response to a single question. She had said she didn't know what she had been doing that day, didn't know when she had been in the house and when out, didn't know how the body came to be in her backyard, didn't know when she had last seen Stuart Rees. She had also said, several times, that she had no bad feelings toward him, no reason whatsoever to wish him dead. That wasn't good. Her lawyer, the blustery young man she vaguely remembered, occasionally intervened and several times advised her not to answer.

At first reading, her interview revealed nothing except perhaps a sense of her numbness at the time. She had obviously been mumbling and incoherent—more than once she was asked to speak up or repeat what she had just said. There were several "ums" and sentences that trailed away.

So far, Tabitha hadn't written a single note. But then, rereading the transcript more slowly, she came to a question that didn't make sense to her. "Why were you anxious to prevent Mr. Kane from going into the backyard?" (The solicitor had told her to say "no comment.")

She rubbed her face with both hands, trying to clear her thoughts, then leafed through the sheets of paper until she found Andy's statement, which she skimmed through until she came across the sentence: "Tabitha called out to me when I was opening the back door. She told me not to go out there. She seemed anxious."

Tabitha laid down the paper. Her heart was thumping with an irregular beat. It was like a heavy object inside her chest, slamming from side to side. She had no memory of saying that to Andy, none at all. She closed her eyes and forced herself back to that dark afternoon. She remembered him coming to the house, but vaguely, as if the details had been erased and all that was left were dark, blurry outlines. She had been lying on the sofa, half awake, listening to the sound of sleety rain falling and trying to push away the thoughts that kept seething into her mind. He had knocked and she had at first ignored him, but finally struggled to her feet when he knocked more insistently. He had brought the weather into the house with him; his long dark hair was plastered to his skull, his face was streaked with rain and his heavy jacket sodden. She remembered him stamping his boots on the doormat.

She thought that he had asked her if she was all right, and then he had talked about the work they were going to do tomorrow. But she couldn't recall what he had actually said; everything had felt an enormous effort that day. She had sat back down on the sofa, and he had opened the back door that led to the yard and the outhouse and the wind had sliced through the room like a knife. Had she tried to stop him from going out there? Her mind was blank; it made no sense. But why would he invent such a thing? She turned to the back of her notebook, wrote "Tasks" in her neat cursive script, underlined it, then wrote underneath: "Ask Andy to visit." Her hand was beginning to cramp with the cold.

She read through the vicar's statement in which she mentioned seeing Tabitha at two-thirty in the afternoon. Apparently Mel was coming out of the shop where she'd just bought a newspaper and she had talked to Tabitha about the tens of thousands of passengers stranded at Gatwick Airport because of a reported drone. According to her, Tabitha had been in a distressed and very agitated state. Tabitha wrote down the time.

There was a brief statement from Rob, the farmer up the road who was always walking around the village, sometimes with his whippet dog, and a sullen expression on his broad, fleshy face. He said he had been in front of Tabitha when she had gone to buy milk in the morning and apparently she had turned to him and said that Stuart was a bastard. She turned to the back of her book and wrote: "Rob Coombe?" Then she wrote "Bastard?" She didn't think that was a word she used much.

None of this felt right to her. Not Andy's account, nor Mel's, nor Rob's, nor Pauline Leavitt's from yesterday. She was reading about a stranger who had her name and her face, but who she didn't recognize.

She came to Laura Rees's statement. For all sorts of reasons, Tabitha had avoided thinking about her, but now she made herself. She realized with a jolt of shame that she had never paid any attention to Laura or thought of her outside of her marriage to Stuart. She had been the wife in the background of his active, busy life, not a woman with her own internal life and her own story. She was a woman who did not seem to want to be noticed; perhaps made a determined effort not to be. She was of indeterminate middle age, wore sensible, rather shapeless clothes in dark colors, had her hair cut into a neat helmet, was invariably polite but wore an inscrutable expression on her face. She kept herself to herself, as they put it in the village. Shona had told Tabitha that Terry had said that Laura had been a bit wild before she married Stuart, but Tabitha had no idea if that was true. It was the kind of thing Terry came out with to liven up the day. She would lean happily across the counter, lower her voice, and offer up tidbits of gossip. She had recently told Andy, who had told Tabitha, that Mel the vicar had taken a shine to Dr. Mallon. Tabitha wondered what Terry said about her.

She read Laura's statement carefully. Nothing leaped out from it. She jotted down times that were mentioned: she had last seen her husband at 9:30 A.M., when she had driven out of the village in order to go to a house viewing, and she had returned about half past three in the afternoon—leaving the estate agent's earlier than usual because their son Luke was expected home for Christmas that day. That was the gist of it.

Owen Mallon, the GP with a practice in town, said he had seen Tabitha in the morning when he was out for his run. It was his morning off and he always went for a long run then. It seemed to Tabitha that she only ever saw Owen Mallon when he was out running. He was small and wiry with a neat beard, and he was constantly dashing through Okeham in shorts and a thin yellow top, even in winter, his eyes fixed on the horizon, his legs all muscle and the sinews in his neck standing out. She found it hard to picture him in his GP surgery in smart clothes, putting a stethoscope on people's backs and asking them to cough.

Owen Mallon said that when he met Tabitha, she was bundled up in a thick jacket and her hair was wet; he thought she looked unwell. He didn't know the exact time, just remembered a helicopter flying over when they were speaking so he couldn't catch what Tabitha had said.

Tabitha stood up and wandered into the workroom once more. She walked up and down, up and down, between the sewing machines, clapping her hands together to get warmth back into them. She tried to picture the village, to picture herself trudging around in it with her head down, feeling invisible but clearly not so. She could almost taste the salty air and hear the waves rolling in, and her tumbledown, gray house with its muddle of outhouses stood clear in her mind. But everything else was indistinct. She concentrated, summoning the almost-sheer cliffs standing like a wall behind it, with the stunted oaks growing impossibly out of the rock face; the sea that every day had a different voice and different face but on that day had been metal-gray and cold and grim. A narrow road snaked into Okeham, and ended a few hundred meters beyond the post office, where it circled back on itself. At the road's end, a gravel track led to her house—and to Stuart's. He and Laura lived in one of the larger places in the village, a symmetrical building that looked naked and exposed in the winter when the trees were bare, with large windows looking out to the sea, a front porch, a separate garage for their two cars and a garden that was mostly lawn.

Tabitha tried to picture the rest of the houses that clustered together on either side of the road. In her mind's eye, she could see the little round-tower church of St. Peter's, a stone's throw from the village shop, and beside it the shabby vicarage where Mel lived. But her mind was full of holes; the village was trickling through them. She went back to her cupboard and started trying to draw a map of Okeham in her notebook but quickly ran out of space. Turning to her list of tasks, she wrote "Ask librarian/Shona/Andy for A3 sheets of paper."

She needed to think about the case as if she weren't involved in it. The obvious thing to start with was the timeline of the day. She turned to a fresh page and headed it "December 21, 2018." Then, checking back to the notes she had made and leafing through the bundle of paper in front of her, she drew up a list:

6:30: Wake up. Lie there for some time (how long?). Not feeling good.

7:30 (approx): Get up. Start making porridge and tea. No milk.

8:00: Go to village shop to buy milk. See CCTV.

She looked at the image and added:

In PJ bottoms and wellies. School bus there. Meet Rob Coombe?

??? A.M.: Go for swim. Meet Dr. Mallon.

She looked at the CCTV images once more and wrote:

10:34: Stuart drives out of village in his car.

10:41: Stuart drives back again in direction of house (blocked by fallen tree).

2:30: Meet vicar.

She chewed the end of her pen. What had she been doing at two-thirty? She had no memory of leaving the house after her morning swim, though she thought she did remember a conversation with Mel about drones at Gatwick Airport; the vicar had said it was bound to be the work of eco-warriors.

3:30: Laura returns. No sign of Stuart.

In her list of tasks, she wrote: "Find out exactly when tree blocked road and when it was cleared."

4:30: Andy arrives at house. Discovers body.

She stood up again and continued her pacing. She had no idea what time it was. The sky outside was heavy with black clouds; it was the kind of day that is never quite light. Perhaps it was lunchtime, but she didn't feel hungry. She went into the cubicle and ate another sugar lump, then jumped up and down on the spot for a few minutes to keep warm.

Stuart had been killed after 10:41 A.M., when he had been seen in his car driving past the village shop, and before about 3:30 P.M.—the forensics made it clear that he had been dead at least an hour and probably longer by the time his body was discovered. Who had been in the village during those times, after the tree had fallen across the road and before it got cleared? That was the question. She started counting off on her fingers, but lost track and so returned to her notebook. She started a new list:

Me
Mel
Shona
Rob Coombe
Andy
Terry
Dr. Mallon
Luke???? (Under her tasks, she added: "When did Luke arrive?")
Pauline Leavitt

Was that all? It was possible: in the summer the village filled up with tourists. Boats bobbed out at sea, visitors came to stand where Coleridge had reportedly stood, the hotel on the outskirts was open and the little café beside the shop often crammed. But in the winter the place was practically deserted. She flicked through all the sheaves of paper again and found in the police report that there had been a delivery driver who had made it into the village minutes before the tree fell. He had handed over an Amazon parcel to Stuart at 9:45

and then got stuck in Okeham until the road had been cleared, so she added him.

That made ten people so far, including herself. Six of them had seen her during the day. Four of them—Mel, Rob Coombe, Dr. Mallon and Pauline Leavitt—had said she had been agitated, or angry with Stuart. One of them—Andy—had said she had tried to stop him from going into the yard where Stuart's body lay. Every finger was pointing at her.

Tabitha put her head on the table. After her mother had died and left her enough money to put down a deposit on a house, she had come back to Okeham on a reckless kind of whim. Now she found it hard to comprehend her decision. She hadn't been happy there as a child or a teenager, although probably she wouldn't have been happy anywhere. She had been a shy, stubborn and angry little girl with no siblings; an awkward, introverted, abrupt teenager who liked math and nature, who wasn't pretty or sporty, had developed late and had had no interest in boys or fashion, more a dread of both. She hadn't known how to get on with people; she still didn't. Her father had died when she was barely a teenager. She'd been horribly bullied from the age of seven till thirteen or fourteen; after that, she had been largely ignored. Except by Stuart, of course. Except by Stuart. And yet she had returned to the place of her unhappiness. Why?

She had told herself it was because of the house, and certainly that was part of it. Something about its ramshackle, worn-out, low-lying charm spoke to her; it had been neglected for decades, left to sink back into the landscape, and she had wanted to rescue it. And maybe she had hoped the village would accept her as an adult and that would somehow make her childhood less sore. Since coming back, she had believed that at least she was a neutral presence—if not liked and welcomed, at least tolerated or ignored. Now, reading through all the statements, she understood that of course the village still didn't want her. She was an outsider and an object of suspicion, even derision. She wore strange clothes and ate strange food and didn't brush her hair or wear makeup and she swam in the sea in winter and was sometimes so sad she couldn't talk in proper sentences. What was there to like?

Tabitha sat up and stacked all the papers together again. Her anger had gone and she felt heavy with foreboding.

Twenty-three

When she got back to her cell, the only sign of a new occupant was a pile of clothes on Michaela's old table. She looked around. Up on the top bunk was what looked like a bundle of blankets. Tabitha realized it was a person. She had a sudden memory of going to the zoo as a little girl. She would put her nose against the glass to see some exotic rodent and all that was visible was a slightly raised pile of straw in a corner.

"Hey," said Tabitha.

No response.

With some trepidation, she nudged the bundle. Perhaps it was dangerous.

"I'm Tabitha. We're sharing a cell. We're going to have to talk sometime."

There was a movement in the pile. The blanket was pushed back and a tiny face, bordered with curly dark hair, emerged. Tabitha almost gasped. She thought there must be some mistake. It looked like the face of a little child. The dark eyes were bloodshot. She must have been crying. Tabitha reached out toward her and then stopped.

"My name is Tabitha Hardy. What's your name?"

"Dana." She spoke in the voice of a small girl.

Tabitha didn't know what she should say next. Was she meant to play the role of the experienced protector? She'd only been in Crow Grange for a few weeks. Was she meant to pass on what she remembered of Ingrid's rules?

"Are you OK?" she said. The words sounded stupid as soon as she said them.

Dana shook her head slowly.

"I know," said Tabitha. "I know it's strange and horrible when you first get here. You can't believe it. It doesn't seem real."

"I can't," said Dana, almost in a whisper. "I can't."

"What can't you do?"

"I can't be here. I just can't."

"How long are you here for?"

"A year." A single violent sob shook her frame. "Why did I do it?"

Tabitha stared at the girl. Her head was pounding. "A year," she repeated. "If you don't get into trouble, that's only six months." She bit her lip, gathering her strength, pushing away her own feeling of fear like it was something solid that she must resist. "And that's about the same amount of time that I will be here. My trial is in June."

"What did you do?" the girl whispered and Tabitha almost smiled.

"You're not supposed to ask," she said, "but it's fine. I didn't do anything. So we will have six months together in this cell. And we will both survive. Do you hear me?"

She was speaking to herself, of course; instructing herself. Dana nodded, her child's face swollen with weeping.

"All right," she said. "Yes."

Twenty-four

Tabitha couldn't quite believe it but there she was, sitting across from her in the visitors' room as straight as a ramrod.

Laura Rees looked like she was dressed for church or for a cocktail party. She was wearing a white blouse with an amber woolen cardigan and an oval brooch at her throat. Her hair looked grayer. Her face was an unyielding square of set jaw and thin mouth and cold glaring eyes.

For several seconds neither of them spoke. Not a flicker of expression disturbed the granite stiffness of Laura Rees's face.

Tabitha coughed unnecessarily. "I'm sorry about your husband."

"How dare you?" Her voice was harsh.

"What?"

"How dare you pretend to be sorry? The nerve of it."

"I didn't do it," said Tabitha.

"Is that why you wanted to see me—to protest your innocence? I should get up and walk out right now."

"I wasn't sure you'd come."

"I needed to look at you."

And Laura did look at her and Tabitha looked right back, in a way that felt rare, neither one glancing away.

"I'm not going to try to persuade you," said Tabitha. "And I'm not going to apologize."

"You're not going to apologize. Not for anything?"

Tabitha felt herself flush. "I was fifteen years old. I was a virgin. I didn't know anything."

Laura gave a sort of snort. "You were a slut," she said.

Tabitha had a sudden flashback, so vivid that it was like she was there. Just once, Stuart had taken her to his house. He had led her up to the bedroom where he had started to undress her. He did it in a businesslike way, as if she were a parcel whose contents he already knew but which needed to be opened. She didn't have any say in it and the unwrapping was a little awkward. He had pushed her back onto the bed so that he could pull her shoes and socks off. Then he had lifted her to her feet and started undoing the buttons on her blouse.

She had looked round and seen his wife's dressing table, pots of cream, lipstick, little jewelry boxes.

When she was fully undressed, he had stepped back and looked at her, standing there among his wife's intimate belongings. Now, all these years later, Tabitha understood that she was an object placed among other objects. Why had she not said no, shouted no? Undressing her there, in his wife's bedroom, that must have been part of the thrill for Stuart; he was treating both her and Laura with derision, and she—usually so surly and stubborn—had let him. She had had no power, maybe just the novelty of being someone helpless and young and unformed compared with the wife he'd grown tired of. A woman of what? Thirty-five, forty?

"I was a child," she replied at last. "He was my teacher."

For a moment something in Laura's face shifted, like the stony mask was going to crack apart. Then it hardened again.

"Fifteen-year-olds aren't children," she said.

"I was."

"I haven't come here to listen to you saying you're a victim."

"Someone wrote a letter to the police," said Tabitha. "Telling them about me and Stuart. Was it you?"

"If I wanted to tell the police, do you think I'd need to write an anonymous letter?"

"So why *didn't* you tell the police?"

Laura's expression became even blanker, almost frozen.

"People always blame the wife. They say she must have known. Or they say it was her fault really. I must have been a nag, I must have been frigid, I must have been boring, I must have been a doormat." She looked at Tabitha contemptuously. "Nobody from the outside can know what a marriage is like. Why would I wash my dirty linen in public? Anyway, I didn't need to tell them; they had enough evidence without it. Now everyone will have to know." She leaned forward. There was a fleck of pink lipstick on her front tooth. "My son will know. It makes a mockery."

"A mockery of what?"

"Of me. A mockery of me."

Tabitha stared at her. "I'm in prison," she said. "If I'm found guilty I'll be here for years and years. And I didn't do it. That's a mockery."

Laura started to speak and then stopped. It seemed to take an effort to say what she wanted to say. Finally she got the words out.

"He said you made the first move. He said you had a crush on him and caught him at a vulnerable time.

You . . ." She hesitated again. "You were intimate just the once and then he ended it."

None of it was true, absolutely none of it.

"Do you believe that?"

"Years ago I decided that it didn't matter what I believed or didn't believe."

"I don't understand."

"No, I don't suppose you do." Her face contorted, became briefly ugly. "I've watched you walking around the village in your torn jeans and ridiculous jacket and with paint in your hair, in your own little world. But people like me—"

"People like you?"

"Decent people," said Laura.

"What do people like you do?"

Laura looked away, out of the window at the blank gray sky. "I don't even know why I'm talking to you." She turned back to Tabitha. "Have you had other visitors?"

"Shona came, Shona Fry. And the vicar."

"Did she offer you religious consolation?"

"I don't believe in God."

"Then that made two of you. A vicar who doesn't believe in God. That's what we've come to."

Tabitha wanted to ask her about the day of the murder, but held her peace.

"It drove Stuart mad," said Laura. She was suddenly almost chatty, in a fierce way.

Tabitha made a murmuring sound to encourage her.

"He actually made an official complaint."

"Really?"

"That was one thing about Stuart, he was very good at making complaints. He always knew who to complain to. He used to say you had to go to the top. He once wrote a letter to the CEO of a DIY chain about poor service."

"Who did he complain to about Mel?"

"The bishop, of course."

"What happened?"

Laura seemed suddenly aware that she was talking to Tabitha as if she were, if not a friend, at least not an enemy. Her face emptied of expression and she drummed her fingers on the table.

"Could you tell me about the day it happened?" Tabitha asked.

Laura shrugged. "I haven't anything to say. I wasn't there."

"Where were you?"

"I had a job."

"I don't even properly know what your job is."

"I'm an estate agent. I was going to show someone a property, along the coast in Denham. I drove there but the client didn't turn up, so I drove back to the office."

Tabitha considered this. "Why didn't the client turn up?"

"I don't know. He just didn't."

"He."

"Yes."

"Have you seen him since?"

"I've never seen him."

"What? Never? He sounds like someone the police should talk to."

"They haven't been able to find him. Yet."

"But isn't that a really big deal?" said Tabitha. "He rings you . . . What's his name?"

"He said he was called Mike Wilson."

"Mike Wilson. That sounds fake."

"Why?"

"It just does. So someone calls you to get you out of the way. That's important."

"That's what it's like being an estate agent. People make appointments and break them."

"I suppose they can trace him through his phone."

"You'd think so."

"Does that mean they haven't?"

"I'm sure they will."

Tabitha wished she had brought a pen and paper with her. She had to trust herself to remember all of this. She tried to think of something else to say.

"Your son," she said. "Luke."

"Leave him out of this."

"He came home that day."

"I said, leave him out of this. You seduced and then killed my husband, but you sit there like a . . ." She searched for a word. "Like a muddy little mole," she said at last. Tabitha almost laughed at that. A muddy little mole. That wasn't bad.

"I just need to know when he came home."

"Stuart used to poison moles," said Laura and she looked at Tabitha with a fixed, glittery gaze. "He was very proud of his lawn. I think he quite enjoyed poisoning them."

"I always thought of Stuart as someone everyone liked," said Tabitha after a pause.

"Did *you* like him?"

"Obviously 'like' isn't really the right word."

"There you are then."

Again Tabitha couldn't make proper sense of what Laura was saying. She felt a need to go away and think about this and get it straight in her head.

"Did *you* like him?" she asked.

"That's a ridiculous question."

"OK, did you love him?"

"I was his wife," Laura said, almost dismissively. She made a motion to stand up and then stopped and sat back down. "They sent a police officer, a young woman of about ten, to see me. I think she was meant to be showing how sensitive they were to the widow. I made her tea and she sat next to me on the sofa and held my hand, which I didn't enjoy. She told me that this was the worst time. But it would just be a couple of months and you would be tried and convicted and given a life sentence and that would give me closure."

"But if I didn't do it, would it give you closure?"

Laura's gaze settled on her. "I might dig up the lawn," she said. Then she stood up.

"You didn't say you loved him," said Tabitha.

"We were married for thirty-five years." She turned away.

"That's not really an answer."

But Laura Rees was already out of earshot, walking briskly across the room, looking neither to the left nor to the right.

Twenty-five

Galia, the librarian, had given her several sheets of A3 paper. Tabitha sat in her icy cupboard and spread one out on the table in front of her. She angled the lamp so it was in brightness, and picked up her pencil. Then she closed her eyes for several seconds, summoning the little village into her mind. First she drew the cliff that rose up like a wall behind the string of houses. Nobody could climb that wall: she had tried several times as a girl, hauling herself up by the stunted trees, grazing her hands and ripping her clothes, and always arriving at an impasse. The only way in and the only way out was by the single-track road that snaked its way down from the west, ending at the small shelf of land and the rocky beach. Tabitha scowled at the cliff for several minutes. Then she drew in Rob Coombe's farmhouse on its top, high above the village, adding a miniature tractor and some sheep.

The road came next. Very carefully, she penciled its bends down the cliff and through the village, ending in a loop at the east of the village where cars could turn. Several times, she used the miniature eraser at the top of her pencil to rub out the faint lines before correcting them.

At the road's loop, she added the track that led to her house and Stuart's.

She stood up and looked down at what she had done. Then she laid a fallen tree across the road at the entrance of the village.

The sea was next, running all the way across the page. She added a little boat in full sail and a couple of gulls flying low across the waves. She shaded in places where you could reach it, including the rocky beach where every day she swam. Used to swim. She put in the flat rock where she undressed and dressed again, and she put in a tiny figure in the water. Her.

Next, starting at the fallen tree, she marked the buildings. There were several small houses on the right as you came into the village; one was apparently only occupied in the summer, and she was pretty sure another was the home of Pauline Leavitt, the old woman who claimed that Tabitha had threatened Stuart. After them, on the left, was the hotel that was closed for winter.

She couldn't remember how many buildings there were until Shona's bungalow on the right and a bit further on Andy's tiny house, set back from the road. Perhaps twenty, she thought, maybe a few more.

More or less opposite Andy's came the vicarage, which was smaller and shabbier than its name suggested. The church was next to it. Tabitha spent quite a long time getting the church right; its round tower and stunted spire.

A few paces on from that was Dr. Owen Mallon's house.

Then the shop, which Terry lived above, and to its side the little annex that served as a café in the summer. Opposite the shop was the bus stop.

She drew the Reeses' square house and then, remembering Laura's words, added a sloping lawn and put a mole in its center.

Finally she made a miniature picture of her own crooked little house. She put smoke coming out of its chimney. She parked a tiny car at the front and then she drew in the shed where Stuart's body had been found.

What had she missed? She was sure there was something. Yes, the camera. She drew an eye over the roof of the shop. A glaring eye.

Twenty-six

Dana was lying as usual on her bed, almost invisible beneath her blanket. She heard a clattering from outside.

"It's dinnertime," Tabitha said.

No response.

She leaned up and touched the bulge in the bed. There was still no response so she pulled the blanket off.

"We're going to get our dinner."

"I'm not hungry."

Tabitha shook Dana. She told her that she had to get up, fetch a dinner tray and bring it back to the cell and if she didn't want to eat it, that was up to her. She had to almost drag her along the gangway, down the stairs and into the queue. They returned with a tray each. Back in the cell they each sat on a chair. Tabitha looked down at her tray; the sight and the smell of it made her stomach heave. There were four compartments, containing respectively vegetable stew that looked like vomit, a bread roll, a foil-wrapped granola bar, and a sludgy stewed apple for pudding.

She looked across at Dana, who had chosen the baked fish instead of the vegetables.

"I think you may have made a better choice than me," she said, not meaning it.

"Take it," said Dana.

Dana didn't eat more than a couple of forkfuls of her meal. But it was something. She was sitting up. She had spoken a few words. She wasn't just lying under her blanket.

Tabitha took the two trays and returned with two mugs of tea.

"I didn't make you eat the food," she said, "but I am going to make you drink the tea. It's about hydration. You should probably have about three liters but you're definitely going to have this mug."

Was there the tiniest hint of a smile on Dana's lips? Tabitha thought that there probably wasn't. But she did start to sip at her tea. Tabitha put her own mug down. She laid a fresh sheet of paper on her desk and started to write. She quickly filled two sheets. Then she looked across at Dana, who was staring at the wall.

"I've written a letter," she said. She placed it in front of Dana. "What do you think?"

Dana gazed blankly at it and then shook her head. "Don't know."

"You mean, you think it's not right?"

"I can't make it out."

Tabitha hesitated for a moment. "Dana," she said slowly. "Can you read?"

Dana shrugged. "A bit. You know. When I need to."

Tabitha pulled her chair closer and picked up her piece of paper and looked at it.

"I've written two letters," she said. "I'm not sure if I've found the right tone. Pull your chair over here."

Dana looked suspicious.

"We could go over the letter, spell it out, word by word." Tabitha paused. Dana still seemed reluctant. "Well, what else have you got to do? Crawl back under your blanket?"

With a scraping sound, Dana eased her chair closer to Tabitha's table.

Twenty-seven

A ndy came into the room slowly and heavily; she could hear his shoes on the floor as he approached. She had made an effort for his visit, washed her hair and put on jeans rather than her shapeless tracksuit trousers, but still she saw he was shocked by her appearance.

He had made an effort too. She was used to seeing him in his working clothes, at ease in old trousers covered in paint and oil that had multiple pockets for tools; rough, often ripped shirts and boots without laces. But today he wore jeans, a round-necked gray sweater that was one size too small, shoes he might even have polished, and he had shaved, which made him look younger and less good-looking.

He raised his hand to her from across the room and kept it awkwardly raised as he made his way toward her. He was tall and solid. She had always looked ridiculously little standing beside him.

"Thank you for coming," she said as he lowered himself onto the chair.

"Oh." He flushed. "No worries."

He didn't like talking very much; he communicated with his hands, with the way he used a saw, or measured up a space just with his eyes, or laid licks of fresh paint over plaster.

He shifted in his chair, nodded. His blue eyes were uneasy and there were purple rings of exhaustion under them. His long dark hair was wet from the rain. The nail on his left thumb was dark purple. He was always picking up bruises.

"I'm sorry about everything you had to go through," she said.

"It wasn't great."

"Are you OK?"

"I guess."

"I'd like you to go on working on the house while I'm in here. I'll pay you, of course. It just might take a bit more time. I'll be able to picture you standing in the kitchen with a mouthful of nails and your radio playing. First of all, we need—that is, you need—to lay the floorboards." She saw the tiny flinch and knew he was thinking of going out to the shed. "And after that, there are the skirting boards and the shelves in that old pantry."

"OK."

"And the window frames need repairing, of course," she continued.

"And the porch."

"Yes, but you can wait till the weather gets better for the outside stuff. I used to walk past it," she continued, "and think it looked so neglected and unloved. Houses need love." Her voice was dusty and her eyes throbbed. "But that's not what I wanted to talk about."

"What then?"

"Did you tell the police I had tried to stop you going out into the shed?"

"Yes," he said slowly. "Yes, I did. He asked me."

"Who?"

He shrugged. "The man in the suit, face like an ax. I had to tell him."

"But I don't understand," said Tabitha. "I don't remember that at all."

Andy stared at her helplessly. "You were pretty out of it. You couldn't really speak."

"I was having a bad day."

He nodded.

"I get them every so often. I just have to weather them. It doesn't mean anything."

"Of course not," he replied, too quickly.

"You know I'm defending myself?"

He nodded.

"So I need to know everything. Help me remember. From when you arrived."

Andy cleared his throat. "I knocked and then knocked again. I knew you were in because a light was on."

"What time?"

"Four-thirty or near enough."

"Go on."

"You opened the door but it was like you weren't really seeing me. Your eyes had a kind of—" He stopped.

"Go on."

"A glazed look. Like you were on drugs."

"What did you think?"

"I thought you had taken something. And that you were unhappy. I was anxious."

"That I'd done something?"

"No! Anxious for you."

"Why?"

"You're my friend," he said simply.

Tabitha's throat hurt. She swallowed hard and said, "Did you notice anything else?"

"Like what?"

"Like did I have blood on me?"

He flinched. "No. I mean, I don't think so. You had the blanket wrapped around you though. It was pretty dark."

"So then what?"

"I asked you if you were OK and you mumbled something and kind of staggered back to the sofa and lay down. I didn't know what to do. I tried to ask you about what we were going to do on the house the next day. I thought that might help. You know. Practical stuff."

"Yes."

"And then I said I'd bring in some of the planks so they wouldn't be all frozen in the morning. I opened the back door. And you told me not to go out there."

"Is that all?"

"I think so."

"Did I sound urgent?"

"Kind of," he said miserably.

"So why did you go out?"

He frowned. "I don't know. I just thought you didn't want me going into the cold."

"Right," said Tabitha. "That's what I must have meant."

"Yeah," he said. He wasn't looking at her. "I guess."

"But I didn't say that."

"No. You were strange. Scary."

"Andy."

"Yes?"

"I didn't do it."

He looked at her. He was a handsome man, with his shaggy dark hair and his blue eyes. Little wonder that Shona had a thing for him.

"Of course not," he said.

"Do you believe me?"

"You know I'm on your side."

"Thanks." Though it wasn't really an answer.

"What did you think of him?"

"Stuart?" He gave a grimace.

"You've done work for him, haven't you?"

"I put up a greenhouse last autumn and laid the new patio."

"How was he?"

Andy shrugged. "I was just the guy doing the manual labor."

"You mean he ignored you?"

"He was good at getting what he wanted out of people."

Tabitha remembered what Laura had said about her husband making complaints.

"So he got what he wanted out of you?"

"That's one way of putting it."

"What do you mean?"

"He was a bit of an asshole, that's all."

Tabitha leaned forward. "Really? What do you mean by that?"

Andy shrugged. "He wasn't the nicest person, that's all. Liked getting his own way. An asshole."

"Did other people think so too?"

"You'll have to ask them."

"When was the last time you were there?"

Andy considered. "I helped move a socking great sofa into the living room a few days before he died. He stood there and told me I needed to find a different angle. In the end, I had to take its feet off."

"You didn't see him the day he died?"

"No."

"Where were you?"

"I was at Kenny's, painting."

"Was Kenny there?"

"No."

They stared at each other.

"Why?" asked Andy at last.

"I need to find out who was in the village and where they were and when, and who they saw."

"Sure. Well, as I say, I was at Kenny's."

They sat in silence, not meeting each other's eye, then Tabitha said, "By the way, Shona came to see me."

"I know." Andy smiled and his face softened again. "She's told everyone in the village. Multiple times."

"Of course she has. What do you think of her?"

"Shona?" A strange expression crossed his face, almost furtive.

"Yes."

"She's OK. Friendly."

"She's very attractive."

"I've never really thought about it."

"She is."

"What's this about?"

"Nothing. She's broken up with her boyfriend and—"

Andy gave a sudden shout of laughter. "I don't believe it!"

"What?"

"Did she put you up to this?"

"I don't know what you mean."

"She did, didn't she?"

"Not really."

"It's never going to happen."

A bell was ringing. Tabitha ignored it.

"Let's talk about something else."

"Time's up."

She looked round and saw the thin warden with the sour face.

"It can't be."

"It is," the warden said.

"I'm getting ready for my trial."

"I don't know anything about that."

The warden had thin cheeks and eyes like raisins. She put a hand on Tabitha's upper arm and her fingers dug in like pincers. Tabitha felt herself grow hot.

"Fuck off," she said, shaking the woman off. Then she said it again, louder. Very loud.

Now there were two more wardens standing at the table.

"The governor's not going to like this."

As she was led away, she turned to see Andy watching her. He didn't look happy.

She sat in front of her opened notebook but she couldn't concentrate on anything. She was remembering the way Andy had looked at her. He had pitied her. The thought of it made her nauseous. She felt suddenly overcome by a heavy exhaustion so that she could barely keep her eyes open. It would be such a relief to sleep. To sleep and sleep and not to wake.

Twenty-eight

"I've got a new idea." Tabitha heard herself. She sounded like the head of a Girl Scout troop, the sort of person that she had always especially hated.

The new idea was that they would work on a letter together but this time Tabitha would dictate it and Dana would actually write it. Dana scowled.

"Is that allowed?"

"Why wouldn't it be allowed? There are people in prison who can't write and there are other people who write letters for them."

"But you can write."

"It doesn't matter. This is good practice for you."

"I'll just feel stupid."

"You'll be helping me. In this letter I'm trying to

persuade someone to do something. It'll be good to have your point of view."

So Tabitha sat Dana down at the table with a pen in her hand and a fresh piece of paper.

"He's the local farmer," Tabitha said. "I saw him down in the village that day."

"What good is that going to do you?"

"There was hardly anyone in the village the day that Stuart Rees was killed. I want to talk to all of them. Someone may have seen something. Or heard something."

"That can prove you didn't do it?"

"That's the idea."

"Like what?"

"I don't know. If I knew, I wouldn't need to ask." She thought for a moment. "'Dear Rob.' Actually his name is Robert but I've never heard anyone call him by that. Rob might be too casual. But then Robert might be too formal."

"Do you want me to write something down?"

"Write 'Dear Rob.'"

And then slowly, Tabitha dictated a letter to a man she had no reason to like, friendly but not over-friendly. Some of the words she spelled out letter by letter. She pondered how to end. "Yours sincerely"? Yours"?

"All the best"? She settled for "with best wishes." She looked it over.

"You did that really well."

When Dana left the cell, Tabitha quickly rewrote the letter on a fresh sheet of paper.

Twenty-nine

Almost by return of post, Tabitha got a letter back from Coombe.

> *Dear Miss Hardy,*
>   *Thank you for your letter. I may be called up to give evidence in the upcoming trial and therefore I don't think it would be appropriate for me to come and visit you.*
>   *Yours sincerely,*
>   *Robert Coombe*

"Fucking pompous idiot," she said aloud when she had finished it. She tossed the letter down and then immediately picked it up again. He was giving evidence for the prosecution. And if it were for the prosecution, it would have to be damaging to her. Was it just that he had heard her bad-mouthing Stuart? Or he said that he had. She didn't believe him, but why would he make up something like that? Would she be informed as part of the prosecution case? Probably.

It was all so confusing. She had thought that in spite of everything Coombe would see her, that he would be curious enough. But just a few hours later, she found herself sitting opposite someone she had never even thought to ask.

"**Long time** no see," said Luke Rees.

And it was a long time. He had been eleven or twelve when she left Okeham, and they were at the same school for only a year. All she'd known about him was that he was Stuart's son, though by the time Luke arrived in secondary school Stuart no longer paid any attention to Tabitha. She remembered him as scrawny and emotional; once she had seen him weeping near the school gates, pushing his knuckly fists into his eyes, trying hard not to cry. To be a boy and cry was to be a baby or a sissy; to be the teacher's son was to be the target for bullies.

Now Luke was tall and rangy, with pale skin, long dark hair in a topknot: he was arresting in a wasted kind of way. He was wearing a purple hoodie and beneath it a red tee shirt. Tabitha tried to make out his expression. Was he contemptuous, amused, distressed or just detached?

"I'm surprised to see you," she said finally. "I mean, really surprised. I didn't write to you. I didn't think you'd want to see me."

"Why? Because you fucked my father? Or because you're accused of killing him?"

He grinned and nodded his head as he spoke, as if he was agitated and trying to keep it under control. He put his hands on the table. They were pale and smooth with long fingers; beautiful hands, except the nails were bitten back almost to nothing.

"Is that what you came all this way to say?"

"I'm not sure why I came. Maybe it was just because I wanted to take a good look at you and hear what you had to say for yourself."

"I'm not sure that I've got anything to say for myself. I know this must be horrible for you."

"Don't pity me," he said in a loud tone that made Tabitha look around.

"You don't want to make a scene here," she said.

"What will they do, throw me in prison?"

Luke Rees was about five years younger than Tabitha but she felt like he was a morose, ironic teenager who was going to be as sulky as he could, simply to make a point. But what point?

"Our paths have never crossed," said Tabitha. "Since school, I mean. Not that they really crossed even when we were at school."

"I didn't know," he said. She liked his directness. "About you and my father, I mean. I only knew when Mum told me a few days ago."

"I suppose she was very angry with me."

"She didn't seem angry. I think she just put up with things. That's what being married means, doesn't it? Putting up with things."

"I don't know," said Tabitha. "I've never been married."

"You don't seem like the marrying kind."

Tabitha didn't know what to make of that. She forced herself to focus. She wasn't sure why Luke had come but she needed to make the most of it, to learn anything she could.

"What did you think when she told you?"

He put his hands behind his head. Underneath his casual manner he was like a coiled spring.

"Think? I thought, poor old Mum, having that as well."

"You weren't surprised?"

Luke gave a harsh laugh. "I'm told it's what men do

when they reach a certain age. I was only surprised it was with you."

"Why do you say that?"

"I remember you. You weren't exactly the most sophisticated girl in the class."

"No. I wasn't."

"So yeah, really I just felt sorry for Mum."

"Have the police talked to you?"

"Why do you care?"

"I want to know who was in the village. Were you there?"

"Sure."

"So you saw Stuart . . . your dad?"

"No, I didn't."

"How come?"

"I came home that day. I took the train to Dormouth, but the bus to Okeham wasn't running. So I walked."

"In the storm?"

"It's a way of thinking, clearing my head. There was almost nobody around. I saw where the tree had blown down and blocked the road. They were starting to work on it."

"I thought there was no way into the village at all."

"There wasn't, except over the tree. I climbed over the trunk with the help of the men, and walked down.

When I got home there was nobody in, the car wasn't there."

"It must have been parked round the back of my house by then. What time was this?"

"Why?"

"Was it morning or afternoon?"

"I don't know exactly. Afternoon, about two or three. Before Mum came back anyway. I wasn't looking."

"So what did you do?"

"Nothing. I was tired."

"Did you see anyone?"

"What does it matter whether I saw anyone?"

"I'm trying to work out who was in the village and who met who and who talked to who and what they said and what they saw."

"Why?"

"I'm defending myself in the trial."

"Yeah, I heard. It's all anyone's talking about. Sounds weird."

"That's why I'm asking everyone."

"You're saying you're innocent?"

"That's right."

He looked at her with frank curiosity.

"I got home and hung around and I didn't see anyone until Mum got back later in the afternoon and we didn't talk to anyone else until the police arrived. Is that any help?"

It felt like he was trying to provoke an argument. There was a silence, during which he tapped his fingers against the table.

"It must have been difficult for you, at school, being the child of one of the teachers," said Tabitha.

"It wasn't perfect."

"You left when you were sixteen, didn't you?"

"That's right."

"I thought you'd be one of the people who went to university."

"I did other things."

"What did your parents think about that?"

"Why do you even ask?"

"Your father was a teacher. I suppose that he thought it was important to pass exams, get good grades, all that sort of thing. So maybe your dad was a bit disappointed when you left school."

"My dad was disappointed with a lot of things."

"Like what?"

"This is my murdered father we're talking about. And you're talking about an ex-lover."

"He wasn't my 'ex-lover.'"

"I thought that was the word for someone you've slept with. How would you describe it?"

"He was my math teacher and almost three times my age, and I was only fifteen." She thought Luke gave an involuntary flinch: perhaps Laura hadn't told him that bit. "What would you call him?"

"I don't know," he said, and for the first time he sounded sincere.

"I wasn't a very mature fifteen either. Looking back, I see I was vulnerable and afraid and he was someone I looked up to and he took advantage of that."

"That sounds like a reason to kill someone."

"It's one of the reasons I'm sitting here," said Tabitha. She had surprised herself by speaking so openly. "All right. What about you?"

"What do you want me to tell you?" said Luke. "You must have heard the story by now. I left school early. I went off the rails. I left home and didn't return. I'm not the son my dad would have chosen. He wasn't the father I would have chosen either."

"Did he bully you?"

"Did he bully *you*?" replied Luke.

"I think he did bully you," Tabitha continued. "I think you were scared of him and crushed by him and he made your childhood miserable." She spoke slowly and held his gaze, willing him not to look away.

For a few seconds she thought he was going to tell her something. She could see his face working with the effort to speak and not to speak. But then his expression shifted.

"Fuck you," he said. "Oh no, I forgot, that was what my father did."

"Fuck you too." She sat back and they glared at each other. Tabitha wanted to shout with nasty laughter. "I need to find out something," she said at last. "Or I'll be serving a life sentence for murder."

"Which is what you should be serving if you killed him."

"But I didn't. Or at least, I . . ." She bit down on the words. "I didn't," she repeated.

"So you say."

"And if I didn't, someone else in the village that day must have. You see?"

Luke let out a breath that was halfway to a whistle. "That's what this is about. You're playing detective."

"It's hardly a game."

"You're trying to find out if the bullied son could have murdered his wicked father. Or maybe just smear me a bit, spread a little doubt about. Would that be enough to get you off?"

"It might be," said Tabitha. "You know: reasonable doubt." Tabitha considered for a moment. "Had you made up?"

"Made up?" Luke gave a peculiar little smirk. "You

mean, had he decided to forgive me for not being the son he wanted?"

"Had he?"

"I'll never know."

"What about you?"

"What do you mean?"

"Had you decided to forgive him for not being the father you wanted?"

Something in his expression changed. He looked sharp and almost ugly. "I'll never forgive him," he said, not angrily but deliberately, like a kind of pledge.

Tabitha felt like she'd been punched. She stared at him and he stared back, then shrugged, regaining his ironic composure: "Fathers and sons," he said. "You know."

"You said your father wouldn't have chosen you. What about Laura?"

"You know mothers. She took my side. At least some of the time." He stopped and folded his arms.

"So why did you come back?"

Luke's face flushed red. "It was Christmas. Mum wanted to see me."

"Was he OK with that?"

"You know what they say, home is the place where when you go there, they have to let you in."

"You hadn't been back for years."

"Have you been checking up on me?"

"I didn't need to. You know what Okeham's like. Everyone knows everyone's secrets."

Who had it been? She thought perhaps Pauline Leavitt, or maybe Terry in the village shop.

"I can imagine. The ingratitude of kids, poor Stuart and Laura, that kind of thing."

"Something like that. But you should hear what they say about me."

"I don't get what you're asking."

"You don't go back for ages, and then when you do return he's killed."

"So?"

"Was his car there when you got home?"

"No. I already said."

"And you didn't see it?"

"No."

"Did the police interview you?"

"They checked a couple of details."

"That sounds a bit casual."

"They were mainly there to reassure my mother. The main man told her that it was OK, that they'd already got the right person. Slam dunk." He pointed an index finger at her.

"Who was he?"

"Someone who liked the sound of his own voice." He wrinkled his brow. "His name was Dudley, I think."

"Face like an ax?" asked Tabitha, remembering what Andy had said.

"More like a hatchet. Or a cheese grater perhaps. He kept patting Mum on the shoulder."

"Are you going to be giving evidence?"

"Why? What about?"

"Maybe they'll want you to talk about the impact on your family."

"I'll leave that to my mother."

"You probably won't be needed," said Tabitha. "I imagine the witness box will be full of people from the village talking about how beloved he was in the local community."

"Yeah, right," said Luke, with a strange sort of smile.

"What does that mean?" said Tabitha. "Does that mean 'yeah, right' meaning yes? Or 'yeah, right' meaning no?"

Luke stood up and leaned toward her. She realized he was very angry. "You're the person who stayed on at school. You're the person he fucked. You're the person who's in prison for his murder. You decide."

The interview was over.

Thirty

When she got back to the cell, she saw that Dana
was away. Was that a good sign? Not necessarily but most of the really bad things people did to
themselves were in their own cells. She sat at her table
and retrieved her list of names. Against Luke's name
she wrote: "At home. No witness. Angry."

When she was finished she lay on her bed and went
over the interview in her mind. Stuart Rees: revered
teacher, beloved husband and father, the heart and
soul of the village. Something Luke had said, a phrase,
floated into her mind: *Poor old Mum, having that as
well.* As well as what? She stood up and opened her
notebook again to write down the words, underlining
"as well."

Then she turned to the page on which she had written the timeline. She inserted Luke's timing.

6:30 (approx): Wake up. Lie there for some time (how long?). Not feeling good.

7:30 (approx): Get up. Start making porridge and tea. No milk.

8:00: Go to village shop to buy milk. See CCTV. In PJ bottoms and wellies. School bus there. Meet Rob Coombe? Insult Stuart?

??? A.M.: Go for swim. Meet Dr. Mallon.

10:34: Stuart drives out of village in his car.

10:41: Stuart drives back again in direction of house (blocked by fallen tree).

2–3: Luke arrives in village (apparently). Climbs over tree (workmen there).

Walks to his house. Says he sees no one at all.

2:30: Meet vicar. Talk about news.

3:30: Laura returns. Luke there. No sign of Stuart.

4:30: Andy arrives at house. Discovers body.

The sky in the small window darkened. Dana returned, shuffling her feet. The key turned in the lock. They ate their supper in silence. Someone screamed and then screamed again. They used the toilet. They brushed their teeth. Footsteps echoed outside. Tabitha lay in her bunk and Dana climbed into hers, a foot or so above her; she could hear her breathing and shifting her position. She imagined the other women lying in their bunks in both directions, and on the floors above and the one below, like they were stacked on warehouse shelves. If she looked carefully, she could see a few pale stars in the small square of window. She thought about there being a moon out there somewhere, fields, woods, rivers and then the sea. She thought about snow falling on the water and frost glittering in the branches. She thought about people in their houses, closing curtains and cooking meals and watching TV, reading a book maybe, sipping tea and chatting about their day.

She needed help and suddenly she had an idea.

Thirty-one

From her icy little cupboard Tabitha could hear the sounds of sewing machines clattering and women talking. She put her hands to her ears and tried to concentrate. She had in front of her the list of names of people who had been in the village on December 21.

Me
Mel
Shona
Rob Coombe
Andy
Terry
Dr. Mallon

Luke
Pauline Leavitt
Deliveryman

If she hadn't murdered Stuart, then one of these people must have. But why? She took the names one by one, adding comments beside some.

Me: Sexually abused by Stuart when 15.

Mel: Disagreement with Stuart over religion. He wrote to the bishop complaining about her.

Shona: ????

Rob Coombe: ???? (Why would he lie about me to the police?)

Andy: Didn't like Stuart.

Terry: Must have been in shop all day?

Dr. Mallon:

Luke: Stuart bullied him.

Pauline Leavitt:

Deliveryman: Who is he?

She looked at what she had written. Her motive was the only one that made clear sense. Her eyes ached, her throat felt itchy and sore. She had the beginnings of a cold. She put her head on her arms and fell asleep.

"You look tired," said Ingrid.

"I am."

"It's hardest in winter. But the days are getting lighter."

"I guess."

It was March 27. Tabitha had been in prison for more than two and a half months. Eighty days. Spring was lying in wait. The snowdrops and winter aconites would be long gone, and the witch hazel would have lost its rusty gold blossom, but there would be primroses and crocuses and daffodils, and tight buds uncurling on the trees. It was time to pick young nettles for soup. Time to mend the porch and paint the windows.

She mustn't think of such things. She turned to Ingrid. "How are you, anyway?"

"My parole hearing's coming up soon."

"That's good."

"Yes." Ingrid smiled. "I'm feeling hopeful."

"It is so nice of you to come."

Michaela sat across from her, a tall, strong figure. She was wearing black jeans and a yellow blouse the color of sunshine. Her hair was held back in a complicated plait. There was something different about her, thought Tabitha, and then she realized what it was: she looked *clean*. Her clothes, her hair, her skin, were fresh. She even smelled nice.

"I said I would," said Michaela.

"How's it going?"

"It'll be better when winter is over. What about you? How's your new cellmate?"

"Dana. Young, like a child really. She cries a lot."

Michaela nodded matter-of-factly. "Early days."

"I need your help."

"Go on."

"You know I'm defending myself. So I need to find out what happened on the day that Stuart was murdered."

"Why?"

"To work out who could have killed him."

"You just have to show it might not have been you."

"Everything points to me. I'll be found guilty unless I can show it could have been someone else."

As clearly as she could, Tabitha spelled out what she knew. How a tree had come down, cutting the village off and effectively trapping only a handful of people. How the CCTV had shown Stuart to be alive at ten-thirty in the morning—so it was just the hours between then and three-thirty in the afternoon that mattered. How his body had been found in her shed, his car in her drive, his blood on her clothes. How villagers had come forward to claim that she had threatened Stuart. How she had a history of depression that counted against her. How—she hesitated for a moment here—Stuart had had sex with her when she was fifteen and he was her math teacher.

She looked at Michaela's expression, which wasn't shocked like she had expected, and continued, telling her about the anonymous letter sent to the police, and the conversations she had had with Shona, Andy, the vicar, Laura and finally Luke.

"So you see, several of the people who were in the village that day had reasons to dislike him, or even hate him. Not just me."

"Maybe," said Michaela dubiously.

"Definitely."

"You've been busy."

"But there are things I can't do while I'm in here. Which is where you come in."

"Go on."

"First off, the farmer, his name's Rob Coombe, he said I was being threatening about Stuart that morning, in the shop. He says I called him a bastard."

"Did you?"

"I don't remember it at all. It doesn't sound right. But he won't come and see me. So I wondered if you'd go and talk to him."

"What would I say?"

"I don't know. Sound him out, see if he'll tell you anything. Just get a feeling if he's lying." It sounded a bit desperate, but then, she was desperate. "You can say you're a reporter or something. People sometimes like talking to the papers."

"I'm not sure I look like a reporter."

"Or you could—" Tabitha stopped. She couldn't think of anything.

"It's OK. I'll do it."

"Really?"

"I can borrow my aunt's car and have a day out. You have to give me the address."

"I don't know how to thank you."

"Then don't try."

Thirty-two

The prosecution delivered its evidence to Tabitha on April Fools' Day, which seemed appropriate.

The giant warden who had first escorted her to her cupboard full of mannequins and whose name, she had discovered, was Barry brought it in. Tabitha was sitting in the semidarkness: the socket the lamp had been plugged into was no longer working and the bulb that hung above her flickered dismally. She had expected a box folder or something like that. Instead, she got two large boxes full of papers, photos and forensic evidence; reports on the fallen tree, the state of the road and on what kind of heavy-duty plastic the body had been wrapped in. There were details of the fibers, hairs, blood types, blood spatter and the outside temperature at various times during the day; the marks made by tire tracks from Stuart's car, invoices, receipts and phone logs. There were statements from people whose names she'd never heard and who hadn't been in the village, all of them rendered into the kind of clunky legalese that made her head bang.

Even at a cursory glance, Tabitha could see that most of it was useless to her. The problem was, anything that might be relevant was buried in the avalanche of spurious information.

She sighed heavily.

"What?" said Barry, pausing on his way out.

"There's too much here."

"They're fucking with you."

"What am I meant to do with it all?"

"I'm just the guy who delivers it." He hesitated, then said, "I could bring you some coffee."

"What! Really?"

"I guess."

"I would love that."

"Maybe it'll help you keep awake."

Tabitha lifted the contents of the first box onto the table and started from the top. She peered at a map of Okeham, although in the dim light it was hard to make it out, and then looked at the transcript of Andy's call to emergency services. She read the officer at the scene's description of the body, and of herself. "Miss Hardy was in an incoherent and agitated state," she read. "She was covered in blood and she repeatedly said, "'I didn't know, I didn't know.'" Tabitha laid aside the sheet of paper and frowned. What didn't she know? Her memory was still a horrible blank and reading about herself was like reading about a stranger.

She came to the photos of Stuart and made herself look at them again—but what could they tell her? That his carotid artery had been severed and he had been stabbed repeatedly in his chest and stomach. The autopsy used the word "frenzied"? Could she have been so frenzied that she had killed Stuart and forgotten? And how had his body got into the shed? He was overweight and she was small.

Several of the sheets of paper had been signed by DCI Dudley.

After several hours of reading she came to the CCTV shots. She saw herself going into the village shop at 08:10 and then leaving at 08:15. She saw Stuart's car drive past at 10:34 and, in the next image, returning at 10:40. That was all.

She looked at the four grainy pictures for a long time. The sewing machines outside had stopped; everyone must have left. She had no idea what time it was. Whoever had killed Stuart had done so after 10:40 A.M., but there were no CCTV pictures for after that. If she was going to get anywhere, she needed to see who had gone past the surveillance camera throughout the day. Anyone who walked through the village toward Stuart's house had to go that way. All of the houses except hers and Stuart's were on the other side of the village shop, so it made sense that the murderer, whoever she or he was, would be on film.

Tabitha flicked rapidly through the pile of paper in front of her, then lifted the second batch out of its box and scrabbled through that as well. There were no other CCTV photos: they had dumped every bit of information they had, however irrelevant, but left those out.

She bundled everything together and opened her notebook to find the card she had pushed between its pages after her court appearance in February. Tom Creevey, liaison officer for the prosecution.

"I need to see all the footage," she said, cupping her hand over the receiver and turning her back on the warden who was standing too close to her.

"All?" Creevey's voice was politely incredulous.

"Yes. From, say, six in the morning of the twenty-first of December until half past four in the afternoon."

"I think that might be a problem."

"It's my right," she said. "The judge said you were to give me everything I asked for. I demand it."

A hefty sigh came down the phone. "It might take some time."

"I haven't got time."

"I need a different room. It's my right." She sneezed loudly.

Deborah Cole stared at her across the polished desk as if she were an alien species, something curious and faintly repellent. "You don't seem to understand the rules," she said. "This is a prison, not a hotel."

"I have the right to see all the evidence I need before my trial."

"You're beginning to try my patience."

Tabitha squeezed her fists together. She knew she mustn't lose her temper but the sight of the governor's blond hair, her impeccably applied makeup, her tailored clothes, maddened her. She pictured all the women prisoners, their night terrors and their private agonies and the mess of their lives, and she looked at Deborah Cole's manicured hands and her shapely eyebrows and thought she might pick up the paperweight and hurl it at her.

"I'm sorry about that," she said in a tight, scratchy voice. "But I do need a space where the electricity works and where I can watch CCTV footage. The judge was very insistent," she added, "that I have everything I require. He made a point of it. I'm sure you don't want to be seen to be impeding the course of justice."

She felt ridiculous using such a phrase, but she saw something shift under the smooth surface of Deborah Cole's face.

Thirty-three

There was no warning. After the breakfast trays had been collected, Mary Guy appeared at the door.

"You're going to see a film," she said.

Tabitha wasn't immediately sure whether this was a question or a statement. Then she realized. She picked up her notebook and a handful of pens. She followed the warden into the library. Mary Guy walked round the desk into the librarian's office. They went through a door at the back, entering a room that was little more than a corridor with the toilet at the far end. A small TV screen had been placed on a narrow table. A DVD player was attached.

"Really?" Tabitha said. "You could have just put it on a memory stick."

"No computer. It's a security issue."

"It would have saved a lot of trouble."

"We're not here to save you trouble."

"So is it on disc?"

"Yeah."

"Have you got it?"

"Yeah."

There was a pause.

"All right," said Tabitha. "I wasn't just asking out of interest. Are you going to give it to me?"

"Them. There are a few of them."

"Are you going to give *them* to me?"

"Hang on."

"What for?"

"It needs to be checked over."

"I know how to operate a DVD player."

"I said hang on."

Mary Guy's tone had grown more menacing, so Tabitha stood and waited, faintly puzzled. Then the door opened and a familiar shaven-headed figure entered. One of the women from the fight, all those days ago. It took Tabitha a moment to remember her name.

"Jasmine," she said. "Are you going to watch TV with me?"

Mary Guy took something from her pocket and handed it to Jasmine Cash. Tabitha couldn't see what it was.

"Two minutes," said the warden and left the room.

"What's this?" said Tabitha. "I don't need help to work a DVD player."

Jasmine ignored her. She sat down and put the DVD player on her lap. Now Tabitha saw that the warden had given Jasmine a miniature screwdriver. With a few deft movements, she was using it to unfasten the screws on the back panel. She didn't remove the panel but loosened it enough so that she could push her fingers inside. She pulled out a small white plastic bag and then Tabitha saw that the plastic wasn't white. It was what was inside the bag.

"What the fuck is this?"

Jasmine ignored her. She put the bag on the table and then pushed her hand back inside the back of the DVD player. When she was done, there were four small bags in a line on the table. She put two in each pocket of her tracksuit bottoms. Then, with a frown of concentration, she refastened the panel. Then she looked round at Tabitha with a smile.

"We owe you one," she said.

"If they found out—" Tabitha began.

"They won't find out. They don't want to find out."

The door opened and Mary Guy came back in. Jasmine handed the screwdriver back.

"All working fine," she said.

"Good," said Mary Guy. "Then you'd better be on your way."

When Jasmine had gone, Tabitha looked at the warden for some sign that she felt guilty or uneasy or acknowledged in any way what had just happened. She saw nothing, nothing at all.

"There are rules," the warden said.

"Rules? What do you mean, rules?"

"I'm told that you're entitled to watch this and you're entitled to privacy. That means I'm outside the door at all times. Don't get up to anything. Just watch your film."

Mary Guy was holding an A4-sized padded envelope. She laid it on the table.

"The discs are in there," she said and then she left the room.

The envelope was stapled shut and Tabitha pulled it open. There were two little stacks of discs, held together with rubber bands. She took the two piles out and examined them. Each one had a label affixed: one said "interior" and the other "exterior." She started with the exterior pile. Each disc was in its own square envelope with a time scrawled on it in thick black marker. She saw "3–4 P.M." on one, "10–11 A.M." on another. She arranged them in chronological order. The first was "6–7 A.M." Wouldn't it be completely dark? The last was "7–8 P.M.," well after the action was over. She opened the envelope of the third disc, "8–9 A.M.," and inserted it into the DVD player. At first the screen was just a fizzing blur and she felt a terrible sense of anticlimax. But after some clicking on the control, an image appeared on the screen, wavering and wobbling and then suddenly, like in one of the dreams she had been having night after night, Tabitha was back in Okeham.

Thirty-four

The image was in black and white and it was a little grainy but she was looking across the main street of the village. There wasn't much to see, the tarmac of the road, the bus stop and the little bus shelter behind it that was built into the sheer cliff side that climbed to the moorland above. If it weren't for the time code in the top left corner of the screen, it could have been a still photograph except that, when she looked closely, she could see the birch tree beside the shelter swaying slightly, its naked leafless branches rippling. Tabitha felt tears coming to her eyes. She could almost feel the northerly wind from the Channel on her cheeks. She could almost smell the salt and the seaweed and the mud at low tide.

She wiped her eyes on her sleeve. *Think, Tabitha,* she told herself. *Calm. Think calmly.* She opened her notebook at a clean page and wrote "CCTV" at the top and underlined it. She looked at the image. Nothing was happening. There was nothing to note down. There was an absurdity about it. A static image of nothing happening in an irrelevant part of the village. What good was that to her?

She mustn't give in to thoughts like that. It would drive her mad. *Think, Tabitha,* she told herself again. She tried to place herself at the scene. If she were standing there, with her back to the village shop, seeing what the camera saw, what else would she be able to see? If she turned right, she would be on the road leading up and out of the village, the road that had been blocked by the fallen tree. What time was that? She looked through the notes she had made. It must have been shortly after nine-thirty.

Next door to the village shop was the church and next to that was the little vicarage where Mel lived. After that was a row of houses and then the hotel, closed up for the winter. On the other side, the side away from the sea, were two rows of houses on the hillside under the cliff.

If you turned left instead of right, you would see the little cove and stony beach down on your left. Tabitha swam there every morning. Just beyond the cove, the road looped round on itself. If you stayed to the left, you went up the broad drive to the Reeses' house. If you veered right, a rough and uneven track led to Tabitha's house. Beyond the two houses there was just the cliff wall as it curved round the bay that Okeham sat in. There was no way up or round. The coastal path didn't go through Okeham, it veered away from it, up on the moors, and only rejoined the actual coastline three miles further along.

But the camera couldn't see to the left or to the right. It just blankly looked straight across at the bus shelter. And then suddenly two girls walked into the frame. They were young, about nine or ten, wearing thick coats and hats. Tabitha realized that this was going to be a problem. The twenty-first of December had been a cold, blustery day. Even if people were caught on this grainy footage, it might be a challenge to identify them. The girls walked across the road toward the camera and disappeared underneath as they entered the shop. Tabitha thought she recognized one of them. Beth Tally's daughter, she thought. She wrote the name down. Another group of children appeared, two boys this time and a girl standing apart. They were waiting for the school bus. The girl crossed the road and entered the shop. Tabitha had got used to seeing them in the shop in the mornings, buying packets of crisps and giggling and escaping the cold.

A car pulled up on the far side of the road and two people got out. Tabitha instantly recognized Rob Coombe. The girl getting out of the passenger side must be his daughter, though Tabitha had never seen her before. The two of them crossed the road and went into the shop. Tabitha noted the name and the time.

The two boys were hunched over against the cold, hands in pockets. One of them laughed, then the other seemed to hear something and looked round to his right. What had he seen?

A compact figure entered the frame, so wrapped up in a heavy jacket and a hat and a scarf that they were almost entirely hidden. For a moment Tabitha wondered who it was and then she felt a rush of emotion that left her feeling faint. She was looking at herself. She seized the control and froze the image.

She looked at the time code: 08:11:44. At that moment, eleven minutes past eight on December 21, Stuart Rees was home, alive, and Tabitha Hardy had walked to the village shop to buy a carton of milk. Tabitha felt a terrible impulse to shout at that woman, frozen there in the street, to tell her to forget everything, to go back home, get in her car and drive out of the village, to go anywhere, just get away. Not that it would have done any good. She had never been much good at taking advice. As she came closer to the shop, unaware she was being observed, she looked as if she were frowning, thinking hard about something. Tabitha wondered what it could have been.

At almost the same moment as Tabitha disappeared into the shop, a huge shape filled the frame. The school bus had arrived. She could see the face of a boy staring through a cracked window of the bus, his face heavily scrawled over by the fractures in the glass. The bus driver emerged and walked past the camera into the shop. Tabitha smiled slightly, despite everything. She remembered it now, even if it was in fragments. As she'd queued for the milk, the children had been chattering, excited. It was the last day of term—that was it. Rob Coombe had bought a packet of cigarettes. Tabitha remembered that it was different from the old days. The cigarettes weren't just stacked behind the counter. Terry, the woman behind the counter, had to open a kind of cabinet to get them. And then there was something else? What was it? Tabitha tried to remember but it was like trying to grasp an image that always slipped away at the last second.

She wanted to follow herself into the shop. So she ejected the disc from the player and replaced it with the 8–9 A.M. disc from the interior pile. She pressed play. The interior camera, which she had never noticed before, was apparently placed at the back of the shop, almost at ceiling height, and looked toward the door. She fast-forwarded, seeing unidentified figures jerking in and out of the shop, until she reached just before eleven minutes past eight. She could see the back of Terry's head and she could see Rob Coombe. The two girls were standing to one side. Like an actor making her entrance at the right time, Tabitha entered the shop and stood behind Rob, almost hidden by him, though it was clear that she was wearing pajama trousers under her coat. Then the bus driver came in and joined the little queue. But Tabitha's attention was on the farmer. He looked like he was in a bad mood and was gesticulating angrily. That was what Tabitha had been trying to remember: what had it been about?

Now Rob Coombe turned so that only the back of his head showed. Tabitha briefly saw her own face, wretched with exhaustion, and behind her the driver. She watched to see if she spoke, said the words that were part of the evidence against her—but then Rob stood in front of her and she and the driver disappeared from view.

Tabitha tried to put herself back there, in her shapeless clothes and pajama bottoms, heavy with wretchedness, the sleety rain falling outside. She imagined herself saying, "Stuart Rees is such a bastard" was that how it was? Or: "That Stuart, he's a right bastard." Or even, "I could tell you a thing or two about Stuart Rees; what a bastard . . ." It didn't feel right, but then nothing felt right. Or was it the farmer turning to her, his face suffused with anger, and saying, "That bastard Stuart Rees." She held all the versions in her mind for a moment and then let them go.

Rob Coombe left with a newspaper and cigarettes; Tabitha noted the time. The two girls left, presumably to get on the bus. She herself bought milk; she saw her lips moving, her hand proffering coins, her bundled-up figure leaving; she wrote down the exact time: 08:15:09. The bus driver also bought cigarettes and some kind of chocolate bar, then he too exited. The camera looked once more at nothing.

Tabitha went back to the exterior disc, picking up at the point where she had left off. She watched the bus pull up, the driver go into the shop, then Rob Coombe leave and get in his car. She watched herself come out of the shop, clutching her small carton of milk and her head down against the hard wind. She watched herself disappear behind the bus. She watched the driver come out. She waited for about thirty seconds. Then she watched the bus leave, sliding out of view, leaving the bus stop deserted. And now the camera gazed serenely at nothing again and the branches quivered in the wind that was blowing from the sea.

She watched as a few flakes of snow fell before turning once more to sleety rain.

She watched as nothing happened, just the little counter at the top of the screen ticking past the seconds and the minutes. She inserted the fourth disk, 9–10 A.M. She thought of fast-forwarding until there was something to look at, but it was oddly hypnotic to be staring at the screen as if she were back there, back in the day that had undone her life. So she just gazed at the tarmac and the bus stop and the cliff and the leafless birch. A bird in its branches and then gone. A large cat strolling past.

At 09:29:43 a small car drove by, coming from Stuart and Tabitha's end of Okeham. That would be Laura Rees. She jotted down the time.

At 09:39:27 a white van pulled up near to the bus stop and a man got out, thickset and with a hat pulled low over his forehead, a scarf wrapped around the lower part of his face. He went into the shop and came out carrying a paper and a bag of crisps. For a moment, Tabitha couldn't think who he was, then she remembered: the deliveryman who had been the last person to see Stuart alive. Or at least, she corrected herself, the last person who had seen Stuart alive apart from the killer.

He got back in his van and drove off in the direction of Stuart's house.

Tabitha waited as the little timer counted off the minutes. At 09:55:17 he was back, parking his white van in the same place and walking to the right of the camera. For a moment she was confused, then she remembered the little café to the side of the shop that people told her was crammed with people in the summer, and served scones and ice cream and coffee and walnut cake, but stood largely empty most of the winter. Perhaps he had been going in there. Something snagged in her brain and she tried to hold on to it, but it was gone.

Now she was on disc five, 10–11 A.M. Not long into it, the familiar figure of Dr. Mallon sped past the camera, bony bare legs and head up in spite of the weather.

At 10:10:19 two young women pushed two strollers into view. Tabitha recognized them: they were twin sisters who lived in the village and were married to men who looked rather similar to each other, and who both had small children. She made a note that they too had been in the village after the tree had fallen, and looked back at the screen in time to see both toddlers raising their heads and pointing at something in the sky. One of the mothers disappeared into the shop while the other guarded the strollers. She was rubbing her hands together to keep them warm. Then the little group left.

Tabitha was starting to feel a bit dazed with staring at the grainy images, but then Andy was on her screen. He was wearing his work clothes and carrying a large canvas bag. He walked toward the shop; the time clicked past; a couple of minutes later he was there again, turning to the right.

Dr. Mallon dashed past in the other direction. Tabitha noted the time: barely enough to reach Stuart's and Tabitha's houses and the solid cliff beyond, however fast he had run. She remembered that he had mentioned seeing her, when she had been agitated and incoherent. It must have been in between these two times. Again, she put herself back there, in the windy coldness, salt on her skin. She would have been swimming at the cove, her hair would have been wet and her fingers numbed. What had she said to him? What had he said to her? She thought she remembered seeing him, but it was like a memory groped at in thick fog, retreating as she reached out for it.

At just past 10:20 A.M., the vicar and her dog, a golden retriever called Sukie, were on the screen. Mel sat Sukie on the pavement, wagged her finger at her to stay still, and went into the shop. She came out holding her paper, and met Shona, well wrapped up in a quilted jacket and mittens and wearing wellington boots. Tabitha watched as the two women walked out of camera in the direction of Tabitha's house, Sukie between them, talking. Almost immediately, Shona came back and went into the shop. A minute or so later the vicar and her dog walked by. That's what people did in villages, Tabitha thought: they took their dog for a walk, or themselves.

Tabitha wrote all the times down. She knew what must come next and sure enough, at 10:34:33 a gray car drove past the camera. Stuart.

And at 10:40:22 it returned. She needed to concentrate because it was between now and half past three in the afternoon that he was murdered. She stood up and jumped up and down a few times, then sat once more.

The deliveryman came out and sat in his van. Nothing happened. No car drove past—but then it wouldn't because the tree was down and so the only place they would be driving to was Tabitha's house or Stuart's. No other person walked past.

The 11–12 A.M. disc showed nothing, except Mel walking past with her dog, and the deliveryman getting out of his van, wandering off in the direction of Tabitha's house and returning a couple of minutes later.

Tabitha went to the door and opened it. Mary Guy was sitting on a chair outside, legs stretched out, chewing gum and staring straight ahead.

"I need the toilet," said Tabitha. "And some water."

Mary Guy pointed. Tabitha used the toilet and drank some water from the tap. What she really wanted was a large mug of coffee but she didn't think the warden was going to stir herself. She must have been watching footage for nearly four hours. What had she learned that she didn't already know?

She went back to her position and sat hunched forward, staring at blankness with her fingers pressed to her temples and willing herself to stay alert.

At 1:05 P.M., the deliveryman got out of his car. He no longer wore his hat and his scarf and Tabitha caught a glimpse of his face. He didn't look impatient, just resigned. He went into the shop, or the café, and stayed there.

At 13:19:38 Shona went into the shop. The interior disc showed her buying a packet of crisps and a can of Coke. She was wearing different clothes: a woolen coat and ankle boots. What had she done that day, when she was stuck in Okeham?

At 13:33:01 Rob Coombe went into the shop. The interior disc showed him buying sandwiches.

Tabitha frowned. He had dropped his daughter off at the school bus at ten past eight and driven off, but the tree hadn't come down till after half past nine. Why had he stayed in Okeham? Everyone else—the vicar, Shona, Andy, Dr. Mallon, the twin sisters, Luke, Terry herself—lived there, but Rob's farm was above the village. Where had he been all that time? She scribbled a note to herself and returned to the CCTV.

The door opened quietly and the librarian tiptoed in, carrying a mug of coffee and a plate with two short-bread biscuits on it. She put it down in front of Tabitha.

"Thank you!"

"You're welcome," Galia said in an exaggerated whisper, and tiptoed out once more.

Tabitha took a gulp of coffee, then another. She had a large bite of the biscuit. The light was fading; the white bark of the birch glowed in the dusk. Snow began to fall once more, melting on the road, quickly turning back into rain. And then a thin figure with a rucksack on his back sloped past. She rewound; he shot backward; she pressed play and there he came again. Luke Rees entering the village at 1:57:49. It matched what he had told her.

She watched as the vicar, in a waterproof jacket, came into the camera's view, and went out again. A few minutes later she reappeared. Mel's day seemed to be made up of walking up and down the village, with Sukie or without. Then she realized that this was when Mel said she had come across Tabitha in great distress. She paused the machine and sat staring at the frozen image of the vicar. Mel said she had talked about the news: specifically, the reported sighting of a drone at Gatwick Airport that had stopped all flights arriving or departing from the airport. That rang a bell. Yet something was wrong with it as well, though she couldn't think what it was.

She finished her coffee and her biscuits with the static image in front of her. A few minutes later she pressed play again. Nothing, nothing, nothing. Then, at 15:34:44, Laura's car went past the camera on her way home, meaning the fallen tree was cleared. Sure enough, the deliveryman got into his van and drove away.

At that point, the afternoon became like a mirror image of the morning. For now the school bus drew up and when it drove off there were the children on the pavement, jostling each other, kicking water up from the puddles, in high spirits for they were on holiday for Christmas. A different boy stared out of the central window.

There came Rob Coombe collecting his daughter.

And now, now it was 16:24:12 and Andy walked past the camera in the rain, still in his work clothes and carrying his canvas bag. On his way to Tabitha's. She felt sick and she bent over for a few moments, squeezing her eyes shut.

She should turn the DVD player off now, she thought. Nothing that came next was relevant. Stuart was dead; soon Andy would be knocking at her door; soon he would step out into the backyard and, reaching down, find the body. But she kept on watching.

The police car came first, lights flashing in the gathering darkness. Then the ambulance. Then another police car.

Only minutes later the vicar could be seen striking purposefully toward the shop. Then Shona, almost running. The twin sisters with their strollers. Their husbands, home from work and keen to be in on the action. That man in his wheelchair whose name she couldn't remember. Pauline Leavitt, amazingly quick on her feet for a woman who usually leaned on a cane. Everyone arriving because something was going on and they were gathering like flies around a carcass.

In spite of herself, Tabitha inserted the interior disc and fast-forwarded to see them all inside. The little shop was crammed with excited people. It was like a party in there: a murder party.

She ejected the disc and sat back. Her head was pounding and her mouth was dry. She didn't want to look at the police car coming back with her sitting inside it. She waited for a long time, and then she got up and knocked at the door. Mary Guy opened it. She was still chewing gum.

"I'm done here."

Thirty-five

Tabitha hadn't had lunch but she didn't want supper. The sight and smell of Dana's minced beef and mashed potatoes turned her stomach. She thought of biting into a crisp, sour apple, or eating toast with a scraping of Marmite on it; drinking a large mug of tea—from her blue mug, she thought, which she had bought in Spain ten years ago. She wanted, she needed, to be somewhere far from the press of people. She imagined herself by the sea, miles from anywhere and not even a boat on the horizon, just the wash of waves over pebbles, the urgent call of the gulls, the bitter wind scouring her face.

"What are you writing?" asked Dana.

Tabitha looked up. "A new timeline," she answered.

"Timeline of what?"

"Of the day the murder took place."

"Can I see?"

Tabitha made room for her on the bed and they both looked at what she had done. Dana's lips moved as she read.

6:30 (approx): Wake up. Lie there for some time (how long?). Not feeling good.

7:30 (approx): Get up. Start making porridge and tea. No milk.

08:11:44: Go into village shop to buy milk in PJ bottoms and wellies. Rob Coombe and daughter. Also, two girls, bus driver and Terry—witnesses?

08:15:09: Leave shop in direction of home.

09:29:43: Laura's car drives out of village.

09:39:27: Deliveryman goes into village shop, then leaves again. Drives off in direction of Stuart's house.

09:55:17: Deliveryman returns (last person to see Stuart?).

??? A.M.: Go for swim. Meet Dr. Mallon.

10:09:14: Owen Mallon runs past, in direction of Stuart's house.

10:10:19: Twins and their toddlers arrive at village shop.

10:19:35: Owen Mallon runs back in other direction.

10:22:51: Mel goes into shop then out again.

10:23:46: Shona talks to vicar outside shop; walk toward Stuart's house together.

10:25:20: Shona back and goes into shop.

10:30:32: Mel walks past.

10:34:33: Stuart drives out of village in his car.

10:40:22: Stuart drives back again in direction of house (blocked by fallen tree).

13:19:38: Shona to village shop.

13:33:01: Rob Coombe to village shop.

13:57:49: Luke arrives in village. Climbs over tree (workmen there). Walks to his house.

14:31:13: Vicar walks past. (Says she met me at this time and we talked about news.)

15:34:44: Laura returns. (Says Luke at home and no sign of Stuart.)

16:24:12: Andy on his way to my house.

16:30: Andy arrives at mine. Discovers body.

"I don't get it," said Dana after she had studied it. "Why do you need to put in the seconds as well as the minutes?"

"I don't," said Tabitha. "It just makes me feel a bit better. Everything's such a mess; this makes it seem less messy. As far as I can see," she continued, staring gloomily at what she had written, "I've learned nothing that can help me. It's exactly like the police said. Except—" She stopped.

"Except?"

"I don't know. I have this ridiculous feeling that if

I think hard enough I'll find something I'm missing."
She shook her head. "I'm just kidding myself."

And anyway, she thought, as she used the toilet, brushed her teeth, pulled on her night things and climbed into her narrow bed, maybe the police were right but her memory was withholding from her. Perhaps she knew but didn't want to know, couldn't bring herself to remember, and all the time, as she had watched people come and go on the CCTV footage, the Tabitha she used to be was crouched out of sight in her tumbledown house, waiting with a knife in her hand for Stuart to come to her door.

Tabitha slept and had a chaotic dream. Then she woke with a small, clear thought. Owen Mallon hadn't been able to pinpoint what time he had met Tabitha that morning after her swim, but he had said that their conversation was drowned out by the noise of helicopters. In her mind, she spooled through the CCTV: those two children in their strollers had both pointed up into the sky. It must have been then. Most probably it meant nothing, but she should remember to write that on the timeline tomorrow.

She couldn't go back to sleep. There had been something else. She rummaged around in the corners of her memory and couldn't find it. Above her Dana whimpered and turned over. Tabitha could hear the rain falling outside. April showers. It came to her that she had to write her defense statement by May. What even was a defense statement? And what was her defense? "I can't remember doing it. I can't remember anything. It must have been someone else, someone who was stuck in the village as well . . ." She went over the names: Rob Coombe, Luke, Dr. Mallon, Mel the vicar, Shona, Andy . . . She needed to talk to Laura again, to Shona. She needed to see Owen Mallon. She lay with her eyes open, staring into the darkness, and the little timer in her head ticked on.

Thirty-six

Tabitha was in a hurry when she almost bumped into Ingrid on the landing. She tried to move past, but Ingrid started talking about a girl who had slashed her wrists.

"She was taken to hospital," she said. "That's when you know it's bad. When they take them to hospital they have to fill out a proper report, it goes on the record. If they can fix them up here, they can fudge it."

"You're a cynic," said Tabitha.

"Just realistic."

Tabitha started to move away. "I've got to go. I've got a visitor."

"I've been meaning to talk to you," said Ingrid, almost physically preventing Tabitha from moving past her. Tabitha shifted uneasily. Laura was her visitor.

Tabitha had been almost startled when she agreed to come back. The idea of being late and that Laura might leave was nearly unbearable.

"We can talk later," said Tabitha.

"I might not be here later. I'm having my hearing."

"That's good, isn't it? You might be getting parole."

"I hope so."

"But they won't let you out right away, will they?"

"No, but they'll move me to an open prison." Ingrid gave a faint smile. "To prepare me for life back in the real world."

"That's fantastic," said Tabitha, trying to edge away. "Really, good luck. You deserve it."

"I just wanted to say that I'm sorry I wasn't more help."

"You were more help than most people."

"And you're really doing this?"

"What?"

"Defending yourself."

"It's starting to look like it."

"You're sure it's a good idea?"

"I'm not at all sure. I wasn't able to convince my lawyer and now I think I can convince a jury. Sounds crazy." She put a hand on Ingrid's arm. "I've really got to go but, as I said, good luck." Then she thought of something. "I haven't got many friends out in the world. If you give me your number, maybe I can give you a call."

"Anything," said Ingrid, putting her hand on Tabitha's. It was a gesture that felt like pity and Tabitha didn't like it at all.

"Sorry, sorry, sorry," said Tabitha in a rush, sitting opposite Laura. She expected Laura either to say that it didn't matter or to issue some kind of rebuke but she didn't reply at all. She looked paler than when Tabitha had last seen her.

"I told people I was coming to see you," she said. "I didn't want to keep it a secret."

"Of course. I'm glad you've come."

"I told Luke and he didn't seem to approve but then he doesn't approve of anything I do, and I told Dr. Mallon at the funeral." She paused. "I suppose I should say that we finally had the funeral."

"The funeral," said Tabitha. "Oh. I didn't know. How was it?"

"It was good, in a way. That sounds terrible, doesn't it?" As Laura spoke, she was looking past Tabitha, as if her attention was on someone standing behind her. "There's so much to prepare and it's all a bit complicated and it becomes easier to talk to people because you're talking about arrangements, not about Stuart dying. The day itself was quite relaxing. It was nice listening to the hymns."

"Did the police come?"

"Just DCI Dudley."

"The one in a suit with the grim face."

"He does wear nice suits, yes. I wouldn't like to comment on his face. He's been kind to me."

What had Luke said about him? Yes, that he'd thought the case was a slam dunk.

"Were there lots of tributes?" she asked.

"The vicar said a few words."

"What did she say?"

"Oh you know, the usual sort of thing. She said he was the heart and soul of the village. She said he kept people on their toes. Including her."

"What does *that* mean?"

"As you know, Stuart preferred his services a little more traditional."

"You told me about his letter to the bishop."

"There you are then."

"What else did Mel say?"

"Just the usual things that people trot out. She said he liked to get things done and that he didn't suffer fools gladly."

"I've heard that before and I'm never quite sure what it means. It sounds like being angry with people who don't deserve it."

"I don't think he was exactly angry."

"So what was he?"

"I think he saw people's weaknesses. He had a sort of sixth sense about them."

"Did he see *your* weaknesses?"

"Mine aren't so hard to see," said Laura. "You don't need a sixth sense for them."

"Did he suffer *you* gladly?"

When Laura answered, it sounded like she was talking to herself. "Marriage is a funny thing. It's strange what you do to the person you're supposed to love."

Tabitha wasn't sure what to say. She wasn't used to people confiding in her like this. Let alone this person.

"I suppose everyone in the village was there."

"Not everyone."

Tabitha wanted to know who had been there and, especially, who hadn't been there, but she couldn't think of a decent way of phrasing it.

"So Dr. Mallon was there."

"Yes."

"That's nice," said Tabitha. "Having your doctor."

"He's not actually our doctor. Not anymore."

"You mean he was?"

"It's not important."

"Another letter of complaint?" said Tabitha.

"It actually makes him easier to talk to, him not being our doctor any longer. I just talk to him like a friend."

"Like telling him you're coming to see me?"

"Yes."

"And what did he say?"

"I think he was surprised. He asked me why I wanted to."

"Did he try to persuade you not to?"

"No. He was just concerned that I was doing it for the right reasons."

"What would the wrong reasons be?"

Laura thought for a moment. "If I had the idea that meeting you would be some kind of comfort."

"Is it?"

When Laura replied, it was pensively, as if she was asking herself the question, not Tabitha. "Why would looking into the face of the woman who's been charged with my husband's murder be a comfort?"

"Wouldn't it be a comfort to know who killed your husband and why? If I had killed Stuart and if I confessed to you, then you could start to make sense of everything. But I didn't."

"I'm supposed to believe you?"

"The problem is that this prison is full of people claiming that they're innocent and that they're hard done by. The further problem is that just a few of them are telling the truth."

"Did your lawyer believe you?"

"I don't think lawyers are meant to say that. My lawyer told me that she thought the case against me was very strong. She thought I should plead guilty and talk about the extenuating circumstances."

"Being abused?"

"That's what she had in mind."

Laura nodded. "Because you *were* abused."

"I'm sorry," said Tabitha after a shocked pause. "Are you saying that as a question?"

"No."

"Last time we met," said Tabitha, picking her words carefully. "You seemed certain that I was responsible for what had happened at school. You said I had pursued him and he had succumbed in a moment of weakness."

"I know what I said."

"So why have you changed your mind?"

"I'm not stupid, you know."

"Of course not."

"Describe yourself at fifteen."

The two women were staring at each other now; it was as if the space between them had opened up so that for this moment only Tabitha felt that she could say anything, ask anything, and Laura would listen and would answer.

"I was small," she said and as she spoke she could see herself then, with her short dark hair and braces on her teeth, her head buried in books because that was where she was safe and the world was welcoming. "Thin. Flat-chested. Plain. Unpopular. Unhappy. Awkward. Quite clever. Angry."

Laura nodded as if everything she had said made perfect sense. "Why didn't you say no?"

"How do you know I didn't?"

"Did you?"

"No."

"Why?"

"I can't explain it to myself. I was fifteen, he was my teacher. I didn't know."

"What didn't you know?"

"I didn't know anything."

"It was more than once, wasn't it?"

"Yes."

"How many times?"

"Eleven, maybe twelve."

"And you never told anyone."

"No." Tabitha looked away at last, wrinkling her brow. "Who would I have told?"

They sat in silence for a few moments. Then Tabitha said: "Can I ask you a question?"

"What question?"

"How was Luke's relationship with Stuart?"

"You know. He came to see you."

"I'd like your view of it."

"Stuart could be a difficult father. But then Luke could be a difficult son."

"How did that show itself?"

"In disagreeing about things. Luke felt that he hadn't measured up to his father's expectations."

"Why did he feel that?"

"Because he hadn't."

"So he was angry with his father?"

"We lived in a house of anger," said Laura.

"Why did he come back then?"

"It was Christmas. Family time," she added, apparently without irony.

"Yeah, but he hadn't come back for other Christmases, had he?"

"Who said that?"

"People in the village. Before all this happened."

"It's got nothing to do with anything."

"It just seems a bit of a coincidence that Stuart's estranged son returns on the same day that Stuart gets killed."

Laura's face became tight with anger. "You're talking about my son."

"I'm just asking."

"Is that your plan? Are you going to throw mud at people? Create confusion?"

"That's what lawyers do. I just want to find the truth."

"All right, then. I'll answer the question you can't quite bring yourself to ask. Luke would not be capable of killing his father and hiding the body and then lying about it. He couldn't do it."

"That's a strange way of putting it."

"How do you mean?"

"You're not saying he didn't do it. You're saying he's not capable of it, even if he wanted to."

"It amounts to the same thing." She leaned forward. "The only thing in the world I am certain of is that Luke didn't kill his father."

"Because you're his mother?"

"I *know*."

They both sat back in their chairs and Tabitha could feel the tension in Laura gradually lessen. She tried to think of anything else she should ask. "Are you coming to the trial?"

"I'm giving evidence," said Laura.

"What about?"

"I'm not sure I'm allowed to tell you."

"I don't think it's a problem. As far as I know, the prosecution have to tell me their case. If I start threatening you or trying to persuade you not to say what you know, then it starts being a problem."

"Are you going to threaten me?"

"You don't need to tell me if you don't want."

"I told them about how he reacted when you came back to Okeham," Laura said in an even tone.

"How did he react?"

"He was very shaken. He said he'd seen a ghost. Then he insisted we put the house on the market."

"Didn't that seem a bit drastic?"

"He was scared. I'd never seen him scared like that before."

Tabitha sat in silence for a few seconds. She couldn't imagine Stuart being scared of her. Disregard or casual contempt seemed more likely.

"What did you think about it all?"

"I forgave him long ago," Laura said, in a voice entirely lacking in emotion.

She stood up, preparing to leave, and Tabitha stood as well. She had remembered something, something she needed to ask.

"I saw the CCTV footage of the village, from the day of the murder. At half past ten, Stuart drove out of the village. As you know, there was a tree across the road and he had to come back. Do you know where he was going?"

"No."

"I looked at the prosecution evidence. There was nothing in his diary for that time. Did he have some regular place he went on that day?"

"No."

"Does it seem strange to you?"

"My only thought is that if the tree hadn't fallen over, he might still be alive."

"That's true. What a strange thought."

"And soon there's the trial."

"Yes, there's that."

As they were starting to say goodbye, Tabitha thought of one last thing and wondered whether she ought to say it aloud and then said it anyway.

"You never said why you came to see me."

"I'm not sure I know."

"I think I know. I think that you believe me when I say I didn't kill your husband."

"I'm not sure what I believe," Laura said and turned away, making her way slowly through the tables of the visiting room.

As Tabitha watched her go, she thought of what she really hadn't dared say aloud. Laura may have believed that Tabitha was innocent, yes; or she may have believed that she was guilty and didn't care.

Or maybe she knew something about her husband's murder. Or maybe she feared something.

Thirty-seven

Tabitha read through her timeline again and again until she knew it by heart. It was almost restful. She could lie on her bunk, close her eyes and play the film in her head, moving outside into the cold blustery Devon day and going inside into the shop. As she played it over and over, it developed its own rhythm, like a piece of music, the school bus coming in the morning and returning in the afternoon, the delivery van coming at 9:40 A.M. and then leaving at 3:34 P.M. Mel and Luke and Dr. Mallon and Shona and the rest of them moving this way and that.

Tabitha created different scenarios in her head. Laura had been conveniently absent during the day, called away by a mysterious client who hadn't turned up. Had the police traced him yet? She needed to check. But then Laura couldn't have known about the fallen tree. That couldn't have been part of any plan.

Always she came back to the video. The video. It was almost nothing and yet it was everything. There was a simple fact and she repeated it to herself. Nobody could reach Stuart's house—or indeed her house—without being seen by the CCTV camera. Unless they flew in, or arrived by balloon or boat. There were of course two exceptions to that. Luke, who had been there at the very end of the time when it was possible. And herself, who had been there pretty much throughout. Which was more bad news.

She considered her meeting with Laura. If Laura hadn't definitely been out of the village, Tabitha would have started to suspect her. Then she thought of someone else, someone else she needed to see. It was a slow process. Finding someone's number, phoning them and arranging a date took days. But perhaps in this particular case there was a quicker way.

Unfortunately, Mary Guy was the warden on duty. Tabitha walked up to her.

"I've got a pain in my ear," she said. "It might be an infection."

Mary Guy seemed indifferent. "You know where to go."

"I'm a remand prisoner. I've a right to see my own doctor."

The warden looked puzzled and then she looked angry. "What are you talking about? It's only your ear. Just go and see the nurse."

"You can check if you want. I've got the right to be seen by my doctor. But if you want to tell me that you aren't going to do it and want me to make an official complaint, then just tell me."

Guy looked to the left and to the right, checking that nobody could hear her. Then she leaned forward and spoke in little more than a whisper.

"You'd better get off in this trial of yours. Because if you're convicted, you've got a lot of people's backs up in a very short period of time. If you're convicted . . ." She paused. "Oh fuck, let's stop pissing about. *When* you're convicted, you're going to find out what people can do to get their own back over five years, ten years, fifteen years."

Tabitha reached into the pocket of her jeans and produced a torn-off piece of paper.

"That's his name," she said. "Tell him it's an ear infection. Tell him it could be meningitis."

Guy snatched the piece of paper. "Fuck you," she said.

Thirty-eight

"I can't see anything," said Dr. Mallon. "No signs of infection. No discoloration."

They weren't in the visitors' room. Tabitha had been led to an examination room in the medical wing. There was none of the usual paraphernalia of a hospital. No posters on the wall. No objects that could be picked up and used as a weapon. There were two battered chairs and an examination couch. Mallon himself was dressed in a faded gray jacket and a navy-blue shirt and dark trousers.

"Sod's law, isn't it?" said Tabitha. "The moment you actually see the doctor, you're suddenly better."

"Well, I can confirm that you don't have meningitis," said Mallon. "That was your self-diagnosis, wasn't it? Meningitis because your ear ached? That's what they said on the phone."

"I mentioned it as something I was worried about."

"She didn't speak very warmly of you."

"We didn't get off to a good start," said Tabitha. "And then it continued not being good."

"She said she thought you were malingering. Malingering." He said it again with a smile. "I haven't heard that word since I was at school. I suppose the mention of meningitis could be a ploy. It more or less forces a doctor to actually examine you, just to make sure."

"The problem with being in here," said Tabitha, "is that you feel ill almost all the time, one way or another."

"When she rang, I could have said something else."

"What?"

"That I'm not actually your doctor."

"You're my doctor in a way. You're the doctor who lives in the village where I live."

"You'd been there for a few weeks. You're not registered with me. But it doesn't matter. I'm here now. What do you want? Apart from examining your uninfected ear?"

Tabitha began a conversation she was getting used to, in which she told Mallon that she was conducting her own defense and it became gradually clear that he knew almost all of it already. What else did they have to talk about in Okeham? Then she told him about the CCTV footage.

"I saw you on it," she said.

He looked faintly surprised. "What, me?"

"Yes, you. You think you got away from it all when you moved to Okeham, but we've got our own little piece of the surveillance society in front of the village shop."

"I didn't even know that we had CCTV in Okeham. So did it show me doing anything interesting?"

"You were running."

"That's not interesting; I run almost every day."

"And I swim. Just a dip. It's good for me. It improves my mood. I go swimming, you go running: we probably do it for the same reasons."

"I do it as a way of thinking."

"Then we don't do it for the same reasons. I mainly do it to avoid thinking. On that day, I went for a swim at about a quarter to ten and on my way back, I met you."

"Yes, I gave a statement about that."

"I've read it. As far as I remember, you said I seemed distressed."

"It was just an impression."

"I was probably just shivering. But I'm not going to argue with you. People tell me I must be careful not to interfere with the course of justice."

"It would be a pity if you got into trouble," Mallon said in a dry tone.

"Is that a joke?"

"Sorry. I didn't mean to be unfeeling." Mallon had been standing up. Now he half sat on the end of the couch.

"So, Tabitha, you didn't have an earache and you've already read my very uninformative statement to the police. What was worth my taking an afternoon off from my practice?"

"Why did you take an afternoon off in order to see someone who isn't even your patient?" asked Tabitha. "Is it interesting to take a look at the person who's the talk of the village?"

"If you're trying to get me on your side, then this is a pretty odd way to go about it."

"Are you giving evidence for the prosecution?"

"Yes."

"Why?"

"Honestly, I don't know. I was just told that I should make myself available."

"I suppose it puts me in the village, walking in the right direction."

"I don't know."

"What did you think of Stuart Rees?"

Up to now Mallon had looked almost amused. Now

he was visibly startled. "What do you mean? What's that got to do with anything?"

"I'm just asking."

"I don't even know why you would ask me something like that."

"It's like this," Tabitha said. "When I first started thinking about my situation, there were several things which made it terrible. One of which was that people thought I had a motive for killing him. I was the"—Tabitha held up her fingers and made air quotes—"abused little girl. I had had my"—more air quotes—"innocence taken from me. And meanwhile, the person I was supposed to have a grudge against was the most popular person in the village. Then I started talking to people and it seems like I'm the only person who didn't dislike him. Or at least, almost everyone turns out to have a reason for disliking him. But you know all about that. You've talked to Laura. Or rather, Laura's talked to *you*. She said you were helpful."

"I can't say anything about that," said Mallon.

"Was it about being ill or was it about something in her personal life? People talk to doctors about all kinds of things, don't they?"

"It doesn't matter how you rephrase the question, I can't answer it."

Tabitha couldn't decide whether he was just being

professionally correct or whether she had touched on an uncomfortable area.

"You were his doctor," she said, "and then you weren't his doctor."

"People change doctors all the time."

"Yes, when I lived in London, changing doctors was no big deal. But in a place like Okeham, changing your doctor is like moving house. Except that your old house doesn't get offended when you move away from it."

"It's nothing like that. I'm not offended."

"I just talked to Laura. She's come to see me. She's not someone who seems desperate to be liked, but I quite like her." Tabitha waited for Mallon to make some kind of comment, but he didn't, so she continued. "The way she talked about Stuart surprised me. People usually idealize the dead, especially when they've just died. But Laura wasn't like that. The Stuart she talked about was someone difficult, a bit of a troublemaker, a stirrer."

"She's upset."

"And I'm guessing that he didn't just move doctors. I'm guessing that he made some kind of complaint about you."

"I can't comment on that."

"You're suddenly sounding like you're already in court."

Mallon stood up and gave a little laugh.

"All I can say is that if someone makes a complaint about you in writing, then murdering them isn't going to be a very clever way of dealing with it."

"So he made a complaint about you in writing?"

"It happens all the time. It's part of the job."

Tabitha now stood up as well.

"When they brought you in," she said, "and they took you through door after door, locking and unlocking them with those big bunches of keys rattling, did it make you feel a bit trapped? Even though you know you can go home?"

"Yes, it did."

"You probably didn't enjoy this much . . ." He made an effort to say something but she shushed him. "A talk like this, whatever else it does, it makes me feel a tiny bit less shut in, just for a few minutes. Maybe you just have a smell of the outside world. Perhaps you could come again, in a doctorish sort of way."

"Perhaps," he said.

Tabitha didn't think it was very likely.

Thirty-nine

Tabitha found it disconcerting to see Terry George sitting across from her in the visitors' room.

"You know, I don't think I've ever seen you outside the shop," she said.

"It's your whole life," said Terry cheerfully. "If you don't enjoy it, then don't do it. Because I live above the shop, I open up at seven and I'm not done till half past six. You've got to like it. And you've got to like people."

Tabitha went through the ritual of thanking her for coming, but she was clearly enjoying herself. She had dressed up in a purple velvet jacket over a tight green blouse, and her eyes were bright with curiosity.

"I've been watching you on the CCTV," said Tabitha.

"I know, I was there when they took it all away. Quite a business."

"So I know that *you* didn't do it," said Tabitha. "The camera shows you were there the whole day."

"I'm lucky if I get two minutes for a toilet break," Terry said, laughing loudly. It felt like a laugh that had been developed for getting through the hours in the Okeham village day, from the groups of boisterous children on their way to school and back from school, the older people in the village who needed someone to talk to as they bought their single baking potato. You couldn't afford to lose a customer. There were only about a hundred of them.

"I'd have brought something," Terry continued, "but someone told me that they don't let you bring anything in."

"That's all right. I just wanted to talk to you. I've always thought that you're the person who knows what's going on in the village."

"I don't know about that. I try to have a word with everyone when they pop into the shop."

"I wanted to ask you about that. When I looked at the footage of the shop on the morning of the murder, I saw that Rob Coombe was talking to you. He looked angry about something. He was gesticulating a lot."

"Sounds like Rob."

"Do you remember what he was saying?"

"No."

Tabitha smiled, although she didn't feel like smiling.

"That's a bit certain. I thought you might take a moment to try and remember."

"I can't tell one day from another. That's what I told the police. The same people come in and out all the time. I remember the odd ones, the strangers. But not my regulars. So I can't tell one day from another; I can't tell one *year* from another."

She laughed again. Tabitha knew that Terry's husband had left her last year. People said it was the strain of running the shop. Tabitha thought it could have been the strain of listening to that laugh day after day.

"All right, you can't remember. But is it possible that he was angry with Stuart Rees?"

For the first time Terry seemed to be considering how to reply.

"The point of living in a place like Okeham is that it's like family. You've to rub along with people because you're all living together, you're seeing each other every day."

"I know that Stuart had complained about Melanie Coglan. And I think he had some problem with Dr. Mallon."

"I'm not going to say anything against Stuart Rees," said Terry firmly. "I never do. And I never speak ill of the dead. I'll just say that nobody went to his funeral who didn't have to go."

"Did *you* go?"

"I have to go. It's part of my job."

Tabitha didn't quite see how it was part of Terry's job as proprietor of the village shop to go to funerals, but she let it go.

"But with Rob Coombe," said Tabitha. "There was nothing specific."

"No." There was a pause. "Except for the land."

"The land."

"You know the bit of his farm up on the cliff, over-looking the bay?"

"I know that his farm is up there."

"He was applying for permission to build some holiday homes. It was going to be his pension. Then it was all halted. There was an objection."

"By Stuart?"

Terry's expression changed to one of disapproval.

"That's what people said. I wouldn't repeat it myself. I don't know anything about it. He was just someone who had his finger in every pie, wanted to be involved in everything." She looked at Tabitha with a sudden expression of alarm. "I didn't mean . . . I mean."

"It's all right," said Tabitha. "I suppose everyone knows now about my . . ." She hesitated for a single beat. "My involvement with Stuart. Years ago."

"I don't know. I don't pay attention to things like that."

"It doesn't matter. But you must pay attention to some things. Did you see anyone out of the ordinary on that day? I saw the school bus driver was in there at the same time as me."

"Sam," said Terry. "He comes in and buys his cigarettes every morning. I always think those bus drivers are a bit dodgy. I think the police should have a word with him."

"Except that he was driving the bus," said Tabitha.

"That's true," Terry said, looking a little disappointed.

"Maybe he heard something."

"I couldn't say."

"Can you tell him I'd like him to visit me? I'll put him on the list and he can come anytime. But as soon as possible."

"I'll tell him."

"There was the deliveryman as well. He delivered the package to Stuart and then got stuck in the village."

"That's true. Polish fellow. Poor love. He sat in the café for hours. He was drinking tea and then he had lunch. The police gave him a right going over. Poles, you know. It's completely unfair, of course."

"Of course," said Tabitha. Then she had a thought. "Rob Coombe was there that day. Was he in the café?"

"No, he wasn't. I'd have remembered, you know, with the Pole being there."

"So where was he?"

"Must have been in someone's house. It wasn't the day to be hanging around outside." She looked at Tabitha suspiciously. "What are you saying?"

"I'm just trying to work out where everyone was on that day."

"You should just ask him."

"I did. He won't come."

"He's moody like that."

"Can you do me a favor?"

"Of course."

"I've tried ringing Shona. She's one of my friends in the village. Can you ask her to get in touch?"

"She's on holiday."

"Holiday?"

"Gone to the Canaries, lucky thing. For a week. She should be back any day. I'll tell her when I see her."

"Oh. All right."

Tabitha always saved the difficult questions till last. "Terry, could you do me one more favor?"

"Of course."

"You know more about the village than anyone. What do they think of me?"

For the first time, Terry looked awkward, ill at ease, evasive. "I don't quite know what to say."

"You don't need to be polite." Tabitha laughed. "Look at me. I'm in prison. Things can't get worse. I just want to know the truth."

"Well, I mean . . ." Terry hesitated, her eyes flickering round the room. "You keep yourself to yourself."

"Yes."

"You don't quite fit in. You're not a joiner-in. You know how people are. They get suspicious. They don't see you as . . ." She seemed to be struggling to find the words. "Your normal kind of . . . you know."

"Yes, I know."

"Like that time you refused to buy a poppy on Remembrance Day?"

"I did?"

"You'd only just arrived then. I'm sure you didn't mean it. Or when Pauline Leavitt took you for a young man when she first met you and then apologized, but you asked her what was wrong with looking like a man."

"And?"

"What?"

"What is?"

"Oh. I mean, if it was just up to me—"

"It's all right. And do they think I did it?"

"Well, you know, people have their own thoughts."

"And what are those thoughts?"

"I don't know, that the police wouldn't do all this for nothing. That's not my thoughts, of course."

"Thank you, Terry. This has been interesting."

"Interesting?" said Terry. She looked momentarily confused, as if she had just watched a film and been told that she'd missed the good bit.

Forty

Tabitha had always loved the spring. In prison, she had missed the snowdrops, the winter aconites, the daffodils and crocuses. Soon she would have missed the last of the tulips and the bluebells that grew in the woods above Okeham. She would have missed the birds building their nests, the swallows returning. But even in prison, spring showed itself: the sky through her small cell window was often blue and the days were longer. From the library she could see trees in blossom and new leaf. And she no longer needed to wear layers of tee shirts, sweaters and socks at night.

Spring didn't necessarily mean hope in Crow Grange. A fifty-year-old woman who had killed her abusive husband hanged herself; a twenty-two-year-old woman who had smuggled drugs cut herself so badly that everyone thought she would die; Vera started attacking wardens and sometimes she would stand in the hall and tear her precious sheets of paper into tiny fragments, tears streaming down her old face.

"That's bad," said Michaela when Tabitha told her this. Her smooth face darkened.

"You look well, though."

"I'm OK. I did what you asked."

"You've been to see Rob Coombe?"

"Yes."

"And you said you were a journalist?"

"Yes. I don't really know what journalists are like, but I know they don't look like me and they don't sound like me."

"So he didn't believe you?"

"You never told me how cool it was there."

Tabitha had never really told Michaela anything. They'd lived side by side for those weeks in silence.

"Well," she said now, "I guess I'm used to it."

"I sat in the car for a long time, just looking." Michaela's eyes were dark, her expression unreadable. "But then I found your farmer, on the top of the cliff with all the mud and the machines."

"Rob."

"Not a very friendly character, is he? I'd bought a notebook and a pen and I got out of the car. It was windy enough to sweep you right off the cliff top. I knocked at the door and nobody answered and then I saw him coming toward me out of this barn. I said I was a journalist and he asked where I was from and I said I was from the *Enquirer*."

Tabitha wasn't used to Michaela talking in long connected sentences.

"It's OK. He didn't ask to see my ID or even what my name was. I said I was writing a story about the murder and he said I should fuck off."

"That's him. Sorry about that."

"I didn't pay him any attention," continued Michaela calmly. "I said I'd heard he'd accused you of threatening Stuart and he asked who I'd heard that from. I said I couldn't tell him, but was it true?"

"And?"

"He told me to get off his land. His wife came back then and parked next to us and asked what was going on. I told her I was a reporter come to ask them questions about the murder and she glared at the farmer like it was his fault I was there. Then she pointed a finger at me and told me I was trespassing."

"And you left?"

"Yes. Though there was a great dumper truck blocking my way so I had to sit there while they watched me."

"Thanks for trying."

"Are you going to ask me if I drove straight home?"

"Did you drive straight home?"

"No. I went to your village."

"Okeham."

"I parked near the hotel and I wandered around. I went into the village shop and I told the woman working there that I was a reporter from the *Enquirer* and she was much friendlier than the farmer."

"I bet."

"She told me how the village was in trauma." Michaela's brow furrowed a bit. "She said that she would prefer not to be named, but that everyone had always thought there was something fishy about you."

"Fishy."

"I think that was the word. It might have been dodgy."

"Right." Tabitha wondered which it was better to be: fishy or dodgy.

"She said you hadn't entered into the village community much. That you wore odd, mannish clothes— well, that's true anyway." And now Michaela smiled

296 • NICCI FRENCH

at her, a large and unexpected smile that showed a chipped tooth. "And you didn't have much chitchat. You just worked on your house or swam in the sea when nobody in their right minds would do that in the winter, or stalked around the village in a dark coat, scowling."

"I get it. They didn't like me."

"Oh, I don't know. They're all just getting off on this. I asked if anyone thought you might be innocent."

"And?"

"She sighed and said the police had been very thorough and she was very sorry to say it wasn't in much doubt. Then she asked if I knew about what had happened between you and the guy you're meant to have killed in the past. I said I knew the bare bones. She lowered her voice and leaned across the counter and got very chummy."

There was a lightness about Michaela that was completely new to Tabitha. *It's being free*, she thought, and a spasm of pain gripped her.

"What did she say?"

"Things like: you never could tell what people get up to behind closed doors, dark horses or something. Then the vicar came in and she told her I was a reporter, and the vicar said nobody in the village would want to discuss something that had been so distressing.

Then she said that she wanted to make it known that she had visited you in her pastoral role or whatever. She said she couldn't reveal what you had told her but she thought it had been helpful to you to see her." Michaela put her head on one side. "Was it helpful?"

"What do you think?"

"That's what I reckoned. The two of them smiled at me so much I thought their jaws would crack. They kept saying it was very sad and smiling at me. They asked when my article would come out. And I said I didn't know. Then I walked to your house."

"What for?"

"I wasn't going to go all that way and not see it. They pointed me in the right direction. It's pretty, but it doesn't look like anyone could live there. There was a man painting the porch."

"Andy."

"I said I was a reporter and he told me he had nothing to say to me. But he was quite polite about it so I didn't mind."

"Yes, he is polite."

"And that was it."

"Thank you, Michaela," said Tabitha. "I'm really grateful."

And she was, although in truth she had learned nothing new. Then a thought came to her.

"What was the dumper truck doing at Rob's? And you mentioned machines as well."

"The whole place is a huge muddy building site."

"What's being built?"

"Houses maybe? That's what I assumed anyway."

"I see," said Tabitha.

Terry's words came into her mind: *He was applying for permission to build some holiday homes. It was going to be his pension. Then it was all halted. There was an objection.*

Stuart.

Forty-one

The bus driver, Sam McBride, looked more like he belonged in prison than many of the actual prisoners did. He was thin, with an unhealthy pallor that made Tabitha think of days spent indoors, and sandy hair that he wore in a ponytail. He was wearing a combat jacket, and when he took it off and hung it over the back of the chair, Tabitha saw that both his arms were thickly tattooed. He reminded her of a fox, quick and watchful, his brown eyes flickering around the room.

"Thanks for coming," she said.

"Yeah, well," he said, his voice surprisingly low. "I don't know what use I am."

"It was just on the off chance. I looked at the CCTV of that day and you were in the shop at the same time as me in the morning. You came in to buy cigarettes and I was in front of you."

"In your pajamas." A little smile chased across his face.

"Right. And I just wondered if you remembered anything."

"Like what?"

"Like, did I say anything?"

"Can't you remember?"

"The man who was standing in front of me claims I said something offensive about Stuart."

"That's not good."

"Did you hear me, though?"

His eyes rested on her face briefly. "It doesn't ring a bell."

Tabitha paused.

"Do you remember me not saying anything or do you just not remember anything?"

He looked puzzled. "I don't know. If you'd shouted or been angry, I guess I'd have remembered that."

Tabitha let out a sigh.

"That's good, I suppose. Did you hear Rob Coombe—that's the guy—say anything? He looked angry on the CCTV. I want to know what he was angry about." She took a breath. "Specifically, I want to know if he was angry about Stuart."

"I see," said the driver slowly. "That's what you want."

"I want the truth."

"Right. You want that to be the truth."

Tabitha smiled, though she felt discouraged. "Sure," she said. "There's a great wall of evidence stacked against me and I want to pull out a few of the bricks. Or loosen them."

"I wish I could help you more," he said and he seemed to mean it. "But I go in there most days to buy cigarettes or a can of Coke or whatever, and I don't really pay attention to what's going on. Now you mention it, it rings a bell—but that may only be because you're mentioning it, if you get me."

"If I asked you to be a witness, would you?"

He gave a tiny, crooked smile. "You must be desperate."

"Pretty much."

He stared at her for a few seconds, considering. "If it'll help."

"And if anything else does occur to you, like remembering the farmer yelling about Stuart, you'll tell me."

"Sure."

"Do you drive the school bus every day?"

"Yeah. I spend from half seven in the morning till about five in the afternoon, five days a week, driving it;

except after the school run, it's the old people going to community centers and stuff like that."

"So you know the area well?"

"I wouldn't say that exactly. I only came to Dormouth in November, five weeks before it happened, so I haven't been doing the job for very long." Before she could ask her next question he added, "I was in the army and driving a bus is . . ." He paused for thought. "Restful. And the kids are nice, mostly."

Time was precious so Tabitha steered the conversation back to December 21. "So do you remember anything about that day?"

"What kind of thing?"

"I don't know. But you were there in the morning and again in the afternoon and I wondered if there was anything you saw that struck you."

He pondered. "That man running," he said eventually. "He's always running in his little shorts with his bare legs even when it's freezing. Terry in the shop says he runs marathons. He probably goes along that coastal path that goes all the way along the cliff. Oh, and there was a little kid who fell over in front of the bus as I was driving into the village and I had to step on the brake. I know it was that day because of the ice on the road. Maybe there was a man carrying a bag."

"What kind of man? What kind of bag?"

He shook his head. "I don't know. It's probably not even true. Or it's true of a different morning. I see him sometimes walking through the village with his holdall."

Andy, she thought.

"Then there were Christmas trees lit up in the windows," the driver continued. "Smoke coming out of chimneys. And the vicar with her dog. I always seem to see them. It's a nice dog, not one of those skinny little things you could put in your shopping bag. This isn't helping, is it?"

"I don't know. Did you see Stuart?"

He shook his head. "Not that I remember."

"Or his wife?"

"I don't think so."

"You mean you might have?"

He gave a small grin. "Don't get your hopes up. I didn't even know what she looks like."

"Nothing else you can think of?"

"It was just an ordinary day. And it was still pretty dark."

"Of course. Did you see anyone coming into the village as you left?"

"You mean in a car?"

"Anything."

"I don't know. Perhaps a van."

"A van."

"I said perhaps."

"I know I'm clutching at straws, it's just—" She stopped and spread her hands in a gesture of helplessness.

"Sure."

Tabitha frowned in concentration, thinking of the CCTV footage. Then it struck her that of course most of this was irrelevant: Stuart had more than two hours left to live after the bus had left Okeham. A feeling of glumness settled on her and she tried to push it away and think of anything she could ask that was of any possible use.

"What about Rob Coombe?" she said eventually.

"I've told you what I remember, and don't."

"No, I mean did you see him after that? He didn't leave the village."

"Maybe he was with his girlfriend."

"I'm sorry?"

"That nice nurse."

Tabitha leaned forward, gripping the table. "Nurse?" she said.

"I think she's a nurse. I've seen her in her uniform."

"Rob Coombe is having an affair with her?"

"I'm just the bus driver. But sometimes after he's dropped his kid off at the bus he drives away and then stops further up the village and walks back to her house."

"How do you know it's her house?"

"I saw her answer the door to him once. I had to stop the bus on my way out of the village because one of the kids wouldn't sit down and there she was. I'm quite high up so I get a good view."

"I see," she said.

There was only one nurse in Okeham.

After he left, Tabitha sat forward, her chin in her hands and her eyes half closed. Rob and Shona, Shona and Rob. Did that mean anything? And if it did, what?

Forty-two

She sat on her bed, knees drawn up, leafing through her notebook. It was more than half filled now with lists and timelines and thoughts, maps and tasks, all written in her meticulous hand.

She examined the map, drew another tiny boat on the sea, hatched the cliff more neatly. She put a small car on the turning circle, and a bare tree at its junction with the track that led to Stuart's house and her own.

She wrote up the notes from her meetings with Terry, Laura, Dr. Mallon and the bus driver. She wrote down what Michaela had told her. Then she looked at the list of the people who had been trapped in the village on the day of Stuart's murder. Surely she could cross off Pauline Leavitt, who was in her eighties and sometimes walked with a stick? And the man in his wheelchair, who wouldn't even make it up her driveway with all its potholes and bumps. And presumably the two sisters with their toddlers. Then there was Terry, who had been in Okeham throughout the day but hadn't left the shop.

That left Shona—and what the bus driver had said about Shona returned to her; Rob, with his holiday homes that Stuart had tried to put a stop to; Dr. Mallon, who had received Laura's confidences and whose practice Stuart had left. Then there was Mel the vicar, who had fallen out with Stuart, and who Stuart had complained about to the bishop. Andy, who had told the police she had tried to prevent him finding the body. Luke Rees, who had been bullied by his father and who was protective of his mother.

Tabitha thought about Laura, so angry behind her very English restraint, so lonely. But she had been away that day, with her failed meeting. Once more, Tabitha thought about both Laura's botched appointment and Stuart's attempt to leave the village. Where had he been going?

And of course, she had been there all day herself. She tapped the pen beside her own name.

She put the names in a circle and Stuart's name in the middle, then drew arrows connecting them: everyone except Terry and Andy had one that joined them to Stuart. Then she linked Shona to Rob Coombe, herself to Andy, because he was her only real friend in the village. She chewed her pen. Was she also linked to Shona because she had gone to school with her? And was Owen Mallon everyone's doctor—and was that even remotely relevant?

What was this stupid diagram doing anyway?

She drew a red line through the whole thing, closed the book and lay down in bed. She closed her eyes, and the grainy film started to play again in her head, figures moving in and out of the frame while the leafless birch swayed in the wind and the sleet fell.

Forty-three

"You look great," said Tabitha.

Shona was glowing from her week in the Canaries. Her face was tanned, there were new freckles on the bridge of her nose, and her chestnut hair had paler coppery streaks in it. She wore a yellow shirt, rolled up to the elbows, and seemed to bring sunshine into the drab visitors' room. Sitting across from her in her grubby gray sweatshirt and jeans, Tabitha felt a stab of pure envy.

"I needed to get away."

"Tell me about it," said Tabitha. "Did you go alone?"

"I went with Jules—Jules Perry. Do you remember her from school?"

Tabitha did, though she tried not to. Tall, long-limbed and mean. She attempted a smile but her mouth felt stiff. "I think she probably arrived after I'd left," she said. "I was only there till I was sixteen."

"She lives in Nottingham now so I don't see her that much. We had such a laugh, remembering old times."

"Good."

"And the sun, oh God, I soaked up the sun. Though it's spring here now as well." She suddenly looked contrite. "I'm sorry, Tabs." (*Tabs?* thought Tabitha.) "Listen to me going on about holidays and spring and all the time you're stuck in here. How are you?"

"All right."

"I mean, really, how are you?"

Tabitha suddenly felt that she didn't want to tell Shona how she "really" was.

"I'm working on my defense."

"How's it going?"

"It seemed like I had ages, the weeks just stretched out in front of me, and now time's running out. My trial is on June the third and we're already almost in May."

Shona nodded. "Tell me how I can help," she said. "I feel I haven't really done anything. Do you want to talk it through?"

"Not really."

"Is there anything you need in here?"

"I'll let you know if I do." Tabitha paused. "I really want to talk about something else. I'm trying to work out what everyone who was in the village that day was doing."

"Why?"

Tabitha couldn't bear the thought of going through the whole case again with Shona. "It could be useful. For example, where were you all day?"

"Me?"

"Yes. It's like putting together a jigsaw puzzle," said Tabitha.

"Right."

"So where were you?"

"At home. I mean, I went to the shop, I think."

"Yes, you did. Twice."

"Sorry?"

"I saw you on CCTV."

Shona looked bewildered. She gave a small laugh. "Then you know already."

"But you didn't go out at all apart from those times?"

"Why would I? It was foul out there."

"Was it a workday?"

"Yes. I was on call. Two of my mothers were overdue, one of them already nine days late. But of course, I got stuck. It was nice really, an unexpected little holiday. Like those snow days we sometimes had when we couldn't go to school, do you remember?"

"What did you do?"

"Not much. Why?" Tabitha waited. "Just pottered. I had a bath—a bath in the middle of the day, bliss. Made myself lunch. Wasted time online."

"Did you see anyone?"

"Apart from when I went to the shop, you mean? Nobody."

"Nobody?"

"No."

"Really?"

"What is this?"

"Did you see Rob Coombe?"

Shona's face turned blank. "What do you mean?" she asked after a pause.

"Honestly I don't care what you do in your personal life. I just wanted to know if he was with you."

"Why would he be?"

"Well, was he?"

"Who's been spreading rumors?" asked Shona. Her face flamed.

"None of that matters," said Tabitha. "But if he was with you then I need to know."

"I think it's time to go."

"Listen, Shona, I don't care who's fucking who, who's betraying who, I only care about where he was and where you were on that day."

"Have you said anything to Andy about this gossip?"

"What's Andy got to do with it?"

"Nothing. Sorry. I just—never mind. I'm a bit confused by this, to be honest, and we're friends but all of a sudden you're not talking to me like a friend." Shona's brown eyes were reproachful.

"You still haven't told me."

"It was just a little fling, after Paul and I broke up and I was a bit of a mess and Rob was nice to me. I didn't mean for it to happen and I really don't want everyone in the village finding out. It's been over for ages and it's got nothing to do with anything."

"So? Was he there?"

Shona fidgeted in her chair. "Maybe," she said at last.

Forty-four

It almost felt like she was being released. Mary Guy collected her from the cell and led her through four doors. Tabitha never got used to the laborious unlocking and locking, the rattling of the keys, but this time they took a different route and she was signed out like any other visitor and emerged blinking into the car park in front of the grand Victorian gateway. Tabitha looked around, but there was only a dark silver sedan with a middle-aged man sitting in the driving seat looking at his phone.

"Where's the van?" said Tabitha.

"Unavailable," said Mary Guy. "We're taking a cab."

They both got in the back seat and the car moved off. Tabitha stared out of the window. Everything she saw looked like something in a dream: a woman pushing a stroller, a man and a woman smoking a cigarette on the pavement outside their office, a few teenagers in school uniform laughing and jostling. All completely mundane and familiar and yet she felt she was moving past them like a ghost.

"Must be weird," said the driver, not looking round. "Working in a prison."

Tabitha flashed a look at an unresponsive Mary Guy. Clearly the driver hadn't been told she was a prisoner. Tabitha was tempted to tell him, just to see the shock on his face. But she didn't. Suddenly she wanted to savor these few moments of being treated as a normal person.

"Yes," she said. "It's pretty weird."

"I suppose it's not like it is in the movies."

"No," said Tabitha. "Not really."

"Showers and strip searches," said the driver.

Tabitha could see in the rearview mirror that he was grinning. She had a strong impulse to say something or even to do something. It might even be worth getting into a row with the driver. It might even end with him stopping and making them get out. How would Mary Guy deal with that? Reluctantly she stayed silent. They were heading to see the physical evidence that the police were holding. Examining it was a right she had as part of her defense, but if she caused a scene, Mary Guy was entirely capable of making things difficult. She could start talking about "security concerns" and going straight back to Crow Grange.

The driver began to describe at length a female prison drama he'd seen on TV but Tabitha let her attention drift and it turned into a comforting background drone like the wind blowing or a radio playing in another room. Instead she just continued to look out of the window. It was all so interesting. The most boring things—other motorists, the occasional cyclist, men dressed in yellow peering into a hole in the road—seemed magical to her, fresh and gleaming. She tried to store them in her memory, something she could smuggle back to the cell with her like contraband.

They were driving on the edge of town past car showrooms, furniture stores, a garden center, a DIY wholesaler.

"Couldn't we stop nearby?" asked Tabitha hopefully. "Go for a little walk?"

Mary Guy looked at her watch. "We're five minutes late. And any road, the answer's no."

The cab pulled into the forecourt of a large yellow warehouse store: "24-Hour Storage Solutions!" was the large, jaunty logo on the front. Next to the logo was

a picture of a cheery, rubicund man in overalls, bran-
dishing an oversized key and smiling a gleaming smile.

"Is this right?" said Tabitha.

Mary Guy got out, so Tabitha followed her, still
thinking there must be some mistake.

"It's storage," said Mary Guy.

"I can see that. I just thought we were going to a
police station or a government facility."

The cab drove away and Tabitha looked around. A
young woman was standing on the steps clutching a
clipboard. She was dressed for business in conserva-
tive navy with a white blouse and black shoes. Tabitha
would have guessed that she was an estate agent. She
stepped forward, looking a little uneasy, and suddenly
very young.

"Are you the . . . you know, the er . . . ?"

Mary Guy showed her pass and a typed letter. The
woman checked the name off on her clipboard.

"It's on the second floor," she said. "It's a bit of a
walk, I'm afraid."

Tabitha looked at the woman curiously as they were
led inside and up a stone staircase.

"Are you police?" Tabitha asked.

"Oh no," said the woman, looking almost alarmed.
"We, I mean Sunburst, that's the company I work for,

we carry out all kinds of services for the police. Catering, logistics, storage like here."

"You own this?"

"No, no. We rent it and arrange the transport and all that."

They reached the second floor and walked past a series of spaces, each locked behind a grille. Tabitha glimpsed piles of furniture, packing cases, an upright piano, a rowing machine, fragments of people's lives, the things that they could do without for a while but couldn't dispense with. The woman looked at her clipboard.

"Two twenty-nine," she said. "This is us."

Tabitha looked through the grille. The space was lined on three sides by very basic shelving. There were objects on the shelves and various bundles on the floor. The woman unlocked the padlock and pulled open the door that was itself just a heavy grille on hinges. The three of them stepped inside. Tabitha looked around.

"A lot of stuff," she said.

The woman looked at her clipboard.

"I think the material relating to your case is over there." She gestured to the left-hand side. "Everything is labeled with the reference number." She read the number off the clipboard.

"Hang on," said Tabitha. She took her notebook from her pocket and got the woman to read the number over again until she had it written down.

"And each piece of evidence has a separate number."

"You mean like "'Exhibit A'?" said Tabitha.

"I think they're numbered actually."

"What can I call you?" said Tabitha.

"Kira," said the woman.

Tabitha looked around once more.

"So, Kira," she said, "if my stuff is over here"—she gestured to the left—"then other people's stuff is everywhere else."

"Yes."

"So other people come in here," said Tabitha. "People connected with other cases."

"Sometimes."

"Doesn't this evidence need to be kept secure?"

Kira was looking more and more uneasy. "It *is* secure."

"But you just said that people unconnected with the case are coming in and out of here?"

"Yes, but it's police and lawyers mostly."

"They could pick things up. They could pick up the wrong things. They could get them mixed up."

Kira gave a nervous little giggle and her eyes flickered between Tabitha and Mary Guy.

"But they wouldn't," she said.

"Who's making sure?" said Tabitha. "Other police?" She thought for a few seconds. "Have you got a business card?"

"What do you mean?"

"I might want to get in touch with you," said Tabitha. "For the trial. Just to ask about storage and security. The sort of thing you do."

Kira fumbled in her bag and produced a card.

"Don't let her get to you," said Mary Guy to Kira.

"I'm just asking for her card," said Tabitha, taking it.

"You'd better get going," said Mary Guy. "You'll run out of time."

There was nowhere to sit, no desk. Kira and Mary Guy just stood awkwardly to one side as Tabitha made a quick initial assessment of what was being stored. It was mainly the contents of her outhouse, the outhouse that she had constantly been planning to clear out. Well, it had been cleared now and put here as evidence against her. She walked along the wooden shelf. She noticed her kitchen knives, wrapped in plastic, arranged in a row. She picked up her bread knife and examined it. She looked round. Both of the other women were staring at their phones.

She had a sudden, terrifying, vertiginous idea. She could jot down the exhibit number of this knife. She could peel the label off, hide it, swallow it, whatever. Then she could move the knife across the room and hide it with the evidence of one of the other cases. She would call for it during the case. She could claim that it was crucial evidence for her defense. And it would be missing or it would be found but without the label.

"What kind of a case is this?" she imagined herself saying. "If they've done this, then what other mistakes have been made?"

Would that sow enough confusion? Would it be enough to create reasonable doubt? She carefully put the knife back on the shelf and almost smiled to herself. Lucky she was an honest woman.

She looked along the shelf and saw the scraps of her outhouse neatly bagged up: a couple of ceramic tiles, a small tin of paint, a small stick that had been used for stirring paint, an old chisel, a bare tennis ball, a double-plug adaptor, a metal bolt. On the ground were larger objects, also wrapped in plastic sheeting, which gave them a sinister, morbid appearance, corpses made of some rolled-up chicken wire, a Christmas tree base. Slightly surreally, there was some plastic sheeting that was itself wrapped in plastic sheeting. Her old paint-spattered stepladder was leaning against the wall.

She felt suddenly disheartened. It was just rubbish, the stuff of her life, the clutter that everyone has at the back of a shed, in a loft or a spare room or by the side of the house, the stuff they mean to get rid of and never quite get around to.

But now they were evidence. Would some of them be produced in court as evidence against her? Presumably some had blood on them and that's why they were here. There had been so much blood around.

There were the objects that would be used by the prosecution. Was there anything that would be any use to the defense? A lawyer or a police officer might know. She didn't have any idea where to begin.

With a feeling of utter pointlessness, she opened a new page of her notebook and began to write a list of everything that was there, along with the exhibit numbers. When she had finished, she noticed a bin bag she had overlooked. She looked into it and saw clothes, the sort you might take to a charity shop, except that these were also wrapped in plastic. She tipped them onto the floor and then saw the dark stains and recognized them with a lurch. These were the clothes and the trainers she had been wearing when the body was found. On top of everything else that had happened, she had been taken to one side by a female officer and made to take them all off. Even her underwear.

She wrote a list of them in her notebook.

The list filled two pages. She looked at it. It all seemed meaningless. She decided she needed to be more thorough. She looked at the knives one by one. Each of them had a maker's name on it. She wrote them down. Perhaps one of them wasn't actually hers. She would check. The chisel didn't have a maker's name. She looked at the plastic sheeting within the plastic sheeting. It was spattered and smeared with blood. There was a paper label on it saying "Reynolds Brown" and a long serial number. She copied it all down.

She looked at the two tins of paint. Umber. Clay. She didn't recognize them although presumably she had chosen them. She wrote them down along with the brand names.

Was that it? She stepped back and contemplated them as a whole. The sight made her feel somehow blank and nauseous at the same time. It was like those few hours of her day, which hadn't mattered to her while she was living through them and now she was trying to retrieve them minute by minute. And there were these scraps from her shed, these bits and pieces on the edge of her life, which had been individually wrapped in plastic and kept in the dark.

She had a painful sense that somewhere among them, there, right in front of her, was something that could be of help, if only she could see what it was.

But she couldn't.

She turned to Mary Guy.

"I guess we can call another cab now," she said.

Forty-five

The letter was very short and written by hand, a spidery and barely legible scrawl with no address and no date.

It's late and I'm pretty stoned so I probably shouldn't be writing this and anyway I probably won't send it, but here goes. You keep asking why I came back at Christmas after so long away. I'll tell you why. I came back to tell Mum to leave him. I never got why she stayed until I talked to you, but now I see she was his victim just as much as me, or you, or anyone. We were all his fucking victims.

We didn't kill him. But I wish Mum had left before he died. I wish she had told him she was

done with him and wiped the smile off his face
and I wish I'd been there to see that.

Something was heavily scratched through here and
though Tabitha lifted the letter up to the light she
couldn't make out the words.

It was probably you, anyway. Everyone thinks so.
That inspector was certain. But I wanted to say
that I don't blame you if you did kill him and I'm
glad he's dead and I'm sorry about what he did to
you and it's not fair.

Tabitha sat for several minutes, holding the letter,
thinking.

Then she wrote a reply.

Dear Luke,
I'm glad you told me that. Will you be one of my
witnesses? Please.
Tabitha

Forty-six

Two days later, she watched the entire CCTV footage once more. She didn't really need to, but she had no idea how else to fill the days between now and the trial. This time, she didn't make notes, she just stared at the grainy film until it became like a dream, or like something that had happened far away and long ago.

The camera gazed at the leafless birch. Figures appeared, disappeared. The bus arrived and left. She saw Stuart's car go by and she saw it return. She saw Mel, Rob, Shona, Owen Mallon, Luke. She saw the deliveryman.

The deliveryman. She had interviewed everyone except him—and he'd been there all day, waiting patiently for the tree to be cleared.

She rifled through all the bundles she had received from the prosecution: Lev Wojcik.

He was solid, with round shoulders, broad hands and brown eyes that were almost green. The lines on his face gave him a worried air. He sat opposite Tabitha and fixed his gaze on her.

"Thank you for coming," she said. "I was hoping you could help me."

He didn't say anything, just waited.

"As you know," she continued, "I've been charged with murdering Stuart Rees on the twenty-first of December. The day you were in Okeham because of the tree."

"Yes."

"You were there practically all day."

"Yes."

"And you were the last person to see Stuart alive."

"No."

"What?"

"The person who killed him was the last."

"Right. Apart from the killer. Who wasn't me," she added a little desperately.

"What do you want from me?" he asked. "The police have already asked me everything." He suddenly sounded grim.

"Did they give you a hard time?"

"What do you think?"

"I see." She gave him a small smile but he didn't smile back. "But you saw Stuart."

"Yes."

"Can you tell me about that? I mean, you arrived in the village at nine-forty," she said. She didn't need to look at her notes; she had that day memorized by heart now.

He nodded.

"And you went to the village shop first."

"To buy a sandwich," he said.

"Nobody else was in the shop?"

"No. Then I drove to the house of Mr. Rees."

"You only had the one delivery in Okeham?"

"Only one."

"Do you know what the parcel was?"

He shrugged. "A book perhaps. Not big."

"So you went to the house and rang the doorbell?"

"I didn't need to ring. He must have heard the van so he opened the door before I rang. I gave him the parcel."

"And that was it?"

"Yes."

"How did he seem?"

"I just gave him a delivery."

"He didn't say anything about going out later?"

"No. How would he, with the tree down?"

"And you just left."

"Yes."

"And went back to the shop."

"Yes."

"And stayed there pretty much all day?"

"Yes."

"What did you do?"

"I bought coffee. I bought a paper. I waited in the van. It was very cold. Sometimes I ran the engine to get warm."

"You got out a few times. Why?"

"It was many hours," he said. For the first time he looked uncomfortable. "I had drunk much coffee."

"You didn't go back to Stuart's house?"

"What for?"

"I don't know."

But she knew, from looking at the CCTV, that he hadn't been away from his van or the shop for long enough to get to Stuart's house and back again. Something nagged at her, but she couldn't put her finger on it. She felt she wasn't asking the right questions.

"Did you see Stuart drive past you at about half past ten and then back again?"

"Perhaps."

"Perhaps?"

"I don't know."

"Did you see me?"

He looked at her with his mottled eyes. "I don't know," he said again. "I wasn't looking. I was just waiting. It was boring. It was cold. I was losing money. What do you want me to say? It was just one of the days when nothing goes right. I was happy to leave."

"How did you know when the tree had been cleared?"

"Like when I came, the woman in the shop told me."

"Terry."

"She didn't say her name."

"So you can't remember anything you saw as you sat there all those hours?"

"I didn't say so. There was the woman with her dog. I like dogs. She walked back and forward several times. There was a man who ran."

"But you saw nothing odd? Nothing that grabbed your attention?"

He shook his head slowly, his eyes resting on her. "Nothing."

Forty-seven

Michaela looked at Tabitha with an expression of concern, almost of dismay.

"You should wash your hair you know, maybe get it cut."

"I know."

"Before the trial, anyway. It's not long to go now."

"Just over three weeks."

"You've got to look smart for that."

"I know."

"What'll you wear?"

"I haven't thought. I don't really have the right kind of clothes. I'm not really a suit kind of person. Or a skirt and blouse kind."

"Shall I get stuff for you?"

"Would you do that? I'll pay you, of course."

"Sure. What size are you?" She eyed Tabitha. "An eight, I think. Or a six. You're tiny. What size feet?"

"Thirty-seven. You're being very kind to me."

Michaela shrugged and looked uncomfortable: she didn't like praise.

"I was hoping you could do a bit more research for me."

"All right. I'm only working shifts at the pub at the moment."

"I made a list." Tabitha handed Michaela two sheets of paper.

"What is this?"

"All stuff the police took from my house. I've no idea why some of them are relevant. They probably have blood on them."

Michaela nodded, giving the list a cursory glance. "What do you want me to do?"

"I don't know really. But look, these knives, say, I want to know if one of them is older than the others, or doesn't fit with them."

"I can give it a go."

"I wrote down serial numbers. Like that paint, or the plastic sheeting. It's probably useless but I don't know what else to do and I've got to do something or I'll go mad just sitting here and waiting and knowing I've got pretty much nothing."

"You're not feeling good, are you?"

"Not great."

There was a pause.

"I feel like I should say something positive," said Michaela.

"Don't," said Tabitha. "I wouldn't believe you."

Forty-eight

Tabitha, sitting in the small room off the library, selected a sheet of paper from the sheaf that the librarian had given her. She unscrewed the lid of the pen and tested it on a page in her notebook to make sure it wasn't about to run out.

She wrote her name at the top of the paper in her neatest cursive. Underneath it she wrote "Crow Grange" and beside that her prison number. On the left-hand side of the paper she wrote the date: May 11, 2019.

Then, in capital letters in the center of the page, she wrote: "DEFENSE STATEMENT."

She paused. She had the strong urge to lie down on the floor and close her eyes. She recognized that urge, the insatiable desire to sleep away the time, a sleep that didn't erase tiredness but added to it. She preferred burning with rage to this heavy weariness. *Fight*, Michaela had said. She rubbed her sore eyes.

What was her defense?

"None of the evidence against me proves that I killed Stuart Rees," she wrote, making sure each letter was clear, each "i" dotted.

She stared at what she had written. What else? She couldn't think of anything but she needed to add something to this single, paltry sentence.

"I intend to show that the prosecution case is built on the fact that I am an outsider in Okeham. Just because I could have done it does not mean that I did," she wrote, just so the statement took up more space on the blank whiteness of the page.

There was nothing else. She had spent all these weeks interviewing people, looking at CCTV footage, going over the facts and the statements again and again, and all she could come up with was this.

She was about to fold the sheet of paper in two and slide it into the A5 envelope when she remembered that she should add the names of witnesses she intended to call. Her head throbbed.

"Witnesses," she wrote. She underlined the word.

She chewed her lip. She couldn't think of a single person. Maybe she should call someone as a character witness, but who? Her old boyfriend, who had decided he wasn't going to see her anymore? Her employer, who she had met twice and who hadn't replied to her letter? Her friend Jane who was living in Japan and who she hadn't seen for three years? She thought of asking Shona—Shona who was having an affair with Rob Coombe. She thought of asking Andy—Andy who had told the police she had attempted to prevent him from discovering the body. The sense of her isolation, her loneliness, flooded into her like ice-cold water. She blinked.

"To come," she wrote.

She folded the paper.

Forty-nine

"What have you got there?"

"Pork pie salad," said Dana, prodding at the mottled pink meat. "You?"

"Soya lasagna. It's horrible."

"It looks it."

"Not long now," said Tabitha. "Just keep going." She was talking to herself as well as to Dana. Her voice seemed to come from a long way off.

Dana nodded. She was like a mole pushing its way through the earth, thought Tabitha. They both were.

After they'd eaten, they sat on Tabitha's bed and Dana read out loud while Tabitha occasionally corrected or encouraged her. It was a fantasy novel, full of dragons and warriors and unsatisfactory magic, and her attention wandered. The sky through the window was still blue, that lovely deepening blue of evening.

They got into their nightclothes; they brushed their teeth. When she spat into the sink, Tabitha saw that her gums were bleeding. Her mouth tasted of iron. Her head ached. She hadn't had a period since being in prison, but now she had a dull ache in her lower back. Ten days to go, she thought. Less. Terror shot through her, turning her insides watery.

She imagined walking into the courtroom, men and women in their stupid wigs, standing in the dock, all eyes on her. She had nothing to say. She had nothing.

She sat in bed with her notebook and turned the pages, looked at the map with its drawings of the boats out at sea and the tractor beside the farmhouse. And of her house with its sheds. She looked at all the names again: Shona, Andy, Rob, Terry, Luke, Owen Mallon, Mel. She thought about Laura and her pursed mouth, that sense of her suppressing the story that was coiled tightly inside.

She thought about Stuart. She thought of him in that small car all those years ago, the stale air, him pulling up her skirt, pulling down her knickers. Why had she passively let him, neither encouraging nor resisting, but limp, almost lifeless, staring out at the trees and waiting for it to be over? Why had she returned to the place where that had happened? Why, when there were so many things that made her furiously angry, had she never been angry about that until now, when like a hot ember, the fact of what he had done smoldered inside the dry tinder of her mind?

What had she done on that day of his murder?

She lay down. From far off, she could hear someone calling out for help, over and over again.

She shut her eyes tightly. *Bluebells*, she thought. *Swallows. Floppy pink quince blossom; clean green leaves unfurling. The dark sea rolling in, tossing seaweed in hissing heaps onto the shingle. A moon. Stars. Out there.*

Ten days.

"Please," she whispered under her breath. "Please."

Fifty

She was sitting in the library with her notebook, the contents of which she knew by heart now, even the crossings out, when Vera tottered in. Tabitha hadn't seen her for days, maybe weeks; the women said she had gone to hospital with a chest infection. They said she was mad and getting madder. They laughed and tapped their temples with a forefinger. Vera looked ten years older, more. Her eyes were red-rimmed and her long white hair was dry as summer hay that you could crunch in your fists.

She came to a halt in front of Tabitha. She was carrying a large bundle of papers in her arms like it was a new baby and now she laid it on the table, where it spread out in a chaotic heap.

"For you," she said. "All for you."

"But it's yours, Vera," said Tabitha in a kind of panic. She didn't want to be in possession of these scrawled sheets of paper. They were like a wild version of her own notebook, a kind of warning of what she herself might turn into. "You've worked on this for years. I can't take it."

"No, no, no," said Vera. "I gift it to you. You can't refuse." Suddenly her face took on a settled look; her eyes stopped darting around the room and met Tabitha's. "It's too late," she said.

"What do you mean?"

"My time's over."

"No, Vera."

"Yours," Vera said and pushed the papers toward Tabitha. Some of them fell into her lap and others to the floor. Like she was uttering a curse, she repeated, "I gift it."

"Then thank you," said Tabitha helplessly.

She watched Vera leave, empty-handed, listing as she walked and her feet sliding on the floor.

"Poor lady," said the librarian.

"Yes." Tabitha looked at the pile in front of her. "What shall I do with all this? I can't just throw it away."

"I'll keep it for you if you want. Put it in a drawer for the time being."

"Thank you."

Galia picked up the bundle.

"This might come in useful, though," she said, and pulled out a dog-eared paperback with an austere dark green cover. "I gave it to Vera myself a few months ago."

She handed it across to Tabitha: *How to Defend Yourself in Court*. Tabitha opened it up and flicked through the pages. Vera had scribbled things illegibly in the margins and turned down the corners of several pages.

"I guess it might," she said. "Thanks."

It gave her something to do. She had lots of time so she read it through slowly, word for word, and she made notes in her moleskin book, which was practically full now and perhaps looked as mad as Vera's pile of papers.

It is vital you understand the law relevant to your defense.

Call Judge "My Lord" or "My Lady."

Never interrupt.

Preparation is the key: work out what your case is.

Support what you say with evidence: witnesses, documents, physical objects, expert witnesses.

Disclosure: you are obliged to set out in a numbered list all the documents that are relevant.

There are serious consequences in making a statement that you do not believe to be true.

Dismantle your opponent's argument.

Fill everything with doubt.

Behavior and intent.

You can bring a friend, known as a McKenzie friend—this can be family or friend. They can help by providing support, taking notes, helping with case papers and quietly giving advice. (They cannot speak in court, except where in rare cases when they have permission from the judge to right of audience.)

Dress smartly.

Arrive early.

Speak slowly and clearly.

*It's all about performance: stand straight, keep
still, use limited hand movements, don't shout.*

Tabitha looked at what she had written. Some of it
didn't apply to her. Some of it was too late—she had,
for instance, already sent off her entirely hopeless defense statement with no supporting evidence, and she
had no control over what time she arrived at the court.
Mostly it didn't tell her what she needed to know; but
then, she didn't even know what she needed to know.

She closed the book.

Fifty-one

"The search took ages. They did it once for security and once for fun. It's that thin warden; she always hated me and she hates me even more now she can't lock me into my cell. What do you think?"

Michaela held up the dark gray suit. The trousers were baggy, cinched at the waist, and the jacket had thin lapels and a ripped crimson lining.

"I think it's nice. How much did it cost you?"

"Fourteen quid. A bargain. And I got these boots."

She pulled some neat black ankle boots out of the bag.

"Size thirty-seven," she said. "Try them on."

"They look brand new," said Tabitha suspiciously.

"I didn't steal them if that's what you're thinking," Michaela said. "They belong to my aunt's partner's stepdaughter."

"That's kind of her."

"She doesn't know. She won't miss them though; she's got a ridiculous number of shoes. You can just wear tee shirts under the jacket. I got a couple of basic white ones from Primark. They're in the bag."

"Thank you," said Tabitha. "I owe you."

Michaela waved her hand airily.

"Any luck on those searches?"

"Searches? Oh, that list you gave me. I'll do it as soon as I leave here."

"I was going to ask you something else."

"Go on."

"You're still not working?"

"Only shifts sometimes. Why?"

"I was wondering if you'd be my McKenzie friend."

"What?"

"I'm allowed to have someone in court. I've been reading up about it. To support me, give me advice, that kind of thing. It's not like being a lawyer, of course; you're not allowed to talk or ask questions."

"You want me in court? Are you joking?"

"Well . . ." Tabitha faltered. "If you don't want to—"

"Want to? I'd fucking love to."

Three days before the trial, Tabitha started to feel sick. She couldn't eat and beads of sweat pricked her forehead. Her tongue felt large and her legs unsteady; her stomach churned with dread.

Her eczema and her mouth ulcers flared up. When she caught sight of herself in the mirror, which she tried not to do, she was unsettled by her thin, hollow-eyed face under the unruly mop of hair. She looked like a prisoner. She looked like someone who was not of sound mind.

Her sleep, when it came at all, was shallow and fitful and full of nasty dreams.

She sat in the library and read through all the prosecution documents. More had arrived over the past weeks, but she couldn't see that they made any difference to anything.

She looked at the lists of witnesses they were calling. Alongside the pathologist, the forensic scientists, the police officers, she saw names she didn't recognize and some that she did. Andy's was among them and her chest ached. She turned the paper over so she didn't need to look at it.

She looked again through her notebook. She still had the itchy sense that she was missing something, but every time she tried to grasp it, it slipped out of her mind.

She tried on the clothes that Michaela had brought in. The boots fitted perfectly, but the suit was slightly too big. She rolled up the cuffs and stood in front of the mirror, looking like a scarecrow. She said, "I swear to tell the truth, the whole truth and nothing but the truth." Her voice rasped. She wondered if it was too late to call Mora Piozzi.

The afternoon before, she washed her hair and combed it straight. She sat in her cell with an egg sandwich that made her stomach heave. She tried to help Dana with her reading, as if this was just another evening, but all the words blurred.

She lay in bed and thought she would never sleep but she must have done because she lurched awake with a feeling of panic and the sky outside her window was a brightening gray. It was today and she wasn't ready and when she stood up her heart bumped and her breath came in shallow gasps.

She washed and brushed her teeth. She put on the new white tee shirt and the suit; she pulled the boots on. She combed her hair until it lay flat on her scalp.

She met herself in the mirror. "Good luck, Tabitha Hardy," she said.

PART TWO

Prosecution

Fifty-two

Tabitha had only glimpsed the front of Harwood Crown Court out of the little window of the transport vehicle. It could have been any modern, public venue with its sweep of steps leading up to plateglass doors. A regional theater, perhaps, a concert hall or library. But the vehicle turned down a side street and, handcuffed to a warden she had never seen before, Tabitha was led in the back way past parked cars and large steel rubbish bins. She was hardly aware of her surroundings, just the squeak of her rubber-soled shoes on lino, the walls painted a glossy institutional cream color. She found herself—almost as if she had just woken up—in a short corridor with two cells on each side. One of them was open, waiting for her. She was led inside, her handcuff was unlocked and she was left alone, locked in.

This cell was utterly bare, with just two molded plastic chairs and nothing else. No sink, no toilet, no window. Tabitha just sat and stared at the wall. She heard the now familiar sound of a key turning in the lock and the door opened inward and two people were ushered into the room. The door was shut behind them.

Tabitha looked round slowly. A middle-aged man and a young woman were looking down at her. The man had a florid face with short curly gray hair. He was wearing a pinstriped double-breasted suit, white shirt, sober dark tie and black leather shoes. The woman was dressed in a navy-blue skirt and jacket, white shirt with low-heeled black leather shoes. Her blond hair was tied back in a bun. She had minimal makeup, the palest of red lipstick and no nail varnish. Both of them were immaculate in almost every detail down to the man's silver cuff links. Their clothes looked as if they had not just been cleaned but brushed. Their shoes were polished so that they shone. There was just a touch of raffishness in the man's hairstyle, a fuzziness, but even that seemed to denote confidence. By comparison, Tabitha's clothes—the clothes that Michaela had bought on her behalf—felt shabby and cheap and even fraudulent, like a badly made costume.

"I'm Simon Brockbank," the man said. "I'm acting for the crown." He paused. "That means I'm the prosecutor. This is my colleague, Elinor Ackroyd. She'll be assisting me."

Brockbank spoke as if he were already just a little bored by the proceedings. His accent, his whole demeanor, immediately made Tabitha feel inadequate, underprepared, undereducated. And then she felt angry with herself.

"I suppose you're here to tell me that I'm stupid to be defending myself."

"It's a little late for that," said Brockbank. "That particular train has left the station."

"I've got a McKenzie friend, though."

"Good for you," said Brockbank. "Some kind of lawyer?"

"My ex-cellmate."

He glanced across at his colleague and leaned back against the door. He unfastened the buttons of his jacket, revealing a waistcoat. He put his hands in his trouser pockets.

"I've been authorized to make you an offer," he said. "More of a suggestion, perhaps."

"What's that?" said Tabitha.

"You plead guilty to manslaughter. The Crown Prosecution Service drops the murder charge."

All that day Tabitha had felt like she was underwater. Everything around her seemed to be blurry and moving slowly. She couldn't make out what people were saying and what she could make out she couldn't understand.

"What would that actually mean?" she said slowly. "I mean for me."

Brockbank looked round at his companion.

"What do you think, Ellie?"

When Ackroyd spoke, Tabitha immediately thought of horse boxes and ski slopes.

"Murder has an automatic tariff of life imprisonment. Minimum of fifteen years before you can be considered for parole."

"What's the conviction rate in the Crown Court?" Brockbank asked. Everything he said was in a bored tone that suggested his time would be better spent doing something else.

"Eighty percent. Probably more than eighty percent."

"What about manslaughter?" asked Tabitha.

Again Brockbank glanced across at the younger lawyer.

"The judge has a great deal of latitude. For a start, you get maximum credit for pleading guilty."

"Maximum credit," said Tabitha. "That sounds like a good thing. What does it mean?"

"Usually it means something like a thirty percent reduction in the sentence. Maybe even a fifty percent reduction. But manslaughter's a special case. You can get a life sentence or you can get community service. It depends if there are mitigating circumstances."

"Mitigating circumstances," Tabitha repeated. "Like what?"

Brockbank pursed his lips. "I don't know. Hypothetically, if the victim had perpetrated sexual abuse against the accused when she was a minor, that might be considered significant. In the current climate. Of course, nothing can be guaranteed."

Tabitha tried to make herself think. She felt hot and cold at the same time. She felt confused. But then gradually a thought took shape.

"It's a game," she said. "It's like poker. You're saying that I should plead guilty even if I didn't do it."

"I'm not saying anything," said Brockbank. "I'm just relaying an offer."

"But what if it were you?" Tabitha asked. "If you were made this offer and you hadn't done it, what would you do?"

"That's an entirely inappropriate question. I'm not your counsel. I may have an opinion as to what your counsel would advise, if you had one, but I'm not going to say anything."

"I know what you're saying," said Tabitha. "I know what my lawyer would say because I know what my lawyer did say."

Now Simon Brockbank looked irritated as well as bored.

"I don't think this is the time or the place for a lecture on the basis of the British legal system. We've come here to make an offer. In my opinion, it is an exceptionally reasonable offer."

"I just want the truth," said Tabitha, almost talking to herself. "I want people to know the truth. I want to know the truth myself."

"Please," said Brockbank firmly. "Time is short. We need an answer."

Tabitha was in turmoil but it was only turmoil due to the knowledge that her choice was really no choice at all. As if she were standing at the edge of the abyss and she had no doubt that she was going to leap off it into the darkness because that was the only way of discovering what lay inside that darkness.

"I'm sorry," she said. "The answer is no."

"What do you mean, no?"

"I'm not going to plead guilty. I can't."

There was a long silence. Tabitha had been staring down at the linoleum floor. She had seen that it was worn in patches and she wondered what had caused the wear. Was it caused by desperate people walking up and down? People like her? She looked up at the two lawyers. Brockbank no longer looked insouciant; there was a glint of interest in his eyes.

"I thought you'd accept," he said. "The prosecution has an exceptionally strong case. You're defending yourself. I'm not clear as to your reasoning."

"This isn't a game to me," said Tabitha.

"Nor should it be. I simply want you to be clear of the implications of your decision. You risk being in prison until you are middle-aged. And I can tell you that at the end of fifteen or twenty or twenty-five years, people don't come out the way they went in."

"You think I'm mad."

"I don't think you realize the situation you're in. I should add that this offer goes away in about five minutes' time."

Tabitha was panting now, as if she were running or carrying a heavy object.

"I can't," she said.

"Fine," said Brockbank. "Then we need to go upstairs and meet the jury."

"One thing," Tabitha said.

"What?"

"What happened to the original McKenzie?"

Brockbank looked puzzled.

"What do you mean?"

"McKenzie. As in, McKenzie friend."

"Oh, he lost the case. Because he didn't have proper representation."

He rapped against the door and then looked back at Tabitha. His expression was almost regretful. "I'm not going to enjoy prosecuting this case. But I'm afraid that won't do you much good."

Tabitha had heard of those dreams where people find themselves on a stage, not knowing the lines, not even knowing what the play is. Tabitha had never been on a stage and she had never dreamed about being onstage, so she had never understood the anxiety behind it.

She understood now.

The previous months had been so awful. The claustrophobia, the sense of unreality, the dread, the sense of sheer physical fear. But it had all been a preparation for the main event, for this.

A female police officer with a round face and crooked teeth led Tabitha out of her cell, along the corridor, turning this way and that, then up some stairs. It all felt strangely dingy and shabby. The paint was peeling on the walls, there were cracks in the linoleum on the floor. At the top of the stairs, the officer paused in front of a polished wooden door. She looked round at Tabitha.

"You call her "'My Lady,'" she said.

"What?"

"The judge. You call her 'My Lady.' Normally it's 'Your Honor' but Munday's a High Court judge. They have High Court judges for big cases like this."

"I knew that," said Tabitha. "It's about the only thing I do know." So this was a big case. She knew it was big for her. She hadn't thought about it being big for other people. Of course it was. Murder. What was bigger than that?

The officer knocked on the door. It opened and they stepped through into the light and, yes, it really was like stepping out onto a stage. Tabitha was in a daze. Everything was blurry. She thought she might faint. They took a few more steps into a little enclosure surrounded by what looked like transparent plastic sheeting. There was just a chair and a simple wooden table. She was uncuffed and she sat down. The officer sat behind her and laid her hands placidly on her lap.

Tabitha thought, and she felt stupid as she did so: *This is really happening.*

She looked around. The large room was wood paneled, but this was not the paneling of an old country house. It looked more like a seminar room from a new university. Below her were three rows of desks. Sitting at them were people in suits and two people in gowns and short wigs. She quickly recognized them as Simon Brockbank and Elinor Ackroyd. Every single person had an open laptop in front of them. Every single person except for her. All the faces looked up at her, as if interested to see what Tabitha Hardy looked like in real life. She had a sudden sense of herself as the star of the show. The bull in the bullfight. One of the faces seemed to come into focus and she saw it was Michaela. She was almost unrecognizable in a dark trouser suit. She was holding a thumb up. Tabitha didn't feel able to hold up a thumb in response.

"All rise," said a voice.

Tabitha looked around, puzzled, and saw the officer gesturing at her to stand. A door in the far wall opened and a figure entered. Tabitha saw a red robe, an off-white wig and a pale face. The figure sat down and nodded at the prosecution lawyers. Everybody in the court sat. When the judge spoke, Tabitha was surprised to hear a woman's voice, although she shouldn't have been. She had been told repeatedly.

The judge put on a pair of half-moon spectacles, shuffled through some papers in front of her and opened a laptop. She looked around and seemed to notice Tabitha for the first time. She frowned.

"Today we're going to deal with some preliminary matters," she said. "Do you understand?"

She sounded like a very grand headmistress. A headmistress from an earlier age. Tabitha's own headmistress had not been grand.

"Not really," said Tabitha.

The judge gave an exasperated sigh.

"This is why we have counsel."

"Counsel?"

"Barristers. Lawyers." She sighed again. "But there's no point talking about that now. You'll just have to do your best. I'll try to give you some guidance but there's only so much I can do. For example, is there any prosecution evidence that you want excluded?"

"I'm sorry," said Tabitha, "but I can't properly hear what you're saying. Am I going to be stuck in this plastic box for the whole trial?"

"You're the accused. The accused sits in the dock."

"So what was your question?"

Judge Munday repeated it.

"Like what evidence?"

"That's entirely up to you."

"I don't know. I don't even know what that means."

Judge Munday took a long slow breath.

"I'll take that as a no," she said and wrote something on a pad in front of her. She turned to the prosecution lawyers. Brockbank stood up. He put his hands in his pockets.

"I'm hoping we can arrange for the witness statements to be read out. To save time."

"What does that mean?" said Tabitha in a raised voice.

"There's no need to shout, Miss Hardy," said Judge Munday.

"*Ms.* Hardy."

Judge Munday paused. It looked like she was swallowing a piece of food that was hard to get down.

"Ms. Hardy," she said finally. "All statements are to be addressed to me, not to anyone else in court. Unless you are cross-examining a witness. Evidence that is accepted as an agreed fact can simply be read out to the court."

"No," said Tabitha.

"What do you mean no?"

"I don't accept it."

"Which evidence don't you accept?"

"None of it."

Judge Munday slowly took off her spectacles.

"Ms. Hardy, you cannot simply waste the court's time."

"I'm fighting for my life," said Tabitha breathlessly. "I'm not wasting anybody's time."

There was a pause. Brockbank gave a cough.

"Perhaps it might help if we went through the witnesses one by one," he said.

He went through them all: the police officers, the forensic investigator, the pathologist, the various fellow villagers, and in each case Tabitha said that she didn't accept it and that they would have to give evidence in person. Finally he sat down and Judge Munday gave another sigh and picked up a piece of paper and scrutinized it for a moment and then looked at Tabitha.

"I have to say that your defense statement was wholly unsatisfactory."

"What do you mean?"

"The purpose of the defense statement is to define the issues on which your defense will rely. There is none of that here. There is nothing."

Tabitha couldn't think of anything to say. Again it felt like she was standing in front of a headmistress being dressed down. Tabitha had never been good in situations like that. Judge Munday put the piece of paper down.

"Ms. Hardy," she said. "I don't know what you've been told about conducting your own defense. Some defendants seem to see it as a way of creating confusion and throwing dust in the eyes of the jury. I can assure you that you will be treated fairly but I will not allow that to happen in my courtroom. Do you understand?"

"I really don't know—"

"Do you understand?"

"Yes."

"Good. We'll begin with the opening statements tomorrow."

She stood up and everybody stood up with her.

Fifty-three

Tabitha clutched her notebook. She stared through the Plexiglas at the court.

There was Michaela with all the files in front of her; today she was wearing a vibrant green dress which cheered Tabitha slightly: she was a flash of color and disobedience in a room of grays and blacks.

There was the jury who had been sworn in that morning, seven men and five women, and Tabitha didn't like the look of that man on the left with a military mustache or the woman with hair like a bowl and a look of disapproval already on her face. Or the young man who kept picking his teeth for that matter. She had thought of objecting, opened her mouth to do so, then stopped: not liking the way someone looked at her wasn't a reason for throwing them off the jury.

There was Simon Brockbank and Elinor Ackroyd in their flappy gowns and their stupid wigs.

And Judge Munday sitting in state, files stacked in front of her. It was hard to believe there was a normal woman under her wig and robe.

There were other people as well, some of them tapping on their laptops. Tabitha didn't know who they all were. She guessed the men and women with notebooks must be journalists. And there were a handful of people up in the public gallery. She met the eye of an old man who was gazing avidly at her and looked away, feeling suddenly nauseous. Then she saw Michael gazing down at her and his face had lost its disapproving expression and was kind. She blinked. The face resolved. Of course it wasn't Michael. Of course he hadn't come. Nobody had come, only curious strangers.

She felt humiliated, utterly exposed and shamed, sitting like an exhibit in this horrible wooden box, everyone examining her and speaking about her and having opinions about her. Her suit itched; it was like thousands of tiny insects were crawling under her skin. The courtroom came in and out of focus. She knew that she had to concentrate but her mind kept drifting. Suddenly she remembered a math lesson long ago, and Stuart Rees leaning over her as she worked, his breath hot and stale on her neck. How had she let him—? She bunched her fists: she needed to focus.

Now Simon Brockbank was standing, pulling down his cuffs ever so slightly, taking a small sip of water from the glass, looking down for a moment at the notes in front of him, taking his time over everything, relaxed and composed. He turned toward the jury, looking slightly sorrowful. Tabitha gritted her teeth; there was a precise nub of pain in her temples. She gripped her notebook, leaned forward slightly.

"Members of the jury," Brockbank said. His voice was rich and sonorous. "Over the course of this trial you will hear the testimony of many witnesses and have the opportunity to consider a great deal of evidence, some of which is straightforward and some technical and complicated. But at its heart, this case is very simple. Tabitha Hardy is charged with the murder of Stuart Rees. There can be no graver crime. There might be times when you feel sympathy for her because—as the prosecution will show—she had good reason to feel angry with the murdered man. But do not let pity divert you from your task, which is to decide whether or not on the twenty-first of December 2018 Tabitha Hardy killed Stuart Rees in a premeditated act of murder."

He took another sip of water and turned back to the jury.

"I have been a barrister for more decades than I like to admit." He gave a rueful smile. "And I have to say that I have rarely come across a case that is so straightforward and so—"

Tabitha rapped on the Plexiglas several times. Everyone looked at her. Simon Brockbank's mouth was open in mid-sentence.

"Ms. Hardy?" said Judge Munday. "You will have your opportunity to respond, but this is the prosecution's opening statement."

"I need a pen," said Tabitha. "I need to make notes and I haven't got my pen. Michaela's got some."

Michaela leaped to her feet. She rummaged among the piles of papers in front of her, looking rather frantic, then held up a clutch of pens held together by a thick elastic band.

Judge Munday nodded at a woman seated at the bench below her who rose and made her way to Michaela. She took a pen and brought it to Tabitha.

"Also," said Tabitha, "I can't hear very clearly from here. It's a bit fuzzy. Maybe he can speak more clearly."

Simon Brockbank looked toward her and gave a tight smile then resumed, talking slowly and carefully. Tabitha opened her notebook and several loose pieces of paper dropped to the floor. She picked them up, ducking out of view for a second. The pen didn't work at once and she had to scribble it across the page.

Now he was saying she had motive. She had opportunity. There was ample evidence. He was going to tell the jury the salient facts of the case that would be laid out during the trial.

Tabitha grasped the pen. Her hand was sweaty.

"First of all, motive. When the accused was fifteen, she was involved in a sexual relationship with Stuart Rees." He put up a hand as if someone were trying to interrupt him. "However complicit she might have been at the time, she was underaged and vulnerable. Her life was blighted by this sorry episode."

Tabitha listened to his words rolling out across the court. Her mouth was dry and the precise pain in her head had widened out into a booming ache. She kept her eyes on her notebook, but she could still feel all those eyes on her.

"You will hear," continued Simon Brockbank to the jury, "how she suffered from severe clinical depression, how she had psychotic episodes, how she was hospitalized and how she has been under a regime of drugs to help her cope. It's a sad story," he said solemnly. "Very sad. But"—and here his voice became firm—"it also gives the accused a powerful motive. Tabitha Hardy believed, with reason, that Stuart Rees had destroyed her life and got away with it."

One of the men on the jury nodded. Another juror wrote something on the pad in front of her. Tabitha chewed at her lip until she tasted blood. She was very hot and then suddenly she was cold and shivery. Her whole body felt wrong. For a few moments, she lost her grip on what he was saying. His words slid off her, his mouth opened and closed and expressions passed across his florid face: sorrowful, knowing, stern. She sat up straighter.

He was describing how she had concealed what had happened when she was fifteen from the police. He was making each point clearly and calmly, laying it down slick and flat like a playing card peeled from the deck. How in the last six weeks of his life Stuart Rees had been visibly anxious and how he had abruptly decided to put his house on the market and move from Okeham. "Almost the same number of weeks, members of the jury, that Tabitha Hardy had been living there.

"You will hear," the barrister continued, "various witnesses testifying that the accused publicly threatened Stuart Rees, even on the morning of his murder. You will hear how on that day, she was in a highly agitated state. You will hear how she even went so far as to make a partial confession to one of the residents."

He paused and looked down at his notes once more, gave a preparatory cough before going on. The lights in the court were sour and glaring. *I could just confess*, thought Tabitha. *Have done with this*. She looked at Michaela and Michaela looked back at her and gave her a nod and a smile, then wrinkled her nose in the direction of Simon Brockbank.

Now it was about the distressing images the jury would have to see. Simon Brockbank's voice dropped and he was looking at the twelve men and women compassionately. Tabitha felt rage bubble up in her. She rapped once more on the Plexiglas, as hard as she could. The performance came to a halt. Everyone stared at her.

"When he does that, I can't hear properly," she said in a loud, harsh voice. "How am I meant to defend myself if I can't hear? I shouldn't be sitting here. I should be down there." A phrase belatedly swam into her mind. "My Ladyship," she added, but that was wrong. "My Lady, I mean."

"You are the accused and you sit in the dock," said Judge Munday. "That is the rule of the court."

"You're the judge. You're in charge. You're like the monarch or the dictator or something and you can do what you want. So you can let me sit down there."

"I am indeed the judge. And you will remain in the dock."

"It's not right. I need to hear what he's saying."

"Miss Hardy."

Tabitha banged against the reinforced Plexiglas with her fist, shaking it. "*Ms.*"

"If you continue like this you'll be removed."

There was a high crack of laughter and she realized with a shock that it came from her. "Removed? How? What happens then?"

"At the very least, you will be handcuffed."

"You can't do that."

"As you rightly pointed out, I am in charge of this court. You need to behave in an appropriate manner. Do you understand?"

There was a pause. Tabitha's hands were shaking. "Yes," she said at last. She swallowed. "My Lady."

"Good."

The prosecution statement continued. The fallen tree that cut off the village, meaning the police knew exactly who was there during the crucial hours. The CCTV evidence that fixed the time of murder after ten-thirty in the morning and before three-thirty that afternoon. Stuart Rees's car at Tabitha's house. His body in the shed. The way she had tried to prevent Andy going out there. The blood on her. Her strange behavior at the police station . . .

Tabitha made herself write down each point in turn, because she knew that what she was hearing were the essential bones of the prosecution's case against her. The motive, the opportunity, the evidence. These were the things she needed to unpick. Her thoughts were jumbled, but her writing was surprisingly clear.

At last it was over. The smooth, over-enunciated voice stopped. Simon Brockbank sat down. Elinor Ackroyd whispered something in his ear and he nodded. Judge Munday looked at her watch even though there was a digital clock on the desk.

"We only have forty minutes remaining. Would you like to stop now, Ms. Hardy, and resume with your defense statement tomorrow morning?"

"No," said Tabitha. The judge looked taken aback. "It won't take long. Nothing like forty minutes. Five maybe. I'd like to get it over with, but I need my papers."

She beckoned at Michaela, who rose, lifting the folders. She carried them toward the dock.

"She's my McKenzie friend," Tabitha said to the jury. She tried to smile at them but her lips were cracked.

She took hold of the folders. One dropped onto the floor and Michaela squatted to gather the scattered papers. There was a titter from the public gallery and Judge Munday frowned upward.

"Right," said Tabitha once everything was in front of her. "Right."

She cleared her throat. She opened the top folder then closed it again, because there was too much in there. She opened her notebook and looked down at it. She turned toward the jury, her eyes moving from face to face. There was a moment of complete silence.

"Well," she said. Her voice was even gruffer than usual. She wished she was taller, more solid, less shabby. "If the prosecution really thinks this is such a slam dunk for them, how come they"—she pointed across at Simon Brockbank and Elinor Ackroyd—"yesterday offered to reduce the sentence to manslaughter? They can't have much confidence in—"

"Stop!" The judge's voice was a shout and her face was white with anger. "What on earth do you think you are doing?"

She turned toward the jury.

"I am very sorry that your time has been wasted in this way. You are discharged."

"What have I done?" asked Tabitha.

The judge ignored her, addressing herself instead to the journalists. "All members of the press are under strict instructions not to report what the accused said."

"But I—"

The judge pointed at her. "Be quiet," she said. "You have done quite enough. You are in serious trouble."

"What, more trouble than being on trial for murder? More than that?"

"I take it you understand that the trial will have to start again with a new jury."

"Really?"

"Yes, really."

"Oh."

"All rise," said the court associate.

Judge Munday swept out of the court. The police officer took Tabitha by her arm and led her from the dock. As she left, she heard someone laugh.

Fifty-four

It was very strange to be in a different prison. There were no faces she recognized, no one else in her cell, which was hot and whose little window didn't show the sky but a gray-brown wall. This was a new prison but cheaply constructed and already starting to crack and peel. She almost missed Crow Grange.

She sat on her bed and tried to breathe steadily. Her head banged and her heart banged and her legs felt weak. She was exhausted. The day was like a dream or like a play that she had watched and also starred in: a small, scruffy figure in the dock, and all those grand, robed, wigged figures looking at her, talking about her, angry or smirking at the idiot she had made of herself.

She forced herself to eat the cellophane-wrapped cheese sandwich, which tasted plasticky and bland; she drank the milky, tepid tea.

She couldn't understand how Simon Brockbank had been so in control of all the information—those hundreds of statements and documents and photos and timings—and he had gathered it all smoothly up and offered it to the jury in bullet points. Glancing at the notes had just been a gesture. Whereas she—who had lived through the events he was only describing, and who had had months to assimilate the information and shape it into some kind of narrative—was still in a fog.

She needed to focus. Michaela had taken the folders, but she opened up her moleskin book that was falling apart and gazed at the notes, the lists, the drawings, the arrows and the graphs and the various timelines. She looked at the asterisks and exclamation marks and circled and underlined words. It looked mad. It was mad. She closed the book and closed her eyes and let sleep swamp her.

She dreamed that she was back in Okeham. She was in her house in the darkness and someone was rapping at her door and she knew she mustn't open it but she did. Stuart Rees was standing there but he was the Stuart of fifteen years ago. He beckoned at her, his finger like a hook. The school bus was behind him. She could see her own face at its central window, scribbled over by the crack in the glass, illegible, soundlessly shouting something. The sea was rolling toward her, hissing and swollen and inky black.

She woke with a jerk and stared around her. Her mouth was dry and her head was full of cobwebs and ghosts.

Fifty-five

When Tabitha was a teenager she had gone to see a comedian who gave a brilliant improvisatory performance, drifting from topic to topic in a kind of random free association, bouncing off comments made by the audience. She had been so dazzled by it that she had gone the next night as well. It turned out that it wasn't improvisation at all. Every cough, every stumble, every little digression was identical. Even the apparent off-the-cuff responses to heckles were identical. She had felt let down and grudgingly admiring at the same time.

She felt much the same when she sat and watched Simon Brockbank deliver his opening statement for the second time. The first time it had felt conversational and relaxed, like a man with complete control of the case was thinking aloud, sharing his thoughts with the jury. There had been a moment where he had mentioned Laura Rees, what it was like for her to have to identify the body of the man she had been married to for thirty-five years, when his voice broke, he paused and then took a sip of water, as if the emotion was so great that it had got to him, a hardened professional. The second time, he did it exactly the same way, the same cracking of the voice, the same sip of water. Tabitha almost wanted to laugh and to get up and shout to the jury that this was a fake, a performance. But she didn't. She didn't want the trial stopped all over again.

Instead, her mind started to wander. She looked around the court that was crammed with journalists who must have heard about this lunatic woman who was defending herself, and then she looked up at the public gallery. It too was crowded; she saw faces peering down at her and quickly turned away.

Next, she looked across at the jury. They were sitting in two rows down to her left. She looked along the back row: balding man, like a middle manager, early forties maybe; frizzy, black-haired woman, late thirties, hippyish, big earrings, Tabitha imagined she'd made them herself; round-faced woman, head scarf, looking round and smiling at nothing in particular, thirties; woman, forties, bright pink cardigan, stern face; young man, twenties, hoodie and tee shirt, blotchy face, clearly bored and it was still only the first day; man in his fifties, dressed for court, thin, serious, kept shifting around—to concentrate? Stay awake?

Front row: serious woman, serious hair, serious small round tortoiseshell spectacles, serious dark clothes, probably a doctor; man, trimmed beard, checked shirt, possible geography teacher; older woman, late sixties, comfy, flowery dress; woman in forties, big brown-beaded necklace, ferocious brow, stared up at Tabitha more than any of the others, not in a friendly way; posh woman, mid-forties, immaculate fawn sweater and discreet necklace, precisely made up, Tabitha could imagine her on a horse in tight white trousers; man in a man bun, but too old for it, late forties probably.

There were different sexes, different ages, different races. Tabitha could imagine an alternative universe in which she would be winning them over one by one, crafting a defense that would appeal to each one of them personally. Probably she should at least separate them in her mind into the friendly and the unfriendly. The problem was that they all seemed unfriendly. Scary brow was probably worst, but they all showed varying degrees of suspicion. When they had looked up at her, Tabitha, in her Plexiglas container, had felt like a creature in a zoo. There might as well have been a label: "Tabitha Hardy. Murderer."

"Ms. Hardy?"

Tabitha looked round. She had almost forgotten where she was.

"What?"

"Your defense statement," said Judge Munday.

"What?"

"It's time for you to make it."

Tabitha looked round in dismay. Simon Brockbank had finished his statement and was seated. Both barristers had swiveled in their chairs and were gazing at her, as were the jury, as was the judge, as was everyone in the court, for once not staring down at their laptops.

Tabitha's mind was a complete blank.

"Am I meant to speak from here?" she said.

"This has already been decided," said Judge Munday in a firm tone.

"It just feels like I'm talking from inside a box."

"Please continue."

Tabitha took a deep breath. What if she just didn't say anything? What if she fainted? She looked at the jury, who looked back at her. They were probably starting to feel embarrassed, like at a wedding speech that had gone wrong. Would it make them feel sorry for her? Probably not.

"It might seem a bit strange," she began. "Me here defending myself, without a lawyer."

"I'm sorry," said Judge Munday. "I have to interrupt here. Please be careful what you say, Ms. Hardy." She turned to the jury. "As you will have seen, Ms. Hardy has chosen to represent herself. And as you may know, this is unusual in a case of such importance but it is her free choice. She is perfectly entitled to make it. I want to say two things: the first is that certain parts of the trial may appear more informal as a result." She looked at Tabitha with a frown. "That will not be an excuse for the breaking of the rules of evidence. And secondly, the fact of her defending herself should have no influence on you, either for or against her." She looked back at Tabitha. "You may proceed."

"Thanks," she said. "I mean, thanks, madam. My Lady. I'm not going to say much." The interruption had helped her to gather her thoughts. "I'm not going to go through the whole case the way the other guy did."

"Please call him Mr. Brockbank," said Judge Munday.

"Sorry. Mr. Brockbank. Obviously I'm not an expert. One thing I know is that technically I don't have to prove I'm innocent. I just have to show that you can't rely on the evidence against me. I know that lawyers do it with tricks and creating confusion." She glanced nervously at Judge Munday, who was frowning at her and slowly shaking her head. She looked back at the jury. "I don't want to do that. I want to show you that I didn't do it."

She sat down and for a moment there was a silence broken only by a couple of coughs. Tabitha looked around. Was something the matter? Brockbank stood up.

"Excuse me, My Lady, but can we send the jury out?"

The jury members looked baffled and displeased as they were led out of their seats, round the side of the room and out through the door. As soon as they were gone, Brockbank stood up and said that Tabitha should have given a detailed description of her defense.

"How can I do that until I've seen what people are going to say?" she said.

"You have seen. It's in the prosecution statement you received."

Judge Munday shook her head. "We can't be too rigid about all of that," she said. Then she looked more sternly at Tabitha. "That does not apply to your treatment of witnesses. There are strict rules about direct cross-examination of witnesses by the accused. About those there will be no latitude whatever."

Tabitha had no idea what these rules were, but she just nodded humbly. Judge Munday looked up at the clock.

"I think we'll have time for the first witness," she said.

Dr. Leonard Garner was a consultant pathologist with an alarmingly long list of qualifications. He was tall, with a long, gaunt, serious face and hair that was almost white. He stood erect in the witness box like someone who had been there many times before. He also had a spotted bow tie and some of his hair was combed across his bald head. Tabitha had never understood either of these style choices. When he started to speak, he gave a small sound at the end of each sentence, a kind of hum, and Tabitha quickly found it irritating. It was difficult not to listen to the hum instead of what he was saying.

Dr. Garner had examined Stuart Rees's body at the scene and he had also conducted the autopsy. With almost maddening detail, Brockbank led Dr. Garner through a description first of his own qualifications, then of the body as he had found it at the scene, then the results of the autopsy. Tabitha had already seen the photographs of the stab wounds, but here they had been blown up and stuck on large sheets of cardboard and put on a trestle at the side of the court.

Dr. Garner described the cause of death, shock caused by catastrophic bleeding. One of the multiple knife wounds had virtually severed the carotid artery. Rees would have died within minutes. The wounds were caused by one knife, a single-edged, non-serrated knife, with a maximum width of 3.4 centimeters. A knife from Tabitha's kitchen was produced. Dr. Garner was asked if it was possible that this knife had been used in the murder and he said, yes, it was possible.

Tabitha looked down at Michaela and hissed at her and rapped on the Plexiglas. She looked round.

"Are you taking notes?" Tabitha said.

"Please, Ms. Hardy," said Judge Munday.

"What am I meant to do?" said Tabitha. "I can't whisper to her. She wouldn't be able to hear me."

"Please let the witness continue without being interrupted."

Tabitha wrote the word "knife" on her pad. It was the first note she had taken. She had been looking at the jury while Dr. Garner gave his evidence. When they were shown the photographs of the wounds, two of the women put their hands over their mouths and the man-bun man rubbed his eyes and went very white.

The only surprise came when Dr. Garner was asked about the time of death. He said that because of the temperature of the body at the scene and the progress of rigor mortis and the pooling of blood in the body, he put the time of death at between about 1 P.M. and about 3.30 P.M. Tabitha wrote a note of that with a question mark.

Simon Brockbank thanked Dr. Garner and sat down.

Again everyone turned to Tabitha. She stood up and for a moment she felt as if the court had rotated slightly. She lurched and had to hold on to her chair to stop herself from falling.

She had a vague sense that she ought to say something to defend herself, but she wasn't clear what Dr. Garner's testimony meant for her. Was it actually that damning?

"All right," she said, starting a sentence that she didn't know how to continue. Suddenly she had a thought and she felt herself clutching at it desperately. "Stuart Rees was quite big and strong, wasn't he?"

"I'm really not sure."

"You did the autopsy. Don't you take measurements?"

Dr. Garner had an open laptop in front of him on the witness stand. He looked down at it and tapped at the keyboard.

"Stuart Rees was just over five feet ten inches tall. I can't speak to his strength."

"But he was bigger than me."

390 · NICCI FRENCH

"I can't really see from here."

"That's because I'm stuck in this ridiculous thing. That's why I have to shout."

"You don't have to shout," said Judge Munday. "We can hear you perfectly well."

"Sorry, My Lady. All right, I'm five foot one, if that. So he was much bigger than me, right?"

"Bigger, yes."

"The stab wounds were all from the front, yes?"

"One of them was on the right side of the abdomen."

"So doesn't it seem unlikely that someone of my size could do that to someone of his size?"

"No."

"No?" Tabitha hadn't expected such a stark response. "Well, maybe other people won't agree with that."

Dr. Garner turned to the judge. "Is it all right if I expand on that?"

"Of course," said Judge Munday.

Dr. Garner proceeded to give a detailed account of a recent autopsy he had conducted. In a gang-related incident, the victim, taller and stronger than Stuart Rees, had been stabbed multiple times by a young woman of about Tabitha's size and build.

"If one person has a sharp knife," he concluded, "and the other doesn't, then size is of less importance."

"Odd, though," said Tabitha, a little desperately.

"I can't comment on that," said Dr. Garner in a dry tone.

Tabitha looked down at her scanty notes in search of inspiration.

"The knife," she said. "The one you said fit the wound. Was it found by the body?"

Dr. Garner paused. "No."

"Where was it found?"

"It was a kitchen knife. I believe it was found in the kitchen."

"It was just a normal knife, wasn't it?"

"Yes."

"There's probably a knife like that in every kitchen, isn't there?"

"In most kitchens, probably. Yes."

Tabitha looked down at her notes again. She felt like there was something that needed asking but she didn't know how to put it.

"I saw a documentary once."

"What?" said Dr. Garner.

"It was about forensics. It was called 'Myth Busting' or something like that. One of the things it said was that all this estimated time of death stuff is all a bit, you know, dubious. Do you know what I mean? I mean, do you agree?"

"No."

The witness box was on the far right of the court-room, just below where the judge sat. Dr. Garner had been looking ahead of him, mainly addressing Judge Munday. But now he turned to look at Tabitha with an expression of distaste. Simon Brockbank had described him as "a leading figure in his field." And now he was having to deal with this.

"You saw the body at about six, right?"

"I arrived at about a quarter past."

"You knew that the police had arrived at about five, so that bit wasn't very hard. But what about the earlier time? You said after one P.M. How did you come up with that time?"

When Dr. Garner replied he spoke slowly and evenly as if he were talking to a small child.

"As I have already explained, there is a formula for the drop in the core temperature of the body."

"If there's a formula, then why don't you give an exact time of death? Two forty-three or something like that?"

"Different bodies cool at different rates. So I put forward a range of possibilities based on long experience."

"Do other things affect it?"

"Affect what?" Dr. Garner was sounding tetchy now. He looked up at Judge Munday. "Is this really necessary?"

She tapped her pen on the desk. She didn't look entirely satisfied with the situation.

"I'll intervene if Ms. Hardy's questions are improper."

He gave another hum. "What was the question?" he said.

"Time of death," said Tabitha. "What other things affect it?"

"Many factors. Surrounding temperatures, the way in which the body was kept."

"You said between one and three-thirty. What about twelve o'clock? Would that be impossible?"

"Unlikely. On the information I was given. Or obtained."

"Impossible?"

"Unlikely."

"Eleven?"

"I'm just giving my expert testimony."

"Ten?"

"Really," said Dr. Garner, "this is absurd."

"Absurd? I'm on trial for my fucking life," said Tabitha.

"Ms. Hardy," said Judge Munday in a raised tone. "You are not to use language like that in my court. And you are not to address a witness like that."

"I'm sorry. But I just wanted to say that this is just guesswork."

"You're not meant to just say things," said Judge Munday. "You're meant to ask questions."

Tabitha thought for a moment. "It's guesswork, isn't it?" she said.

"No," said Dr. Garner.

She sat down. She didn't feel pleased with her performance. She had done what she had promised not to do: she had created confusion for its own sake.

Fifty-six

"Look what they let me in with," said Michaela the next morning, shouldering her way into the cell with her files under one arm and her canvas bags slung over the other shoulder. She was wearing a pinstriped jacket and leopard-print leggings and her hair was tied back in complicated braids. She smelt of tobacco and a perfume that was musky and reminded Tabitha of dark basements.

"Real coffee!" said Tabitha, as Michaela held out a cardboard cup.

"And"—Michaela put down all her burdens and rustled in one of the bags—"cinnamon buns!"

"Amazing," said Tabitha, though she had no appetite. Her stomach felt loose with the anticipation of the day ahead.

She took the coffee. It was strong and bitter and gave her a welcome jolt.

"There is a queue going all the way along the side of the building."

"What do you mean?"

"People queuing up to get a seat in the public gallery."

"Why?"

"I think you've made a bit of a stir the last time. Word must have got around. Someone told me they started queuing at six."

"Christ, that's all I need."

"Are you ready for the day?"

"I've felt readier. Remind me of the schedule."

Michaela opened the first file and took off the top page.

"I put everything in order last night," she said. "It took ages; everything had got in a bit of a mess what with you dropping things. Here. First off, Pauline Leavitt, whoever she may be."

"Someone who doesn't like me," said Tabitha.

"Oh." Michaela held out a bun encouragingly. "And then it's Laura Rees. Have you worked out what you want to ask them both?"

"No."

"Playing it by ear?"

"That's one way of putting it."

Pauline Leavitt walked with a stick. It seemed to take a painfully long time for her to reach the witness box. Tabitha glanced at the jury: the serious woman looked even more serious; Blinky in her hippyish clothes was blinking more than ever and slightly nodding as if to encourage the old lady; the ponytail man was chewing his thumb reflectively; the smiley woman in the head scarf was gazing at Pauline Leavitt with an expression of intense sympathy, while beardy guy steepled his hands and rested his chin on them and looked sad. For the briefest moment, Tabitha's eyes met those of Scary, whose expression was wrathful, the storm clouds gathering.

There was a lot of unnecessary fussing. Pauline Leavitt was asked if she was quite sure she was comfortable. She was handed a glass of water. She was thanked for being in court. She was told that if she needed a break at any point she should simply say. Tabitha felt her irritation growing: it wasn't as if Pauline Leavitt had witnessed anything unpleasant or suffered some kind of trauma, and yet because she had white hair and limped—limped, what's more, like she never did in

Okeham—everyone was treating her with exaggerated deference and care. Tabitha realized that her face had become scrunched up in a scowl. She tried to soften her expression.

Pauline Leavitt took her oath on the Bible. She was led, with infinite gentleness, through the throat-clearing bit about who she was and where she lived and how she knew Tabitha.

"I wouldn't say I know her really," she said and gave a sweet smile that to Tabitha seemed a small curl of sheer malice. "She doesn't exactly mix with the rest of us. We pride ourselves on being a welcoming community in Okeham, but she has never been very friendly."

Tabitha stood up and rapped on the Plexiglas.

"Yes?" Judge Munday looked at her with her eyebrows arched.

"That's not true, they're not at all welcoming, or not to someone like me who doesn't—"

"Please be quiet, Ms. Hardy. You will get your chance later, if you choose to cross-examine. If you feel that the witness's remarks are prejudicial or irrelevant you may object."

"I object."

"Ms. Hardy, this isn't an American courtroom. We don't have objections and we don't have gavels. If you want to raise a legal point, then you can stand up and make it courteously. But mainly you should wait until it's your turn."

"I always had only friendly feelings toward her," Pauline Leavitt continued complacently. "I felt sorry for her." Tabitha bunched her fists. "She was obviously lonely, but I'm afraid she was her own worst enemy."

The comfy juror gave an understanding nod. The blotchy young man yawned.

"On the twenty-fourth of December you went of your own volition to the police station and made a statement. Is that correct?"

"Yes."

Simon Brockbank made a great show of finding the statement. "Page twenty-three in your folder," he said to the jury. He cleared his throat. "The relevant part is very short. I am going to read it out to you. 'Sometime in the days before the twenty-first of December I saw Tabitha Hardy talking to Stuart Rees while I was out walking with my dog. They both seemed agitated. She was saying something like "I'll get you. I promise that I'll get you." Do you remember making that statement?"

"Yes, I do."

"And you stand by it."

"Most certainly. I remember it like it was yesterday. I am old but I have an excellent memory," she added, addressing the jury.

"Thank you," said Simon Brockbank. "So to be absolutely clear, you saw the accused talking to Stuart Rees in the days leading up to his murder, and you clearly heard her verbally threatening him."

"That's right."

"'I'll get you, I promise that I'll get you,'" he said, very slowly and very clearly.

"Yes."

Tabitha rapped on the Plexiglas. The judge looked toward her.

"Or something like that," said Tabitha. "That's what the statement says: 'or something like that.'"

"That's right," said Judge Munday, and Tabitha felt a surge of triumph: for the first time, she wasn't disapproving.

"I was coming to that," said Simon Brockbank smoothly. He turned back to Pauline Leavitt. "'Or something like that': I take it you meant that was the gist of the accused's words?"

"I'm sorry?"

"What did you mean when you said 'something like that'?" asked the barrister patiently.

Tabitha scribbled a note on her pad.

"I wanted to be very truthful and not say anything to the police that might not be completely accurate. I just meant that she might have used ever-so-slightly different words. Like, 'I promise I will get you soon' or 'I swear I will get you' or 'I promise I will get you for what you did,' or even—"

"Thank you," said Simon Brockbank, cutting her off. "And what was the manner of the accused when she was saying these words?"

"She looked angry. And—" She stopped for a moment.

"Take your time."

"A bit frightening, if I'm honest. Out of control."

Tabitha lifted her hand to knock against the Plexiglas but let it drop.

"And what about Stuart Rees?" asked the barrister, after a pause to let Pauline Leavitt's words sink in. "How did he respond?"

"I don't know. His back was to me."

"I see. So what did you take from the exchange?"

"I took from the exchange that she was angry and threatening him. But I never thought she would actually kill him."

"And did you repeat what you had heard to anyone else? I mean, it must have been rather shocking for you to hear such words."

"It was shocking. It was very shocking. But I didn't tell anyone else."

"Why not?"

Pauline Leavitt pursed her lips and looked solemn. "I'm not a gossip," she said.

Tabitha let out a small snort and Judge Munday glared warningly at her.

"I thought it best to keep quiet," the old woman continued. "Though of course if I'd believed for a single minute that . . ." Her voice wavered. She took a sip from her glass of water with a trembling hand. "If only I'd known," she said.

It was Tabitha's turn. She stood up and looked toward Pauline Leavitt, who looked calmly back at her. In a rush, Tabitha understood the old woman actually hated her. She took a steadying breath and turned slightly toward Judge Munday.

"How far from me were you standing?" she asked without raising her voice.

"Sorry? Can you repeat that?"

"It must have been substantially further away than you are from me now," Tabitha said in the same even tone, still looking toward the judge.

"I didn't quite catch—" said Pauline Leavitt. She halted and looked at Brockbank.

Tabitha grinned. "Thank you. I have no further questions, My Lady."

She sat down. Someone in the public gallery gave a loud guffaw and out of the corner of her eye she saw Michaela give one of her thumbs-up signs again. Brockbank rose swiftly.

"The accused cannot seriously be suggesting that there is no difference between hearing a heated argument on the street and hearing someone talk from the dock, with a wall of Plexiglas seriously impeding audibility."

"I'm just saying," said Tabitha, getting to her feet again, "she and me are much closer to each other now than we were then and she obviously couldn't hear me so why should anyone believe what she's saying? I don't. What's more, she"—Tabitha pointed to Judge Munday—"Our Lady, that is, or sorry, My Lady, has already said very emphatically that my audibility is not impeded which is why it's all right for me to be up here, so are you saying the judge is wrong?"

"You were deliberately lowering your voice," said Brockbank. On his face was an expression of studied outrage.

"That's enough," said Judge Munday.

"I'm just—" began Tabitha.

"I know exactly what you're doing. I do not need

your help, thank you. I do the ruling in this court." She took off her glasses and rubbed her eyes, looking suddenly older and less impregnable. "Very well, we will break for lunch and after that you may sit on the bench."

"Really?"

"Does that mean, My Lady," said Simon Brockbank quickly, "that my point about the inaudibility of the accused from the dock is accepted by the court?"

"No, it does not. It simply means that the accused can take her place on the lawyer's bench."

Fifty-seven

"Well played," Brockbank murmured an hour and a half later as she took up her new position.

"This isn't a game."

"You should learn how to take a compliment."

"Fuck off."

"Ms. Hardy," Judge Munday said and Tabitha looked round. Had she been overheard?

"Before the jury come in, I want to warn you. I have grave concerns about allowing you to cross-examine Laura Rees." She pushed her wig back slightly to scratch her head and Tabitha was startled to glimpse short red hair.

"I have to," she said. "It's my right."

"It's for me to decide what your rights are. She is the wife of the man who you are accused of murdering. There are strict rules about this kind of thing. If you step out of line, I will come down heavily on you. Do you hear?"

"I don't know what the rules are."

Judge Munday sighed. "Keep to your brief. Don't ask questions that are irrelevant or unnecessarily distressing. Basically, behave like a decent and rational human being, if that's not beyond you. If you step out of line, I will force you to have representation."

"Can you do that?"

"As you so usefully reminded Mr. Brockbank, I rule this court."

Laura Rees made a good witness. She was dressed soberly, in a dark suit that she probably wore to funerals, with low-heeled shoes and a flowery blue scarf tied carefully round her neck. Her hair was neat but softer than usual. She looked like what she was: a solidly respectable, trustworthy, unflamboyant Englishwoman in her middle age who would tell the unvarnished truth and be incapable of lying.

The press gallery was crammed and the public gallery too. Glancing up, Tabitha saw strangers looking down at her with greedy curiosity.

There was complete silence as Laura Rees was led through her testimony. Elinor Ackroyd was asking the questions, woman to woman. She had a beautiful voice, low and clear. Her face was eloquent with sympathy. Tabitha, seated at the bench with a pile of papers in front of her and her notebook on her lap, could hardly bear to listen.

It began, as she had known it must, with the abuse of fifteen years ago. She kept her head ducked down as Laura Rees answered the questions, but even so she felt dozens of eyes watching her, examining her, undressing her until she was naked and a wretched teenager again, and she had a sense of such shame and vulnerability that if she could have crawled under the desk she would have done.

Yes, Laura Rees had been aware of the episode at the time. (Tabitha scribbled a note on the use of the singular noun.)

Yes, her husband had confessed to her. He had been very upset and contrite. He had promised nothing like this had ever happened before and it would never happen again.

Elinor Ackroyd asked, very delicately, about the illegality of it: he was in his forties and her teacher; she had been fifteen. Laura Rees answered her steadily, though her voice was slightly hoarse and every so often she stopped to take a sip of water. It was very wrong, she said. But her husband had sworn that Tabitha had initiated it and he had been weak and foolish. Michaela hissed something inaudible under her breath.

Yes, Laura continued, she had chosen to believe him. (Tabitha scribbled another note about the wording.)

And she had forgiven him because she was his wife, stayed with him because she was his wife: as wives do all over the world, she was implying, and Pinky and Smiley, and Blinky, Posh, Comfy and Doc all leaned forward slightly, united in their shared understanding of what wives do and what wives knew. Tabitha scowled down at her ringless hands with their bitten fingernails. Michaela calmly put a tab of chewing gum in her mouth.

"It was a relief when she moved away," said Laura Rees. "We could go back to normal."

Tabitha wanted to leap up and howl: "What about me, what about what I felt, what about me never being able to go back to normal?" But though she visibly squirmed in her seat she kept quiet.

Now they had jumped forward to the weeks leading up to the murder and Tabitha's return to the village.

"You were suddenly neighbors," said Elinor Ackroyd.

"Yes."

"How did you feel about that?"

Laura Rees hesitated for a moment. "I'm not sure," she said. "It had happened so long ago. You just get on with things, don't you? Make do."

"How did your husband feel?"

"He didn't talk about it and I didn't ask him. But I know he felt very anxious."

"How do you know?"

"Because he told me that we had to leave the village."

"Let me get this absolutely clear: you are saying that as soon as the accused returned to Okeham your husband decided you had to leave?"

"Yes."

"Are you quite sure that the two things are connected?"

"What other reason would there be?"

"Did you ask him directly?"

"No."

"Why not?"

Laura Rees took another drink of water. "Because I already knew," she said. "So why confront him? It would only muddy the waters."

"Did you put your house on the market?"

"Yes. We were going to have viewings early in the new year."

They moved on to the day itself. Tabitha flicked through her notes but couldn't find the pages where she had written things about Laura. Her hands were sweaty. Laura's uninflected, hoarse voice and Elinor Ackroyd's clear, low one went on, back and forth: how Laura had left home at 9:30 A.M. to see a client; how she had returned at 3:30 P.M., earlier than usual because her son was coming home for Christmas; how her husband wasn't there and nor was his car in the drive, but she hadn't thought anything of that.

There was nothing that Tabitha didn't already know, hadn't read several times. Laura Rees even used the same phrases she had used in her statement to the police. Everyone's memories, thought Tabitha, were just memories of memories of memories of what they had said six months ago.

It was very hot in the court. There was a fly buzzing nearby though she couldn't see it. She twisted her head and found herself looking at a journalist on the press bench with small eyes and a double chin and he stared back then wrote something down. She returned to doodling in her notebook. She drew her house. She drew a fly. She drew a face and put a wig on it. She could feel her eyes grow heavy and she forced them wide. How could she be in danger of falling asleep when she was on trial for murder and the widow of the man she was meant to have killed was giving evidence a few feet from her?

Then suddenly it was over. Elinor Ackroyd sat down. Laura Rees smoothed her hair and fiddled with her scarf and her eyes flickered briefly across to Tabitha. The judge ordered a break. The court all rose.

"I know this is hard for you," said Tabitha. "And it must feel really weird as well. It does for me too."

"Ms. Hardy," came the judge's voice.

"What? Is that a wrong thing to say? I don't know how this works," she said to Laura, "but I need to ask you a few questions, so well, yes. Here goes."

She cleared her throat. Her mind had gone horribly blank. Along the bench, Simon Brockbank was gently bouncing a pen on the desk. The sound of it ticked in her head.

"Can you stop that?" she said and he serenely laid down his pen and folded his arms.

"Yes, as I was saying. Just a couple of things. First off, the abuse, affair, whatever." Her whole body was hot and itchy; she could feel her face become scarlet. "You said it was just once."

"Did I?"

"Yes. You said 'episode.' That's singular. Do you still believe it was just once?"

"I don't know," said Laura.

Their eyes met, and it felt neither hostile nor friendly.

"Do you accept it might have been more?"

"It might have been, yes."

"If I said it was multiple times, would you be surprised?"

"I don't know."

"Thank you. And also . . ." She glanced down at the scrawled notes she had made. "You also said you *chose* to believe your husband when he said I'd started it."

"Yes."

"Do you still choose to believe that?"

"I don't know," Laura said again.

"So if I were to—" Tabitha felt Michaela pulling on her jacket. "What?" she said, breaking off. "Sorry," she said to Laura. "Hang on."

She leaned toward Michaela, who whispered urgently, "I think this is making it worse."

"What do you mean?"

"Don't you see, all this—him coming on to you, it going on for longer—makes it more likely you'd want to kill him, not less?"

"Oh."

She stood up straight again, faced Laura.

"Can I ask you about this business of moving? Does it really make sense that it was because of me?"

"Yes."

"I mean, did he ever say I had threatened him?"

"No."

"Because whatever Pauline Leavitt said, I hadn't."

"Ms. Hardy!" reprimanded the judge at the same time as Simon Brockbank got to his feet.

"Sorry. OK. So he never actually said I'd been threatening him, is that right?"

"All I know," said Laura Rees, "is that you arrived in Okeham at exactly the time he became anxious and decided to move."

"I want to ask you about the day itself. You went to meet a client?"

"Yes."

"But you never met him?"

"No."

"Isn't that a bit odd?"

"Not really."

"*I* think it's odd."

Brockbank was picking at his nails and half smiling to himself.

"What is your point?" asked Judge Munday.

"I'm just saying it's a bit fishy," said Tabitha. "And then your husband also had a meeting he didn't get to."

"I don't understand what the question is."

"Do you have any idea of where he was going that morning?"

"No."

"Isn't that a bit strange?"

"Not at all."

"It's a bit of a coincidence, isn't it? That neither of you got to your meetings?"

Laura looked at her with something approaching pity. "A tree prevented him leaving the village, that's all."

There was a titter from the public gallery. Tabitha looked up and tried to see where it came from and met row upon row of faces gazing down at her, craning their necks to get a clearer view. She'd lost track of where she was heading.

She rifled uselessly through the papers in front of her. "Most of what you've told us is about what your husband told you."

"I'm just answering questions," said Laura Rees. "As best as I can."

"But what if you can't trust him?"

"I've warned you, Ms. Hardy." This from the judge.

"It's all right, I can ask this. It's relevant. Did you trust your husband not to lie to you, or to tell you things that were important and that you had a right to know?"

There was a long silence. The fly buzzed. She

could hear the faint, tacky sound of Michaela chewing her gum.

"I was married to him," Laura said at last.

"I know, and I know you believe in duty and stuff. But was it a good marriage?" Vaguely, she heard the judge speaking sternly and Brockbank objecting, but she plowed on. "Or did he treat you badly too?"

"He was my husband," said Laura. A single fat tear began to roll down her cheek.

"Sorry," said Tabitha. "Sorry, but this is my life on the line."

"No more questions," said Judge Munday.

"I think he was a bully and cruel to you and you were unhappy; I think he was cruel to lots of people; I think lots of people wanted—"

"Stop right now!"

"Can I ask her one more question?"

"Certainly not."

"Do you really think I did it?" she asked Laura.

Michaela was tugging on her jacket urgently again, trying to shut her up.

"Clear the court."

Laura looked directly at Tabitha. "Didn't you?"

"That was really stupid," said Michaela grimly.

"What?"

416 · NICCI FRENCH

"Asking if she thought you did it."

"You're probably right."

"What were you thinking?"

"I don't know."

"Promise me never to ask that question again."

"OK."

"No. I mean it. If you want me to do this, promise me."

"I promise."

Tabitha leaned over the toilet bowl and vomited, until she had nothing left in her stomach and was only retching. When she was done, she washed her hands and her face; she felt frail and used up and grimy all over.

The police officer stood by and watched, without saying anything. Then she took Tabitha out to the van and the van took her back through the gorgeous June day to her cell.

Fifty-eight

When Tabitha saw Dr. Owen Mallon in the witness box, she realized that she wasn't the only one who was nervous. It was almost touching. She was used to seeing him in his running clothes or a casual shirt and jacket. He'd been a friendly face and displayed a feeling of assurance that came from a doctor who knew people's secrets, who looked beneath the surface. But now he was wearing a slightly ill-fitting suit and sober tie; his hair was brushed. He wasn't sweating, but there was a stiffness about his expression that made him look different. And he was in court to give evidence for the prosecution.

He affirmed rather than taking an oath on a Bible and as he took the card, Tabitha noticed that his hand trembled slightly and he glanced round, caught her eye and looked back at the card.

"I do solemnly, sincerely and truly declare and affirm that the evidence I shall give shall be the truth, the whole truth and nothing but the truth."

He looked back at the card as if not sure what to do with it. The court usher took it from him. Then Simon Brockbank stood up and gently began questioning him and Tabitha learned things about Dr. Mallon she hadn't known. He'd been trained in Nottingham, he had an extra degree in community medicine, and he'd taken a year off to work at a hospital in rural South Africa. She looked over at the jury. They looked blank, as usual, but surely they must be impressed. This prosecution witness was not just a doctor but a doctor who had spent a year treating the poor in Africa.

"Would you describe yourself as a friend of Ms. Hardy?" Brockbank asked.

Mallon looked doubtful. "An acquaintance, I suppose. We used to meet in the village. When I was out running and she was returning from a swim, that sort of thing."

"How would you describe her normal demeanor during these meetings?"

"Objection!" shouted Tabitha.

"Please be quiet," said Judge Munday. She looked at Mallon. "Please proceed."

He seemed shaken by the interruption and the question had to be repeated.

"I would say that she seemed moody, agitated."

"Could you be specific?"

He thought for a moment. "She'd only been there for a few weeks. We nodded at each other, the way you do in the village. But there was one particular conversation we had when I asked her how things were going. She said that things weren't going well, so I asked why she'd come back and she said 'unfinished business.'"

"Hmm," said Brockbank. "Unfinished business. That's an interesting phrase. What did you make of it?"

"I wasn't sure what to make of it."

"Did it make you feel concerned?"

"I was concerned for *her*."

"Thanks very much," said Tabitha in a sarcastic mutter that came out louder than she intended.

"Please, Ms. Hardy," said Judge Munday. "You can address witnesses through me—when appropriate—or you may address the court, but must not make comments like that."

"Sorry," said Tabitha in a sulky tone.

She was about to raise herself up to start questioning, without any clear idea of what question she was going to ask, but Brockbank started speaking again.

"You were saying that Ms. Hardy seemed agitated?"

"Sometimes."

"But being agitated is one thing. Another issue is whether Ms. Hardy had a propensity to violence." Brockbank paused as if deep in thought. "Did you see any suggestion of that?"

"Yes."

Tabitha felt a jolt of alarm. What was this?

"I was coming back from a run, running along the road near the beach, and ahead of me I saw Ms. Hardy and this local man, Robert Coombe. They were having, well . . ." He was searching for the right word.

"An altercation?" said Brockbank. "An argument?"

"I only came as it was ending. She was walking away. I had to help him."

"Help him? Why?"

"His nose was bleeding. I had to check that it wasn't broken."

Brockbank turned to the jury with a theatrical expression of surprise and dismay.

Tabitha had been sitting, stunned, when Michaela leaned across and hissed in her ear, "That wasn't in the statement."

It was like she had woken Tabitha from a dream. She immediately called out, "What's going on? That wasn't in his statement. What's going on?"

"Please," said Judge Munday. "If you have something to say, you stand up, Mr. Brockbank will yield to you and then you can speak. In a level tone."

"All right," said Tabitha, standing up and taking a breath. "That wasn't in Dr. Mallon's statement. Is that OK?"

Judge Munday glanced sharply at Brockbank. "Is that true?"

Brockbank coughed. "Well, I, er . . ." He coughed again.

"Right," she said. "Clear the court."

The jury members got to their feet, gathered notebooks, pens and water bottles and trailed out of the court. The public gallery and the press gallery also emptied. Finally there was silence.

"Mr. Brockbank," said Judge Munday. "What's going on?"

Simon Brockbank and Elinor Ackroyd had been huddled together, whispering urgently. Now he looked round and hastily stood up.

"I'm sorry," he said, in quite a different tone from any he had used before. "There must have been a fail-

422 • NICCI FRENCH

ure of communication. Dr. Mallon was reinterviewed. Someone must have forgotten to, er . . ."

"Follow their legal responsibility to send it to the defense? Is that what you mean, Mr. Brockbank?"

"I apologize to the court," he said, bowing his head slightly. "I'm minded to stop that entire line of examination."

"What good's that?" said Tabitha. "You've said it now. You told the jury that I got into a fight. What are you going to do? Tell them that they have to forget it because of some technicality?"

Everything about Judge Munday looked very stern, her tightened lips, her furrowed brow. And for once it wasn't aimed at Tabitha.

"Ms. Hardy is absolutely correct. I think we'll have to proceed. But"—and she rapped her knuckles on the desk—"if you try this one more time, there will be trouble. Do you understand?"

"Yes, My Lady."

She turned to Tabitha.

"You're entitled to a recess, if you want, to go over this evidence. Would you like that?"

Tabitha looked at Michaela, who shrugged. She felt shocked and jangled and she could do with a rest. But Simon Brockbank looked a bit shaken as well and Mallon was probably worrying about what had happened. Besides, she knew what he was going to say.

"We might as well go on," she said.

When Brockbank resumed his examination, it was in a more routine tone. He established that Coombe had been bleeding and Mallon had helped to stanch the bleeding and Coombe had been shaken by the experience and no, Dr. Mallon had never seen an act of violence like that in the village before. Had it raised a concern in his mind about Ms. Hardy's psychological state? Yes, it had.

Michaela leaned over and whispered in Tabitha's ear:

"So what did he do? Did he call the police? Call an ambulance?"

"All right," Tabitha whispered back. "Good. All right."

She looked round. She realized that Judge Munday and the members of the court were looking at her. Brockbank had finished his examination. She stood up and stared straight at Dr. Mallon. He glanced away and then back at her. He looked unhappy.

"Did you call the police?" she asked.

"What?" said Mallon. "No."

She looked down again. "Did you call an ambulance?"

"It was just a nosebleed."

"Nosebleeds can be serious."

"This wasn't a serious nosebleed."

"Did Rob Coombe tell you what had happened?"

"No."

"Did you ask him?"

"No."

"How long were you with him?"

"I don't know, a couple of minutes."

"And then you left him?"

"Yes."

"Weren't you worried I might come back and hit him again?"

Mallon gave the faintest of smiles but didn't reply.

"You've got to give an answer."

"I didn't think about it."

Tabitha couldn't think of any more questions about this. Michaela nudged her elbow and she looked round. On her pad, Michaela had written in capital letters: "2ND INTERVIEW. WHY?" Tabitha looked questioningly at her but Michaela just nodded. Tabitha turned back to Mallon.

"Why did the police do a second interview with you?"

"You should ask them."

Tabitha felt a moment of panic, as if she had forgotten her next line, and then suddenly she had an idea of what Michaela had meant by her note.

"Hadn't they got enough from the first one?"

There was a moment of hesitation before Mallon answered. "They didn't say."

"Well, what *did* they say?"

"They said to tell them anything I could think of."

"Why didn't you tell them about the thing with Rob Coombe in the first interview?"

"I didn't think of it."

"Because it didn't seem important?"

"I just didn't think of it."

Tabitha felt she'd run out of questions again. She picked up her notebook and flicked through it. Somewhere she had made some notes about when Mallon had come to visit her in prison. She couldn't find them. She remembered a few sketchy details. She wasn't sure they'd be much help.

"Were you Stuart Rees's doctor?"

"Yes."

"That's kind of true and not true, isn't it? I meant, were you Stuart Rees's doctor when he died?"

"No."

"Because he left you."

"He changed doctors."

"And was it a friendly changing of doctors?"

"It wasn't friendly or unfriendly."

"But he didn't just leave. He wrote a letter of complaint, didn't he?"

Mallon gave a nervous smile. "It's more complicated than that."

"You have to answer the question," said Judge Munday.

"He did make a complaint."

"But you stayed friends with Laura Rees?"

"I wouldn't say friends."

"She told me that she talked to you about things. Is that true?"

"We talked a few times."

"What about?"

"I'm a doctor, I can't talk about that."

Tabitha thought for a moment. She felt she was just randomly throwing things at a wall, hoping something would stick.

"So Stuart Rees left and Laura Rees stayed?"

There was a long pause.

"No. Laura Rees left as well."

"Why?"

"She said that her husband . . ." Mallon gave a helpless shrug.

"Insisted?"

"Something like that."

Tabitha thought for a moment. "So obviously I won't ask about when you were her doctor. I'll ask about when you weren't her doctor. Was she unhappy with her husband?"

"You can't just answer a question like that yes or no."

"Did she love him?"

"I don't know. She stayed married to him for many years."

"Was she frightened of him?"

"I don't know what you're trying to say," said Mallon, raising his voice now. "If you're making some kind of accusation, just make it."

Tabitha felt so startled that she couldn't think of anything else to ask. She looked round at the jury and several of them looked visibly startled as well, or at least puzzled. She looked back at Dr. Mallon.

"She wasn't in the village when it happened," Mallon continued, almost plaintively.

"I don't know what you're talking about," said Tabitha. "Who said she was? I'm asking you questions and you keep not answering them."

"Please, Ms. Hardy," said Judge Munday. "You're walking a fine line here. As the accused person defending herself, you have to be careful in your treatment of witnesses."

"He's not a victim," said Tabitha. "He's a doctor. He should be able to look after himself."

"Stop," said Judge Munday. "This is my court." She turned to Mallon and spoke to him courteously but firmly. "Nevertheless, I think this is a reasonable question. Was Mrs. Rees frightened of her husband?"

"Frightened? I don't know. He was controlling."

Judge Munday turned to Tabitha. "Any further questions?"

Tabitha looked at Dr. Mallon. He seemed a diminished figure. When she had arrived in the village and seen him running through the village, exchanged the odd word, he had seemed her sort of person. She could imagine him as a friend. That seemed a long time ago.

"That official complaint," she said. "If it had succeeded, what's the worst that could happen?"

"It wouldn't have succeeded."

Tabitha didn't reply. She just stood there, waiting for him to realize that he would have to answer the question. She looked at him. The silence felt awkward to her, but she knew that it must feel worse for Dr. Mallon.

He gave a cough. "It would—maybe—be some kind of reprimand."

"At worst?" said Tabitha.

"Well, obviously," said Dr. Mallon in an angry, sarcastic tone, "the worst that could happen is that you'd be struck off but that couldn't have happened in this case, so there's no point in mentioning it."

"You're the one who mentioned it," said Tabitha as she sat down.

The judge looked at Simon Brockbank, who just shook his head. More mud on the wall, Tabitha thought to herself, as Dr. Mallon shuffled out of the witness box and passed her, not meeting her eye.

Fifty-nine

Rob Coombe was a big man, not fat but muscled, with broad shoulders, a jowly and slightly florid face and full lips. He had always made Tabitha feel a bit queasy. Whenever he stood near to her, she had caught a rich, pungent smell coming off him: of the farmyard and the gym and the bedroom.

He wasn't wearing a suit, but a pair of dark trousers, a jacket and a tie that she was pleased to see was done up a bit too tightly. He spoke in a loud voice, but she could tell he was anxious. His Adam's apple moved when he swallowed and he grasped the edge of the witness box in both his large hands.

After the traditional précis of who he was (a farmer, like his father, grandfather and great-grandfather before him), where he lived (in the large farmhouse above

Okeham), and his relationship to Tabitha (none, except they lived in the same village and he had always tried to be friendly when they met, "though that hasn't always worked," he added with a smile that was meant, Tabitha imagined, to be ruefully charming), Simon Brockbank asked him about the "altercation."

"It came out of the blue," said Rob Coombe. "I met her outside the shop and I think I asked her about swimming or something, how cold it must be in the water. Just being friendly, the way you are if you live in a village like Okeham. We all have to get on with each other, that's how it works. Except she doesn't seem to understand that. And she punched me."

"Fucker," said Tabitha under her breath and she heard Michaela snort.

"Let me get this straight," said Brockbank with a look of righteous indignation on his face. "You asked her about swimming and she punched you."

"Yes."

"That must have been very shocking."

"It was deeply shocking."

"What did you do?"

"Do?" He looked at the jury and the jury looked at him. Wriggly twitched and Blinky blinked and Beardy stroked his beard. "I'm a big man, as you can see. Well able to look after myself. But I would never hit a lady, especially not a lady who was frail, vulnerable."

"Oh, for God's sake," muttered Tabitha.

"So you're saying you did nothing?"

"That's right."

"How do you explain what happened?"

"I can't. I just think she's always in a bit of a rage, a bit of a wild cat."

Tabitha jumped up. "Wild cat?"

"I've told you how to proceed with your objections, Ms. Hardy," said Judge Munday.

Rob Coombe's dark eyes settled on Tabitha. "Always ready to boil over. Everyone says so."

Judge Munday interrupted.

"Mr. Coombe, it's important that you only talk about what you yourself witnessed, not what other people have said."

"But I witnessed the way people talked about her."

"That's not the same thing."

It took some time to settle this and at the end of it Coombe still didn't seem convinced. Tabitha thought it probably made Coombe look bad, but she wasn't sure it made her look good. The jury had got the (accurate) sense that the people of Okeham didn't much care for her.

"It might be thought," said Brockbank, "that after

this regrettable incident you have a grievance against the accused. Is that the case?"

Coombe shook his head. "Not at all. I felt sorry for her, not angry. I figured I was just in the way. I didn't take it personally. I wished her well. I just hoped," he added virtuously, "that she would be able to sort her life out a bit. You only have to look at her to know she is clearly angry and unhappy."

Before Tabitha could react, Michaela stood up. "You can't say things like that."

"Please sit down, Ms.—"

"Horvat. Michaela Horvat. And he can't say things like that."

"McKenzie friends are not allowed to address the court. And I think the statement is allowable."

Coombe looked across at Tabitha and smiled nastily.

"Now we've got that over," continued Brockbank blandly, "we can move on to the morning of the murder, which is why you have been called to give evidence by the prosecution. You say in your statement to the police that you saw the accused that morning."

"Yes."

"Can you describe what took place?"

"It was around eight," he said. Tabitha scribbled a note. "I was buying a paper and she comes in."

"The accused."

"Yes. And she starts going on about Stuart."

"For the record, Stuart Rees, the victim?"

"Right. She was in one of her moods and she called him a bastard."

"A bastard," repeated Brockbank.

"Right."

"Can you remember in what context she made this comment?"

Coombe shrugged his large shoulders. "It was morning. I was dropping my kid off. I wasn't paying attention. I just remember that. She called him a bastard. I think she said other things about him too, but I can't be sure. She wasn't a happy bunny."

"You are absolutely sure that the accused called Stuart Rees a bastard."

"Yes."

"Did you mention this to anyone?"

"The police obviously. Before them, you mean? Why would I? I mean, if we told each other every time she went off on one, that'd be all we ever talked about. But she said it."

They broke for lunch. Tabitha paced up and down the little cell while Michaela ate her chips.

"I'd like to punch him again," she said.

"Right," said Tabitha. "Let's start with the time I punched you."

He nodded and folded his arms across his chest.

"I'm not disputing it," she said. "I did punch you. You did have a bloody nose." She tried not to smile. That wouldn't look good. "You say you can't remember what you said to me before?"

"Right."

"But you think you said something about me going swimming and how cold it must be?"

"Right," he said again. "Not much of a reason to hit me, was it?"

"You did say that, it's true," said Tabitha. "You said you knew it must have been cold because you could see my nipples through my jersey." A little murmur ran through the court and out of the corner of her eye she could see the jury slightly rearrange itself on the two benches.

"Rubbish," said Rob Coombe. "I wouldn't speak like that to a lady."

"You don't think of me as a lady, though, do you. You think I'm a wild cat."

"That's just a figure of speech."

"Yeah. Then I told you to fuck off and you said

you'd never thought of me as having proper breasts but my nipples looked like bullets and could you feel them to test their hardness."

"That's a lie!"

"You don't remember that?"

"I don't remember it because it never happened."

"I hit you because you asked to touch my nipples."

"This is just desperate."

"And if I'm honest, I'm glad I hit you."

"Why would I want to touch someone as ugly as you?"

Judge Munday intervened like someone trying to stop a pub brawl. When Tabitha resumed, Coombe's voice was even louder now and his face a beefier shade of red.

"You say you were in the shop at shortly after eight?"

"Right."

Michaela handed Tabitha the timeline she had made and she glanced at it.

"I came in at eight-eleven, so that makes sense. And you say I was angry. That was your word, right? And I called Stuart a bastard."

"Right."

"Are you surprised that no one else heard me say that?"

He shrugged. "Not really."

"Or that I don't remember it?"

"That's what you say."

"There was Terry and she hasn't said anything about it, and the driver of the bus and he hasn't said anything. And me. And I don't remember."

"I'm just saying what I heard. You called him a bastard. I'm not going to change my mind, you know."

"I'm sure you're not. But the jury might."

A ripple of laughter went through the public gallery. And the immaculate woman in the second row of jurors actually smiled. Tabitha felt a moment of giddy triumph.

"Where was I?" she said.

Michaela tugged at her sleeve and whispered something.

"Oh yes, I remember now. I need to show the CCTV footage," she said to the judge.

Judge Munday nodded then looked at her watch.

"We will break early," she said, "and meet again on Monday, when we will start with the relevant CCTV footage."

"What! Do you mean I have to come back?" asked Rob Coombe. "I'm a very busy man."

Judge Munday looked at him for a few seconds. Her face was quite blank. "Yes, you have to come back," she said.

Sixty

Tabitha's mood of exhilaration seeped away quickly, leaving her drained and stale. The weekend was a strange interruption. She spent many hours in the library, which wasn't as pleasant as the one in Crow Grange and had no view over fields and woods, trying to prepare for the week ahead, but she was so tired that she couldn't focus on anything. Her thoughts were confused and her eyes heavy. Several times she fell asleep at the table, jerking awake to stare in bewilderment round the unfamiliar surroundings.

She leafed through all her documents. She phoned Michaela. She slept alone in her cell and dreamed she'd had a baby, but a woman in wellington boots and a nun's wimple was trying to take it away from her. Only when she woke did she think it was strange that she had dreamed she had a child.

Then it was Monday, and she was both appalled and relieved that it was time to be in court again.

This time Rob Coombe wore a suit and shiny shoes. Tabitha thought he looked like a boxer, bulky and tense and waiting for the fight to begin.

They started with the CCTV. Tabitha had asked for it to start at 08:05, so the court spent a few minutes looking at the grainy space of empty shop before the door opened and Rob Coombe came in with his daughter behind him, almost hidden by his bulk.

There he was at the counter, gesticulating angrily, his face broken into myriad tiny gray squares so it was hard to make out his expression.

And there she was, entering the shop, in her jacket and her pajama trousers, her face a briefly glimpsed pinch of distress.

The bus driver came and stood behind her.

Rob Coombe was still talking. He took his newspaper and a packet of cigarettes that Terry had to open the little cupboard for. For a few moments he turned and Tabitha saw the back of his head and her own face, pale with tiredness, and her slumped shoulders. She could recognize her own wretchedness as if it was in the court beside her.

Rob Coombe shouldered past her, out of the shop.

She gestured at the clerk and the CCTV was halted.

"Right," she said to the farmer. "I don't know what you just saw, but I saw you doing all the talking."

"Ask a question, Ms. Hardy," said Judge Munday.

"OK. Wasn't that you doing all the talking?"

"No."

"No? We just saw you and you looked really grumpy and you were waving your hands and talking."

"You talked as well. I heard you."

"But you were facing the other direction."

"I didn't say I saw you, I said I heard you. I heard you say Stuart Rees was a bastard. Definitely." He gave a firm nod.

"The camera doesn't show that."

"Just because we can't see you talking doesn't mean you weren't talking."

"You have a loud voice."

"Ask a question," said the judge warningly.

"Wouldn't you agree you have a loud voice?"

"Sometimes. Like everyone else."

"Booming, even." He shrugged. "And do I?" she asked.

"What? I don't get you."

"Do I have a loud voice too?"

"It's a bit scratchy," he said. "Like you've had a cold or something."

"So how could you have heard me while you were booming away there and I was apparently saying something in my scratchy little voice?"

He looked at her. She could imagine him hitting her. She could imagine him doing worse things than that.

"I just did," he said sullenly. He pointed his finger at her. "I heard you abusing Stuart Rees and a few hours later he was dead."

"Maybe it was you who said it." She shot a look at Judge Munday. "I mean, didn't you say it yourself?"

"No."

"It looked like you were saying something angry."

"It was you. End of story."

"Because isn't it true that you were angry with Stuart?"

"No. We got on fine."

"That's very noble of you," said Tabitha, "considering he'd blocked your application to build holiday homes on your land."

Rob Coombe glared at her. His face was flushed. "Be careful," he said.

"But it's OK now," said Tabitha. "It's all going ahead, isn't it? Now he's dead."

"Ms. Hardy," came the warning voice of the judge.

"You watch out," said Rob Coombe in a nasty growl.

"It's OK, you would never hit a lady, would you?"

She was about to sit down when Michaela hissed: "Ask him where he was."

"What?"

"Ask about that day. Like you said you were going to."

"Oh yes, I nearly forgot," Tabitha said to the court. "You dropped your daughter off at the bus stop at about ten past eight so why didn't you go back to your farm?"

"I had a few things to do."

"Like what?"

"I went for a wander, had a cigarette, read my paper in peace, stuff like that. What?" He glowered at her. "You're in a great big hole and you want to smear other people in the muck that's covering you."

"Until the tree came down."

"Yep."

"So you were there all day?"

"So?"

"So where were you?"

She knew of course where he was. He had been with Shona—for some of the time at least. For a moment, she thought she would say it out loud, but she stopped herself, and not just because she couldn't see how it would help her case. The events of the past months had shone a bright and unforgiving spotlight on how people saw her: as plain or even ugly, as mannish, weird, ridiculous, dysfunctional, angry, pathetic, capable of killing someone. But Shona and Andy didn't see her like that.

"Here and there," he said. And then he added, "But nowhere near the Reeses', and if you don't believe me, watch the CCTV, why don't you, and it'll show you I never went in that direction and whatever you're trying to suggest is crap."

And it was true, thought Tabitha, as she sat down, feeling like everything was askew. He might be a sleazy, lying lecher, but the CCTV showed that he hadn't gone beyond the village shop during the day. The jury might not like him much after his time in the witness box, they might not entirely believe that she had called Stuart Rees a bastard, but it didn't alter the solid, unshakeable fact that he couldn't have done the murder. And she could have.

Sixty-one

Tabitha entered the court, but she didn't even get a chance to sit down. An usher came across and touched her on the arm.

"You're to come with me," she said.

"Where?"

"Just follow me."

Still handcuffed to the police officer, Tabitha followed the usher across the court and through the door that was usually reserved for the judge. It felt like going backstage. They entered a corridor that was notably smarter than the one she generally used. There was a carpet, the wall was painted a smooth, smoky blue and there were watercolors on the walls with elegant frames. They reached a brown wooden door with a brass handle. The usher rapped on it softly. There was a murmur from inside which Tabitha couldn't make out, but the usher seemed to understand because she turned the handle and pushed the door inward. She leaned into the gap.

"She's here," she said, stepped aside and gestured to Tabitha to enter.

Tabitha and the officer walked into a room that was so different from anything else Tabitha had seen in the court that it was difficult to believe it was in the same building. Tabitha just saw it in fragments: a richly decorated carpet, heavy furniture, oil paintings on the wall, dark wooden panels, a large window. Through it she could see the branches of a tree. Three faces looked round at her and she didn't recognize them at first. It was only when one of them spoke that she realized it was Judge Munday, not wearing her wig. She had fading ginger hair, cut very short. For the first time, Tabitha thought of her as a real person, eating a boiled egg for breakfast, going on holiday, having friends, having fun, maybe having a family.

"I think we can lose the handcuffs," the judge said.

The officer removed them.

"And perhaps you can wait outside," Judge Munday continued.

The officer looked puzzled by the request. She looked at Tabitha.

446 • NICCI FRENCH

"Behave yourself," she said and left the room, closing the door behind her. Tabitha looked around and saw that the other two people were Simon Brockbank and Elinor Ackroyd, also without their wigs.

"Please sit," said Judge Munday, gesturing at a large armchair.

Tabitha sat and almost sank into it. It felt like they were in a sort of gentleman's club that she had only ever seen in films and that they ought to be smoking cigars and drinking brandy. But she didn't feel relaxed, not at all. Something was up. She could see it in the three faces that were looking at her.

"The prosecution have a new witness," the judge said.

"You mean someone who hasn't been mentioned before?"

"That's right."

"I thought they weren't allowed to do that."

"It's allowed in exceptional circumstances," said Simon Brockbank. Elinor Ackroyd was sitting in another armchair, right on the edge, looking tense, but Brockbank was standing, hands in pockets. "Apparently this witness has only just come forward. It's very regrettable."

He didn't sound as if he really felt it was regrettable.

"Who is it?" said Tabitha, her mouth suddenly dry.

"A woman called Ingrid Bennet. Someone you know apparently."

Tabitha was about to say that she'd never heard of this woman and then she remembered.

"Ingrid," she said. "She was my friend. She helped me, gave me advice. I don't think I'd have got by without her. What's she doing here?"

"I think she's just talking about certain conversations you had."

Tabitha turned to the judge. "I'm sorry, could I have some water?"

Judge Munday filled a glass from a jug on her desk and handed it to Tabitha, who gulped it down so quickly that she had to wipe her chin with the back of her hand.

"I thought you weren't allowed to do that," she said.

"It's an exceptional case," said Brockbank.

"So you can keep ambushing me with different kinds of evidence," said Tabitha. "Is that how it goes?"

There was a pause. Judge Munday looked at Simon Brockbank.

"That seems a fair point to me," she said. "What do you say to that?"

"I'm sorry. I know it's unfortunate. But if new, relevant evidence is given to me, it is my duty to put it to the court."

"Can I object to it?" said Tabitha.

Judge Munday took a deep breath. Tabitha could see that she was angry. There was a steeliness in her expression that was almost frightening.

"Mr. Brockbank is correct," she began slowly. "As far as it goes. But this is the second time this has happened in this trial and I am not pleased about that. I want no suggestion that the prosecution is playing games in my court."

"Of course not," said Simon Brockbank soothingly.

Judge Munday didn't seem to be soothed. "I'll allow this witness. But I'm going to make sure that Ms. Hardy is not unfairly disadvantaged by this." She turned to Tabitha. "If you want a day to prepare for this, I'll give you one. This witness can always appear later."

Judge Munday was still obviously furious. If something bad was coming, then it might be useful to have her slightly on Tabitha's side.

"What would I prepare for?" she said.

Back in court, she sat down next to Michaela and told her what had happened.

"What the fuck," said Michaela rather too loudly and Tabitha saw various officers of the court looking round. "Do you know what she's going to say?"

"I've no idea," said Tabitha. "I guess she'll talk about meeting me in prison. I don't know why that's relevant."

Michaela thought for a moment. "I know what she's going to say," she said.

She started frantically writing notes on her pad. Tabitha couldn't make out what they were.

Suddenly it was like opening time. The public gallery and the press gallery filled up, the jury walked in, looking sullen. Tabitha gave them what she hoped was a friendly nod, but none of them responded. They all rose, the judge entered and they sat down. The new witness was announced and everyone looked round, including Tabitha. She was genuinely curious.

As Ingrid entered the court and was led by an usher to the witness box, Tabitha was impressed, despite herself. She was dressed in a dark suit with a white blouse and a coral brooch at her throat. Her hair was immaculately styled. She seemed as much at home in a courtroom as the lawyers. As she passed the desk where Tabitha and Michaela were seated, she turned and gave a smile and a little twitch of her shoulders as if there was a shared understanding of how comic this was, how slightly absurd. Tabitha started to smile back and then stopped herself, remembering that Ingrid was appearing for the prosecution, not the defense. What was this about?

Ingrid swore her oath on a Bible and she spoke it with a furrowed brow and an expression of concentration as if she was considering every word as she spoke it.

"I swear that the evidence that I shall give shall be the truth, the whole truth and nothing but the truth, so help me God."

Tabitha looked across at the jury. Would the mention of God strengthen their belief in this woman? Probably.

Elinor Ackroyd stood up. So she was going to take the examination. Woman to woman, like with Laura, Tabitha thought. Maybe that was also meant to be more convincing somehow.

"How do you know the accused?"

"We were in Crow Grange Prison together. I was there when she arrived. She was in a distressed state and I think I was someone she could turn to."

Other people giving evidence had seemed nervous, intimidated by the setting. Tabitha was struck by Ingrid's confidence and clarity. She seemed strong, the sort of woman a vulnerable person might lean on.

"So you had personal, private conversations with the accused?"

"Yes."

"Did you talk about the crime she's accused of here, in this trial?"

"Yes."

"What did she say?"

Up to this point Ingrid had been looking toward Elinor Ackroyd. Now she turned her face directly to the jury.

"She confessed to it."

"What?" said Tabitha in a loud, angry tone.

Judge Munday rebuked her sharply. "Please, Ms. Hardy. You will have your own opportunity to question the witness. But you must keep quiet."

Elinor Ackroyd turned to the jury with a wide-eyed expression as if Ingrid's statement had come to her as a total surprise.

"Really?" she said. "Could you remember exactly what the accused said?"

"I remember every word."

"Please. Can you tell the jury?"

Ingrid paused for a moment as if she were trying to gather her thoughts. "She told me that she had had a sexual relationship with the victim when she was a teenager."

Oh, Tabitha thought to herself. *Oh right. I can see what's coming.*

"She said it had ruined her life," Ingrid continued. "She came back to her home village with the idea of punishing him for what he had done. She said she had planned it all. She said she had confronted the man and threatened to make it all public, go to the police. She arranged to meet him at her house and she stabbed him there. She had a plan to get rid of the body but before she could do it, a friend of hers found the body by chance."

"Was that all?"

Ingrid thought for a moment. Or, as Tabitha bitterly saw it, pretended to think for a moment.

"She also said that her lawyer didn't believe that she was innocent. She said that she had no choice but to defend herself."

"Thank you," said Elinor Ackroyd. "I have no further questions."

Tabitha stayed seated for a few moments. She felt like she was in a fever. How was she going to think? How was she going to ask questions? She looked helplessly at Michaela. Michaela put her hand on Tabitha's. It made her feel just a little bit better. She forced herself to stand up and still her legs felt shaky and she had to steady herself by leaning forward against the edge of the desk.

"This is a bit of a surprise," said Tabitha.

"I can see it must be difficult for you."

"Do you?" said Tabitha sarcastically. "That's really kind of you."

"Please, Ms. Hardy," said Judge Munday. "You're to ask questions, not to make vague statements."

Tabitha had so many thoughts. She just didn't know how to formulate them into a question.

"That was quite damaging, what you just said." Still no question, Tabitha told herself angrily. "Didn't you miss something?"

"I don't think so."

"I said a version of what you just said, but you left out the important bit, the bit where I said that this is what the prosecution case against me is."

"No, I didn't. Because you didn't say that."

"I thought that if I were going to defend myself, I needed to be clear about what the prosecution case against me was. And I thought it would be useful to think aloud with a friend. Someone I thought was my friend."

"I'm afraid that's not true," said Ingrid, glancing at the jury.

"Look," said Tabitha, "if I really had committed this crime, why on earth would I confess it all to *you*? What would be the point?"

The moment the words were out of her mouth, she silently cursed herself. What a stupid, stupid question. A question that was so easy to answer.

Ingrid gave a sympathetic smile. "It's strange, I know. But I think people sometimes feel a need to confess to someone. It lightens the burden somehow."

Tabitha felt a sense of humiliation and knew that it must be visible to everyone, including the jury. Her face had probably gone red. She could feel it. She turned toward Michaela and saw that she was gesturing at her notes. She saw the word "parole" written in capital letters. Right, she thought. Right. And even in her confusion, she understood how competent and how clever Michaela was. She turned back to Ingrid. She had an idea of what she wanted to say but she knew it had to be phrased as a question and she didn't know how to do it.

"When I was talking to you, as a friend, you were waiting for your parole hearing, right?"

"Yes."

"Was there a connection?" said Tabitha. "I mean: give the authorities something they want and they'll give you something *you* want."

Ingrid shook her head. "No, not at all."

Tabitha tried to gather her thoughts. "All right. Can I put it like this? When you went to whoever you went to with this made-up story about me—"

"It wasn't made up," Ingrid interrupted with a new edge in her voice.

"Whatever," said Tabitha. "When you told your story, was it before you were given parole or after?"

Tabitha noticed a hesitation in Ingrid's manner.

"Before you answer," Tabitha continued, "you should know that this is something that can be checked."

Ingrid looked at Simon Brockbank and at the judge and back at Tabitha.

"Before," she said slowly. "But that doesn't mean anything."

"That's really interesting," said Tabitha, "because I was told that the prosecution had only just learned about this."

Simon Brockbank sprang to his feet.

"I think Ms. Hardy should confine herself to asking questions."

"You'd like that, wouldn't you?" Tabitha said angrily.

"Stop that," said Judge Munday in a stern voice. "Both of you. Ask questions, please, Ms. Hardy." She turned to Simon Brockbank. "However, I have noted Ms. Hardy's point."

Brockbank went very red and sat down.

"Any more questions?" Judge Munday asked.

"One second," said Tabitha.

456 · NICCI FRENCH

She leaned down and whispered urgently to Michaela. "Can you think of anything?"

"Fucking grass," Michaela hissed.

"I can't say that," said Tabitha, glancing round to see if anyone had overheard.

"Please, Ms. Hardy," said Judge Munday. "The court is waiting."

"Just a moment," said Tabitha.

"Ask her about her crime," said Michaela.

"What do you mean? She told me she got tangled up in her work's financial difficulties and was made a scapegoat."

"Just ask her."

Tabitha straightened up and swallowed nervously and felt her heart beating. She didn't know where this was going. She cleared her throat.

"You told me that your crime was taking money from your work? Is that right?"

Ingrid looked at the judge. "I've served my time. I've got parole. I shouldn't have to talk about this."

"You have to answer the question," said Judge Munday.

"I had a cash flow problem," Ingrid said. "I borrowed some money. I intended to pay it back as soon as I could. But it was wrong and I paid the penalty. Rightly. I'm truly sorry."

Tabitha couldn't think of anything more to say. She felt Michaela nudging her.

"Go on," she mouthed.

"Erm," Tabitha began helplessly. "Could you maybe say something more about it?"

"Like what?"

"What was your work?"

"I worked for an organization."

"Just tell us what it was."

Ingrid took a breath. "A charity making logistical arrangements for migrants."

"Logistical arrangements?" said Tabitha. "What does that mean? Find them somewhere to live? Giving them money for food?"

"Yes."

"It sounds like a good thing. How much did you steal?"

"I didn't keep an exact count."

"Some figure must have been mentioned in court."

Ingrid started to say something in a mumble that was barely intelligible.

"Sorry," said Tabitha. "Could you speak so we can hear you?"

"They said three hundred and seventy thousand pounds, but I think it was an exaggeration."

"Three hundred and seventy thousand pounds?"

458 · NICCI FRENCH

said Tabitha in a startled tone that was entirely genuine. "Did you have to pay it all back?"

There was no answer.

"You did pay it back?" said Tabitha.

"I couldn't."

"You mean you'd spent it all? Three hundred and seventy thousand pounds?"

"It was complicated."

"So, stealing this money from a charity for refugees, you probably had to lie a lot, fake documents, that sort of thing, is that fair?"

"It was a difficult time."

"Well, I'm having a difficult time at the moment," Tabitha said. "That's all."

She sat down. As Ingrid was led back across the courtroom, Tabitha avoided meeting her eye. Instead she leaned across to Michaela and whispered in her ear:

"You should be a fucking lawyer."

Sixty-two

There followed three days of expert witnesses. They gave evidence on blood type and tire tread and fibers and much else, which Tabitha sat through without asking a single question.

Then came the psychiatrist, Dr. David Hartson. Tabitha heard her medical history being read out once again, and couldn't object because it was all true. And she couldn't object when he said that she had a problem with authority figures, because she reckoned that she'd shown that to be true as well, during these past weeks in court.

There was also a man with a long thin nose and high forehead who tapped on a computer in front of him, while large-scale maps and close-up photos of Okeham appeared on the large screen. He was there to establish that nobody could have got to Stuart's house or Tabitha's without passing in front of the CCTV camera outside the village shop.

Tabitha kept glancing at the jury. They all seemed staid and unremarkable, but she knew it went to the heart of the case, because when all was said and done, all the ugliness and rumor over with, the insinuations, bad feelings, suspicions and lies, it was still a fact that she had been in the right place on the day and she couldn't see how anyone else could have been. The jury looked untroubled. The young man in the hoodie was obviously doodling on his pad, the smart woman had had her hair cut and highlighted. Her nails were painted orange. Tabitha opened her notebook and stared at her annotated, scribbled-over and amended timeline until her brain hurt. What was she missing? Something. Surely there was something.

On Friday, at the end of the third week of the trial, it was the vicar's turn to take the stand. Tabitha, glancing up at the public gallery, was startled to see familiar faces in the front row. Terry from the village shop had come. Tabitha wondered who was covering for her. And Laura was there too, right at the edge and accompanied by Dr. Mallon. She sat very straight and her face was pale and stern. Tabitha felt her throat constrict so that she could barely swallow. Little beads of sweat broke out on her forehead. She had almost become used to being in court, but now the terror she had felt during the first days of the trial surged back. She could feel the stuttering gallop of her heart, and her thoughts became a loose muddle of panic. She took a mouthful of water, holding the tumbler in both hands to hide her trembling, and tried to focus.

Mel took her oath on the Bible with a heartfelt sincerity. Her voice was strong and clear. She was wearing a blue blouse with a pattern of swallows on it, and of course, her dog collar. Her hair, tied back as always in a simple ponytail, was lighter, bleached by the June sunshine, and her freckles, which had been pale in winter, were coppery blotches. Tabitha thought of her striding round the village in her stout shoes, her dog beside her. A woman of country lanes and village churches, cottages and fields.

Yes, she said, her name was Melanie Coglan. Mel, she added. Yes, she was the vicar in Okeham and also in surrounding parishes: she had several churches on her patch. Most people, she explained, didn't understand how hard a vicar had to work these days and how much ground they had to cover. No, she hadn't always been a vicar. Before she was called, she had been in sales for a pharmaceutical company in the southeast of England.

She had earned much more, she said, but soon she had realized that her life had little meaning. Her expression as she answered Simon Brockbank's questions was friendly. She looked at the jury and smiled and her teeth were square and white. She had been a vicar for a decade now and had been in Okeham for seven years. She lived in the vicarage that was next to the church and very near the village shop—bang in the center, she said, and gave a warm laugh though Tabitha didn't see why it was funny.

And yes, she had been there all through the day of Friday, December 21, when Stuart Rees had been murdered. She confirmed that she had seen the accused during that day. Her benevolent gaze rested on Tabitha as she spoke, and Tabitha stared fixedly back until she felt Michaela prodding her.

"What?" she whispered.

"You look really scary. Stop it!"

They were coming to the crucial bit. The barrister leaned forward slightly. He spoke slowly.

"Can you tell me when you saw the accused?"

"I can't say the exact time, obviously. The first would have been midmorning, I think, after I'd been to the shop."

Simon Brockbank glanced at his notes. "The CCTV

shows you there at ten twenty-two. Would it have been then?"

"Yes."

"Did you talk?"

"Not really. I would have greeted her, of course. I always make a point of greeting everyone." Again, she smiled her wide, trusty smile.

"Did you observe her demeanor?"

"Fucking demeanor," hissed Tabitha to Michaela. "Always my fucking demeanor."

"Shh," whispered Michaela. "Why are you letting this woman get to you?"

"I did," said Mel. "She was obviously in a bad way. She was walking fast and hugging herself and I think she was talking to herself as well." She lifted her eyes to the jury. "I should have stopped her. I should have asked her if I could help her. I'll always regret that I didn't."

Tabitha was about to hiss something again, but then she stopped. Mel looked genuinely troubled: what if she was simply being sincere? What if she actually was a good woman who wanted to help people? Tabitha clenched her hands together, seeing herself from Mel's point of view—a furious, damaged, lonely young woman in the grip of her own demons.

"The next time," Mel was saying, "was in the early afternoon."

"That would be at two-thirty," interposed Simon Brockbank, consulting his notes.

"That sounds right. This time we did talk."

"And can you tell me what you talked about?"

"Yes. I stopped her, because she still looked really wretched and in a bad way, and I wanted to help her however I could. I tried to make conversation, draw her out of herself. So I pointed to this story in the papers about the reported drone at Gatwick Airport that had stopped all flights arriving or departing from the airport. She didn't really say anything. I asked her if she didn't think it was awful to do that kind of thing as a prank, something like that."

"Did she reply?"

"Not really, not in the way I expected. She had a strange look about her."

"Strange in what way?"

"Blank. Fixed. It was like she wasn't really seeing me. Then she said, well, she said, excuse me." She looked directly at the jury again. "She said, 'I've f-ing ruined my life and you expect me to care about f-ing drones?'"

"I see," said Simon Brockbank solemnly. "I see. And was that the end of your conversation?"

"I'm afraid not. I asked her what she meant, and she said something like, 'You're a vicar, you've got God on your side, but I don't believe in God and anyway, if there was a God he would hate me.'"

"She said God would hate her?"

"Yes."

"What did you make of that?"

"I didn't know what to make of it. I felt deeply concerned for her. I told her it was never too late to turn to God and open her heart to him, and that God was about love not hate. I was actually scared of her. She said I didn't know anything and it was too late for her now. She said she had wrecked everything and her life was over."

"Too late," repeated Simon Brockbank. "She had wrecked everything and her life was over. Hmm. Can you tell the jury how you interpreted those words?"

"At the time, I thought she was a soul in despair. I felt extremely sorry for her." Mel's eyes settled once more on Tabitha, who felt she would jump up, scream and hurl something just to stop the pity she saw in them. "Now, I think she was making a confession."

"And what do you think she wanted to confess?"

"She wanted to confess to the murder of Stuart Rees," said Mel softly.

The court was completely quiet. To be outside, Tabitha thought. To be somewhere else. She thought of the great waves rolling in toward the shore; their shining smooth darkness rising and gathering power. She could walk into that water and be carried far away.

"And you are sure that what you have remembered is accurate?"

"I may have got one or two words slightly wrong," said Mel. "But I have sworn an oath to tell the truth. I feel certain now that she was in a state of guilt and despair and self-horror, and that she was confessing to me. That is the truth."

Sixty-three

"What are you going to say?" asked Michaela.

"Sssh."

"You have to say something."

"I'm thinking."

"And you need to eat as well. I got a sandwich for you."

"I can't eat anything. I'll be sick."

"You need to keep your strength up."

"No."

"You have to say it isn't true. You wouldn't have said all that to her."

"Maybe it is true."

"Stop it! You've been doing so well. Don't go all gloomy and self-harming on me, Tabitha."

"I'm thinking."

"Cheese and onion marmalade. Here, have a bite at least. You can ask about how she and Stuart fell out. That's what you were going to do, isn't it? That letter he wrote about her. Make her look suspicious."

"That's not the point."

The buzz of a fly on the wall high above her. Tabitha rose and looked at Mel where she stood in the witness box. She cleared her throat unnecessarily.

"It wasn't half past two that we talked," she said. She heard her own voice, loud and harsh.

"That's not a question," said the judge.

"It wasn't half past two that we talked, was it?"

"What do you mean?" Mel looked bewildered.

"You say we talked about that story about drones in the paper, right?"

"Yes."

"But you bought the paper in the morning, didn't you?"

"I've no idea."

"I have. You did. You are on CCTV at ten twenty-two going into the shop and a few minutes later you come out carrying it."

"All right," said Mel in a conciliatory tone. "Maybe I bought the paper in the morning."

"And at two thirty-one you're seen again on CCTV *not* carrying a paper. That's when you say you talked to me, but I think we had that conversation, or whatever you want to call it, in the morning. And if it was in the morning I couldn't have been confessing because Stuart was still alive. That's a question, I guess."

Mel nodded and looked thoughtful but not flustered. "Well," she said. "You might be right, of course, and you were talking about something you were going to do, rather than something you had done. But I tend to think it was in the afternoon. Maybe I still had the paper with me."

"You didn't. We can look at the CCTV if that helps."

"No, I'm sure you're right," said Mel. "But I don't see why that means I wouldn't have mentioned the drone at Gatwick Airport anyway. I didn't need to be holding the paper, did I?"

"But you said you pointed at the story."

"Maybe I just mentioned it because I remembered it."

"So what you said wasn't true?"

"Everything I've said I believe to be true. But it could be that I wasn't actually carrying the newspaper and I didn't actually point at it. I'm not sure that's a very grave error." She looked at Tabitha with her cheerful kindness. "I was just trying to connect with you, in your distress. That's all."

"Yes," said Tabitha through gritted teeth. "So let's talk about that conversation. The one where I'm apparently confessing. At the time, you didn't think I was confessing, did you?"

"But I did, though."

"You did?"

"Yes."

"So why didn't you call the police at once?"

Mel gave a small clucking laugh. "I didn't think you were confessing to murder, obviously. I thought you were confessing to a sense of self-loathing and despair."

"But that's not a crime, is it?"

"No," said Mel cautiously. She was about to add something but Tabitha cut in.

"You only thought I was confessing to an actual crime once you knew about the murder, right?"

"That's true."

"So I'm someone who suffers from depression and I say I've wrecked my life. As a vicar, you must have heard countless people saying things like that." She waited a beat. "Haven't you?"

"People bring all manner of sorrows to me," said Mel earnestly. "Things they cannot carry on their own."

"Good. And they're not criminals either?"

"Of course not."

"So the only thing that makes what I said to you that day suspicious is the fact that someone was found dead later in the day, is that it?"

"It's for other people to judge what that means."

"Right," said Tabitha.

She looked at the jury and they looked at her. She didn't think she was convincing them. She glanced up at the public gallery and met Laura's gaze. For a moment, she considered just sitting down and putting her head in her hands and saying she was done. They would lead her away and put her in a cell and she would hear the lock turning and the struggle would be over.

She felt a hand on the small of her back.

"Ask about the feud," Michaela murmured. "Go on."

Tabitha turned back to Mel. "Can you tell me about your relationship with Stuart Rees?"

Mel looked puzzled by the question. "I don't know what you mean by relationship. He came to church on Sunday, helped out at the church fete, and we met at the parish council and in the village sometimes." For the first time, she seemed cautious.

"Was he a regular churchgoer?"

"Regular as clockwork," she said, and there was a hint of acerbity in her voice.

"Were you on friendly terms?"

"Of course."

"Really? I've heard that the two of you didn't see eye to eye." Before the judge could intervene, she added: "Is that correct?"

"No. I mean, it is true that Mr. Rees disagreed with me about some doctrinal issues." She smiled. "But goodness me, if I fell out with everyone who disagreed with me on such things, there would be no one left in my church."

"But isn't it true that Stuart Rees thought you didn't even believe in God?"

"That's absurd."

"It may be absurd, but is it right?"

"He thought that my version of Christianity was too liberal, certainly. Happy-clappy, he called it." Her face had become flushed; she was almost angry, thought Tabitha.

"That sounds rude."

"I have to accept things like that. It goes with the job."

"Was it just a disagreement?"

"What do you mean?"

"Is it true that he wrote to the bishop, complaining about you?"

Simon Brockbank at last rose to his feet. "I've been lenient with Ms. Hardy, but I think that is called leading the witness."

"It seems proper enough," said Judge Munday.

"He did write to the bishop," said Mel.

"Was it upsetting?"

"I always tried to remain friendly with him and not take it personally."

"That must have been hard."

"Not really. I knew his hostility came from a deeply troubled place, so really, I felt sorry for him."

Sorry for Stuart, sorry for me, thought Tabitha.

"A deeply troubled place?" she asked.

"Yes. Once he—" She stopped.

"Yes?"

"He was very heated. I'm afraid I had spoken words that perhaps were not wise. I said something along the lines of his version of God being rather angry and unyielding, and he laughed and said he was damned whatever he did now."

A murmur ran through the court. The reporters were scribbling away furiously. Tabitha glanced up and saw Laura leaning forward, her face in a thin line and her eyes shining oddly in her drawn face.

"Damned," she said. "He told you that?"

"You have to remember it was in the heat of the moment," said Mel. "But yes. He said he was damned for what he had done."

Tabitha felt a bit giddy. A few minutes earlier the vicar had told the court that she, Tabitha, had said she was beyond hope and forgiveness, and now she was saying that Stuart had also said as much. As if the two of them were in the same pit of despair and self-hatred.

"Why would he say that?"

"Perhaps he was thinking of what he did to you all those years ago."

Once again, Tabitha didn't know if what Mel was saying helped or damaged her case. Probably neither, but this sunshiny woman had brought a darkness into the courtroom, as if the trial was no longer just about murder but about sin and depravity.

"Thank you. I don't have anything else to ask you," she said.

Sixty-four

Tabitha could hardly bear to look at Andy when he gave his evidence, standing in the dock in his cheap, badly fitting suit, newly shaved, looking like he wanted to be somewhere else. On several occasions the judge told him to speak up.

But it didn't really matter that he mumbled and looked shifty. His evidence was solid enough. Tabitha knew exactly what he was going to say, but she was still dismayed by it.

He told the jury—although he didn't look in their direction, but down at his feet or sometimes at the woman sitting beneath the judge's bench—who he was, how long he had lived in Okeham (all his life), what he did and how he knew Tabitha. He described the work they had been doing on her house, and he grew more confident as he talked about joinery and damp courses and leaking gutters. He talked about how he had been working up the road that day at Ken Turner's house, though Ken hadn't been there, and had gone to Tabitha's when he'd finished, at about half past four.

"Sunset was at fifteen fifty-three that day," said Simon Brockbank. "So it would have been dark, I presume?"

"Yes," said Andy. Dark, cold and sleety; filthy weather. His voice became a mumble as he told the court how Tabitha hadn't answered the door at first and when she had, she had been odd.

"In what sense odd?"

"Not herself," said Andy and when Simon Brockbank waited, he added, "Maybe she'd been crying, or something. Her eyes were bloodshot. Not herself."

Again, he cast his wild look at Tabitha. She wanted to smile at him but her lips were stiff.

"And then what happened?"

"I went inside. I wanted to talk to her about the work we'd planned. We were going to lay floorboards. But she wasn't right in herself," he said uselessly. "I thought she was ill maybe."

"And then?"

"Then I went out the back door to get the wood."

"Where was the wood kept?"

"Shed," muttered Andy.

"In the shed at the back of the house, is that right?"

"Yeah."

"But did anything happen before you went out there?"

"She said not to go."

"Can you speak up, please?"

"She said not to go out there."

"She said not to go out there," repeated Simon Brockbank. "I see. And what was her manner when she said this?"

"How do you mean?"

"Did she say it calmly?"

"No."

"So how did she say it?"

"She shouted it."

"I'm sorry. Please can you say that more clearly?"

"I said, she shouted it. Like she was in a panic."

"But you went anyway."

"Yes."

So it went on. His faltering words, the barrister's fluent ones, back and forth. The body. The blood. The staring eyes in Stuart's dead face. What Tabitha had done, had said, how she had seemed almost drunk with the horror. How he had called emergency services. Tabitha had lain on the sofa with blood on her face.

"Did she say anything?"

"She was kind of gabbling stuff. Like she was in pain."

Tabitha shielded her face with her hand. She felt eyes on her. They were imagining her smeared in blood and wild. She was imagining herself.

At last it was over and it was her turn. She stood up and faced Andy. Their gazes locked.

"Sorry about all this," she said.

Andy half smiled. For a moment his face was handsome again. She didn't know what to ask him. In the silence she could hear Simon Brockbank tapping his pen on the table: tick, tick, tick.

"Do you think I killed him?" she asked.

Beside her, Michaela let out a loud groan. "You promised never to ask that again," she said, in a voice loud enough for everyone to hear.

Andy stared at Tabitha, horrified. In that brief moment Tabitha understood that he did. And she knew that everyone else in the court also understood.

"Oh," she said.

"I mean, of course I didn't think . . . you're my friend. It's just . . . look, I don't think you would hurt a fly unless . . . well, unless you weren't yourself."

He was saying other things, about how the body was in her house and that was strange, but that didn't mean . . . Tabitha couldn't hear properly for the roaring in her ears. The room was going in and out of focus.

She whirled round toward Simon Brockbank and Elinor Ackroyd, though their faces weren't properly in focus, just bland circles of discreet pleasure.

"You fuckers," she shouted, so loudly the words ripped at her throat. "He was pretty much the only good relationship I had left in my shitty, stupid life and you've fucked that as well. What have you done? What have you gone and done to me?"

She went on shouting as she was led from the court, and her last sight was of Andy, bent over in the witness box, his face screwed up as if someone had punched him.

Sixty-five

E ven sitting alone in the quiet of the holding cells, Tabitha felt like she was surrounded by a swarm of wasps. They were inside her head and outside her head. They were buzzing and they were crawling on her skin and they were crawling inside her skin. She felt an urge to tear at herself or to smash against the wall, anything that would just put an end to this fever of anger and agitation that was like an unbearable itch that she couldn't scratch. She only had the dimmest memory of the previous minutes, of being dragged like an animal through the court, along the corridors into the cell.

She stood up and faced the white concrete wall. She slowly clenched the fingers of her right hand and raised it. Just one punch would do something to break the fever.

"Don't," said a voice behind her.

She looked round. Simon Brockbank was leaning in the doorway of the cell, his wig in his hand, his robe over his arm. There were two chairs in the cell. Brockbank walked inside and sat on one of them. He draped his robe across his lap and placed his wig on top.

"I did a case a few weeks ago," he said. "A fight outside a pub. My client took a swing at another defendant, missed, and hit a brick wall instead. So I'm a bit of an expert on hands and walls. There are twenty-seven bones in the human hand and if you do what you're thinking of doing, they're difficult to fix."

He gestured toward the other chair. Tabitha glared at him. She was seriously thinking of punching Simon Brockbank instead of the wall. She looked at Brockbank's face with its slightly sarcastic smile. He'd probably like it if she took a swing at him. It would show he had got to her. So she took a slow, long breath and sat down opposite him.

"Have you come to gloat?"

Brockbank thought for a moment. "That would be one idea," he said. "You did me a favor up there. I imagine the jury had been thinking, this Tabitha Hardy, she's a bit prickly, a bit angry, but would she really be capable of killing someone? You've dealt with that little problem."

Tabitha knew he was probably right. "Andy was my only friend," she said. "And look what you all did to him."

"That sounds like a conversation you should have with someone," Brockbank said, not sounding very concerned. "Meanwhile you have a decision to make."

"What's that?"

Brockbank sniffed. "It's not really a decision. It's more like an acknowledgment of reality. You can't just sit here forever. You have to do something."

"Such as what? Plead guilty? Is that what you want?"

Brockbank seemed to consider this, as if it was an entirely new idea.

"It's never too late to do the right thing. The judge might give you a certain amount of credit." He looked at Tabitha, whose expression was entirely impassive. "I thought not. In that case, what you really should do is go back upstairs and make a full, unconditional, sincere apology to the court."

"Fuck that," said Tabitha.

"All right," said Brockbank, looking more serious. "I really should let you do this to yourself. But first I'm going to spell out in detail what will happen."

"Go on then," said Tabitha. "Spell it out."

Leaning closer in, gesturing with both hands, Simon Brockbank spelled it out.

"**Have you** anything to say, Ms. Hardy?"

Tabitha stood up and faced the judge. She had a sudden flashback to apologies when she was at school, to a teacher or, on occasion, to the head. Those apologies were normally delivered in a faintly ironic monotone. It was generally accepted on both sides that Tabitha wasn't really sorry but it was a form of theater that had to be gone through so that life could proceed.

This was different. If she was going to do this, it had to be convincing. It had to be real. It wasn't real, of course. But it had to convince both the judge and, even more important, the jury.

She clenched her fists so that her fingernails bit into her palms so hard that they actually hurt.

"Yes, I do have something to say. I don't want to make excuses for what I did. I don't want to say that I'm feeling stressed by this whole situation, I don't want to say that I was upset by having a friend appearing for the prosecution—" She stopped herself, realizing that she was making the excuses she'd said she wasn't going to make. "I just want to say that I'm truly sorry. I know that you're meant to behave in a certain respectful way in court, quite rightly, and I didn't live up to that. I'm sure I've broken some law and I'm completely willing to acknowledge that and pay the penalty." She turned to the jury with an expression that she hoped wasn't obviously hypocritical. "I just hope that you can all accept this apology and that I'll be allowed to carry on representing myself. I absolutely promise that nothing like it will happen again."

She turned back to the judge. *Too much?* she wondered. Actually, she *was* regretful. She'd lost all control. She'd let everyone see something that should have been kept hidden. She waited, looking at the judge, who was looking down at her notes, frowning. What would be truly galling would be if she had groveled and humiliated herself and it didn't get her anywhere.

Judge Munday looked up. "Ms. Hardy, your outburst was a disgrace. I seriously considered citing you for contempt of court and appointing a counsel to act for you."

Tabitha gave an inward sigh of relief. But she knew she mustn't look relieved. She must continue to look penitent.

"I want you to be clear," Judge Munday continued. "I won't tolerate anything like this again. No outbursts, no swearing, no shouting. Do you understand?"

Tabitha nodded humbly and sat down beside Michaela, who was sitting with her head in her hands.

"I'm sorry," she whispered.

Michaela lifted her head. She looked grim.

The court then stood up as Judge Munday adjourned for the day and the police officer approached to take Tabitha away.

"Just give me a moment," said Tabitha.

The officer looked at his watch. "Two minutes," he said.

"That's ridiculous. I need to talk about the case."

He looked at his watch again. "One and a half minutes."

Tabitha turned to Michaela. "Sorry," she said again. She felt like a little girl who was losing her only friend.

"How can I be your McKenzie fucking friend if you do things like that? I told you not to."

"I know. I was stupid."

"Bloody stupid. Do you ever listen to anyone?"

"I won't do it again."

"That's what you always say. But you lose your temper and then say whatever comes into your head."

"I know. That's why I need you to be here as well." There was a silence. "You will keep on coming, won't you?"

Michaela sighed heavily. "What else have I got to do?"

"Thank you." She waited a few seconds. "Tomorrow's the crime scene officer."

"Anything you're worried about?"

"I'm worried about everything. All the time."

"I mean, is there going to be anything new?"

Tabitha thought for a moment. "I read the report. It's just about what was at the scene. They didn't find a weapon. I don't know if that's a good thing or a bad thing."

"You want me to do anything?"

"I don't know what would help," said Tabitha desperately. "I don't know what we're looking for. You could take a look at that list of things they had in storage. You've done so much already. I don't know what to say."

She looked round at the officer. "Is my time up?"

"More than up."

Tabitha looked back at Michaela. "Or have an evening off. Whatever."

The next morning when Tabitha was brought into the courtroom, there was no sign of Michaela. Perhaps she had decided not to come after what had happened the previous day: she felt nauseous at the idea. The jury came in and then the judge. The scene of crime officer, Dr. Andrew Belfry, made his way into the courtroom to the witness box and still there was no sign of Michaela. Tabitha looked around for her. Perhaps she had overslept. Perhaps she had just given up on all of this and returned to her old life. Tabitha had been let down by so many people, why not Michaela as well?

She turned her attention to Dr. Belfry, dressed in a rumpled gray suit that seemed a size too small for him. He was largely bald with frameless spectacles and he was carrying a bundle of files and a small bag from which he extracted a laptop. He opened it and started tapping at it until the usher brought him a Bible to swear on.

Elinor Ackroyd stood up and elicited from him that he was not a police officer but hired on a contractual basis. He had a degree in organic chemistry and had twenty-six years of experience in his job, which took him all over the southwest region.

Ackroyd began to take him through the details of his report, the position of the body, the bloodstains on the plastic sheeting that the body had been lying on, the bloody footprints leading back into the house. It should have been horrifying but Dr. Belfry spoke about it as if he were discussing the construction of a model railway. He kept referring back to obscure paragraphs of his report, which he always had trouble finding. Also, he had a strange voice that sounded as if his tongue was too large for his mouth. Tabitha became so preoccupied with this that she found it difficult to pay attention to what he was saying. She had to force herself to take the occasional note. There didn't seem anything especially damaging about the report apart from the basic, central, horrible fact of it happening in the outbuilding of her home.

She sensed a movement behind her, looked round and saw Michaela tiptoeing forward, mouthing an apology at Judge Munday, who glowered back at her. She sat down next to Tabitha, breathing heavily.

"You all right?" said Tabitha in a whisper. "I thought you weren't coming."

"Sorry I'm late, I had to make some calls. I found out something weird. It's about the sheet?"

"What sheet?"

"The one the body was wrapped in."

"Please, Ms. Hardy," said Judge Munday, breaking in.

"What?"

"There is a an examination going on here."

As the examination continued, Tabitha tried to make sense of Michaela's scrawled notes.

"Are you sure?" she whispered.

"I rang the delivery firm."

Tabitha thought so hard that it almost made her head hurt.

"So what does it mean?" she whispered, with her lips actually touching Michaela's ear.

Michaela shrugged. "I don't know. Just ask that guy."

"Finally," said Elinor Ackroyd, "I have one final question. Dr. Belfry, you have supervised all the evidence connected with the crime scene. Have you found evidence of anybody else's presence? I mean beyond the victim, Tabitha Hardy, and Andrew Kane, who found the body."

Belfry turned to the jury before answering. "No," he said, in a louder voice than before. "None whatever."

"Thank you for your help," said Ackroyd, sitting down.

Tabitha stood up with that familiar lurching feeling. She looked down at her notes. She had written two words: "prints" and "blood." It didn't seem like very much.

"Is it surprising that my prints and traces and whatever were all over the place? I mean, it was where I lived."

"There were prints on the plastic sheeting he was lying on," he said.

Belfry raised his eyebrows as he answered and gave a little nod toward the jury. It made Tabitha want to shout at him or hit him.

"Andy and I found the body. We pulled the sheet off him."

"Ms. Hardy," said Judge Munday severely, "you're meant to be asking questions, not making statements."

"All right," said Tabitha. "Er . . . like, could the prints be there because Andy and I pulled the sheet off to see if he was still alive?"

"That would be one possibility," said Belfry. "Not the most likely one in my professional opinion."

"You're not here to give your opinion," said Tabitha.

"Yes, he is," Judge Munday interrupted. She turned to the jury. "Dr. Belfry is absolutely entitled, in response to cross-examination, to offer his opinion, where relevant. Continue, Ms. Hardy."

Tabitha was so flustered by this that she couldn't think of what to say. She looked down at her notes.

"Blood," she said.

"What?" said Dr. Belfry.

"There was blood on the plastic sheet," said Tabitha. "And there were footprints going back into the house. And there was blood on the sofa in the living room. Anywhere else?"

"There was blood on your clothes," said Dr. Belfry.

"And on Andy's clothes. Because of finding the body." She realized that wasn't a question. "That's right, isn't it?"

"Yes."

"Anywhere else?"

"There were traces on the floor."

"Those were the footprints, right?"

"Probably."

"Stuart Rees had his throat cut, right?"

"Yes."

Tabitha turned to the jury. "I'm sorry, this is going to sound really gross. But I can't think of a non-gross way to ask it." She turned back to Belfry. "There are arteries in the neck, aren't there?"

"The carotid arteries, yes."

"And if they were cut, wouldn't they make a mess everywhere? I mean all over the floor and on the walls et cetera, et cetera."

"But they didn't."

"But didn't you think that was weird?"

"I just describe the scene as I find it."

"It didn't trouble you?"

"No."

Tabitha felt she'd hit a brick wall. A question occurred to her and she asked it without considering whether it was a good idea.

"Did you find the murder weapon?"

"It hasn't yet been found."

"Does that seem strange?"

"You had plenty of time to dispose of it."

Tabitha felt like she'd been struck. "Me? Did you say that *I* had plenty of time?"

"The murderer, I should say."

"At what point did you decide that I did it?"

"I merely assess the evidence," Belfry said stiffly.

"Were you thinking that right from the beginning? As you were going through the evidence? Were you fitting everything around that idea?"

"No."

"Yeah, right," said Tabitha loudly and sarcastically.

"Careful, Ms. Hardy," said Judge Munday sternly.

Tabitha looked down at Michaela's notes and tried to formulate a question.

"Could you tell me about the sheet?" she said.

"What?"

"The sheet the body was found in."

Belfry thought for a moment, for the first time seeming at a loss.

"It was a heavy-duty piece of plastic sheeting."

"Anything else?"

"I don't know what you're talking about."

"There's a label attached. It says 'Reynolds Brown.' And underneath it says . . ." Tabitha picked up the notes and read out: "'FRC569332.'"

"I'll take your word for it," said Belfry.

"What do you mean, you'll take my word for it? That's supposed to be your job. You're meant to check things like that."

There was a pause.

"I'm sorry, is there a question?"

"My friend, Michaela, did what you should have done. She googled it. Reynolds Brown is a furniture company. And the FRC thing is a reference number. So she phoned them up. This sheeting was used to wrap a sofa."

As Tabitha paused to give Dr. Belfry a chance to react, Simon Brockbank stood up. He spoke warily.

"I'm sorry but the defense can't just spring undisclosed evidence on a witness."

"I don't know what you're talking about," said Tabitha. "This is evidence that this guy wrote his report about. I'm just asking him about it."

Judge Munday waved her hand wearily.

"Just continue, Ms. Hardy, but please call him Dr. Belfry and not 'this guy.' It's just a matter of courtesy. And please, at some point, ask a question."

"All right. As I said, Michaela rang up the company, which is what you should have done. She quoted the reference number. It was delivered on the seventeenth of December to Cliff House in Okeham. Do you recognize that address?"

"No."

"It's Stuart Rees's home address. Does that seem interesting to you?"

Belfry coughed and when he answered it was in such a low voice that the judge had to ask him to speak up.

"I can't really comment on that."

"But you didn't find that out? Yes or no?"

"No, but I don't really—"

"What else didn't you check up on?"

"That's an insulting question."

"You know what I think?" said Tabitha.

There was a pause.

"That's not really a fair question," said Judge Munday.

"Sorry, it was like a preparation for a question. What I think is that you just assumed it was me and that you didn't look at anything that went against it. Is that fair?"

"No. It isn't fair."

"That's all I've got to say," said Tabitha, sitting down with the feeling that there must have been more that she should have pressed harder.

Elinor Ackroyd started to get up but Brockbank put his hand on her shoulder, preventing her. He stood up instead and stepped forward.

"Just one more question," he said. "Tabitha Hardy has been trying to confuse things and throw dust into the faces of the jury. So can I just make something clear in case the jury have forgotten it? Did your investigation find evidence of anyone else at the crime scene?"

"No."

As Brockbank sat down, Tabitha leaped up.

"Since we're all asking just one more question, I'll ask one: was it even a crime scene?"

Dr. Belfry looked utterly confused. "I'm sorry," he said. "I don't know what you mean."

"Exactly," said Tabitha and sat down.

It was left to Judge Munday to tell him that he could go. As he passed Tabitha, he gave her a look of pure loathing. She forced herself to smile back at him.

Sixty-six

"No no no no. Please no. Oh Christ. Don't let this be happening."

The voice filled the courtroom, slurred and guttural, and it went on and on, words and nasty sounds grinding out into the silence. It sounded like the voice of a hellishly drunken man, florid and abandoned, shouting at the voices in his head. But it wasn't a man.

Tabitha propped her head on one hand and closed her eyes and wanted to disappear. She knew if she looked up she would see everyone staring at her in horror. She had almost no memory of her first interview at the police station, just dark fragments: the stickiness of the table where she rested her head, the look on the face of the police officer that was both polite and triumphant. She had gone through the transcript, of course, and she had it in front of her now, but she hadn't understood the damage it could do her. Just the sound of her voice was bad enough. Now she saw why the prosecution had been so insistent that the recording be played. To read her saying: "What have I done?" was one thing; it could be the straightforward question of an innocent woman finding herself being questioned by the police. To hear her howling it like a beast at bay was quite another.

Someone was asking her about her movements during December 21 and she was saying "fuck off'" repeatedly. The duty solicitor was reminding her that she was allowed to remain silent and she was telling him to fuck off as well.

"Where were you all day, Tabitha?" a voice asked.

"I don't know." The words slid into each other, barely comprehensible. "I don't know anything."

"Do you have any idea of how the body of Stuart Rees came to be on your property?"

"I don't know."

"Did you see him?"

"Blood," she said. "I was covered in his blood."

"Did you kill him, Ms. Hardy?"

And the duty solicitor was urgently telling her not to answer and her voice was saying she couldn't remember anything.

"You mean you can't remember if you killed him?"

"I just want this to be over."

"Please try to answer our questions, Tabitha."

"Sorry. I'm sorry."

"What are you sorry about, Tabitha?" asked a female voice that oozed with sympathy. Tabitha couldn't remember a woman being there as well.

"Everything. Every fucking thing. I'm just tired. So tired."

And the woman said, still in the same concerned voice, that of course she must be tired and that once she had told them what she had done, then she could rest.

The voice said something incomprehensible. Tabitha opened her eyes briefly to look at the transcript. "How can I escape?"

She closed her eyes again.

"Can you repeat that, Tabitha?" said the man.

"No. I can't do this anymore. I can't. I have to go home. Please let me go home."

At last there was silence. The voice had stopped. Tabitha opened her eyes. She looked round to see Michaela's troubled face. She looked across at the jury and they gazed back at her. She turned slightly to where the reporters were crowded onto their benches and then to the judge, who looked like a carved effigy on her raised bench.

She stood up, keeping a hand on the table because she wasn't sure her legs would hold her. She cleared her throat.

"That," she said in a raspy voice, "is called depression. It's called trauma."

With no warning, she felt her spirits lift. Everyone had listened to her howling out like a beast. She had heard herself, but she was still here. She hadn't died of shame. She stood up straighter.

"Depression is an illness," she said and her voice rang out. "I was ill. And the body of a man I had once known was found in my outhouse. It was terrifying."

Simon Brockbank was bouncing his pen again: marking the seconds. Time passing and outside the year and the world were going on without her.

Tabitha fixed her eyes on Judge Munday. "It wasn't a confession. It was just human distress."

Then it was over. The case for the prosecution had been made, the court was adjourned until the following morning and Tabitha was led out. She was taken straight to the van, briefly seeing the blue sky and feeling summer on her skin, and driven back to her cell whose walls were sweaty in the heat. She sat on her bed and buried her head in her hands and tried to gather her thoughts into some kind of coherence.

How had she done? She supposed she had done pretty well, if doing well meant bringing to harsh light how hostile the village was to her; if it meant smearing everyone, making them all seem suspicious and dishonest and acting in bad faith. She felt like she had lifted a stone on Okeham, so that the pretty little village by the sea where visitors came to eat ice cream and stand at the spot where Coleridge had once stood, where everyone knew each other and helped each other, was revealed as a place crawling with petty resentments, jealousy and malice.

A thought came to her that felt like a physical blow. Her head rang with it. It was Stuart who had done that to the community, who had turned people into their worst versions of themselves. That was what he did: he saw people's weaknesses and exploited them. He had done it to Rob Coombe, to Mel, to Owen Mallon. He'd done it to his wife and to his own son. He'd done it to her all those years ago, recognizing the power he could have over a lonely, prickly teenager.

She was glad he was dead.

She sat with that thought for several minutes, still enclosed in the darkness of her cupped hands. Did that mean that she had killed him after all? Listening to herself being interviewed at the police station, her unhinged words, she had felt briefly certain that for all her success in weakening the case against her, she was the killer.

Abruptly, she stood up. No. No, she wouldn't have killed Stuart because she hadn't understood until after he was dead how much damage he had done to her. And she wouldn't have killed Stuart because she wasn't a killer.

She walked back and forth in her cell; three steps one way, three the other. She knew that she had chipped away at the case against her. But it wasn't enough, because she had played the CCTV over and over in her head, and she knew what even the prosecution seemed ignorant of: no one else could have been there. So no one else could have done it. And if it was no one else, that left her.

The door of her cell was locked. She dutifully ate her cheese sandwich, the white bread sticking to her teeth. She undressed and stared down at her strong, pale, hairy legs and her white stomach with the large mole just above the belly button. Her feet looked too big for her body. She remembered how when she had first arrived at Crow Grange she had been struck by the pallor of the women prisoners: now she was one of them. She washed vigorously, brushed her teeth, pulled on her night things and climbed into bed, where she curled under the scratchy blanket and looked up at the ceiling that was veined with dirt.

Her case for the defense started tomorrow. She went through the names of people who would take the stand after she had given evidence: Shona (and she grimaced to herself at what the fifteen-year-old Tabitha would have thought of Shona, one of the in-crowd who used to whisper about her bad haircut and her temper, being her character witness); then Sam McBride and, last of all, Luke, who she still felt guilty about calling. She knew that it was a paltry list of witnesses who at best would muddy the waters a bit more.

She turned on her side to stare at the wall. There was a rusty smear a few inches from her face that looked like blood. She rolled the other way, pulled her knees up. She could hear someone laughing, but it wasn't a happy sound. It made the hairs on the back of her neck bristle. She tried not to hear the sound of her own slurred and horrifying voice, but it boomed and jeered inside her. "How can I escape?" she had shouted.

Sleep when it came was shallow and fitful, full of chaotic fragments of dreams. And then suddenly she was wide awake, sitting upright in bed and holding on to the memory that had somehow found her and now mustn't escape. She swung her legs out of bed, stood up and turned on the light. She dug her notebook out from her pile of papers and found a free space on its scrawled and crossed-out pages, where she wrote down what she remembered, a little scrap gleaming in the mud. She wrote a name underneath and circled it several times. Her hands were shaking with hope: how could she have missed it? How could everyone?

Shona, Sam and Luke would still appear for the defense—but there was someone else, someone crucial, that she needed to call as a witness.

PART THREE

Defense

Sixty-seven

When Tabitha first found herself in the witness box, even though she had only walked a few steps across the courtroom, it all felt completely different. Now she was looking straight across at the jury. Judge Munday was to her right, above her; Michaela was seated to her left, below her, staring up at her with a frown. *She's probably even more nervous than I am*, Tabitha thought to herself. *She can't pass me a note, can't whisper in my ear.*

The atmosphere was different too. There was a new tension, an air of expectancy. The public gallery and the press box were both full. People were leaning toward her, waiting for something; something dramatic.

She affirmed, stumbling over the words, even though she had heard witnesses say them several times before.

Then, just as she started to speak, Judge Munday interrupted her.

"I need to tell you, Ms. Hardy, that you are now appearing as a witness. That means what it says. You are only to report what you have personally witnessed, not what other people have told you."

Tabitha thought for a moment. She was finding this unexpectedly confusing.

"But if someone tells me something, then aren't I witnessing what they're telling me?"

"Just give your account," said Judge Munday. "I'll determine what's admissible. Just try and keep it relevant." She gave a kind of faint sigh. "And decent."

Tabitha took a tissue from her pocket and blew her nose. It was as much to steady her nerves as anything else. She had been lying awake in her cell for most of the night, occasionally thinking of something she ought to say and then thinking she ought to get up and write it down. But she never did and now she was having trouble remembering anything.

She looked across at the jury for hints of friendliness or hostility.

"I'm not going to say very much," she began. Her voice sounded too high, too loud. "I don't know much about doing this. But I've heard that I don't have to prove that I'm innocent. I don't even have to give evidence at all, if I don't want to." She gestured across at Simon Brockbank, who was leaning back on his chair, his eyes looking up at the ceiling. "But I will say a few things."

She took a piece of paper from her pocket and unfolded it and placed it on the little ledge at the front of the witness box, flattening it with the palm of her hand. On it was a numbered list she had written in her cell. It didn't seem much, looked at in daylight, in the courtroom.

"I came back to Okeham when I bought the house. My plan was to do it up and then see how it all went. I could make a go of it in Okeham or I could rent it out as a holiday home or I could sell it."

That was number one on her list. She looked down. She suddenly felt almost paralyzed by the idea of talking about her life in public, describing motives she hadn't actually thought through at the time.

"Some nice person wrote a letter to the police telling them about whatever it was that I had all those years ago with Stuart Rees. I don't know—abuse, seduction, teenage romance, rape, whatever. Looking back, I understand it wasn't good for me. At all. I think it may have affected me, you know, in relationships, that sort of thing—" She stopped herself. She wasn't meant to be saying this sort of thing. She was sounding more like the prosecution. "But all I can say is that I didn't hold a grudge. It sounds stupid, but I didn't understand what it had meant to me until this happened. I didn't know what Stuart Rees was really like until I heard in this court what he'd done to other people."

"Please, Ms. Hardy," said Judge Munday. "This is not your closing statement. Just describe your own relevant experience."

"That's the problem," Tabitha said. "I'm trying to think of what's relevant."

"Just tell us about your day," said a voice.

Tabitha looked around to see who had spoken. She saw that the young juror in the second row had put his hand up.

"It's all very well for you to ask that," said Tabitha. "I bet you couldn't remember every detail of some day three months ago."

"I bet I could if I'd been arrested for murder," the man said and was about to say something else when Judge Munday, whose face had been frozen in horror, interrupted.

"Stop," she said. "For goodness' sake, Ms. Hardy, you can't just start having a conversation with a member of the jury." She turned to the man. "You can ask a question, if you absolutely have to, but you should address it to me, not to a witness. And it would be preferable if it were written down, in case it's prejudicial in some way." She turned back to Tabitha. "However, that is a reasonable thing to say. You can, if you wish, tell us your movements on the day in question. I should warn you that you can then be questioned about any of these statements by the prosecution."

"All right," said Tabitha, gathering her thoughts for a moment. She looked at the jury. "Look, I'll say what I can remember and you can ask about it, if you like."

"Through me," said Judge Munday quickly. "And only if absolutely necessary. It is the job of the jury to assess the evidence, not to cross-examine."

"OK, OK," said Tabitha. She paused again. "Right. Lots of this you've heard in bits anyway. There's not much to say. I woke early. I just lay there. I wasn't feeling good. It was one of my bad days." She looked up at the jury. "If I'd only known. I got up about half past seven. I started making my really basic breakfast, porridge made with water and tea." She stopped. "I don't mean I make my porridge with tea. That would be weird. I make it with water and then I have a mug of tea by the side."

"Ms. Hardy," said Judge Munday. "Only what's relevant, please."

"Sorry, My Lady. It's hard to turn your life into a story. Anyway, I'd run out of milk, so I put a coat on over my PJs and went to the village shop. It was the one busy time of the day, the school bus was there, I actually had to queue to pay for my milk. In the queue was Rob Coombe, who I didn't have an argument with. I headed back for breakfast."

Tabitha thought for a few seconds before continuing.

"In a way, this is all pointless," she said. "I'm just going to be describing a run-of-the-mill, grimly depressing day in which I didn't kill Stuart Rees. I had breakfast and didn't kill Stuart Rees. I went to have a swim and didn't kill Stuart Rees. After my swim, I didn't kill Stuart Rees."

"Please, Ms. Hardy," said Judge Munday. "You're here to give evidence, not just to repeat your plea of not guilty."

"Sorry," said Tabitha, actually grateful that the judge had interrupted her. She turned almost pleadingly to the jury. "My problem is that I have difficulty in having a specific memory of the things I do every day. For example, I can say that I had some scrambled eggs on toast for lunch, but that's only because that's what I always have. Unless I have nettle soup. What I can remember is that it was one of my bad days. Sometimes swimming in cold water makes me feel better, but it didn't really work that time. I remember meeting

Dr. Mallon and meeting Melanie Coglan and I thought I was having friendly, trusting talks with them. But most of the day I was at home. I was meant to be working, or getting things done in the house, but mainly I just lay on the sofa. I felt too tired even to make myself a cup of tea or read or . . ."

While she was speaking, Tabitha started to listen to herself as if she were another person and she started to think of the strangeness of her situation, standing in a courtroom, everyone staring at her, and then, quite suddenly, she couldn't think of what to say.

"Well, anyway, then Andy came round, Andy Kane. He was going to help me with some of the work on the house but I wasn't really in the mood. And then it all happened. And now I'm here."

She paused again, trying to think of a way of coming to a close. She should have planned this better.

"I'm sorry. I don't have a killer fact that somehow proves that I'm innocent of this. I don't even know what that would look like. But I didn't want any of you people thinking I was hiding away and hoping that I'd get off on some kind of technicality. I've probably made things worse by standing up like this and talking. God knows, I usually do. Anyway, sod it, that's all I've got to say."

Tabitha started to leave the witness box.

"Please, Ms. Hardy," said Judge Munday. "We need to hear from the prosecution."

Tabitha silently cursed herself. She'd forgotten that. Simon Brockbank stood up with a solemn expression on his face.

"I'll try to be brief," he said. "I don't want to try everyone's patience." He put his hands in his trouser pockets. "I hoped we could just clear up a couple of points. You have just said in your testimony that the police learned of your intimate relationship with Stuart Rees because of an anonymous letter from a member of the public. We need to be clear about that. This letter was written because you hadn't told the police yourself, is that right?"

"I don't know why it was written."

"But you didn't tell the police yourself?"

"No."

Brockbank's face assumed a puzzled expression and he gave a slight sniff as if this was a damning admission. Perhaps it was, Tabitha thought. She was tempted to start protesting but she had discussed this with Michaela. They had agreed that she should answer any questions as briefly as possible. "Don't give him anything," Michaela had said.

"The jury have heard the tape of your police interview," Brockbank continued. "We all remember that you said many things in response to police questions. However, the jury may be struck by what you didn't say. You didn't say that you were innocent. Why not?"

"You don't know what it's like." Tabitha shook her head slowly, almost talking to herself. "Nobody can unless they've experienced it. I was in a state."

"Because you'd killed Stuart Rees?"

"Because I'd just found a dead body in my house," Tabitha said, more loudly. "Because I realized they thought I'd done it."

"All it took was a clear, ringing statement of innocence. Why didn't you make it?"

"I've said. I didn't know what I was saying."

"Indeed," said Brockbank, savoring the word, running it over his tongue. He seemed to be pondering his next question, although Tabitha was nervously aware that everything about him was prepared in advance. "I have just one question about your testimony. You told us a lot that, quite frankly, we didn't really need to know. But when you came to what we really did need to know, you were strangely silent."

He paused and looked from Tabitha to the jury and then back to Tabitha. She felt a sudden lurching sensation in her stomach. What had she forgotten? What was the trap he was laying for her?

"You briefly mentioned Andrew Kane's visit to your house, but you didn't mention the crucial detail of his testimony. He told this court that when he announced his intention to go out to your shed in search of some building material, you tried to prevent him. The obvious explanation for that is that you knew that Stuart Rees's body was lying on the floor in the shed and that if he went out there he would find it before you had the opportunity to dispose of it. That, as I say, is the obvious explanation. What's *your* explanation?"

"I didn't try to prevent him."

Brockbank's theatrical expression of puzzlement appeared once more.

"Are you saying that Mr. Kane was lying to this court and lying in his statement to the police?"

"I didn't try to prevent him. I told him not to go."

Brockbank gave a heavy, disapproving sigh. "Very well, Ms. Hardy, I stand corrected. Why did you tell him not to go?"

"Look," said Tabitha desperately, "sometimes when I look back at it, it's like looking at someone else and trying to work out why they're doing what they're doing. In all the stress, I'd forgotten saying that to Andy. It was in his statement, so I guess it happened.

The fact is that I didn't know the body was there, so I must have had some other reason."

"Such as?"

"I didn't want him to work on my house that day. I didn't feel up to it. I wanted to be alone."

"Why didn't you tell him as soon as he arrived?"

"I don't know," said Tabitha. "I wasn't in a good condition . . . I wasn't thinking straight."

"Ah, yes, exactly," said Brockbank, almost in a drawl, turning once more to the jury. "You weren't thinking straight." He said each word distinctly, then turned directly to Tabitha. "What else weren't you thinking straight about on that day? Was it your meeting with Stuart Rees? Was it your wish to revenge yourself on him? Was it the problem of disposing of the body?"

Tabitha's answer when it came sounded frail and defeated.

"No," she said. "I couldn't do any of those things. I've thought about it, over and over. I couldn't."

"That's all I wanted to know," said Brockbank. "You can go now."

Tabitha walked back across the court to her table. It felt a long way.

Sixty-eight

"How long have we known each other?"

"How long? I'm not sure. I'm no good at dates. Did we start secondary school together?"

Tabitha was having difficulty remembering why she had thought calling Shona as a character witness was a good idea. Shona was obviously very nervous, and that was making her ricochet between different forms of communication: one minute she was monosyllabic and expressionless, the next gabbling. To make it worse, she would occasionally give a high, anxious giggle. She wouldn't meet Tabitha's gaze. Instead her eyes flickered around the courtroom.

"Yes," said Tabitha shortly. "We did."

"Well, so that would be, what?"

"Nineteen years."

"Oh my God, that's strange." Shona put her hand to her mouth, like a surprised child. In spite of her makeup and her glamour, she did still look a bit like a child, thought Tabitha: wide-eyed and pretty. She was wearing an ivory-colored blouse that set off her tan; her hair gleamed softly. Facing her, Tabitha felt like a hobgoblin, small and grimy and pale. "Are we really that old?"

"Yes."

Giggle.

She's scared I'm going to tell the world about her affair with Rob Coombe, realized Tabitha. *That's why she's being so jumpy.*

"So," she said, trying to meet Shona's skittering gaze, "we've known each other for about nineteen years. How would you describe me?"

"What?"

"I want you to describe me," said Tabitha.

"Really?"

"You're my character witness. What did you think you'd be doing?"

She heard a bark of laughter from the public gallery.

Shona had heard the laugh too and she looked annoyed. "You've always been—" She stopped dead.

"Yes?" said Tabitha after a pause that went on longer than felt comfortable.

"Well. Clever, of course. And stubborn: when you set your mind to something, you'll do it. An awkward person and that makes you a bit prickly sometimes. When you were at school, we used to call you Tabby cat and say you had claws."

There were many things Tabitha wanted to say in response to that but she said none of them.

"Would you say I was trustworthy?"

"Yes," said Shona, though her tone sounded unsure.

"Is there anything you'd like to add to that?"

Shona chewed the side of her thumb. "You speak your mind. You don't let yourself get pushed around. You never have. That's why it was so surprising to learn about Stuart Rees carrying on with you when you were just a kid really, let's face it."

Tabitha didn't know if this was helping or damaging her case. She wanted Shona to say outright that she wouldn't be capable of killing anyone but didn't know how to phrase the question.

"Would you—" she began, then stopped. She felt like something had detonated in her brain. She grimaced, feeling its aftershock work through her.

"You said Stuart was 'carrying on' with me?"

"I don't get what—"

"Wait. Hang on. Pass me that folder. That one there!" she said to Michaela.

She started fumbling through it. Michaela was whispering urgently to her but Tabitha couldn't hear anything. Her hands were clumsy and she dropped several documents onto the floor and it took an awful few seconds to gather them but she found what she wanted and held it out.

"Will you read that out loud please?"

The piece of paper was delivered to Shona, who stared at it, and then at Tabitha.

"Please read it," said Tabitha.

Shona licked her lips. Her eyes flickered around the court then back to the papers.

"'FYI,'" she said. "'It is my duty to inform you that Stuart Rees was carrying on with Tabitha Hardy when she was underage and he was her teacher. This is true.'"

"It was you, wasn't it?" said Tabitha. "It was you who wrote that letter to the police. Of course it was you. How could I have been so stupid?"

She banged the heel of her hand against her head. "Stupid," she said. "Who else would it have been?"

There was noise going on around her. Michaela was saying something, and someone in the gallery was calling out and Judge Munday was asking her to please control her behavior. Meanwhile, Simon Brockbank was leaning back and smiling broadly and Shona, standing in the witness box, had both hands to her face, one at her mouth and the other to her temple, like a caricature of helpless fear.

"You never liked me," said Tabitha to Shona. "You always thought I was weird, didn't you? Not cool or glamorous. Not one of the in-crowd."

"What's this about?" asked Shona.

"You're my witness. I want to ask you a single question and you have to answer it. Did you write that anonymous letter to the police pointing out that Stuart Rees had been *carrying on* with me, as you put it, when he was my teacher?"

Shona stared at her and then her eyes darted around the court. It was as if she was trying to work out how to escape.

"Answer the question please," said Judge Munday calmly. "And it's important you answer truthfully."

Shona didn't look like a pretty child anymore. Her face was blotchy and scared.

"I thought they should know," she whispered.

"That's a yes, is it? What the fuck?"

"Please, Ms. Hardy, you must curb your language."

Shona lifted her head higher. "It's true. It was my duty as a citizen," she said primly.

"Yeah, yeah," said Tabitha. "Very honorable."

Shona flushed. Tabitha could see the red seeping under the golden tan on her throat, and another thought flashed through her.

"How did you have the money to go on your holiday?" she asked. "You were in debt when I talked to you, you couldn't even afford to pay for my notebook, and then you swanned off on holiday all of a sudden."

"Is this really relevant?" said Judge Munday.

"Someone's paid you, haven't they? Some tabloid."

"What?" said Shona. Her mouth was gaping open; her face was shiny with sweat.

"How much? How much to give little tidbits about my life?"

"Stop now," said Judge Munday. "This is a serious allegation you're making. Against a witness you yourself called to help you in your case, by the way."

"I know. You ask her then."

The judge glared at her. "I do not need you to instruct me how to run my court. Which you are, by the way, turning into a public brawl." She turned to Shona. "Miss Fry. A serious allegation has been made and it is my duty to pursue it. Have you received any money or payment in kind from any outlet for your story?"

"She's the one on trial, not me."

"Can you answer the question?"

"I haven't done anything wrong. I've just tried to behave like a decent member of society."

"Just say yes and get it over with," said Tabitha.

"I have given a short interview," said Shona, "and why shouldn't I?"

"Because," said Judge Munday, "you cannot be an impartial witness if you have been paid for your story."

"That's just unfair," said Shona. "Why is it wrong to tell my story? It's mine. Anyway," she added, her voice loud and high with outrage. "She obviously did it. That's what everyone thinks and it's what I think and if you want the truth, even at school we all said she was mad."

"Clear the court," barked Judge Munday.

She turned to Tabitha. "I take it you have no other character witnesses appearing in your defense that you want to demolish, Ms. Hardy?"

"That was awful," Tabitha said. "Horrible."

"It wasn't what I was expecting," said Michaela. She was eating a blueberry muffin and drinking a cappuccino. There was foam on her upper lip.

"At least I didn't say anything about her and Rob Coombe."

"Why didn't you, while you were at it?"

"I almost did—and then I saw us from the outside and felt ashamed."

"You know what I think?"

"What?"

"I think some of the jury are beginning to like you."

"Really?"

"Yeah. That one in the hoodie who spoke to you, he was laughing. And the woman in the front row with the beads."

"Blinky."

"Sorry?"

"It's what I call her. She blinks a lot."

"Don't say that in court. Anyway, when the trial started all of them looked grim, but now that's changed. At least some of them are on your side."

"Maybe."

Sixty-nine

S am McBride was smaller and slighter than Tabitha remembered. He looked vulnerable in the witness box in a cheap blue suit that was baggy on him, with an orange tie that he had knotted too tightly. His voice wavered when he took his oath and when he took a mouthful of water Tabitha saw that his hands were trembling slightly. But once he got going, he answered steadily enough, though Tabitha felt so weary of everything that she barely had the energy to ask him anything.

He explained to the jury that he was a bus driver. He had only lived in the area for seven months—and at the time of the murder, had been there for five weeks. Before that, he'd been in the army. He'd come to Devon to get away from things. He was a stranger to the area and had been working for the bus company for three and a half weeks. He'd driven lorries in the army so it wasn't that different. He described his average day: collecting kids up on his route, dropping them at school, picking up the old folk and taking them to their community centers for lunch, returning to the school for the home run, before taking the bus back to the depot.

He'd been in Okeham on December 21. It was a normal kind of day—except for the ice, he added, plus the kids were pretty hyped up because it was their last day of term. He'd got there at about a quarter past eight, his usual time. He'd gone into the village shop to buy cigarettes.

"I keep trying to give them up," he said, shrugging his thin shoulders.

"Do you remember seeing me?"

"You were wearing pajamas."

"Did I talk to you?"

"I don't think so."

"Did I talk to anyone?"

He shrugged. "I guess you maybe said something to the woman, you know, the woman behind the counter."

"Do you have any memory of me saying anything about Stuart Rees?"

"No."

"What about Rob Coombe? Did he say anything about Stuart Rees?"

"I don't know."

Tabitha had been hoping for a different answer. She pressed on. "When you say don't know, do you mean he might have done?"

Sam McBride shook his head. "I wasn't paying attention. Maybe he said something."

"Can I put it the other way round? You didn't hear me bad-mouthing him?"

"I didn't." He paused for a moment. "I think I would have remembered if you had. You were inches from me."

It was more than he'd said before and Tabitha felt pathetically grateful. She asked for the CCTV to be played. First they watched the images filmed by the camera outside. The digits at the bottom showed it was 08:10. Two young girls walked into the frame in their bulky coats. Three more kids appeared. A car drew up and Rob Coombe and his daughter got out. A figure entered the frame in a heavy jacket and pajama trousers. Herself at 08:11:44. She knew all this almost by heart. She watched herself disappear into the shop. The bus pulled up; there was the face of the boy staring out through the cracked glass of the central window. Sam

McBride appeared and also went toward the shop and out of the frame.

She asked for the interior clip to be played. There was the back of Terry's head and Rob Coombe. Then came Tabitha. The bus driver came in and joined the little queue. Rob was gesturing angrily, briefly turning so that they could all see Tabitha's face, smudged with tiredness. Rob Coombe left with a newspaper and cigarettes. She herself bought milk and exited. Sam McBride also bought cigarettes and some kind of chocolate bar, then he too left.

"There," said Tabitha to the jury. "Does that look like I'm yelling about Stuart Rees? Doesn't it look more like I'm saying nothing and that Rob Coombe is doing the shouting?"

She thanked the skinny figure in the witness box. She didn't know why she suddenly felt so frail and weepy: perhaps it was that Sam McBride made her feel sad, because in his solitariness he reminded her of herself; perhaps it was simply the sight of herself on that icy December morning, heavy with exhaustion and defeat, blundering toward disaster.

Seventy

When Luke was in the witness box, Tabitha never once looked up at the public gallery, but she could sense Laura's eyes on her and she saw the scene as if from above: her in the increasingly baggy and creased suit she had worn for weeks now, like a uniform, with wild hair that needed washing and cutting; Luke facing her, tall and angular, with his pale face and dark hair tied in a topknot. Of all the people who had given evidence, he was the only one who had made no effort to dress up for the occasion. He was dressed in old jeans and the same red tee shirt he'd worn when they first met in prison.

"Can you tell me about your relationship with your father?" she asked.

Judge Munday was practically quivering with vigilance. Tabitha knew she had to tread carefully.

"It wasn't good," said Luke matter-of-factly. He seemed unnaturally calm, much more so than the times he had come to see her at Crow Grange. "I wasn't the son he wanted."

"What kind of son was that?"

"Obedient. Traditional. One of the lads."

"And you weren't?"

"Look at me. I was a crybaby. That's what he called me." He lifted his face toward Laura. "I was bullied at school and I was bullied at home."

He still spoke without anxiety, almost as if it was a relief to him.

"You dropped out of school early, didn't you? Why?" Tabitha asked.

"I had to get away from him. I felt badly about leaving Mum. It wasn't her fault. She tried to stop him sometimes and then she paid for it."

"What do you mean by that?"

"He didn't just bully me. He bullied her too. I don't think he hit her but he controlled her. She was scared of him."

Tabitha glanced across at Simon Brockbank, wondering why he didn't intervene. He was sitting back in his chair with his eyes half closed.

"Why did you come back?" she asked.

"I wanted to persuade Mum to leave him. I never got why she stuck it out. I mean, I know they were comfortably off and had a nice house and all the stuff that goes with it but she had a terrible time of it. I never saw her happy." Again, he glanced up and away. "She didn't laugh or even smile much. She just got through life, like a robot. It made me mad. I wanted her to leave and start again."

At last Simon Brockbank rose to his feet.

"I fail to see what relevance there is in smearing the good name of a murder victim."

"Really?" Tabitha put her hands on the table the way she'd seen him do and leaned toward him. "*Really?* One reason I'm on trial here is because I had a motive. But don't you see, loads of people had a motive. I'm just showing the jury that Stuart damaged people. He made an entire village toxic. He ruined lives. Not just mine. Even his own son's."

She waved her hand toward Luke, who looked back at her with a small, ironic smile. And, *Oh Christ*, she thought, noticing his large pupils, *he's stoned*. At eleven in the morning.

"Did your mother know why you were coming back?" she asked him.

"Yeah."

"Did your father?"

"No." He frowned. "Maybe. You know, he had a way of finding things out. Secrets and weaknesses and things that made you ashamed. He had a nose for them."

Tabitha stared at him hard. "You're saying that he collected secrets?"

He pushed his hands deep into his pockets and once more glanced toward Laura. Tabitha saw an expression she couldn't read flicker across his face. "He liked controlling people. He liked them knowing he had something on them, seeing them squirm."

"So do you think—?" she began, but he cut her off.

"Loads of people would have wanted him dead, or at least not be sad that he was," he said. "You're just in a long line of them."

Tabitha took a sip of water.

"Did you?"

"Want him dead?" He looked suddenly young and vulnerable. "I'm glad I'll never have to see him again."

Seventy-one

Lev Wojcik looked like he was wearing a suit that belonged to someone else. It wasn't too small nor too big but somehow both at the same time. The trousers stretched over his thighs as he walked to the witness box, while the sleeves reached to his palms. Tabitha looked at him for a moment before speaking. He was probably the last person who had seen Stuart alive—apart from the killer. The police had interviewed him, but the prosecution hadn't called him. Was that simply because they didn't think he had anything relevant to say?

She stood up.

"I'm sorry," she said. "I don't know how to pronounce your name."

"Voy-chick," he said with a slow weariness. Tabitha thought of how often he must have to go through this, pronouncing his name, spelling it out.

"Mr. Wojcik," she said carefully, "you were interviewed by the police, right?"

"Yes."

"What did they want to know?"

"What time I deliver package."

"And what time was that?"

"He sign on my manifest so I have exact time."

"Manifest?"

"Mobile thing. For signature."

He took a piece of paper from his pocket and looked at it. "Nine hours and forty-six minutes."

"Is that all the police asked you?"

"They just want the time."

Tabitha paused. She really only had one question to ask.

"How did he seem?"

Wojcik gave a little shrug. "Nothing big."

"And then you were stuck in the village. That must have been a pain."

"Yes. Big pain."

"When did you realize that the tree had blocked your exit?"

"When?"

"Yes."

"When I go to shop and they say."

"But aren't I right to think that you went there on your way to Stuart Rees's house, and then on your way back?"

"That is right."

"So were you told about the tree before you went to the house or after?"

She tried to speak calmly, but she could feel beads of sweat on her forehead.

"The woman say before. When I buy cigarettes. It must have fallen just behind me."

"Let me get this straight," said Tabitha. Her legs felt funny. "You knew before you got to Stuart Rees's house that you were trapped in the village?"

"Is right."

"And, um." She licked her parched lips. "Did you say anything about the tree to Mr. Rees?"

"Oh yes. When he is signing, I tell him I'm stuck in the village because of tree and they say it will be hours, and he tells me about the café."

"So he knew."

"I'm sorry?"

"Stuart knew that the tree had blocked the village."

"I tell him so."

"He knew," repeated Tabitha.

Lev Wojcik looked at her in puzzlement. "I tell him," he repeated slowly, as if to a child.

"And the police didn't ask you about this?"

"No. Small thing."

Tabitha hesitated. She looked round the court and didn't understand why everyone wasn't whispering to each other or staring in astonishment. She couldn't think of what else to say. When she spoke it was almost reluctantly.

"All right," she said. "Thank you."

She leaned over to Michaela.

"There's something I should have said," she whispered. "There's something—" And then it came to her. She didn't have to ask. She just needed to remember. She wrote frantically on the pad in front of her.

Seventy-two

It was the weekend. She had two whole days to think, to plan for the last days of the trial, to ready herself.

Tabitha walked up and down the prison yard. It was smaller than the one at Crow Grange and surrounded by brick walls. It was muggily hot. The air pressed down on her, her skin felt clammy and she longed for wind, for the salt spray of the sea. Up and down, up and down, trying to hold on to the thoughts that hissed through her mind and evaporated.

Lev Wojcik's evidence yesterday in court had given her a glimmer of hope that was almost terror. There was a chance, maybe only a small chance, and it almost hurt. The time of being free seemed far off, and all that seemed real was her sweaty cell and her journey to the court and back in the van that smelled of other people's bodies, and the days, the weeks, spent in that high-ceilinged space where people with well-bred faces under bristly wigs used pompous words, while her own heart galloped with fear.

But whatever happened, she still wouldn't know who had killed Stuart Rees. She wouldn't know that it wasn't her. The case against her might be less robust than it had seemed when she first stared at the bundle of evidence laid out against her, but the question remained, a fist round her heart: who else could it have been? She didn't understand why the prosecution didn't seem to realize what she herself so inescapably knew—that only she had been on the right side of the CCTV camera for long enough to kill Stuart. There was nobody else, just her.

Up and down, up and down, while she tried to find a way out. The film ran through her head, grainy black-and-white images of figures moving jerkily across the frame; of the branches of the tree swaying slightly; of a child staring down through the cracked window of the bus; of the vicar and her dog; of Rob Coombe gesticulating wildly; of Owen Mallon running past; of Stuart's car passing and repassing; of herself dragging her unwilling body along the road; of herself, dazed with tiredness and defeat, looking unknowingly into the eye of the camera; of sleet and snow and darkness drawing in. Fast forward and rewind, and time passing and time frozen on sky and on tree and faces.

She stopped abruptly.

"What you staring at?" said a woman, shouldering her. "What's so interesting?"

"There isn't a coastal path," she said dreamily.

"What? Are you on something?"

"Wait," said Tabitha. "Wait a moment."

She held on to a face. She closed her eyes so she might see it more clearly. A bell was shrilling somewhere.

"Time's up," said a voice.

"Wait."

It took several hours for the discs to arrive and for the TV screen and the DVD player to be set up in the small room near the prison officers' cloakroom that was full of metal lockers. But no one had objected to her request: it was common knowledge that Tabitha was conducting her own defense and not being utterly demolished in the process, and she was suddenly a figure of something that was almost respect. Someone even brought her a mug of coffee and a packet of digestive biscuits.

She began from the beginning, just as she had done all those weeks ago, when Mary Guy had handed her the stapled A4 envelope of discs: two little stacks, held together with rubber bands. Tabitha inserted the first one and pressed play. Once again, she was in Okeham on a winter's day. The birch tree beside the bus shelter moving slightly in the breeze, two young girls in their winter coats walking into the frame, a car pulling up and Rob Coombe and his daughter arriving. Then it was her turn, half hidden in her jacket and scarf, head down. Then came the school bus, the boy staring out through the cracked window, his face looking like it was drawn on.

Like that first time, she slid in the interior disc and watched yet again the scene inside the shop: Rob, herself, then Sam. They all arrived, they left, the snow fell in flurries and then turned to sleet.

A bird. A cat. Laura's car. Lev's van. Owen Mallon sprinting past. The mothers and their toddlers, fingers pointing to the sky at the unseen helicopter. Andy, the return of Dr. Mallon, Mel and Sukie, Shona.

Tabitha's eyes felt tired from staring. She didn't write anything down, but she leaned forward as if as long as she concentrated hard enough, then she would see.

Stuart's car passing. Returning.

The deliveryman and Mel once more. Shona and then Rob.

Luke bowed under his large rucksack. Tabitha watched as he trudged past, kicking up slush.

Mel once more—as if her job consisted of walking round the village looking cheerful and ready to help.

Laura's car arriving. Lev departing in his van.

And the bus returning, sliding past the camera. A different child's face clear at the window. Children running into the street, in Christmas spirits.

Rob collecting his daughter.

Andy walking past on his way to Tabitha's house. Then the police car, blue lights in the darkness. Then the ambulance. Then another police car.

And then people gathering at the shop like flies round a carcass. Because someone was dead. Someone had been murdered.

She finally pressed pause and the film froze on the birch tree in the empty darkness. She could almost hear the sea, the shining black waves rolling in, curling down on the shingle and rock, and feel the bitter sting of salty wind on her cheeks. She was done. And she knew. At last she knew.

Tabitha thought she would feel exhilarated or at least relieved, but she didn't. She felt drained of all emotion.

She sat on the edge of her bed and made herself breathe deeply, in and out like a tide ebbing and flowing, and gradually it came to her that she didn't know what she was going to do.

It was a question, she thought, of how much she prized her freedom. When she had first arrived at Crow Grange, over six months ago, she had thought she would go mad in prison, that she would suffocate there. But now she had to ask herself if she valued her own freedom more than someone else's, which was a way of asking how much she valued herself: that misshapen, botched, heavy thing she had dragged along through the years of despair and anger and satisfaction and moments of hope and release. She thought of herself hammering nails into the wall, hauling timber across the yard, building herself a life that she wasn't sure she wanted to live in.

She would have asked God what to do, but she didn't have a god. Or her parents, but she didn't have them either. If she turned to Michaela she knew exactly what her response would be—incredulity and anger that Tabitha was even thinking she had an option. Nobody could tell her what to do, because it was her own freedom and life that was at stake here.

She found her battered notebook whose torn and scrawled-over pages were a record of the past months and also felt, in their mess and urgency and erasures, like the inside of her brain: maps and timelines and crossings out and doodles and notes to herself and names and lists and questions and night terrors. There were only a couple of blank pages at the end, but this was the last time she would need to write in it. She uncapped her pen.

The question was this: would she be found not guilty anyway, without revealing what she now knew? She wrote everything down, unnecessarily neat, numbering points, and then she sat for a long time staring at what she had. She knew that she had done all right in discrediting some of the less important evidence: the old woman who claimed to have heard her from a distance threatening Stuart but who turned out to be rather deaf; Mel, who had her times muddled up and who was involved in a feud with the murdered man; Rob Coombe, who bore a grudge against both Stuart and presumably Tabitha herself—she had after all punched him in the face. She had confused the assumed timeline, thrown not only the time of death but the place into doubt.

But at the start of the case the prosecution had talked about the three cornerstones of their case against Tabitha: evidence, opportunity and motive. She had the opportunity and the motive remained. Even if Stuart had been killed in his own home, rather than in Tabitha's, she had been nearby and she couldn't work out how anyone else could have been. And he had abused her when she was fifteen and his student.

So had she done enough? She thought of the twelve jurors. What would they think? What would Scary think, or Posh, or the ponytail man or Smiley? Sometimes they had looked hostile; sometimes amused, interested, curious, pained, disgusted. She couldn't read them. Michaela said that some of them were beginning to warm to Tabitha, but she had no idea if that was true or if that made any difference in the end, because it came down to cold facts, to the balance of probability, to whether or not they thought that Tabitha had murdered Stuart.

She wondered what she would think, if she were a member of the jury. Would she believe that the small, unkempt woman who had been abused by the murdered man when an unhappy schoolgirl, who had been depressed and angry for years, who shouted a lot and swore and punched people on the nose when they offended her, who swam in icy seas to try to keep sane, who had tried to stop Andy from discovering the body, who even the one person she called a friend believed had probably done it . . .

She stood up abruptly, slightly dazed by what she was about to do. Of course she couldn't know what verdict the jury would reach. It wasn't possible to make a rational calculation, because this was a decision that was not based on reason or logic or even an educated guess. It was a leap in the darkness; an act of faith or of selfhood. It was about who she was and who she wanted to be.

Seventy-three

Detective Chief Inspector Keith Dudley was in some way the most smartly dressed witness to appear. Luke and Andy had both mentioned his sharp style and today his dark suit looked brushed, like a politician's. His cuff links gleamed. His dark hair was parted in a line that was geometrically straight. As he stood in the witness box, he looked around the courtroom with an almost amused expression. He seemed more at home than anyone there. When he turned toward Tabitha, she saw that his eyes were a startling gray color, almost beautiful. She could imagine being questioned by him. The idea of it frightened her.

Tabitha had thought for days and days about whether it was sensible—whether it was sane—to call the man who had been in charge of the inquiry, the man who knew all the evidence against her; who had a face like an ax or a hatchet. She had talked it over with Michaela. It felt like a desperate last throw of the dice. This was the last thing the jury would hear. If it went wrong, if he had something damaging and new it could ruin her.

But she had her list of questions. She picked up the piece of paper and it shook so much that she had to put it down just to be able to read it. She picked up a glass of water. She sipped from it and replaced it on the table. The courtroom was so quiet that the sound of the glass on the wood was clearly audible. She looked round. The public gallery and the press gallery were packed, people crammed together, leaning forward. She felt like the victim of an accident with onlookers ghoulishly curious to look at the damage.

"You were in charge of the inquiry," said Tabitha.

"That's right."

"But it's the first time we've met."

"We're meeting now. And I've seen you of course."

"Seen me?"

"When you were in police custody and being interviewed. You were in a state of considerable agitation so I am not surprised you don't remember."

"Oh," said Tabitha, wishing she hadn't asked.

There was a silence. Tabitha knew that Dudley was a professional. He would keep his answers short. He wouldn't say anything he didn't have to say. He didn't need to.

"But you weren't there when I was charged. Isn't that unusual?"

"Not particularly."

"But you were like . . ." Tabitha paused, looking for the right word. "Responsible for the case, right?"

"Yes."

Dudley was standing with his hands on the edge of the box, the fingers of his right hand drumming silently. Tabitha looked down at her piece of paper and then back at Dudley.

"Was I your only suspect?" she asked.

"We always keep an open mind."

"I don't really know how to ask this," Tabitha said. "I mean, when did I become the suspect, or the main suspect?"

Dudley's expression turned to puzzlement and then to something like amusement. It made Tabitha feel slightly sick.

"Are you serious?" he said. "Do you want me to spell it out?"

"All right," said Tabitha, her voice suddenly feeling dry. She took another drink of water.

"It just became clear as we went on. The body was found in your house, you tried to conceal it from the man who found it. There was enough evidence as it was. Then it emerged that you had a motive and that you had lied about it."

"I didn't lie about it."

"All right, you concealed it."

"I don't think 'concealed' is the right word."

"That's a matter of opinion."

"I'm sorry," said Judge Munday. "I need to say something at this point." She turned to the jury. "This may be a difficult point to grasp, but you need to consider this: an innocent person is not required to give possibly damaging information about themselves. I hope that's clear. Continue, Ms. Hardy."

Tabitha wasn't clear whether the judge's intervention had been helpful or unhelpful. She looked down at her questions.

"You haven't been in court. So maybe I can tell you some of what you missed—"

Judge Munday interrupted sharply. "You're to ask questions, Ms. Hardy."

"All right, all right, I'll try and do it as questions." She looked down at her piece of paper. "It's obvious that right from the beginning you were so sure that it was me that it stopped you looking in other directions." Tabitha paused and remembered that she needed to ask a question. "Is that right?"

"No, it isn't right."

"I want to ask you a couple of things about the evidence that the scene of crime person gave."

"I can't comment on scientific details," Dudley said, with just a hint of uneasiness.

"These aren't very scientific. The first is about the blood. Stuart Rees's throat was cut. There was blood on his body, on the plastic sheet that had been wrapped around his body, on me and on my friend Andy. But the interesting thing is where the blood wasn't, which is basically everywhere else. There was no blood on the floor, on the walls, on the ceiling."

"From what I remember there *was* blood on the floor."

"Those were shoe prints from where we trod in the blood. But nowhere else. Doesn't that seem a bit strange to you?"

Dudley gave a sniff. "Not really. Every crime scene is different."

"Fine," said Tabitha. She looked back down at her notes. "All the stuff you took away, you stored at a warehouse." Dudley waited. "Not a police station or a government building or whatever. Just an ordinary commercial storage place." Again Dudley waited. "Right?" she asked.

"Yes."

"Isn't that a bit risky? I mean, evidence could get contaminated, couldn't it?"

"Not on my watch," said Dudley.

"But I went there and there was other stuff in there as well as things connected to this case."

"Your point being?"

"Things could have got mixed up."

"Are you suggesting that happened?"

"Well, not really, I'm saying it *could* have." A pause. "Is that right?"

"But it didn't."

Tabitha felt her cheeks burning. "It just suggests a slapdash operation," she said. "No one cared really. You thought you just had me and it didn't matter." Dudley looked at her without speaking, and Tabitha, leaning forward, practically shouted: "Wouldn't you agree?"

"No."

"How about this? I just mentioned the plastic sheeting. My friend Michaela here did what you should have done: she found out where the sheeting came from. It was from a delivery company and it was used to deliver a sofa."

Dudley shrugged. "All right," he said.

"Yes, but not to my house. The sofa was delivered to Stuart Rees's house. Does that seem interesting?"

Another shrug. "I suppose it was in Mr. Rees's car."

"That's an idea," said Tabitha. "So did you check the car?"

"We checked it, yes."

"No, I mean a full search, blood and fibers and all that kind of stuff you see on *CSI*."

Dudley looked hesitant. "I'd need to check the file."

"We already did," said Tabitha, "and—spoiler fucking alert—you didn't."

"Please, please, Ms. Hardy," said Judge Munday. Tabitha looked over at the judge and her head was resting in her hands. She raised her head wearily. "In any other case, Ms. Hardy, I would have you hauled off to the cells. I know it's a lot to ask, to keep on asking, that is, but could you treat this courtroom with some remnant of respect?"

Tabitha took a breath. "Sorry, I got carried away." She looked down at her piece of paper and across at Michaela and back at her paper. There was only one question left. She had been thinking of it ever since Lev Wojcik had left the witness box. She had talked it over with Michaela. She was almost afraid to ask it. She needed to lead up to it.

"You sent an officer to interview Lev Wojcik, the man who delivered a package to Stuart Rees on the morning he died. Why didn't you do it yourself?"

"Because I don't do all the interviews. It's not necessary."

"Your officer just asked one question, which was basically, did he meet Stuart Rees and at what time. But she forgot to ask a second question: what did they talk about?"

Tabitha waited. Dudley looked impassive but she could see from a slight flicker in his eyes that he was wondering what was coming.

"You want me to tell you what they talked about?" Tabitha continued.

"Just say it," said Dudley irritably.

Tabitha knew she had got under his skin. It made her feel better.

"Wojcik is adamant that he told Stuart Rees that a tree had fallen across the road and that he was stuck in the village for several hours."

Dudley looked puzzled as if he was wondering: *Is that it?*

"What do you think of that?" Tabitha asked.

"Not much."

"Well, I'm going to give you a moment," Tabitha said. "I've spent months in prison and you put me there."

"I did not put you there."

"I lie awake every night, looking at the ceiling.

Sometimes I'm wondering who's going to be the next person to die in the prison and whether it'll be me. But mainly I think about the case, over and over."

"Please, Ms. Hardy," said Judge Munday, "ask a question."

"This *is* a question," said Tabitha. "I just haven't got to the end of it yet. So, Detective Chief Inspector Dudley, I've mentioned the plastic sheet, I've mentioned the bloodstains and I've mentioned Lev Wojcik's conversation with Stuart Rees. What does that make you think?"

There was a long pause.

"Nothing in particular."

"Can I say something that maybe you should think about?"

Dudley didn't reply. He just made a dismissive gesture with his hands.

"I'll start with the last bit. Have you seen the CCTV footage?"

"I've seen the relevant bits."

"You saw that Stuart Rees drives out of the village at"—she looked down at her notes—"ten thirty-four."

"I don't remember the exact time."

"And drives back just six minutes later. That's barely enough time to get out of the village. Why did he come back?"

"Because the road was blocked."

Tabitha didn't speak. She just waited. Someone coughed in the public gallery. She could hear traffic outside.

"Ms. Hardy?" said Judge Munday.

"Yes?"

"Do you have a question?"

"I'm just waiting for the detective to think about his answer."

"We're not here to watch people think. Please ask another question."

"All right. Why would Stuart Rees try to drive out of the village when he knew the road was blocked?"

"Because he forgot," said Dudley.

"Forty minutes after being told?"

"He did, though, didn't he?"

"You mean Stuart Rees?"

"Who else would I mean?"

"I want to show you something." She turned to Michaela. "Have we sorted it?"

"I think so."

It turned out that it hadn't entirely been sorted. They had a laptop connected to large screens on two walls of the court. As Michaela tapped on the keyboard all that was visible on the screen were the desktop files.

"It's at about ten thirty-four," said Tabitha in a hiss.

"I know. I'm clicking on the file but nothing's happening."

There were whispers around the court. Someone gave a single snort of laughter.

"Have you tried restarting it?" said Tabitha.

"Hang on," said Michaela and then suddenly the image was there, and once more, even in the courtroom, Tabitha felt she was back in Okeham. There was only the movement of the tree branches to show that it wasn't a fixed image. Tabitha looked at the time code. It was coming, coming and then, with perfect timing, the car swept across the screen and disappeared. Tabitha looked at Michaela.

"Can you go back and freeze on the car?"

She did so. Then she fast-forwarded six minutes and showed the car returning and she froze on that as well. Nothing could be seen through the car, not even an outline.

"You can't make out Stuart Rees as the driver, can you?"

"Who else would it be?" said Dudley.

"Can I suggest a different version?" said Tabitha.

"You can suggest anything you like."

"My suggestion is that the murder wasn't committed in my house. It was committed in *his* house. That's what the plastic sheeting suggests. Did you search Rees's house?"

"No."

"Did you do a forensic analysis of his house?"

"No."

"Then the killer wraps the body in the plastic sheeting and puts it in the boot of Rees's car. The killer drives the car out of the village to dispose of the body but the road's blocked and he or she has to turn back. They arrive back in the village. But where to leave the body? The immediately obvious hiding place would have been my house. Near Stuart's house, a shed outside. The killer dumps the body, intending to come back for it later. What do you think of that?"

Dudley took a long time to answer. He seemed to be going over it in his mind. "It sounds ridiculously far-fetched."

"It fits with the evidence," said Tabitha loudly. "The evidence that you didn't manage to find."

"You're just trying to stir things up," said Dudley. "None of this shows you didn't do it!"

"Look, don't you understand what you've done?"

"I don't know what you're talking about. Nor do you."

"Your whole investigation was wrong. You just assumed it was Stuart Rees driving out of the village and back and because of that you put his murder after that time. But I'm saying—*suggesting*—that it happened before his car was captured on CCTV. His body was in that car. It took place between nine-fifty and ten thirty-five, which is a much smaller window of time than the one you've been working on. And one that you completely ignored. The time you thought it couldn't have occurred in was precisely the time it must have. Your investigation all happened in the wrong place and it was based on the wrong time. What a farce. No wonder you ended up with an innocent person in prison."

The air felt electric; she could almost feel everyone in the court holding their breath.

"That's crap," said Dudley finally, and very angrily. His gray eyes looked like gunmetal.

"Fuck you," said Tabitha.

"Ms. Hardy," said Judge Munday, almost shouting. "Stop that. And you too, Inspector. You will maintain decency and respect in this courtroom. Ms. Hardy, have you any more questions?"

"No, I'm done with him," Tabitha said angrily and sat down.

Seventy-four

Tabitha sat down next to Michaela.

"Are you all set?" Michaela said.

Tabitha looked across at Simon Brockbank. He was due to start the summing up for the prosecution but he was leaning back in his chair, hands in his pockets, chatting with Elinor Ackroyd as if they were about to play a game of cards. Tabitha couldn't make out what he was saying but she saw Ackroyd grin in response.

"They look like they're in a good mood," Tabitha murmured.

"Don't think about them," said Michaela. "Think about what you're going to say."

"I don't really know. I need to hear what Brockbank says."

Michaela started to speak and then stopped. She seemed hesitant.

"What is it?"

"I don't know. I don't know if this is a good idea."

"What?"

"I thought it might be a help. For the summing up. Or it might not be a help."

"What?"

"I can't ask you because then you'll want to see it and then—"

"Oh, for God's sake, what is it? Just show me."

Michaela started fumbling through her files.

"I've been collecting the reports," she said. "In the papers. I thought you might want to see them."

"Why didn't you show me before?"

"I thought it might put you off."

"Just show me."

Michaela pulled the file from the heap and pushed it over.

"They're only allowed to report," she said. "They're not allowed to make comments."

Tabitha opened the file. Inside was a thick pile of newspaper clippings and she immediately saw the large headline: "I was covered with his blood." Below, the story began "A court heard . . ." and was followed by quotations from Tabitha's own testimony. Her attention was caught by two photographs. The first was of Stuart Rees. It was recent, he was standing outside, probably in his garden, squinting into the sun, and Tabitha thought it made him look old and harmless. The second was of Tabitha herself, an older image, square, staring straight at the camera, glaring almost. Tabitha couldn't remember exactly when it was taken, but it must have been for a passport or a railcard or something like that. It looked uncomfortably like a mug shot.

She flicked through the cuttings. Another huge headline: "I slept with my teacher." Again the story beneath began: "A court heard . . ." Accompanying this article was a preposterous sketch of her by a court artist. It didn't look like her. It looked like a short-haired witch, with an angry expression, gesturing wildly. She flicked through page after page. Where had they got all these photographs of her? There was Tabitha, wearing a blazer in her class photo. There was Tabitha caught with a glass and a cigarette at a college party. There was Tabitha on a beach somewhere.

At first she was struck by the headlines: the sex and the blood and the murder. But then she was struck by the sheer amount of attention, reports covering a whole page, a double-page spread. She thought about the people across the country sitting with a cup of tea and reading about her sex life and her mental troubles and why her neighbors thought she had committed a murder. She had gone through her life without many friends, without making much of a stir, and now there were thousands and thousands of people across the country who knew about her, who had an opinion about her. There were people who thought she was a murderer, people who thought she was an abuse victim, people who were for her, people who were against her, all these people she would never know.

She closed the file. She felt suddenly nauseous, as if an abyss had opened at her feet and she was staring down into it.

The door opened and the court usher entered the court, but the judge didn't follow her. The usher walked through the court and stopped next to Simon Brockbank and spoke to him in a low voice. He looked round at Tabitha. Then she came across to Tabitha and leaned down and spoke as if she didn't want to be overheard.

"Judge Munday wants to see you and prosecution counsel in her chamber."

Tabitha started to speak, but the usher just gestured her to follow. Brockbank and Ackroyd walked after her. As they made their way in single file out of the court and through the corridors, Tabitha tried to think of something to ask, some question, but nothing oc-

564 • NICCI FRENCH

curred. She had an ominous sense that there was an
aspect of the case she'd missed, something damaging.
The usher opened the door and Tabitha walked past
her into the sumptuous room where Judge Munday
was sitting behind her desk. She wasn't talking on the
phone or pretending to be busy. Her hands were laid,
one on the other, on the table surface and she was looking directly at her visitors. Three armchairs had been
arranged in front of the desk and she waved Tabitha
and Brockbank and Ackroyd toward them. They sat
down.

"If there's some new witness—" Tabitha began.

Judge Munday raised her hands, almost in prayer.
"Please, Ms. Hardy, just once in your life, could you
keep quiet until you have something to say."

"Sorry," said Tabitha sulkily.

"Good." Judge Munday put her hands together once
more. "Now we need to be clear—and by this I mean
that you, Tabitha Hardy, need to be clear—that any
discussion we have here is privileged and is not to be
referred to in open court or indeed anywhere else. Do
you understand?"

"Fine."

"Not only understand but agree."

"All right, yes, OK."

Judge Munday paused, gathering her thoughts.

"I've been thinking," she said. "I spent yesterday and most of the night going through the relevant transcripts. I paid particular attention to the forensic evidence, to the testimony of the delivery driver and finally yesterday's testimony of the detective in charge of the investigation."

Tabitha had a slow, awakening sense of what was coming. She looked round at Simon Brockbank. He looked indifferent, of course, but there was also a faint smile forming on his face.

"The case against Ms. Hardy," Judge Munday continued, "was always circumstantial but, on the face of it, compelling. It seemed to me that these testimonies exposed gross errors and omissions in the investigation." She paused and looked fixedly at Simon Brockbank. "I have come to the conclusion that the prosecution case, as it now stands, is such that a jury, properly directed, could not convict. I believe it is now my duty to stop the trial."

"What?" said Tabitha. She felt a ringing in her ears. Her whole body was suddenly glowing with heat. She wasn't sure of her surroundings. She couldn't properly follow the meaning of what was being said. "What? What are you saying?"

"Wait," said Judge Munday. "This is a matter for the prosecution. They are entitled to contest this."

Tabitha turned once again to look at Brockbank. He and Elinor Ackroyd had leaned in together in muttered conversation. He looked back at the judge.

"You've heard all the evidence," he said. "Nobody else could have committed this crime."

"I have no need to tell you," said Judge Munday sternly, "that Ms. Hardy has no need to prove her innocence. The prosecution has to prove her guilt and not just by a process of elimination."

Brockbank turned to Tabitha, who suddenly felt like a small animal being observed by a fox.

"Have you looked at the jury?" he said.

"I've been staring at them for weeks," said Tabitha. "I've even got names for them."

"I mean really looked at them. After a bit, you can almost smell what they're thinking. I'm not sure they like you very much."

"I think a couple of them might," said Tabitha. "A bit."

"They saw that the police made some mistakes but these are people who think that if the detective believes you did it, then you probably did it. I think if this case goes before a jury, it could go either way."

"I'm not so sure about that," said Judge Munday. "They'd hear my direction first."

Brockbank looked thoughtful. "I wonder what the police would have found if they had made a proper forensic search of Rees's house and car."

"But they didn't," said Tabitha.

Brockbank smiled. "You're right. They didn't."

He held his hand out to her and, feeling like she was in a dream, Tabitha shook it and then almost recoiled.

"What does that mean?" she said.

"It means the prosecution won't object. But I'm afraid the members of the jury will feel cheated."

Judge Munday got up and walked to the far side of the room. She picked up a cut-glass decanter.

"Do you want a drink?" she said.

"It's eleven in the morning," said Tabitha.

"We're about to go into court and I will make my announcement and you will walk straight out into the world with no preparation. You might want to take a moment. I'm certainly having a drink. You, Ms. Hardy, would drive anyone to it."

Judge Munday poured whisky into four tumblers and handed them round. Brockbank raised his glass in Tabitha's direction.

"I suppose I should offer you congratulations," he said and took a sip.

"Like a game," said Tabitha. She wasn't feeling

any sense of triumph. She wasn't even feeling happy. "Some you win, some you lose, no hard feelings, you have a drink afterward. This is my life."

"I think it is a sort of game," said Brockbank. "I put my evidence, you put your evidence, see who wins. What would you prefer? Would you like it decided by people like Chief Inspector Dudley? He doesn't think it's a game. He goes by his professional experience and his gut feelings and both of them told him that you did it. If it was up to him, you'd be going down for fifteen years."

"If it was up to my lawyer, I'd be going down for fifteen years as well. She wanted me to plead guilty."

Brockbank laughed. "You should have had *me* as your lawyer."

Tabitha drained her glass. It was the first alcohol she had drunk for months and it made her cough and then it made her feel dizzy. She looked at Judge Munday.

"So are you going to say something?" she said. "Give me some wise advice?"

Judge Munday shook her head. "If you're expecting me to pat you on the head and say well done, you're going to be disappointed."

"I don't generally get patted on the head."

"You got away with it," said Judge Munday. "I don't mean with the crime. That's not our concern. Your defense was unruly, uncouth, chaotic and at times verging on the disgraceful, but you got by with it, just about." She paused. "I will give you one piece of advice. When you get out there in the world, it will all be strange and new. A lot of people will want to talk to you. Be careful. Their interests are not your interests." She finished her drink and stood up. "I think we should go."

The four of them looked at each other, as if waiting for someone to make the first move.

"I've got something to say," said Brockbank, "while we're still here." He looked at Tabitha with an expression of amused puzzlement. "Actually, two things. The first is that being found not guilty is not the same as being found innocent. And second and finally, if asked, I'll stoutly deny ever having said this: well done, Tabitha, if I may call you Tabitha. I thought this was a piece of cake for us, but all on your own, you destroyed the case against you, you destroyed that detective, you single-handedly made the prosecution look ridiculous."

Tabitha nodded. "I did more than destroy the detective and the case," she said. "I destroyed everything. My relationships with everyone in the village, my possibility of a future there, of a home even, my friendship with Andy, my belief that at long last I could be accepted and even welcomed. Everything."

"True," said Brockbank cheerfully. "Life, eh? Win some, lose some."

Tabitha and Michaela walked out of the front exit into the surge of a crowd. The buildings tipped toward her and the sky was a blue lid with a hole cut in it for the glaring eye of the sun.

Nobody noticed her at first; everyone was gathered round DCI Dudley and he was evidently at the end of making a statement.

"I deeply regret that mistakes were made so that a strong case was weakened and Tabitha Hardy gets to walk out of here a free woman," he was saying. "I want to be clear that there will be a review of the case but also that nobody else is under suspicion. There are no further lines of inquiry."

"Are there any other suspects?" a reporter shouted.

"No."

"Fuck you," yelled Tabitha, stepping forward into the glare of light and liberty. "You fucked up and now you're trying to smear me to cover it up."

Cameras flashed and snapped and mics were thrust forward and she heard people calling her name.

"*Murderer,*" a voice shrieked, and turning her head, Tabitha saw the furious face of a woman who had been in the public gallery day after day.

"Piss off," said Tabitha.

"The police have just said they have no further lines of inquiry." A voice from her left; a woman holding out a mic. "What do you say to that?"

Tabitha thought of Brockbank's words—*being found not guilty is not the same as being found innocent.*

"They failed," she said. "They failed in there and they're failing out here."

"How does it feel?" someone shouted.

"Say something to them," said Michaela hoarsely. "I'll get us a taxi."

But Tabitha, standing on the steps in the unreality of her freedom, had no words left.

"Please, all of you go away," she said.

"What will you do now?"

"I think I'll go for a swim."

But she wouldn't have a swim yet. There was something else she needed to do first. Everything else could wait.

PART FOUR

Outside

Seventy-five

Tabitha was sitting on a train. She stared out of the window, and through her own faint reflection—a small, pale face and a mop of wild hair; *witch*, she thought—she watched the sea in the distance, glittering and foaming. Fields and small woods and folded hills rolled by. The green of summer was tired now; the leaves on the trees were limp in the heat.

She got out at Truro, where she bought a small mug of bitter coffee and then waited half an hour for a bus. When it arrived, it was empty. It trundled her along Cornish lanes, through sudden towns and past lonely churches, and finally deposited her on a dusty road.

It took her over an hour to walk the last stretch. She didn't mind. For half a year she had been dreaming of walking through deserted landscapes, feeling the ache in her calves and the wind in her face. There was no wind today. The air stood hot and still. Seagulls pecked at a carcass on the road. She knew she should be thinking about what she was going to do, but she didn't, just let half-formed thoughts drift through her mind.

The caravan park was on the edge of a town. There was a grocery store at one end and what perhaps in rainy seasons passed for a stream, but was now a dried-up ditch, at the other. One of the caravans had a small garden at its entrance, with bright flowers and a miniature picket fence. One had recently been burned out and was just a charred remnant. There was a van with broken windows, through which Tabitha could see multiple crushed cardboard boxes. One of the caravans had closed curtains and a motorbike parked at its door. Another had a mountain of a man sitting on the small steps who raised his beer can toward her as she passed.

Tabitha was looking for a camper van and she saw it at the far end of the plot, facing the perimeter ditch and the fields beyond and in the distance the glitter of the sea. She walked over to it and it was as if she were in a dream, suddenly slow and without volition.

She knocked at the back door and stood back, and the door swung open.

He looked down at her and he didn't seem surprised

or upset or angry or even scared, but almost relieved, like he had been expecting her all along.

"How did you know?" he said at last.

"Hello, Sam."

They sat together on two rickety foldout chairs that he pulled from under the van. He looked more like a fox than ever, thought Tabitha: mangy and neglected. But he had strong arms along which his tattoos rippled, a mermaid's tail and a full-blown rose, and she remembered he had been in the army. He was scrawny but strong. Much stronger than she was. She twisted her head round, but the big man had gone from the steps and there was no one around.

"How did you find me?"

"It wasn't that hard. You didn't leave a forwarding address with the coach company, but I talked to Joe Simons." McBride's eyes flickered but he didn't answer. "I talked to this woman in the office at the coach station and I looked at the schedule. Joe was the one who was driving the bus that day. You were just a passenger. You got off at Okeham and you didn't get back on."

"How did you know?" he said.

He took a tin from his pocket and rolled himself a thin cigarette; his fingers were yellow and his teeth stained.

"I kept seeing it," said Tabitha, "but I didn't *see* it. It was in plain sight and nobody noticed. It was the bus."

"What do you mean?"

"On the CCTV. When it arrived in the morning, there was a cracked window. I watched it over and over again."

She could see it now: a boy was staring out of it and his face was crisscrossed by the spider's web of glass.

"But in the afternoon, when the bus returned, the window wasn't cracked anymore."

A different boy was staring into the camera through a clear pane of glass.

McBride wasn't looking at Tabitha, but at the baked earth.

"You told me you drove that bus all day. You said it twice. As soon as I realized about the window I looked at the CCTV properly and, sure enough, it was a different bus. You didn't mention that."

Sam started making another cigarette. She watched his long fingers deftly rolling the piece of paper round the shreds of tobacco.

"It was driving me crazy," Tabitha said. "Everybody hated Stuart except for me but nobody apart from me could have done it. And now there's you. You were his passenger that morning. You got off the bus at Okeham, the way you often did, bought cigarettes in the village shop, went back behind the bus and anyone seeing it on CCTV would automatically assume it was you driving away. The bus hid the sight of you walking in the direction of Stuart's house."

Sam didn't speak. He was smoking steadily and gazing out toward the distant sea.

"You killed Stuart," said Tabitha. She waited and he didn't react. "You planned it in advance. You made arrangements with your friend to drive the bus that day. You called up Laura a few days before and made an appointment for a viewing, just so you knew she wouldn't be there. After the bus left, you must have holed up somewhere out of sight and watched the house. There are several places round there, in the trees by the cliff. You waited till Laura had left and then the deliveryman arrived and you waited till he went as well. You went to the house and you killed him and you wrapped him in the plastic and put him in the boot of his car and drove away with him. But of course the tree had come down and you realized you were stuck. What is it? Sod's law? Murphy's law? If anything can go wrong, it will."

Still nothing from Sam.

"So you came back and dumped him in my house."

"I didn't know anyone was there. It looked a wreck. I didn't mean for it to fall on you."

For a moment Tabitha could barely speak. "You didn't do much about it when it did fall on me, did you? I guess your plan was to drive Stuart's car somewhere, dump the body and leave the car somewhere else. You had to think of a plan B. All you had to do was hide out and then do what you did in reverse. When the bus came back in the afternoon, you just walked behind it, out of sight of the camera again, and stepped aboard."

Sam looked around warily, dropped the glowing end of the cigarette onto the earth and carefully ground it out. "Now what?"

"What do you mean?"

"Why's it you're here, not the police?"

"I knew before the trial ended," said Tabitha. "I realized after the deliveryman's evidence."

"So why?" he asked again.

"When you were talking about seeing Dr. Mallon running, you said something about how he was probably going along the coastal path. But the coastal path is closed off round Okeham. Years ago part of the cliff collapsed and they had to divert it inland. But when you knew it, when you were a boy, the path was still there."

McBride gave a faint smile.

"So I knew it was you," Tabitha continued. "But I didn't know why. I think I do know now. The thing is, I was puzzled by Joe Simons. All right, I can imagine him giving you a lift in the coach and covering for you. But once he heard about the murder, why wouldn't he go to the police? What was in it for him? Unless he was a real friend and you had a good reason and you told him the reason."

She looked him full in the face. A spasm of pain, or maybe it was more like a recoil, gripped his features. There was something feral about him, she thought, and then she remembered the court drawing in which she had looked so savage: was she like him, then?

"He did it to you as well, didn't he?" she persevered.

There was a long silence. Sam sat leaning forward on the chair, looking at his hands that were folded loosely on his knees.

"Yeah," he said at last.

"Was he your teacher?"

"Sports club."

"How old were you?" she asked.

"Nine."

"Jesus."

"The first time," he said. It was obviously an effort for him to talk; the words came in small spurts. "It went on."

"You never told anyone?"

"I lived with my nan and then with foster parents. Who would I tell? Who did *you* tell? You're the first person I've said it to." He thought for a moment. "The second, after Joe."

"So you came back to the area to kill him."

"At first I thought I'd just give him a fright."

He said he'd seen a ghost, Laura had told her. Everyone had thought it was Tabitha he was fearful of, but it had been Sam: one thing to have sex with a fifteen-year-old girl, quite another to rape a nine-year-old boy. The respectable Mr. Rees, pillar of the community, churchgoer, member of the parish council, finger in every pie.

"He put the house on the market. He was going to get away with it all over again. I had to do it before the school holiday, see, while he was still there and I still drove the bus into the village every day."

Tabitha nodded. "Can I have a cigarette?" she asked.

He rolled her one and then lit it, lifting his hand to shield the flame. The acrid taste filled her mouth and she coughed violently.

"I thought I'd feel better somehow, once I'd killed him," said Sam.

"But you didn't?"

"I don't feel guilty, if that's what you're thinking. He was wicked. What he did to me—" He stopped, unable to find the words. "I was never right after," he said instead. "So he got what he wanted in the end."

"What did he want?"

"I don't know. Turn me into rubbish. I used to be sick sometimes; he liked that."

Tabitha stared at the smoke curling between her fingers.

"That day, when he opened the door," Sam continued in a low, flat voice, "and saw me, he seemed, like, almost relieved."

"What do you mean?"

"Like he'd been waiting for me. Like he didn't mind."

What was it Stuart had said to the vicar? *He said he was damned for what he had done.* She thought of him in his little car, looking at her without expression, lifting up her skirt: it had nothing to do with sexual desire. It was something else. Some kind of power.

"Well," she said eventually, "it's over, anyway."

"I didn't mean for it to harm you," said Sam. "That's why I turned up in court for you. I wanted you to be OK."

Tabitha considered this. He had been quite prepared for her to spend six months in prison and be tried for murder in a case that had seemed cut and dried. Turning up as a witness in her defense, with a paltry bit of supporting evidence, didn't seem like much. She thought of saying so, but what was the point?

"The police have no other lines of inquiry," she said instead.

"Unless you give them one."

"If you think I'm going to tell you that people know where I am, you're wrong. Nobody knows I'm here."

He could strangle her, she thought. Or drag her into the van and kill her there. They sat in silence. The sun was low in the pale sky and there was a smudge of mosquitoes above them. He shook his head.

"I'm done," he said.

"I've brought something with me," she said.

"What?"

She opened up her little rucksack and took out a sheet of paper.

"I wrote down in advance what I thought had happened and it's pretty much right. I want you to date and sign it."

"A confession." Sam's face darkened.

"I won't show it to anyone unless you do anything else."

"Like what?"

"I don't know. But if you do anything bad, then I'll go to the police with this."

"You're blackmailing me." He sounded aggrieved.

Tabitha started to laugh. It hurt the back of her

throat and made her eyes sting and it felt unpleasant, but for several minutes she couldn't stop.

"You killed a man," she said at last. "He might have been a bad man, but you killed him. And you were going to let me go to prison for years in your place. This"—she waved the paper before his face—"is just a guarantee that you won't harm someone else."

"I'm not like that."

"No one's like that, until they are."

She handed him a pen and watched as he read the words slowly, his index finger moving along the lines. He put the paper down and wiped the back of his hand across his forehead. Then he signed his name.

When she left, she didn't look back, not once, though she felt his eyes on her as she walked away.

On the shore, the sun nearly set and the tide coming in, little waves licking at her boots, she took out the piece of paper and read what was written on it. Then she tore it into tiny shreds, which she scattered into the sea. They drifted pale on the dark surface of the water amid the straggle of seaweed, and after a while they disappeared.

"Home," she said to herself, though the word held no meaning for her.

Seventy-six

Tabitha went back to Okeham one more time. She couldn't avoid it. She had put the house on the market and an estate agent had managed the process, arranged for the house to be cleaned, shown prospective buyers around, everything. He was very enthusiastic about the property.

"Short walk from the sea, perfect," he'd said. "Any preferences?"

"What do you mean?" Tabitha had said.

He had explained that some people preferred to sell to local people, even if it involved taking a slight loss. It was to do with maintaining the community.

"No preferences," Tabitha had said.

Within a few days, she accepted an offer for the full asking price. She didn't know anything about the buyer except for the name and she didn't care.

But she still had her possessions in the house, her furniture and other stuff. So, one dawn in early October, she drove back to Okeham in a van she hired for the day. She had asked Michaela if she wanted to come with her.

"You don't have to," Tabitha said. "It'll probably be boring."

"Are you kidding?" said Michaela.

It was before seven o'clock on a Tuesday morning when they drove into the village. There was nobody around. Tabitha felt like she was returning from the dead, a ghost that nobody could see. She pulled up outside her house.

"We'll be in and out before anyone knows we've been here," she said. "Except for the CCTV."

She unlocked the front door and they stepped inside. There was a smell of emptiness and abandonment.

"Do you want some tea?" asked Tabitha.

"All right. Have you got milk?"

Tabitha shook her head. "I haven't got tea either." She rummaged in her jacket and produced a five-pound note. "I don't want to show my face, but you could go to the village shop and buy some tea and milk. Biscuits as well, if you want."

While Michaela was gone, Tabitha looked around. It was all rubbish really. She should probably just have thrown it in a Dumpster. She started piling plates into a cardboard box. She shook open a bin bag for mugs and plates that were chipped or cracked or just too awful to take. She put the kettle on and it had come to the boil when Michaela arrived back with a box of tea bags, a carton of milk and a packet of chocolate biscuits.

"They seemed a bit suspicious," Michaela said. "They asked me what I was doing in Okeham. I told the woman I was here with you. Then she got very interested."

"Terry." Tabitha nodded.

They walked round the house with their mugs of tea and decided to leave the beds and sofa and the kitchen table.

"Some people take the light bulbs with them," said Michaela.

Tabitha looked around. "You know I still wake up in the middle of the night and for a moment I think I'm back in the cell and I want to scream out."

"Yeah, I know. Think of the ones who are there for decades."

"I can hardly bear to."

"What happened to that girl you shared with after I left?"

"Dana?" Tabitha looked away, out of the window toward the gray water. She could see Dana's woebegone face, hear her halting voice as she sat beside Tabitha and spelled out words. "I don't know. I wrote to her in prison but she never replied. She would have been released just a few weeks after the trial. I don't know how to find her."

"Maybe she doesn't want to be found. You have to let some things go."

"I'm not so good at that."

In the end, they didn't take much at all. Half of Tabitha's clothes ended up in bin bags. They took towels, rolled up a couple of rugs. Of the furniture, they took only four kitchen chairs and a workbench and a piece of driftwood Tabitha had found washed up on the beach and had thought of carving into something, someday.

When they were done, it was only midmorning.

"We hardly needed the van," Michaela said.

Then Tabitha thought of something. She stepped inside the back of the van, retrieved a towel and her swimsuit.

"We're going for a swim," she said.

"You're going for a swim," said Michaela.

_____

Down on the beach, Tabitha took off her clothes and pulled on her swimsuit. She had lost so much weight in prison that it hung off her, absurdly.

"Fuck it," she said and in front of Michaela's amused gaze slipped it off and ran naked into the sea. The water was cold, like a steely grip on her body. It was also rough and she had to push through the breakers until she was away from the shore. She felt like a creature being born into a new element and she let herself slip under the surface. It was suddenly so dark and quiet and cold and good that she felt an impulse to stay there, to breathe the water in. They said that to drown was strangely peaceful, it took just that first breath of water rather than air.

But she couldn't do it. She didn't want to do it. Not really. She burst up into the light, spluttering, and turned to the shore and saw a shape standing beside Michaela, a shape that she couldn't make out. She swam toward the shore and just as she was approaching it, she was overtaken by a huge wave that turned her over and landed her on the pebbles on her back. It felt undignified and comic and she stood up dripping and laughing and looking into the slightly bemused face of the Reverend Melanie Coglan. She was wearing a heavy-duty anorak and a woolen cap and Tabitha was wearing nothing, until Michaela stepped forward and wrapped a towel round her.

"It's a bit rough," said Mel.

"I like the sea like that."

"I heard you were here."

"Through the grapevine."

"Someone said they had seen you."

Tabitha dried herself, let the towel fall and dressed herself.

"I should have got in touch," said Mel. "To see how you were."

"That wasn't necessary. But I'm fine. How are you?"

"I'm fine too. I'm transferring. To another parish."

"I would have thought your parishioners needed you," said Tabitha. "At a time like this."

Mel flexed her jaw. She looked pale.

"The people in this village do have certain issues, conflicts, problems, call them what you will, but I'm too . . ."

"Involved," said Tabitha.

"Yes."

"Embroiled."

"Well, there have been various kinds of conflict, you know, between people, in the . . ." Melanie seemed to be searching for the right word. "Aftermath of . . . er—"

"Me. The trial. All that."

592 · NICCI FRENCH

"Good," said Tabitha. "Good. They deserve it."

She was all dressed now. She looked at Michaela. "Shall we head off?"

Michaela nodded in response.

As they turned to go, Mel put her hand on Tabitha's shoulder.

"The police," she said. "They're not going to find the truth, are they?"

"How should I know?" said Tabitha, then gave a little shrug. "Probably not."

"That's going to be a torment," said Melanie. "They'll never know. They'll suspect each other."

"That sounds awful," said Tabitha and she and Michaela left Melanie Coglan there on the beach, staring at the waves.

"What are you thinking?" asked Michaela as they drove out of Okeham: past the village shop and the bus stop and the camera, past the church and the vicarage, the row of small houses where Andy lived, where Shona lived, up the hill with the cliffs rearing up on one side, where the tree had fallen. The sea was beneath them now, and from here you couldn't tell how cold the water was and how the undertow sucked you into its churning depths.

She was thinking she would never go back. She would never hammer nails into wooden boards, with Andy working at her side in companionable silence; never make porridge and sit at her kitchen table looking out onto water and sky, or wake in her little gable room in the watches of the night and hear the roar and shush of the waves; never walk down to the cove and take off her clothes and slide her body into the vast darkness of the sea; never suffer her demons and herself in this place that she had thought she could rescue but which had nearly destroyed her. She had been wrong to imagine she could return to call this place home or could ever put the past safely behind her, when all the time it lay inside.

"What am I thinking?"

She glanced in the rearview mirror and saw the village dwindle into nothing; just a few lamps winking in the morning and smoke rising from a chimney. For a brief moment, she thought a small, scowling girl with a mop of dark hair was standing on the shoulder, holding a sticky fistful of blackberries, but it was just a trick of the light.

"I'm thinking that this is where I start."

Acknowledgments

As always, we owe so much to so many.

At United Agents, thanks to dear Sarah Ballard, always our first reader. (Needless to say, everyone that follows is dear as well.) Eli Keren and St. John Donald are a constant support.

We're grateful to Sam Edenborough and Nicki Kennedy and the rest of the team at Intercontinental Literary Agency for their guidance and friendship over many years.

We are hugely grateful to our wonderful American publishers for their clarity, patience and support, especially Emily Krump, Julia Elliott, Christina Joell and the eagle-eyed Katie Shepherd and Stephanie Vallejo.

At Simon & Schuster: Jo Dickinson read the book just before heading off to fresh woods and pastures new and then handed it over to Suzanne Baboneau. We know how lucky we are to have (or have had) both of them—for their intelligence, sensitivity and ability to spell words like "acknowledgments."

Thanks to Hayley McMullan for her passion and imagination. Thanks to Jess Barratt for indomitably and cheerfully accompanying us down some very mean streets around the United Kingdom.

And thanks to Ian Chapman for benignly watching over us.

HARPER LARGE PRINT

We hope you enjoyed reading
our new, comfortable print size and found it
an experience you would like to repeat.

Well – you're in luck!

Harper Large Print offers the finest in
fiction and nonfiction books in this same larger
print size and paperback format. Light and easy to read,
Harper Large Print paperbacks are for the book lovers
who want to see what they are reading without strain.

For a full listing of titles and
new releases to come, please visit our website:
www.hc.com

HARPER LARGE PRINT